I0590680

IN SEARCH OF SISTERS

MARY ELLEN BRAMWELL

Black Rose Writing | Texas

ISBN: 978-1-68433-691-3
PUBLISHED BY BLACK ROSE WRITING
www.blackrosewriting.com

Printed in the United States of America
Suggested Retail Price (SRP) $19.95

In Search of Sisters is printed in Baskerville

*As a planet-friendly publisher, Black Rose Writing does its best to eliminate unnecessary waste to reduce paper usage and energy costs, while never compromising the reading experience. As a result, the final word count vs. page count may not meet common expectations.

To all the female voices in my life,
you make me whole.

IN SEARCH
OF
SISTERS

CHAPTER 1

The two women were sisters. Mira could tell. She was standing on the corner of a busy intersection waiting for the light to turn green, for the walk symbol to tell her everything was okay, that she could cross. The sisters were on the opposite side of the street, approaching the corner at the end of her crosswalk, walking, or rather moving, in a subtle, graceful rhythm in her direction. Her breath caught as the blonde extended her arm toward the crosswalk button. When the chirp signaled all was safe, they would step onto the same crosswalk as Mira, closing the gap between them, crossing paths in the middle while the traffic stopped and waited. They're sisters. Sisters. The thought repeated itself in her head, and she couldn't help but smile.

They are sisters—a pause. *They* are sisters. And the thought undid her.

She watched the hand she'd thought was reaching for the button swing in a carefree arc as the two turned the corner, moving down the opposite sidewalk in unison. Slowly, they glided farther and farther away.

They were definitely sisters. One was a brunette while the other blonde, but that didn't matter. They shared the same nose and the same smile. It's not that the nose was perfect or cute or smaller than Mira's; it's that it was familiar—a family trait. It said they shared something more than friendship. They had a bond, a history, a connection that couldn't be broken by distance or time. They would always be sisters.

Even their gait matched—somewhat choppy, yet lilting at the same time, as if the burdens of one were shared by the other. Walking was easy, progress possible—because they were not alone.

Mira hastily brushed the moisture from her eyes, turning away from the corner just as the walking figure flashed its permission. She stumbled through the people, brushing against several without so much as an apology.

It was late spring on the outskirts of Chicago, and the air was shimmering with newfound warmth, but Mira was shivering. Despite the stillness of the air, she kept pushing brown hair out of her eyes as if the wind kept tossing it into her face. Strands of it soon stuck to her moistened cheeks.

The first bus to arrive was heading generally in her direction, so she climbed aboard, not caring how long the ride would be. She found a seat in the middle with nothing but empty rows around it. She folded in on herself, working to steady her shaking hands.

Much as she tried to wipe the image of those sisters from her mind, it's all she could think about. Their conversation must have been:

"Hey, it's my turn to host movie night, do you want to bring that caramel marshmallow popcorn? Jake loves it."

"Sure. It's so easy to make. Do you have any leftover Chex Mix?"

"Are you kidding? That was three days ago. It's long gone. I can make more. Or even better, I'll buy some."

"Sounds good. Just don't pick a sad movie. Tyler rolls his eyes every time I cry through a movie. I can hide that in a darkened theater, but not so much in your family room."

"Do you really care about that?"

"Oh, you're right. I don't. Chick flick it is!" And they laughed.

No, that conversation seemed too mundane. Maybe it was more solemn, and they were smiling to boost each other's spirits.

"Let's hurry. The nurse called again. The accident was more serious than they first thought. He might not—"

No, now she was imagining soap opera material. Sisters weren't like that, were they? Blood doesn't distinguish between days of tragedy and days of hope and days that are simply days. Sisters are sisters every day of every month of every year.

Maybe sisters fought. Maybe they held grudges and jealousies. Maybe they were estranged and didn't talk to each other for years. Maybe they were even sworn enemies. Maybe.

But just as likely were the other maybes. Maybe they took your phone call, even when they were in the middle of something. Maybe they cried when you cried and laughed when you laughed. Maybe they listened, offering advice when you wanted it or even when you didn't. Maybe they cared about what happened to you. Maybe your life was an extension of their own, impossible to distinguish where one ended and the other began. Maybe they made difficult times bearable.

.　　.　　.

"Where have you been? Are you okay?" Warren took her into his arms as soon as she fell through the front door, his tall frame enveloping her smaller one. "I've been trying and trying to call you. What happened?" He pulled back so he could see her face. Gently he lifted her chin with one hand while brushing her hair back with the other. The tears had dried, but her cheeks were streaked, and her eyes were puffy. "Babe, what's wrong?"

The pleading in his eyes pricked her heart. How could she tell him he wasn't enough? How could she make him understand something she couldn't understand herself? His wavy auburn hair was disheveled with worry lines on his forehead showing between the wayward strands. Mira shook her head, having no words.

"Hey, where's the car? Did you have car trouble?" Warren peered past her through the open door at the empty driveway.

Mira's mouth dropped open. She'd driven downtown. That's why she was waiting for the light to change, so she could cross the street. Her car was in the parking garage she'd used every day since starting her accounting job three years ago. "I … I took the bus. The car's fine. I just took the bus." Then she brushed past him, unable to process the love and concern etched on his face.

.　　.　　.

The plan was Warren would drop her off at work the next morning. Then she could drive her car home at the end of the day. It would take him in the opposite direction from his work, but he didn't bring that up. He was worried about his wife. Mira was always put together and never missed an appointment, all without outside reminders. It was a source of mild annoyance to him actually. "Just put it in your phone, so you don't forget." It was one of the few things he ever got on her case about. But, without fail, she always remembered. And of course, she would remind him of joint engagements—right before his phone did.

"See. I don't need my phone to tell me what to do." She would wear that beguiling half-smile on her face when she said it. He wanted to be annoyed, but that half-smile always won him over.

When morning came, plans changed. "Hey, babe. Are you getting up? We need to leave soon." Mira rolled over to face him, but she said nothing, just like the previous evening. "Mira, talk to me." He brushed the hair back from her face and kissed her forehead. It was hot to the touch. "Mira! You've got a fever. Where's the thermometer?"

She vaguely heard him in the bathroom, scrounging through the drawers, but her mind was elsewhere. *Why now? Why did something so simple push me over the edge?*

Only a week before, she and Warren had gone on a stroll. Hand in hand, they'd wandered through the park. It was the first warm day in months, and the world had exploded with people—especially children. Children were everywhere. Mira had paused, taking in their faces—big, inviting eyes, lips moving in giggles or simple words, long eyelashes any woman would envy, and life radiating from every bit of their being.

She'd had to turn away, blinking back tears. She'd glanced at Warren without moving her head to see if he'd noticed. He was transfixed by the children too. They didn't elicit a smile from him like they used to. Instead, a shadow had crossed his face ... but then it passed.

Seeing all those children tore a little piece of her heart away, but for some reason it hadn't been her undoing. *Why not? Why the sisters?*

"Mira, Mira?" Warren was trying to call her back from somewhere, but she didn't want to come. She instinctively curled into a fetal position, letting the world fade away.

.　.　.

"Is she going to be okay?" She could hear the strain in Warren's voice coming from somewhere both near and far away. "I don't understand.

What do you mean nothing's wrong with her? She has a fever. She isn't even conscious!" His voice was rising the way it did when he got worked up by a tight scoring football game or when a customer service rep didn't respond the way he wanted. But it had an edge to it she hadn't heard before.

"Clearly you don't understand the gravity of the situation." She smiled despite herself. His voice had changed to the strong bass note that had always kept her steady in life. "My wife is lying there in a hospital bed, only she's not there. I don't know where she's gone, but you need to help me figure that out. And if you're not going to do it, I'll find someone who will!"

"Warren." She could only muster the faintest of whispers. "Warren," she tried again.

She heard quick footsteps approaching as the familiar smell of Warren enveloped her like a warm blanket. "Mira? Mira? Are you there? Are you okay? Mira, babe, I love you."

She slowly opened her eyes. It was Warren's eyes that were puffy now. She forced a small smile and lifted a hand to cradle his cheek. It was still wet.

"Oh, babe, don't ever do that to me again." He gathered her up in his arms. "Where did you go? I worried I might lose you. Please, please, don't ever leave me again."

CHAPTER 2

Mira moved through security faster than she'd expected. Usually that was a good thing, but not for Mira, not today. Warren had kissed her when she entered the cordoned-off security line, but he hadn't left. Time was adding up in parking fees, but he didn't budge from his spot. Turning every few minutes to see if he was still there, she often caught him off guard, and he would quickly exchange his forlorn, lost expression with a huge grin. Then he'd run a hand through his rusty-brown hair in that characteristic, nervous habit of his.

He was too far away to hear her voice above the airport noise, but she texted him, "Don't worry. I'm coming back."

"I know," he texted back. "But seeing your face always lights my world."

She couldn't turn to look anymore. The tears pooling in the corners of her eyes would flood her face, and he'd see them, even from a distance. She couldn't do that to him, and it was not an emotion she wanted to admit to herself. As discreetly as possible, she wiped them away, put on a brave face, and turned one last time. He was still standing there, getting harder to see through the crush of people, but he was still there. Standing on tiptoes to be above the heads of those around her, she mouthed, "I love you." He answered by blowing a kiss then running his hand through his hair once again.

It had been a whirlwind month filled with more emotions than she thought possible. Once she'd recovered from her fever and been able to form a coherent sentence, Warren sat down at her bedside and said, "We need to talk."

"About what?" Mira said, although she knew playing dumb wouldn't work.

"What happened to you? You disappeared inside yourself, and I don't even know why."

Mira sat up on the bed, touching the hand of this man she loved more than life itself. He was her everything. But in ways she didn't understand, that wasn't enough. Without realizing it, she laid her free hand on her flat belly. "Do you remember that day in the park?" He nodded. She didn't need to clarify further. "I know we both want children."

"Yes, but we've barely scratched the surface of that, babe. We haven't started infertility treatments yet, but we're saving for them. We have lots of options still. The doctor said—"

She gently lifted a hand, covering his lips. "I know. I know. Just listen to me for a minute, because it isn't about that, or not exactly about that." She slowly lowered her hand, waiting to see if he was ready to listen instead of talk. His mouth remained closed, and he stayed still, allowing her to continue. "As I said, I know we both want children, but I realized it hits you differently than it does me. It never leaves me. I listen to my body every day. Am I feeling ill, tired, … different? That day in the park … It wasn't the last straw, but it was a straw nonetheless. Yes, the sight of the children was a reminder, but I saw your face. The hurt it caused you was fleeting. It passed."

"But you know I want—"

"Please, Warren, let me finish. I'm not angry with you. I'm not even disappointed. It's not about a baby, not really. That's simply a context. There's plenty of time still for children. I know there are things we can do that we haven't begun to tap yet, things we've talked about with the doctor, and like you said, we're saving for them. But I don't think you understand how this hits me. It says that something is wrong with me, or us. It says I've somehow failed."

He opened his mouth, surely to contradict her, but Mira again gently put a hand on his lips. "I'm not saying my thinking is correct or even rational. It's just my thinking. You are the kindest, sweetest man I have ever met." She took a deep breath before fully diving in. "You just don't understand how this rips me up inside, and I don't think there's anything you can do about it."

"What are you saying? I don't understand."

"Exactly." Then she blurted out what she'd been holding in since that day. "I wish I had a sister."

"A sister?" He furrowed his brow, becoming more confused by the moment.

"Warren, I need to be able to talk about things with another female, someone who deals with the same hormones that I do, someone who can see it from my perspective. I need *that* connection to make *this* connection," she indicated the two of them, "function how it should." When he said nothing, she continued. "The baby thing isn't the real problem, Warren. It's that I've been shutting up emotions that are fighting to come out. I know you would listen to them, happily even, and comfort me and encourage me, but you will never fully understand them."

He sheepishly said, "How about a good therapist?"

Mira laughed. "Yes, that would work on some level. But the long-term issue would still exist. I need connections that I'm not paying for."

He was hurt, but she couldn't stop until he understood this need, this longing. "I haven't told you what brought on the fever or why I left the car."

"No, you haven't. I just assumed ... I mean, you *know*?" She could hear the hurt in his voice that she hadn't shared this with him yet.

"I barely figured it out myself. I knew what triggered it, but I didn't know why. Lying in bed recovering from a fever gives one time to process things. I think it finally makes sense to me." She had been fidgeting, staring more at her hands than at Warren, but she forced herself to look up into his eyes. "Warren, I saw two women who were obviously sisters. They were walking in unison, and their mouths were moving so much it was impossible to tell which one was talking at any given moment. They had each other, and they could talk about anything. I need that. I saw those sisters a few days after our walk in the park. It made me realize I need another female to talk to, someone who sees the world through the same set of glasses I do.

"You," she reached for his hand, "you are the best thing that ever happened to me. I can talk to you and tell you anything and everything, but some things just don't register. It's like I don't understand your fascination with all things sports, or belching, or the humor in bodily emanations. I appreciate that you appreciate those things." She stopped when she saw his raised eyebrows and had to laugh. "Okay, maybe appreciate is the wrong word, but you get my point. They just don't mean the same thing to me. It's like a chick flick doesn't hit you the way it does me. There is, after all, a reason they call it a chick flick."

He shrugged slightly. "I suppose I can see what you're getting at. But all kinds of women don't have sisters, and they don't … they don't …"

"Fall apart?" He nodded. "I know. And it's not as if I can suddenly have sisters. That ship sailed a long time ago. I have a brother, whom I love, but it's not the same. Maybe it wouldn't matter so much if my mom was still alive, but she isn't, so I'll never know.

"Warren, I'm not sure what to do at this point. I just know I need a healthy outlet for what I feel. I need someone who understands how different things affect me without having to explain them. Women need other women. Most of the people in my office are men. You're a man, obviously. I'm missing something that will make me whole, but I don't know what to do about it." She'd started to cry at that moment. She hadn't wanted to, but the ache for what was missing was more than she could hold in.

Warren was quiet for a long time. He didn't try to wipe away her tears as he often did. He let them flow. But he held tightly to her hands, never taking his eyes off her. Eventually his tears joined hers and they touched their foreheads together, silently weeping in unison.

"Mira." The sound was so quiet yet bright that she wasn't sure she'd heard it. "Mira," now brighter and stronger, "I know what to do."

She pulled back to look at him. "What? What can you do?"

"No, I mean, I know what *you* can do. Write, babe. Just write. Quit your job, or take a leave of absence, and write!"

"How will that help?" But she was beginning to understand why it would.

"You've been writing for as long as I've known you, until recently anyway. Your emotions, your feelings, they spill out onto the page. I know the page doesn't speak back, but it helps you understand them." She paused, considering his words.

"Why do you think you haven't written much lately?"

"Well, I haven't had much to—" His raised eyebrow stopped her. "No," she finally said, "it's not the lack of material to write about, is it? I suppose the feelings are just too raw. It's easier to bury them than acknowledge them."

"Mira, consider something for me. I have an idea, but you need to promise me you'll think about it, not reject it out of hand."

"What is it?" she said, but Warren raised his eyebrows. It wasn't enough. "All right, I promise."

He squeezed her hands. "Babe, I want you to go away somewhere. Meet people. Meet other women. Talk to them, and write about it. Write about *them*. Write about your feelings and their feelings. Fill a book. Maybe you'll publish it, maybe you won't. But write a book full of feelings and thoughts, a book that you'll always have—filled with sisters you can visit within its pages anytime you want, for the rest of your life."

"But—"

"You promised."

"Okay, but let me ask how in the world we'd pay for such a thing. We can live on your salary, but how would we pay for a trip, especially for the length of time you're implying?"

"Our baby savings, the savings for infertility treatments. I know that's one of the issues we've just been talking about. But—"

"But ... I'll need those other voices, other women, even more when I'm a mom," she finished before he had a chance to. "First things first."

"Yes. We can keep saving. It will delay it but not stop it."

It made sense, maybe the first thing that had made sense in a long time.

"But, babe, you have to promise me one thing."

"What?"

"That you'll call me every day you're gone, or text me, or message me, or something. You're my everything, and I will miss you more than I can say." And this time, she was wiping away his tears as well as her own.

OCEAN

"You can never cross the ocean until you have the courage to lose sight of the shore."

—Christopher Columbus

CHAPTER 3

Mira was greeted with "Welcome aboard," but she merely nodded in return. Her seat wasn't the cheapest but not the most luxurious either. At least it reclined a bit more than some. She was hoping to sleep away at least part of the trip.

After stowing her carry-on suitcase, she sat down to examine the bag Warren had shyly handed her as they were leaving for the airport. She had merely peeked inside before giving him a quizzical look.

He shrugged and smiled, his dimples showing. "I wanted to send you off with something. So, I wandered around the store for a couple hours. Every so often, something would jump out at me, so I'd put it in my cart." He shrugged again. "I can't explain it. It just seemed like a good idea, like you might need those things." Then he'd ushered her out the door before she could object or ask anything more.

Now that she had time, she carefully opened the drawstring bag. Each item was hastily wrapped in tissue paper, and Mira gently unwrapped each one and laid it in her lap. No woman would ever think to put together the odd assortment of things he had gathered. They were so Warren, and she shook her head, smiling at the same time.

She picked up the camera to examine it. It made the most sense of any of the gifts and was certainly the biggest splurge—probably the only splurge when it came down to it. She had planned on using her phone to take pictures, but it made a lot more sense with a trip like this to be able to take better quality photos.

Carefully setting the camera aside, she picked up a small compact. It popped open like a clamshell to reveal two small mirrors on either side.

She glanced at herself in them and smiled. This might appear practical to most people, and while it was in a sense, she knew that's not why he'd given it to her. Warren loved to tease her with, "Mira, Mira, on the wall, you are the fairest of them all." She would protest altogether too much when he said it, inwardly smiling. She didn't always feel pretty, but Warren made her feel like she was—outside as well as in. Why hadn't that been enough? She shook her head as if she could shoo the thought away like an errant house fly, her hair flipping around her in the process.

Her seatmate made a small squeak, and Mira jerked around to face her, her hands covering her mouth. "I am so sorry. Did my hair … Did I just … hit you with my hair?"

She got an eye roll for a response. This might be a very long flight.

Careful to keep her hands and arms—and hair—in her own seat, Mira continued her discovery. She had seen something that would be useful about now. She found it at the bottom of the stack—a bright red scrunchie. She quickly secured her hair in it, being aware of her elbows as she did so.

Now acutely conscious of her seatmate, she made a cursory look through the remaining items. They ranged from a key chain, a favorite childhood candy to a stuffed animal, and even included an empty water bottle. It was pink with blossoms trailing up the side. Her favorite color was purple, but pink was a close second. Like many of the items, she couldn't explain why he'd chosen it, other than his simple explanation that he wanted to send her off with something. The thought made her smile and miss him.

She already had a water bottle, which Warren clearly knew. He usually reminded her to fill it up on her way out the door to work, although she never forgot. It was as much a part of their routine as their kiss goodbye. This morning, however, she'd been so focused on her mental checklist before leaving that Warren had to gently remind her to leave it empty so she could take it through security. She'd filled it up at a drinking fountain near her gate and had been sipping from it ever since. Maybe he thought it was time for a new one. Regardless of the reason, it was a sweet gesture. She could always fill them both up for long days or swap them with each other.

The other items made less sense, but knowing Warren, they'd likely come in handy at some point. He had a sixth sense about these kinds of things—like the time he decided they needed to take an umbrella on a picnic when the skies were clear. Mira felt smug when not a single rain cloud appeared. Halfway through their lunch, however, they'd discovered their perfect spot under a flowering pear tree wasn't so perfect. With even the slightest breeze, a cascade of petals showered down upon them. Mira suggested they move, but Warren merely smiled, opening the umbrella with a flourish as if he were her knight in shining armor. Laughing, they huddled under the umbrella while enjoying the rest of their lunch.

Lost in these pleasant memories, the flight attendant's reminder to prepare for takeoff startled her. She quickly rewrapped each item, returned it to the bag, and safely stowed it at her feet.

It was to be a long flight, so she pulled a book out of her purse that she'd purchased on a whim at an airport we-can-charge-anything convenience store. Even though it was a straight-forward mystery, it felt like a guilty pleasure. She'd been reading e-books lately, but the feel of the glossy paperback cover in her hands was comforting, like when she was a child reading the latest offering from her favorite author on the school bus to and from school.

Mira finished the last lines of chapter two, "Only his name wasn't actually Dr. Simmons. He wasn't even a medical professional, at least not of any reputable kind," when the flight attendant reached over to hand her some pretzels. The woman seated next to her used that moment to sigh.

Noisily opening her pretzels, Mira turned back to her book. "Ralph Simms was his real name," she read.

"Is your book any good?"

Mira wanted to say, "I'm reading it to find out," but instead she simply turned and smiled.

"Hi, my name's Dylan. Have you ever been to London before?"

"No." She was going to leave it at that, and turn back to her book, but the plaintive expression staring back at her changed her mind. She could spare a few minutes. "Honestly, I've never left the United States. I haven't even seen the ocean before, let alone cross over one."

"Did you start from Chicago today? I mean it wasn't a connecting flight for you? Is that where you live?"

"In one of the outlying suburbs, not in Chicago itself," Mira said, shifting in her seat.

"I grew up in Ohio, but I'm living in California now." Dylan laughed nervously. "I've flown to Hawaii, so the ocean isn't new, but I've never gone this direction over the Atlantic.

"Are we over the ocean already? I thought it would still be a while." She lifted her shade to get a better look, but all that was visible were white fluffy clouds in every direction. "I can't tell." She turned to her seatmate as if for answers. Dylan put her hands up and shrugged.

Mira hadn't really noticed Dylan before. She looked young but was probably around Mira's own age. Whether Mira looked it or not, lately she felt the weight of life had aged her, without the added benefit of any greater wisdom or knowledge.

Beyond a similarity in age, she could detect no similarities between the two of them. Dylan had bright red hair, a perfect complement to her creamy brown skin. One ear held several piercings while the other was pierced once with a large hoop hanging from it.

Dylan noticed the stare and raised her eyebrows. "And what do you think?"

"I ... I didn't mean to stare," Mira said, but Dylan narrowed her eyes in reproach. "I'm sorry. That's not really true. I was staring at your earrings and honestly wondering if you liked having all those earrings in at one time. I get irritated with one pair sometimes."

Dylan's head went back, and she let out a long, deep-throated laugh. "I honestly forget about the earrings unless I'm looking in a mirror. I thought you were staring at the color of my skin or my choice of hair color. I don't suppose you noticed that?" She had a slight challenge in the tone of her voice, her head cocked waiting for a response.

"I have many faults and probably more prejudices than I realize, but I don't see why skin color should be part of them. It's not like you get to choose it." Then she covered her mouth, realizing what she'd said. She put her hands up in surrender. "Okay. I just put my foot in my mouth. You did pick your hair color. I happen to like it, but that isn't the point. It's your hair. Your color."

"If you like it so much, how come your hair isn't the same color?" Mira didn't know how to respond. Dylan snickered. "I'm just messing with you. You're cool."

Mira relaxed and let out a sigh, relieved she hadn't offended the person she'd be stuck sitting next to for several more hours.

"You too, huh?"

"What?"

"Your sigh. You nervous too?"

Mira decided not to correct Dylan's misperception. "Well, you know." She shrugged. "What are you nervous about?"

"Oh, just about a million things," Dylan said, rolling her eyes.

Mira put away her book. This might take a while, which she soon discovered she didn't mind. Dylan had a lot of history packed into her twenty-five years, it turned out. She'd been a foster child because of an alcoholic mother, then adopted at the age of 11, "an amazing feat," she said. Dylan's voice was clear and strong, projecting an image of strength, but her words implied something else. Her newfound family gave her stability and love, which in time she learned to give in return, but those 11 years had burned scars that were hard to ignore.

"When I turned 18, I figured I was an adult, so after high school graduation, I moved out." Dylan pulled out a picture to show Mira. "This is them—my adoptive mom and dad." They appeared happy together, smiling at the camera and holding hands.

"I never would have guessed you were adopted. You look so much like them."

"A lot of people have said that." Dylan's eyes were glued to the photo, with a touch of something Mira couldn't yet identify. "They were sad to see me go but supportive at the same time. I guess I never really got over my mom not being there, not fighting to get me back. So, even after seven years, I kept wondering when they'd be done with me too, you know?"

"What did you do then?" Mira was entranced by the story but also by the fact Dylan was so willing to share it.

"I enrolled in a community college. Everyone told me that I could handle a bigger university, and I could have—intellectually."

"Did you even apply?" Dylan didn't answer, still staring at the picture. Mira surprised herself by adding, "Were you afraid they'd reject you too?"

Dylan lifted her head, eyeing Mira. "Yeah," she slowly said. "My friends didn't get that. I think my mom, my adoptive mom, did though. She never said anything bad about my choice. She just kept trying to help me talk things through." She paused and wiped a tear away. "It broke her heart when I left—not because I was leaving, she knew that would happen at some point, but because I left still doubting my worth. She thought she'd failed me."

Mira ventured to put a hand on Dylan's arm, which she didn't shrug off. Dylan began to shed her story piece by piece, unburdening herself. School was soon joined by jobs, boyfriends, more jobs, eventual university studies, and graduation. It was a meandering journey that led Mira to realize she'd misread Dylan. Her self-confident voice wasn't the lie. The lie was what Dylan had fed herself for years.

"I lived with my family for seven years, and now that I've been gone for seven, I see things from a different perspective. They have always been there for me. Allowing me to leave simply meant they trusted me. It didn't mean they stopped caring about me or loving me. I've met some truly messed up people. I'm lucky. I hadn't realized that until recently."

"Wow. So, what now?"

"London." Dylan laughed at Mira's puzzled look. "London is the best part. My mom and dad and my brothers and sisters—oh! I didn't even tell you about my amazing siblings! Well, anyway, everyone is meeting in London to celebrate Mom and Dad's fortieth anniversary. Mom thinks it's only the two of them, but we're all flying in to surprise her." She teared up. "And I am so nervous because I'm going to tell her how much she has meant to me, how much I love her. I'm just afraid I'm going to miss something, that I'm not going to say it right."

Mira had no words. Her eyes were filling with tears as well.

"Oh no!" Dylan gasped. "I left their presents on my kitchen counter."

"Oh, I'm sorry. What did you get them?"

"It's kind of silly, I guess, but the fortieth anniversary is supposed to be the ruby anniversary. So, I bought my dad a men's ruby ring and my mother a ruby necklace. Their anniversary isn't actually until next month, so I guess I'll give them their presents once we're back in the States." She tried to put a smile on her face as she slumped in her seat.

They sat quietly for a few minutes then Mira burst out in laughter.

"What's so funny?"

"I can help you. Actually, my husband can help you."

"What are you talking about?"

"Are your parents good sports? Can they take a joke?" Dylan nodded. "Then I have a present for each of them. She pulled two things out of the bag Warren had given her. Unwrapping the first, she handed it to Dylan. "When I was a kid, I loved ring pops. My husband gave me this ring pop right before I left. It's strawberry, my favorite flavor. Will that substitute for a ruby ring for your dad?"

Dylan laughed her deep-throated laugh. "He would love it! Probably more than the real one I'll give him later. He has never met a form of sugar he didn't like or a joke that didn't make him laugh."

"Great! Okay, now the next one is even better." She could barely contain her smile. "Open this."

Dylan unwrapped the small bundle. Inside was a key chain. Hanging from it was a distinctive pair of red shoes and a small pendant. Dylan gasped. "Ruby slippers! Rubies!" She squealed with delight. "Oh, there's more! There's a quote from Glinda, the Good Witch. 'You've always had the power, my dear, you just had to learn it for yourself.' Oh, that's perfect! Thank you!" Dylan surprised Mira by throwing her arms around her. "You know, that's kind of what I want to tell her—that she's always loved and accepted me. She's always treated me like I was lovable, that I was capable of being loved simply for being me. That's what I've finally learned for myself. Thank you, thank you, thank you!"

The smiles rarely left their faces as Dylan told Mira about each one of her siblings. There were five of them, two of them adopted like her. They had wonderful and interesting lives.

Mira listened with wonder while Dylan continued to bare her soul, but Mira felt guarded. She didn't have a nice neat finish to her story. Her happy ending hadn't happened yet. So, she listened but rarely spoke.

Dylan was yawning more and more, and her speech slowed then stopped altogether. Before long, Dylan was quietly sleeping.

Mira was tired too, but her mind was racing. Now she *was* nervous. What was she doing? She'd had a wonderful conversation with Dylan, and learned so much about her. The conversation, however, wouldn't have happened if Dylan hadn't started it.

Who was she kidding? She wanted to have so-called sisters she could talk to. Not only had she not initiated the conversation, she'd told Dylan nothing about herself, choosing to stay bottled up and private, refusing to allow this kindest of strangers in by even a drop.

"I can't do this. I can't do this," she muttered over and over to herself. Unable to contemplate sleep now, she pulled out her journal from her bag. At least she could write about the exchange, even her own frustrations. That way she'd have written something when she landed in London and made a beeline for the ticket counter to book the earliest possible return flight.

When the announcement came they would be landing soon, Mira woke with a start, her journal open on her lap. She glanced at where she had left off, hoping she hadn't revealed too much in case Dylan had seen, but she needn't have worried. Dylan was asleep in much the same position as before.

Returning her journal to her bag and straightening herself up, she lifted the window shade to see what was visible. She had missed the ocean entirely, of course, and now long stretches of green patches passed beneath her.

When the city began to appear, Dylan yawned, "What can you see?"

"Here, take a look, if you can," Mira said, leaning back in her seat. Together they watched the serpentine Thames River come into view, winding its way through miles and miles of city. Old and majestic buildings blended in with more modern architecture nearby. But Mira hadn't picked London as a destination so she could see office buildings; she wanted to see its rich history.

"Hey, is that London Bridge?"

"I think so." And a few minutes later, "Oh, there's the London Eye!"

Mira's heart raced at the thought of seeing these famous places in person. Maybe she'd stay for a bit after all.

The city sights soon gave way to an occasional green swath, a park perhaps. And more often small buildings, likely homes, could be seen in neat lines with what appeared to be red or brown roofs. Dylan had settled back into her seat, but Mira couldn't take her eyes off the sights below. It was new, different, and yet not. People, people just like her lived here, worked here, raised families, cooked meals, love, fought, laughed, cried here, just like anywhere else. Everyone had their own life story. They were people just like her. Somehow, she wanted to meet some of them, to learn even a piece of those life stories, and try hard to share a piece of her life story in exchange. She'd managed half of that with Dylan.

The landing was smooth. Finally, the fasten-your-seatbelt light went off and the passengers stood as if on cue by a music conductor. Mira was amused that the British flight attendant mentioned retrieving their things from the "overhead locker," what she'd always known as overhead bins. Locker was probably a more accurate term, but it made her realize that she was in for more of a culture shock than she had imagined.

"I can grab your bag for you," Dylan said, standing with everyone else.

"Thanks. It's the blue one. I wanted to be different."

Dylan laughed. "Well, I'm not sure you understand the meaning of that word," she said as she lifted down her own bright orange suitcase complete with a purple seahorse zipper charm.

"Yeah, Dylan, maybe not so much," Mira laughed.

"Hey, we talked for hours and I never got your name," Dylan said as she handed over one blue suitcase.

Wow, she hadn't even shared her name. The task Mira had set for herself was going to be harder than she'd imagined. "I guess not. It's Mira."

"That's a cool name. What does it mean?"

Mira started to answer but stopped. She had no answer. She'd never thought about what her name meant, never looked it up, never wondered, never asked. The thought struck her. How could she not know or even care to know? Here she was searching for connections with others, connections to make herself whole, and ironically, she didn't know the most basic thing about herself. It's hard to share something with others that you don't have in the first place.

She met Dylan's gaze, planning to give her a shrug only to be met with a quick hug instead. "Thanks again for everything, Mira. You'll never know what it means to me." And before she could even reply, Dylan was carried away by a flood of people flowing down the aisle. Dylan stuck out her hand to wave a last goodbye as her bright red hair disappeared in the sea of passengers.

Mira's first friend on this difficult journey was gone, simply here and gone in a bright flash of red hair.

CHAPTER 4

Before Mira disembarked, she decided the next time would need to be different. Her journal entry about Dylan showed a lopsided interaction with an incomplete connection. Dylan had given her plenty of openings, asking about her siblings, her parents and upbringing, and so on. Mira's answers were short—one or two words only, squelching further elaboration. She had let the perfect opportunity slip through her fingers. It was a great testament of how not to proceed. Determining how she would accomplish a different outcome, however, would have to wait as she emerged into the busy airport.

If you've seen one airport, you've seen them all. At least that's what Mira had thought—and it was true, in part. The building was different. The directions were different. But the slightly organized chaos was the same. And thankfully, at this point in her travels, the language was the same.

Mira had been smart enough to heed the advice she'd gotten from others and from reading guidebooks to travel light. She'd likely get tired of the same few shirts, but hopefully, that would be more than made up for in the ease of moving from place to place. With no checked baggage to hassle with, she squeezed her way in and out of the crowd to the taxi stand.

In a whirlwind of efficiency, she was soon traveling to the small apartment she'd rented for her duration in London. It had seemed like a great idea when she booked it—stay in a neighborhood where she could meet people, live like a Londoner. But when her driver dropped her off, it felt lonely—no concierge or doorman, no front desk staff, only an empty London street.

Used to delays in traffic, she'd told the flat owner to meet her at 1:15, but she was early with nothing to do but wait. Having gotten little sleep on the plane, Mira knew if she sat down, she'd be asleep in no time, even if she just sat down on the front steps of her new temporary home. But what to do in a strange city?

Leaning against the wrought iron stair railing, Mira took in her surroundings. Down either side of the street stretched what she knew as townhouses or row houses. Her initial impression when she'd hopped out of the car was that they were virtually identical, but now she could see how unique each was. What had appeared as one long monochrome building was actually separate residences, painted various pastels that gracefully blended from one to the next. The colors were light and airy as if they were an extension of the sky above.

A myriad of other differences existed too. One door was painted dark blue, another a rich burgundy color, and still another was hunter green. Each had a bay window, some with window boxes housing a diverse selection of flowers and plants. All these differences complimented each other like a grand symphony. She could understand why she'd initially seen it the way she had because it was one harmonious and very charming whole.

However, Mira had been mistaken in one regard. The street wasn't empty as she'd first thought. Across it and several doors down, a little girl was sitting on the front steps. Her head was down and she was fingering what appeared to be a stuffed animal or a doll, Mira couldn't tell from her distance.

The child, it appeared, had started the day with two braids, but wisps of loose blond hair now glinted with sunlight in scattered arrays around her face. The child must have had a busy morning. Mira watched the young girl. She didn't budge from her spot yet managed to be in unending motion—her hands busy with the toy, her legs swaying back and forth, or her feet hosting their version of a thumb wrestle.

The child, Mira realized, didn't make her wistful for one of her own. Instead, her curiosity was piqued. What had she done that morning to undo her hair so thoroughly? And why was she sitting in one place right now? Was it a lack of playmates, or perhaps a time out?

Lost in these inquisitive thoughts, Mira didn't see the woman approaching from the other direction. The first "Hullo," made her jump.

"Hello," she said once she'd collected herself, but she glanced quickly back the other direction, saddened to see that the little girl had disappeared. She turned her attention back to the woman who had greeted her.

"You must be Mira!" The voice was more than lilting, almost quick and bouncy as if each word was an excited puppy jumping up to greet her. "You must be so tired after such a long trip."

"Yes, I am," Mira barely got out before the woman continued.

"I'm Cordelia if you hadn't guessed by now. I won't bother you while you're here, but you can bother me anytime you like, and I guarantee that won't be a bother." She laughed at her own joke. Scooping up Mira's bag, she hauled it up the front steps as if it were merely a handbag.

Mira watched her dumbfounded. She'd never seen anyone over the age of eight with so much energy before. She had to be in her forties and barely over five feet. Her clothes were ordinary enough—jeans and a blue jersey top, but they didn't look ordinary, probably because on her they were in constant motion.

Mira hurried up the stairs to catch up. "I was just admiring the townhouses."

"Townhouses?"

"The houses along the street," she said, motioning behind her.

"Oh, terraced houses, luv. Yes, they are nice, aren't they?" Cordelia said as she unlocked the flat. "Now let's get you settled inside."

Cordelia hardly took a breath as she set down Mira's bags and started talking about the flat, but Mira was more interested in Cordelia. She wasn't skinny, but she wasn't fat. Her hair was brown, but not dark brown. In fact, everything about her appearance should have made her fade into the background. Cordelia, however, did not fade. She shone. Her voice was bright and energetic. She didn't walk as much as she bounded, as if on springs. But with all of that, her most distinguishing feature was her smile. It was full and warm, not even relaxing when she spoke.

"What do you think?"

"What?" Mira had been so busy observing Cordelia, that she hadn't bothered to listen or attempt to keep up with her words. "I'm sorry. You're just so ... so ..."

"I know. I can be hard to handle and not very stereotypically British if you know what I mean."

Mira didn't know what she meant, but she'd figure out that meaning later. "No. It's not that at all. You're incredible. I don't talk well to strangers, and you, well, you're so friendly and nice even though you've never met me before. I guess I was expecting someone more standoffish, to be honest. I guess someone more like me. You're rather delightful."

"Oh, luv, I do like you. As I said, I promise not to bother my short-term tenants, but you, you're going to have to make sure and bother me. Now, let me give you the quick tour."

It *was* quick. Cordelia's walking, hand motions, and everything were quite as swift as her talking. "And here we are, back in the kitchen again. Here's a list of local eateries. I especially like this pub. It's my favorite, and Bill there will treat you right proper, he will. I've stocked the fridge with some basic supplies, but you're going to want to fill it with what you're familiar with. I've learned you Americans don't know how to indulge in a proper breakfast, so buy what you're used to." Then in a conspiratorial whisper, she added, "I don't go for the full English breakfast myself unless it's a holiday or my mum is around. Then I don't have much choice. It is lovely, but it leaves me full for a week." She rolled her eyes. "Anyway, there's a supermarket around the corner. I've drawn a little map here so you can see exactly where, and I put the public transportation stops on it too, along with other sights. You'll only have a five-minute walk to the nearest tube station, but take a brolly along all the same." Mira didn't know what a brolly was until the next sentence. "The rain can get you coming and going."

"Oh, an umbrella."

"What, luv? Oh, that's right. You Americans don't know how to use proper English. If you haven't got a brolly of your own, there's one by the front door." She laughed, clearly not offended. "You have my number, but here are some other numbers to ring up if I don't answer right away."

Then as quickly as she came, Cordelia was gone.

Mira felt the tiredness seep through her body. She'd never dealt with jet lag before, but she'd read the best thing to do was to get busy and spend the day doing things, then go to bed in the early evening.

The one thing she wanted to do was call Warren. Glancing at her watch, she figured it was close to eight in the morning for him. He'd just be getting to work and settling in. While he'd be happy to hear from her, she was reluctant. How would it look? Like she couldn't even handle the plane ride and checking into her place? She had her own doubts about forging forward, but she didn't want to worry Warren with those doubts, at least not yet. She'd call him in a few hours. She could wait that much longer, she told herself.

She did quickly send him a text: "Made it safely here. Cordelia, the property manager, is a human version of the Energizer bunny. Going to go out and try to stay awake. Talk later. Love you!!!" She wanted to add, "Thanks for making me do this," but she wasn't sure in that moment if she was grateful or not. Then she put away her phone before giving in to the temptation to call and hear his voice.

It was her first day in London. What to do now? She only needed to make it a few hours until dinnertime and then she could crawl into bed and give in to the sleep that kept calling her. An open, double-decker tour bus sounded enticing. She could get the lay of the land, so to speak, but then she pictured taking the tube to where she could hop on one of those tour buses. Sitting down, with the rhythmic movement of the subway would surely lull her right to sleep.

So, she settled for exploring her neighborhood with the main goal of stocking up at the supermarket Cordelia had mentioned. That seemed like a worthwhile goal, and the walking would help keep her awake.

The hand-drawn map Cordelia had left showed a large park not far away—The Regent's Park. A nice stroll through that might be just what she was looking for.

Growing up in the Midwest had not prepared her for Regent's Park. Maybe if she'd ever been to New York City and visited Central Park, she wouldn't have been so surprised. Little neighborhood playgrounds or city parks with a bandstand were the extent of her experience. They stretched a city block at most, but Regent's Park appeared to stretch for miles.

It was a pleasant afternoon, and she observed couples, children, families, runners, nappers, bikers, and walkers. It wasn't overly crowded, as there was plenty of park to go around, but she couldn't look in any direction without seeing people of all ages and races. It was delightful.

Along the bank of a meandering river spread a grassy expanse dominated by a massive weeping willow. She loved the graceful flow of its branches, reaching out a friendly bough to the ground, connecting them together, conveying a sense of peace. The scene reminded her of a Seurat painting, something about a Sunday morning. The painting, as she recalled, showed a similar grassy slope at a water's edge, people milling about enjoying the day. Trees provided a nice backdrop, like the willow tree she'd been admiring. Seurat, she knew, was French, but surely that painting wasn't far off from this.

A jaunt into France was on Mira's agenda, but how different would it be from England? A whole list of differences came immediately to mind – the language, of course; the culture; the style of the buildings; the food; and on and on. But sitting down on the grass and gazing around her, she couldn't help but feel that maybe the similarities, not the differences, were more pronounced than people typically recognized. If she could picture this scene in front of her as matching that painting from a different country and century, then maybe other connections existed as well.

People were people, weren't they, with their ups and downs? She remembered the thought she'd had on the plane that everyone has a unique life story.

Mira certainly had her own story. But that thought, instead of making her feel part of the world around her, troubled her slightly, causing her to question the conclusions she'd drawn. But why?

The answer was apparent in every person around her. It was in the young couple, sitting not far away, lost in conversation. What did she know about them? They looked like they were together, but were they? What were their hopes and dreams? It was in a group of young boys bounding past. Were they friends with each other, or was one running from the others who were bullying him?

Everyone did have his or her own story, but she didn't know what any of those stories were, and, what made it worse, she was too afraid to ask. For that matter, these people knew nothing about her. They didn't know her challenges, her fears. How could they?

She shivered even though the sun was out. The scene before her, that only a few moments earlier had reminded her of the similarities of mankind, now screamed out their differences. She didn't know any of these people. Surely, they didn't like the same things, know the same things, feel the same things as she did.

Confused by her thoughts, Mira abruptly stood, fished Cordelia's map out of her purse, and made a beeline to the supermarket for some groceries. It was just around the corner from the flat as Cordelia had promised. The items were more expensive than she'd thought but not more than she'd budgeted for, thank goodness. She grabbed meat, cheese, bread, and a smattering of other supplies. About ready to check out, she passed a display of cookies, or biscuits, she had to remind herself. So, she added a sampling of the most interesting looking ones to her basket, all the while trying not to feel so incredibly out of place.

By the time she got back to the flat, it was 5:00 pm. Warren would have his lunch hour right around her dinner hour. If she could wait a mere hour, she could "eat" with him. The plan was to eat out most nights, thinking that might be the best time and place to meet people—at the end of the day when they were relaxing. However, she didn't want to struggle to hear Warren over a noisy crowd, and it's not exactly like she'd be meeting people if she was talking to him.

She puttered around the flat, unpacking—slightly, in case she decided to leave tomorrow—opening cupboards, flushing the toilet to make sure it worked, and opening then immediately closing shutters.

At 5:20, she gave in and called Warren.

"Hi." The sound of his voice flooded her with homesickness. She just wanted her life back, the way she knew it. She could make do without sisters. She could go to her job day in and day out. It was familiar and comfortable. And she did talk to her colleagues, even if they were mostly men. In that environment, she wasn't this scared little girl, afraid of her own shadow, unwilling or unable to say hi to anyone in her path. Warren's voice interrupted her thoughts. "Mira? Are you there?"

"Uh … yeah, I'm here." She was working hard to steady her voice. "So, how are you?"

His familiar laugh came through the line. "I'm in the same place, doing the same thing. The only difference is I slept a little better not having to share any covers—and worse because I'd rather share them." He laughed again. "The real question is, how are you? What's London like? How was the flight? What are the people like? Tell me everything."

"Are you sure? I know it's not your lunch hour yet."

"Are you kidding? I've been waiting for you to call. I just didn't want to bug you in case you were in the middle of something. And, honestly, I've gotten almost no work done. I'm excited for you, babe, but I miss you like crazy already."

Mira smiled and tried to hold back the tears, determined to put on a brave front. "Well, it's, I don't know, it's a change."

"It's a change?"

"Umm, yeah. Like an umbrella is called a brolly, and the flight attendant called the overhead bins overhead lockers."

Warren was silent for a minute. "Okay. Anything else? Did you talk to anyone on the plane? What did you do today?"

Dylan, at least Dylan was a safe subject. A change crept over her as she told him about Dylan, every last detail she knew. She ended with the ring pop and the key chain. "I hope it's okay that I gave them away. They just seemed so perfect."

"That's wonderful. I'm glad you did. You sound more like yourself now, but what happened the rest of the day. Something's off. I can tell."

How could she have even thought this man wasn't enough? He could read her like a book, a well-loved paperback at that. "Warren, Dylan was so nice, but I didn't tell her anything about myself. I think I've made a big mistake. I can't meet people. I can talk to people I already know, but I don't talk to strangers. I don't know how. I am completely out of my element here. I thought I was fairly self-confident, but I feel so small and insignificant right now." She paused and wiped her eyes. "I miss you. I miss home."

"Okay. At least you're talking about it. You haven't shut down. That's good."

She nodded even though he couldn't see it. Yay for me, she thought sarcastically. At this rate, she'd make a new friend in a year—if she was lucky.

"Tell me about Cordelia. You mentioned her in your text."

She felt like a small child being prodded to do a chore, but, at the moment, that's probably the level she was at. "She's outgoing and bubbly. I feel like you could tie a string to her like a helium balloon and she'd bounce up and down in the air above the rest of us. She's probably never had an unhappy moment in her life."

"Did she show you around the neighborhood?"

"No, but she drew a map for me. I followed it to Regent's Park, which is a lovely, very large park. I'm pretty sure there's a lot more to it than what I saw. I'll have to explore it another day. Her map showed me where a grocery store was or, as she called it, a supermarket, so I've bought some food for the next few days."

The conversation eased as they slipped into their familiar back and forth. If Mira concentrated on his voice, she could forget, for a minute, her fears and doubts.

All too soon, they ended the call. Neither wanted to, but the call was costly, and they were both getting hungry.

Mira contemplated going out to grab a bite now that it wouldn't compete with her phone call, but the yawns she couldn't suppress convinced her otherwise. Tiredness washed over her, making coherent thought difficult. So, she slapped some meat on a piece of bread, ate it, then collapsed on the bed without even changing her clothes or pulling back the covers.

CHAPTER 5

When Mira awoke the next morning, it took a few moments to register where she was and why she was fully dressed. Reality hit her like a punch in her stomach. It wasn't being in England that bothered her so much as being in England alone. It was antithetical to the goal for this trip, surrounding herself with other women. All she'd accomplished so far was a fueling of her desire to hide from anyone she didn't know—and since that described everyone in England, things weren't going as planned.

At least she was more well-rested than she'd thought possible. She planned to shower and grab a quick breakfast, but what she really wanted was to talk to Warren over that breakfast like she always did. Calling him was out of the question, though, since it was the middle of the night back in the States. She sent him a text instead that he would see when he woke: "Love you. I'm leaving the flat today. Wish me luck."

Mira spent a wonderful day sightseeing. She tried one of the hop-on, hop-off buses, which worked remarkably well. Growing up in a country with a 250-year history as a nation simply couldn't compare to the sights in England. Buckingham Palace itself was older than that, but it was nothing compared to the Tower of London which had sections that dated back as early as 1066. It was hard to wrap her mind around something that was nearly 1000 years old.

The day was a whirlwind. Only by referring to the pictures she'd taken could Mira remember the order in which she'd seen everything. It had given her merely a taste of what was possible. She was already planning in her head the places she wanted to revisit and spend more time, adding them to the list of places she wanted to see that hadn't been on the bus tour.

She had just enough time before getting something for dinner to write in her journal. Only, what should she write? Mira had seen plenty, but this journal was supposed to be her "sister" journal. The only times she talked to anyone were when she was buying tickets and to say, "Excuse me," as she moved through the crowds. The ticket buying had been fine—nothing to write about in that regard. And every time she'd said, "Excuse me," or, "Pardon me," she had gotten everything from stares to snickers. That didn't make any sense. She was simply trying to be polite. Again, however, it was nothing to write about.

She quickly jotted down a travel log of what she'd done and seen before closing the journal and stowing it, not wanting its sight to remind her of the complete lack of progress towards her goal. That morning, she'd wanted nothing more than to call Warren, but tonight she wanted nothing more than to avoid that call.

She texted him instead: "Had a super busy day sightseeing. Going to try eating tonight at the pub Cordelia recommended. Maybe I'll make friends." She hesitated before sending it, knowing the only way she'd make friends is if other people initiated it, the way Dylan had.

Poking her head out, the sky was grayish, definitely questionable, so she grabbed the brolly Cordelia had left by the front door, just in case. It was only a short distance to the pub. While she walked, she wondered about Dylan. She imagined the whole family had arrived by now. Had Dylan been able to tell her parents what was in her heart? She hoped so. Mira wished, not for the first time, that she'd opened up to Dylan, or at the very least, they'd exchanged contact information.

Stepping into the dim light of the pub, her phone lit up with a text from Warren. "Love u 2 babe. Open your mouth and say hi. It'll be okay. I promise."

The pub, called *The Red Fox*, was starting to fill. People were greeting each other like family, and Mira thought about ducking back out. But before she had the chance, some of the pub employees had seen her. She didn't want to appear rude by leaving before eating something.

Not quite knowing how to proceed, she watched what others were doing, trying hard to observe without being observed. It wasn't too hard to do. The place was dimly lit and sounded a bit like a crowd at a football game. "All right, Joe?" "All right, Roger?" "Hey, how's that little 'un doing these days?" "Can you believe that match last night?" The din was an effective cover.

After their greetings changed to updates, Mira saw them disperse—seating themselves at the bar or empty tables, depending on their reason for being there. She followed their lead and did the same.

A menu sat perched on the table, waiting for her. She wasn't sure what *toad in the hole* and *bangers and mash* were. She'd try those when she'd gotten more comfortable, assuming that ever happened. For now, fish and chips sounded perfect. She didn't see anyone coming around to collect orders, and wondered what to do next. Just then, one of the people she'd followed to the tables got up and went to the bar to place an order for himself and his companion. Getting up to do the same, she noticed a line at the bottom of the menu: *Order at the Counter.* She chuckled to herself as she made her way over to the bar. Apparently, it wasn't that hard to figure out after all.

Returning to her seat, she passed a man moving between tables, greeting people, mostly by name. In response, she heard, "Thanks, Bill. Great as usual." Bill was the man Cordelia had mentioned would take good care of her here, but the last thing she was up to doing about now was introducing herself to Bill and asking for any favors. Feeling small and insignificant, she slid back into her seat and tried to all but disappear.

She only got up twice more—to pick up her food when her number was called, and when she got up to leave. The meal was delicious. It was also plentiful. She thought about taking part of it home to eat later, but she didn't see anyone else pack up leftovers to go, so she was reluctant to ask. Instead, she ate way too much, leaving only a small bit behind. Next time maybe she could ask for a kid-size portion. And maybe next time she'd actually speak to someone other than the person taking her order.

She walked home swiftly in the gathering darkness, not sure exactly how safe it was to be out this time of night alone. Nearing her flat, she noticed light pouring out from a window across the way. Glancing up, she saw a small face watching her intently. Plucking up her courage, she lifted her hand to wave, but the little girl's face darted away before she had the chance. Next moment, the curtains were drawn, blocking any further light inside from finding her.

It was the same little girl she'd seen before, and she wasn't smiling.

CHAPTER 6

A text was waiting for Mira when she awoke. "Call me over dinner tomorrow—today by the time you see this. I miss hearing your voice. I can't wait to hear who you've met."

She knew Warren was trying to help, but it wasn't actually helping. Who goes on a vacation to meet people? She should have just signed up for a gym membership back home or joined the local Kiwanis club.

Seeing her journal nearby reminded her why that option hadn't come up. Warren was right, writing was her outlet. It had been since she was a teenager, until recently anyway. If her emotions were too raw to write about, only something as memorable as a trip such as this could jump-start her writing again.

She flipped open its pages, reading what she'd written the day before.

...The tower of London is really big—and old. I didn't know that before. Lots of people have lived there and died there. Who knew? Well, I guess just about everyone, but oh, well. And Buckingham Palace is also big and quite impressive...

The sights she'd visited were so fascinating. She'd taken lots of pictures. But her recollection of them on the page was as dull and uninspiring as possible. They screamed at her that she was broken—not because she wasn't conceiving a child without help, but because she felt so alone and incomplete.

It dawned on her she was looking at things backward. Jump-starting her writing wouldn't help her feel whole. Finding ways to feel whole would jump-start her writing. Any progress she was making would show in her writing. But how could she do that?

Her plans for the day included Westminster Abbey and the National Gallery. She had been looking forward to visiting the famous church then seeing paintings by Leonardo, Van Eyck, Rembrandt, Van Gogh, and others, having a hard time fathoming such works could all reside in the same place. Exciting as these things sounded, how would they come out on the written page at the end of the day?

"Well, only one way to find out," she said, attempting a quick pep talk. Mira reached out a hand to turn the doorknob to the outside. She took a deep breath and sucked in a giant lungful of self-doubt. She did need other people, and the one person she was comfortable with was back in the States. She knew no one here, even though that was the whole point of her trip.

She took another breath, shallower this time, to avoid any more of those poisonous, self-destructive wisps. Nervously, she let out a small laugh. "Of course I don't know anyone. It's just a matter of not knowing them *yet.* I'll say, 'Hi, I'm here for a bit and want to meet people. My name is Mira.'" She stopped abruptly, her hand slipping off the doorknob.

Mira, her name. "How can I get to know anyone, when I don't know myself? What does Mira even mean?" she muttered under her breath. She pulled out her phone and googled the meaning of her name.

The name Mira has two main origins. The first is from South Slavic languages, coming from Mir which means world or peace. The other is from Hindi, originally from Sanskrit, where its meaning is sea or ocean.

Mira didn't need to read further. Her name meant something as large as a world or an ocean. How could that be? She was small and insignificant. An ocean seemed so vast and unknowable. Mira felt like a tiny drop in that ocean, certainly not the whole ocean itself. "What am I doing here? I should just go home. I am in way over my head, drowning even, in that very ocean!" she ranted out loud while pacing around her rented flat.

This whole thing seemed pointless. She tromped from kitchen to bedroom to bathroom in a neat little circle. The irony was she presented herself as a neat little package—suitcase stowed beside the closet, clothes hung up in a row, toothbrush laid on the sink, groceries hidden from view. Orderly, organized Mira, that's what she was. What did that matter? She didn't need to visit London to organize her things. And visiting London wasn't helping her organize her life.

Her breathing grew rapid as she clenched and unclenched her fists. For as put-together as she had made her surroundings, Mira herself was a jumbled mess. She was insignificant, not vast and powerful like an ocean. Flying to London had thrown teeny little Mira into an even bigger sea of people, one where no one knew her, no one needed her, no one cared that she was here.

Desperately, she picked up her phone. All she wanted to do was talk to Warren. The time on the screen stopped her. It was 9:15 in the morning, meaning it was the wee hours of the morning back home. Warren would be asleep, no doubt again getting some of his best sleep without her there to hog the covers. Instead, he'd be tangled in them like a kitten caught in a ball of yarn. The sight of him in her mind's eye almost brought a smile. He'd be on his back, with one arm above his head on the pillow, his mouth open, vibrating with his usual snores while trails of drool leaked out—things that usually annoyed her. Then he would make some grumbly noise, roll over, disappearing even more into the comforting blankets except for that raised arm and typically one bare, exposed foot.

Surprised, Mira found herself in front of the kitchen sink—and she was standing still. Just the thought of Warren had calmed her down enough to stop the pacing.

She reached into the closest cupboard and pulled out a drinking glass then mindlessly watched as she filled it with water. The stream twisted and danced like a ribbon as it moved from tap to cup, following no discernable pattern other than obedience to the law of gravity. Water. She was back to the water, the substance of oceans.

Mira slowed the flow to a trickle as her glass filled to the brim. She moved the faucet to the side but didn't shut it off. Instead, she traced her fingers through it. She could feel it, but she couldn't grab hold of it. She could let it puddle in her palm but not pick it up. It was knowable and yet not knowable, within reach and yet not reachable. Maybe she was like an ocean after all.

She lifted her wet hand and watched the drops of water slide down and off the tips of her fingers. Carefully she dripped water, drop by drop, into her already full glass. One after the other, the drops stayed in the glass, surface tension holding them hostage—until it was one too many.

The last drop broke the tension, just barely. Instead of staying on top, it ran a ragged path down the side of the glass. A tear did the same down the side of her face, just as it had when she had finally opened up to Warren. That talk had led to this—this trip, this place, this troubled moment, this beginning, this adventure, this journey. Maybe she was only a single drop in that vast ocean, but one drop could make a difference. One drop changed things. One drop mattered. She would matter. She had to, or nothing else would make any sense. With shaky determination, Mira grabbed her rain jacket, keys, and purse again and marched out the door into the waiting, sometimes scary, world on the other side.

.   .   .

Once outside, the encroaching gray sky dampened her enthusiasm. Rain was certainly in the forecast. What was she—one drop? Who was she kidding? She plopped down on the front stoop, ready to give up, when she noticed she wasn't alone.

Across the street stood the same little girl she'd seen in the window last night and when she first arrived. She was playing on a scooter, but she kept glancing Mira's way. Mira caught her eye and smiled. The child smiled shyly back.

After a few exchanged smiles, Mira slowly got up. She didn't want to frighten the child away. Children were safe and innocent. If she could talk to a child, then maybe she could try talking to an adult.

She again made eye contact with her. The wind was picking up and the child tossed her head to move her hair out of her eyes. Mira sucked in a breath, for a moment fearing the child was fending her off. Then a sly smile appeared on the small face, inviting, beckoning Mira to join her.

Mira slowly crossed and moved down the street. The child stood still with one foot on her scooter, watching and waiting for Mira to join her.

"Hi," Mira said. "How are you?"

The child wrinkled up her nose. "You sound funny," she giggled.

"Yes, I suppose I do. I'm from America."

"I've never been to America."

"Well, this is my first time here, my first time outside of America. You kind of sound funny to me too." That made the little girl really laugh. "Is your mom or dad close by? I don't want them to worry that a stranger's talking to their little girl."

"My mum is inside." She pointed to the nearest window. "She won't mind."

"Okay." Mira sat down cross-legged on the ground to be closer to the child's level. "My name is Mira. What's your name?"

"I'm Kailani. I like your name."

"I like yours too. How old are you?"

"I'm eight. I'm on my summer break from school. Are you on holiday from school?"

"No. I'm done with school. But I'm not done with learning. I came here to learn."

"Really? What are you learning?"

"That's a very good question. I can't say that I've learned a lot yet." She looked down at her hands in her lap, wondering what she *was* learning here. A drop of rain fell into her open palm. "You know, I did learn something, today in fact, although I didn't need to come to London to learn it. I learned that my name means ocean. I guess I'm a little drop in a huge ocean."

Kailani tipped her head sideways with a puzzled expression. "What do you mean a little drop?"

"Well, I'm not big and important like an ocean. I'm just one drop is all."

"But if there weren't drops, there wouldn't be an ocean in the first place."

It was as simple as that.

"I … I never thought of it that way before. You're right, Kailani. You're exactly right."

Then before they could talk further, the nearby door opened. "Kailani, inside."

Mira's quick "I'm sorry. I didn't mean to …" didn't have a chance to reach inside before the door was shut tight.

Despite the abrupt end to their conversation, this young girl had touched Mira's heart—warmed it, changed it even. A child had given her more wisdom in one sentence than she'd given herself in all the pep talks she could imagine. With more certainty than she had felt in a long time, she hurried back to her flat, with a new strategy forming.

Back in the bedroom, she had a neat little pile of information from Cordelia, and in the middle of it was the card with her phone numbers. She hoped the first one she tried would work so she wouldn't have to pluck up her courage over and over until she'd tried them all. She may not know Cordelia well, or to be honest, much at all, but they had met, and Cordelia was friendly.

Cordelia, gratefully, answered on the second ring. "Hullo."

"Hi, Cordelia?"

"Yes, and who is this?"

"This is Mira, your tenant? I thought I'd call and … well, bother you."

"Oh, sure. How are you getting on? Is something broken that needs fixing?"

"Oh, no, nothing like that. I simply have a whole city to discover on my own, and I was looking for a bit of company," Mira said, before hastily adding, "if you're interested or not too busy."

"Oh, blinding, luv!"

Mira didn't know how to respond, not sure what that meant, but the cheerful tone gave her hope. She paused hoping Cordelia would keep speaking and make the meaning clear.

"I am rather busy today," she said. Mira's face fell, thinking she now understood, until Cordelia continued, "but I'd be delighted to have a chinwag with you while we do some exploring. I can move things around tomorrow. Does that work for you?"

Picturing a chinwag made its meaning clear. Talking was just what she needed. "That would be great!" Mira was surprised by how genuinely pleased she was. After making arrangements, they hung up, but Mira's step had a lightness to it that had been missing for far too long.

Returning the papers from Cordelia to the bedside stand, Mira caught sight of the bag from Warren out of the corner of her eye. A smile spread across her face. She knew exactly what she needed.

Reaching inside, she pulled out the red scrunchie she'd used on the plane. She went into the bathroom to carefully put her hair into a ponytail, securing it with the red scrunchie from her husband. She had missed its significance before, but now she knew why this gift had appealed to Warren. He had a habit of gently brushing the hair off her face with his hand. He once told her, "I just want to see your face, every bit of it."

"Why?" she had asked.

He hadn't answered right away, trying to attach words to a feeling that was difficult to explain. "You are vibrant and beautiful and kind and giving, and you have so many other wonderful qualities. I see those things in your eyes and your smile, in the gentle slopes of your face. They are as much a part of you as your very skin. Sometimes, though, you're afraid to let people know those things about you, or simply know you, because you can't know one without the other. But you can't hide them from me—not even behind your hair."

A feeling of warmth seeped through Mira as she examined the now secured scrunchie in the mirror. She took in a deep breath—a pure, invigorating breath this time. She could do this, by herself. And if self-doubt tried to worm its way back in, she would remember the scrunchie and know that Warren always had her back. Red was, after all, Warren's favorite color. The red didn't match anything in her outfit, but, "Who cares? It matches me, and that's good enough," she said aloud as she strode out the door with confidence.

The rest of the day went by in a blur. Mira didn't introduce herself to anyone, but the lightness of step hadn't left her. For the first time, she held out hope that she could handle this trip, even though it was such a contrast from what she was used to. Back at the accounting office where she was in her element, she'd been quite comfortable and friendly, and she was well respected for her work ethic and attention to detail.

Here, in a foreign country, however, attempting this vast project on her own ... well, that was a different matter. She was a drop in that vast ocean. (Mira was beginning to like that word *vast*.) Yet every time she thought of that, Kailani's words came back to her—an ocean only existed because of all those individual drops. While these thoughts swirled in her mind throughout the day, she often found herself mindlessly touching the red scrunchie around her hair.

Even though she hadn't met anyone other than Kailani, she'd thought about it, and the thought hadn't terrified her. That was a huge step forward. Tomorrow would be another day. There was Cordelia, not to mention a whole host of people she had yet to meet. The idea of it gave her butterflies, but she told herself they were gorgeous butterflies, and tomorrow she might just set them free and watch them fly away.

· · ·

"Warren, you won't believe it, but I made a friend today."

"That's fantastic!"

"She's not what you would think of as sisterly age, but that's okay."

"Why? Is she old enough to be your mother?"

"Nope, quite the opposite. She's eight."

"Wow. Not what I was expecting, but your voice tells me the age difference doesn't matter."

"It doesn't. She did something for me that I was having trouble doing for myself." Mira wasn't sure she could adequately explain the realizations that had come about that day, but she tried to put them into words. She could almost see him nodding as she spoke.

"Good for you, babe. I love you."

"I love you too, Warren."

· · ·

Before she climbed into bed that night, she pulled out her journal to write.

Today was such an amazing day. I took a river cruise up the Thames (it's pronounced tehmes, which sounds so much more regal than thaymes). Anyway, I watched the London sights go by, but I also watched the water.

It's not that the water was pretty and clear—because it wasn't. In fact, it helped that it was kind of messy because life is messy. I have strengths and weaknesses, but then so does everyone else. I'd started to doubt myself, but a little girl, Kailani, put it into perspective for me. I matter. I am important. Without individuals like me, there would be no whole. It's easy to forget that in the mad crush of humanity that surrounds us. But children often cut through all that.

I also know I'm fortunate. Many people suffer from debilitating self-esteem that a drop of water and a red scrunchie won't cure. My heart goes out to them. I hope they're able to find the help they need. I didn't appreciate that struggle until now, and I only got the smallest taste of it.

For those of us not in that category, I imagine at one time or another we have to face our fears with trembling hearts. Thanks to Kailani and Warren, I was able to step into the dark today, and in the dark, I discovered light and a new perspective. Hopefully, stepping into it tomorrow won't be nearly as hard.

Oh! I haven't even mentioned Westminster Abbey and Big Ben and the National Gallery. I took pictures and bought books that attempt to do them justice, although nothing's like seeing them in person. I suppose they resonated more with me than they might normally. I was seeing them through eyes without scales, and I allowed myself to enjoy what was in front of me. (Although I still got stifled laughter when I said, "Excuse me." Who knows?)

Part of her wanted to write more, while the other part was exhausted—from the day and from the effort of putting pen to paper. She'd missed feeling the desire, the need, to write. Now that it was coming back, she was wary of it, as if it were a broken promise. She wanted to embrace it, but she'd held it at bay so long, she was afraid of opening her heart before she was ready, not wanting to feel betrayed or be the betrayer of such a gift.

Hesitantly, she reread her entry, and with a sigh of relief saw that she was beginning to sound like herself again. Her "sister" journal was far from what it needed to be, though. Up to now, she had written about Dylan and briefly mentioned Kailani although she knew virtually nothing about her. Mira didn't know if she could change that given Kailani's mother's reaction to her, but she'd try. And tomorrow she was going to spend time with Cordelia. Things *were* looking up. Mira closed her journal, held it close to her chest like a forgotten teddy bear, and fell asleep.

CHAPTER 7

Mira had made no plans for the day other than meeting Cordelia. She had barely scratched the surface of London, so she figured anything Cordelia suggested would be just fine with her. It went against her organized nature, but she was trying to embrace this for the adventure it should be. She was still working on finding her sea legs anyway—not in terms of being comfortable in London, but being comfortable in her own skin in London. She was excited by the prospects for the day while hoping she wasn't creating unrealistic expectations.

Mira answered the door almost before Cordelia had a chance to finish knocking. "Hullo, Mira. I must admit it's strange knocking on the door of my own flat, but I'm glad you're here. Are you ready, luv?"

"Absolutely. What do you mean your flat? You used to live here?"

"Yes, I did. It will forever hold a special place in my heart. I manage several places now, but this is the only one I've ever lived in." Cordelia ran a hand along the doorframe, smiling until her finger brushed against the cavity for the deadbolt. She paused as her face clouded over.

Then as quickly as it came, it was gone. "Well, shall we go? What would you like to see?" The bouncy voice and nature were back.

"I … Are you okay?"

"Certainly, luv. Now, what did you have in mind? I've got the whole day." Then with a wink she added, "I'm classifying this as guest relations, so we may as well live it up."

"Okay, then. What haven't you seen in a while that you'd like to see? I've only been to a few places, so most likely, it will be new to me."

"Hmm. Have you checked out the London Eye yet? We can see so much of the city from there, and then check out the aquarium. Or we could try the British Library and the British Museum."

"Let's go for the London Eye. I saw it from the plane when I flew in."

After taking the time to buy tickets online, "to save ourselves from the horrendous line," according to Cordelia, they made their way downtown. Mira hadn't been on a Ferris wheel since she was a kid. That memory was nothing compared to the London Eye, and unlike that experience with legs dangling in the open air and fear of dropping something never to be recovered, they found themselves in an enclosed bubble. The view was incredible.

"I can see for miles! Or I guess I should say kilometers."

Cordelia laughed, "Nope. It's miles here, luv. We're just as backward as you are."

Mira shook her head. "Just when I thought I knew something." She threw her hands up in mock exasperation and, in the process, accidentally bumped someone next to her. "Oh, excuse me. I'm sorry. Pardon me." Cordelia snickered. "What? I keep saying that to be polite, and people laugh exactly like you did."

"Oh, luv. Here you only say excuse me if you've burped, and pardon me if you broke wind or farted."

"You mean ..." Cordelia nodded. "Oh, my. I've been saying that all over London—both of those! No wonder people were laughing." Mortified, she covered her mouth with her hand. But as the ridiculousness of it settled in, she started to snicker then laugh outright. "I can't believe that. I forget that even though we speak the same language, it's not completely the same."

"Yes, I wonder how I'd do in America. I'd likely have similar problems."

"You know, I have one for you. What does 'homely' mean to you? You described your flat that way."

"It means cozy, comfortable, like a nice place to call home. Isn't that obvious? What does it mean to you?"

"Homely means plain or ugly. If you describe a girl as homely, it's not a compliment."

"Oh! We get a lot of people from America wanting to rent from us. Do you think ..."

"I'm sure, like me, they figured out from the context what you were saying. Although, the first time I saw the term, I figured it was a mistake by someone who didn't speak English very well." They both laughed at the irony of it.

By the time the two of them had made it to the aquarium nearby, they had been having a lovely chinwag. While the aquarium was enjoyable, it wouldn't have been nearly so to Mira if she'd seen it on her own.

They parted ways in the early afternoon, Cordelia expressing her regrets that she did need to get some office paperwork out of the way. "I love my work, but sometimes it gets in the way of my fun," she said, pretending to frown.

"Well, thank you so much for keeping me company. Could I treat you to dinner tonight as a thank you?" Mira hastily added, "If you're not too busy or worn out."

"I do need to eat, so company for dinner sounds lovely. Then maybe you'll tell me why you came to London in the first place. You're not the typical tourist."

"I ... you're right. I ... I will if you'll tell me how you knew that."

"Deal."

"Would you mind going to *The Red Fox* with me? I ate there night before last. It was great, but I'd like to meet your friend there if you don't mind."

"Not at all, luv. I'll see you around 7?"

"Sure. See you then."

.   .   .

Mira still had some time left to explore London, but she decided to head back to the flat. She could rest for a bit or head out to Regent's Park again before dinner, and since Cordelia was coming back at 7, that would give her time to talk to Warren over his lunch hour. She couldn't wait to call him.

When she arrived at her flat, she peered back over her shoulder, hoping to catch sight of Kailani. A slight curtain flicker at her place was the only thing she saw. She waved in case someone was watching, but Mira was inside before she saw the small fingers reach through the break in the curtain to wave back.

•   •   •

Cordelia stopped by shortly before 7:00 to get Mira so they could walk over to the pub together. Mira had just finished with Warren on the phone, and she was aglow with the good news she'd been able to pass on to him.

Making their way down the street, Cordelia said, "You look like you're in an exceptionally good mood," while raising her eyebrows.

Mira couldn't contain her smile. "I was talking to my husband back in the States. It was nice to share some good news with him. That I'm making progress."

"Progress?"

"Okay, you made me promise to tell you why I'm here, but first—how did you know?"

"It's not that hard really. I'm used to seeing tourists. That's what I do is manage properties, most of them short-term stays. So, I get tourists staying in them from all over the world, and they are concerned with making the most of their time. London is an expensive city, so they try to squeeze as much as they can into as short a time as possible.

"I've found they have loads of questions, and I often see their itineraries, some of which are pretty loose while others are incredibly detailed. But what those people have in common is they are here to see things, and so they plan to spend as much time as they can doing that." She was nearly poking Mira with her finger to drive home her point. "You can see it by the look in their eyes—driven, desperate even. They ask me where the tube station is, how many minutes it takes to get there, and how long it will take to get downtown or which line will take them where. They want to know how to avoid lines and when's the best time to visit certain sights. They either pepper me with questions or tell me their plans in an offhand way while fishing for my acknowledgment that they are certainly the most prepared guests I've ever had." Cordelia rolled her eyes. "People are so funny. At any rate, while they may range in their approach, they're not here to casually hang out in the flat."

Cordelia stopped in mid-stride to look at Mira. "But you, you're different. You enjoyed learning about 'excuse me' and 'homely' as much as you did seeing London from the Eye. You had no questions for me when I showed you the flat. When I gave you a map of the area, you nodded but didn't even so much as ask for any clarification. I've only had that happen one other time."

"Oh, what happened that time?"

Cordelia waved a hand dismissively and, while starting to walk down the street again, said, "That was nothing. It was just a man here to carry out a contract murder."

Mira stopped abruptly, her mouth open. "You're kidding, right?"

Cordelia turned back to face her. "Oh no, luv. The police caught him as he was getting ready to check out. I saw the whole thing. Last I heard, he'd been found guilty, but not before he ratted out those who had hired him. It all led back to the Italian mob. It was an international incident." She'd turned away before adding, "But you don't seem the type, so I haven't rung up Scotland Yard on you like I did him."

Mira's eyes had grown wide. She furtively glanced around to see if anyone had overheard their conversation, not that it mattered, but she felt exposed somehow even if she'd done nothing wrong. Cordelia, on the other hand, didn't seem the least bit ruffled, walking along with the usual bounce in her step. Without a better option, Mira hurried to catch up.

"Cordelia, I ..." She didn't know if she should defend herself, explain herself, or accuse Cordelia of something, although she wasn't sure what.

"Oh, luv. Everything is tickety-boo. Don't worry."

She said it with a smile and such enthusiasm so as to settle Mira's nerves, although she reminded herself that Cordelia said everything with a smile and enthusiasm. If she cut herself or burned herself on the stove, she'd probably say the same thing. Mira took a deep breath, shrugging the whole thing off, and followed Cordelia into *The Red Fox*.

"Bill! All right?" Cordelia greeted the man Mira had seen moving among the guests on her previous visit. He was middle-aged with thinning hair, but what hair he had was bright red. Now that Mira could see his face, he appeared to wear a permanent smile because the laugh lines at the edges of his eyes were pronounced.

"Cordelia, so good to see you. Come in. Come in."

"Bill, this is my friend from America, Mira. She's staying in my place around the corner. I told her you'd take good care of her whenever she came in. So, don't make me a liar, luv."

"Oh, absolutely, absolutely." Mira noticed he had a habit of repeating himself, and she found it charming. "Have a seat," he said, indicating anywhere they chose, adding, "Have a seat," as he moved to greet another guest.

Cordelia leaned in close to Mira. "There are those who say Bill is the red fox who gives this place its name. You saw the red hair, and he is rather clever."

"But isn't a fox considered clever in a sly, even underhanded way?"

"Yes," Cordelia said with a wink.

"Oh, okay," Mira said, wide-eyed.

After a minute Cordelia burst out laughing. "I'm just being a bit cheeky, luv. He's the kindest man you ever could meet."

Mira let out a weak smile. "Okay."

"Really, Mira. This pub is over 200 years old, and it's had the same name the whole time. They keep repainting or replacing the sign, but it's always been *The Red Fox.*" She laughed at her joke. "Now, if you'll forgive me. Let's order our food then you can tell me why you're here."

Mira decided to be more adventurous and try bangers and mash this time. The bangers, aka sausages, with mashed potatoes and onion gravy were flavorful—and filling, even though she'd asked for a smaller portion. In between bites, Mira told Cordelia what had led up to Warren suggesting a trip.

"The funny thing is, I'm a very organized person. Those detailed itineraries would usually describe me, but my goal is different, and I haven't found a way to organize that. But you were right," she concluded, "I didn't come for the usual reasons, but I'm still glad I came here. I've been fascinated with England and the rest of Europe since I was a teenager. Your countries have been established for so long. By comparison, the United States is a baby country. So, when it came down to it, Warren and I figured if I was going to travel anyway to meet people, why not go somewhere I'd always wanted to go." She paused before admitting, "A part of me, too, knew I needed to be far enough away that I wouldn't run home after the first day. Even with that, I almost did anyway."

"Really, why?"

"Well, I told you what brought me here, but my first experience didn't go so well. My seatmate on the plane was so friendly and nice. I learned so much about her, but … but I told her nothing about myself. I wouldn't have even talked to her on my own. She's the one who started the whole conversation." Mira shook her head in regret. "The sad thing is, I liked her. I wrote about her in my journal. She's great 'sister' material. Only I don't have any way to ever contact her again, to find out how things are going, to find out how her family get-together here in London is going." She sighed. "When I got off the plane after that, it struck me that I couldn't do this. It's taken a lot of guts to stay."

Cordelia studied her. "You're quite the contradiction. Most Americans come here so friendly and outgoing. To some Britons, that's strange and off-putting, but most find it refreshing. Then here you are. You're not overtly friendly, but you want to be." She surveyed her for a minute longer. "You're actually friendlier than most."

"What do you mean?"

"You may have trouble meeting people, but once you do … well, Bob's your uncle."

"Cordelia, you know I'm American. That doesn't help. What does that even mean?"

Cordelia laughed lightly. "It means, it's all done and everything is okay. Once you get past the meeting part, you've very friendly. It's who you are. I've met a lot of Americans who are friendly on the surface, but they're too busy with sightseeing or their own agendas to make or be a friend." She nodded her approval at Mira. "And now, if you don't mind, I'm going to spend a penny." When she saw Mira's arched eyebrows, she added, "It's a polite way of saying that I'm off to use the loo."

Mira nodded as if she'd known that's what it had meant all along, even though both knew that wasn't the case. When Cordelia returned, Mira said, "So, tell me about yourself. This has been the flip side of my experience on the plane. You now know all about me, and I know almost nothing about you, other than that you manage multiple properties, used to live in the flat I'm leasing from you, and that you've been to *The Red Fox* enough to be on a first-name basis with Bill."

"Oh, well, Bill was here when I needed him. He's like a protective older brother."

Mira could see that now. Bill had hovered around their table, making sure their food was good and their seats comfortable. With realization dawning, Mira said, "During our meal, Bill was checking on you, wasn't he? Why? Are you okay? Do you ..." Mira wasn't sure what to ask.

Mira's easy laugh came again. "I'm tickety-boo now, but old habits die hard. Bill will forever be watching out for me. It could be a lot worse than having someone who cares almost too much, couldn't it?"

"Yes, I guess so." Mira wanted to ask her more, but Cordelia, perhaps sensing that, abruptly got up to find Bill to wish him goodbye. Stepping into the dark night a few minutes later, they discovered it was raining ... and they'd both forgotten a brolly.

"I can duck back in and borrow one from Bill if you'd like."

"No, we won't melt, will we?"

"No," Cordelia said, her brow knit. "I wasn't very concerned about that actually."

"Oh, I'm sorry. It comes from the movie *The Wizard of Oz.* You know, the wicked witch melts?"

"Okay, if you say so."

Mira laughed. "I guess it's like tickety-boo and spend a penny and Bob's your uncle."

Cordelia joined in her laughter. "I guess so."

Walking back to the flat, the rain falling gently upon them, Mira said, "Do you ever think much about water? My name means ocean, and that got me thinking about the significance of a single drop of water."

"Well, earth, air, fire, and water are the basics of life, aren't they? A drop, a whole ocean—what's the difference? Water is essential regardless."

"You're right," Mira said, nodding. "Kailani, my new eight-year-old friend, of sorts, pointed out something similar. I was feeling insignificant, but I'm getting the sense that's just not the case."

"If my name meant ocean, I'd be chuffed! Water is life sustaining—to people, animals, plants. But think of its power too—destructive perhaps in terms of flooding, but have you ever been to the Grand Canyon? I hear it's brilliant! All that beauty was formed by the persistent work of water."

Mira hadn't visited the Grand Canyon, but she suddenly had a desire to go there. She walked on in silence with a smile playing on her lips as the rain dripped off her hair and down her cheeks.

Before long, they'd made it back to the flat. "I've got a towel inside if you want to dry off before getting in your car. I mean, *you've* got a towel inside. It is technically yours in the first place."

"Thanks," Cordelia laughed, "but I don't think I'll melt," she said with a wink. "So, am I going to make it into your journal tonight?"

"Of course you are, even though you haven't told me your story yet," Mira said with an arched eyebrow. "I noticed. When you're ready, okay?"

Cordelia's face was expressionless for a few moments. "Okay. When I'm ready."

Mira nodded before thinking of one last thing. "Hey, you used to live in this flat. Do you know the little girl that lives across the street? She's the eight-year-old I mentioned, Kailani. She has a mop of blond hair, cute as can be. Quite honestly, she's the one who convinced me to stay."

"No, sorry. It's been a few years since I lived here. Some of the neighbors are the same, but a fair amount of turnover has occurred too. You'll have to introduce me."

Mira smiled at the thought. If only it were that simple.

CHAPTER 8

The next morning, Mira reread her journal entry from the previous evening. She had written about the London Eye and the aquarium she and Cordelia had visited, including her favorite animals. She even wrote about bangers and mash. And then this:

Cordelia has a way of putting the world at ease around her. She's such a calming influence. She leaves you feeling as if you've been tucked into bed with a nice warm blanket up around your chin. Yet, something is underneath her façade. She has clearly had significant life experiences. But, depending on how you define that, haven't we all—I mean in our own ways? It's like each of us having our own expressions such as, "Bob's your uncle." Instead, I might say, "The rest is history," or, "There you have it," but they share a common thread.

I know I haven't experienced infertility like many women do, and we haven't started down the rabbit hole of medical science in that regard yet. But I still understand the dashed hopes of waiting, waiting ... only to learn I need to wait some more. The endless up and down of it is wrenching. What must it feel like to try something like in-vitro fertilization only to discover it didn't work? I don't even pretend to understand.

But do you need to experience something to be of help to others experiencing that thing? I hope not because that would mean I couldn't help someone unless their lives mirrored my own. So, maybe I can't completely understand what it's like to be someone else, to walk the proverbial mile in their shoes, but I can care. I can listen. I can run towards them instead of retreating in the other direction at the first sign of trouble.

I suppose it's enough to have suffered in one way or another to want to love and help someone else as they too suffer. And, of course, we can celebrate the joys and the triumphs with each other in the same way.

It comes down to one thing—love one another. Yes, love one another.

It wasn't turning out to be the journal she expected it to be, but then again, that was the point, wasn't it? She was here to experience life and meet people to understand how they experienced life. She couldn't have known ahead of time how that would turn out, could she?

Mira put her journal away, turning her attention to her plans for the day. Today she'd decided to tackle the British Museum. When she'd pulled it up online, it amused her that she could look through the Americas' exhibit. She'd come all this way to Britain, would be visiting the British Museum … and seeing American items? But, of course, American museums owned items from Europe and all over the world. So, why not? Still, the whole way there, she kept chuckling to herself about it.

The museum was only a short walk from the tube station, and gratefully, the day was nice and clear—although Mira had a brolly just in case. Nearing the museum, she heard the distinct sound of English spoken with an American accent. Much as she loved a British accent, it was a welcome sound.

It sounded almost … almost like Dylan's voice! It wasn't, of course, but Mira hurried her pace to catch up with the sound anyway. Sure enough, it was a woman who looked nothing like Dylan. Mira stopped to catch her breath—from running, she told herself, instead of from disappointment. Then the woman said, "I hope the British Museum isn't too busy today."

The last time she'd heard someone mention the British Museum without a British accent was on the plane here. When Dylan was telling Mira about her siblings, she also mentioned their plans in London. She'd said they were staying at a hotel not far from the British Museum and even told Mira the name of it, but Mira couldn't think of what it was, although she remembered it being a familiar name.

Rushing to the entrance of the museum, she made a beeline for the information desk. She almost started by saying, "Excuse me," but caught herself in time. Instead, she said, "Would you be able to tell me what hotels are close by here?"

"Sure, let me see ..." The attendant began rattling off quite the list of places, but once he said, "The DoubleTree," she stopped him.

"That's it. That's the one. Thank you so much. Could you, perchance, tell me how to get to the DoubleTree?" The directions were quite simple, and it was surprisingly close.

As much as Mira wanted to wander through the British Museum, she wanted to connect with Dylan even more. It had only been a few days since they'd both arrived, so she imagined Dylan's family was still around. At least, that was her hope.

The DoubleTree was a short five-minute walk away. Making her way through the arched entry into the elegant lobby, she was grateful she'd chosen the living arrangements she had. This hotel was very nice but reminded her of her visitor status. It's not that she would ever be mistaken for a Londoner, but her choice allowed her to mingle among them.

"How may I help you?" The front desk attendant's name badge identified him as Arthur.

"I'm searching for a friend of mine. Her name is Dylan ..." She realized, for the first time, that she didn't know Dylan's last name. "Well, not exactly a close friend. We met on the plane here, and I was wondering if she's still here."

"If you can tell me her last name, I'll ring her room, or you could leave a message," Arthur said.

Mira winced. "I didn't get her last name, but she's meeting up with her family here. They're celebrating her parents' 40th wedding anniversary." She could see recognition dawning on his face, but he hesitated. "Please. I don't know how else to get a hold of her. It would mean a lot to me. We had a great conversation on the plane. I even gave her a strawberry ring pop to give her father." She stopped herself. The more she talked the nuttier she sounded.

But when she glanced at Arthur, he was fighting a smile. "He thought the ring pop was hilarious, had to show it to everyone. He was even wearing it." The smile turned to a titter, and soon he was laughing unrestrained. When he calmed down a bit, he said, "I'm sorry. I've never seen a grown man wearing a candy ring. Funniest thing that's happened all week." He had to wipe his eyes before continuing. "They're still here, but they're out for the day. I saw them leave not half an hour ago. Would you like to leave a message?"

"Yes, that would be great, Arthur. Thank you."

Mira penned a quick note: *Hey, Dylan, this is Mira—remember from the plane? I enjoyed meeting you and hope you're having a great time with your family. My husband encouraged me to go on this trip to make friends— surrogate sisters. I'd love to stay in touch if you wouldn't mind.*" She added her phone and email and signed the note. Rereading it, she was struck by the fact that in a short note she'd told Dylan more about herself than she had on their entire flight. She nodded to herself. It was a good step forward.

After handing the note to Arthur, she made her way back to the British Museum. She still had most of the day ahead of her, and it appeared she would need it if she wanted to do the museum justice.

Mira wandered through gallery upon gallery, hour after hour, fascinated by the variety of items on display. One of the most interesting to her was the Rosetta Stone. Critical to deciphering ancient language, it was bigger than she'd expected. Somehow, though it made no logical sense, she'd expected it to be the size of a book, maybe because that's what she equated with learning. Instead, it stood over three feet tall. What struck Mira, however, was what she heard while standing in front of it. She heard French being spoken and Japanese, German, and, if she wasn't mistaken, Italian.

The museum held an amazing and varied representation of places and cultures from around the world but clearly not only in the exhibits. People from all over were there, speaking a myriad of languages, some of which she could identify and many she couldn't.

She held several small conversations with people when they appeared to be as fascinated with an item as she was, but mostly she smiled at others—something that, regardless of language, others could understand. The Rosetta Stone indeed.

While finishing her purchases at the gift shop, Mira got a text. A smile spread across her face when she saw it was from Dylan.

"Sorry I missed you today. So glad to hear from you! My dad already loves you, even though his ring is long gone. ;-) He insists you join us for dinner. Are you free? Are you still close by? If not, we could try another night. We're here for a few more days."

Mira quickly texted back, "I'm super close—at the British Museum. Just let me know when and where, and I'll be there!"

"We haven't decided where yet but probably about 7. Come to the hotel anytime you want. We're all here."

Leaving the museum, Mira practically skipped down the steps. The day had turned out to be pleasant and inviting. She stopped to peel off her jacket, letting the sun take over warming her skin.

While stuffing her jacket into her backpack, she glanced around at the people who had come to enjoy the museum today. They came in all shapes and sizes—some talking; some in quiet, hurried groups; others leisurely strolling. Then she heard a small sound not far away. Turning every direction to locate it, she saw a mother bending over her child who was crying. She approached, and asked, "Do you need any help?"

The mother's head came up at her words, and Mira could see past her a little Japanese girl sitting on the ground with two scraped and bloodied knees. Her mother's eyes were pleading but hesitant. "Do you need help?" Mira repeated. The mother shook her head and shrugged. She wasn't declining help. She just didn't understand English.

Mira sat down on the ground beside them. She knew what she needed. Searching around in her backpack, she found some tissues and two additional items—all from Warren.

The first was the extra water bottle—pink with blossoms down the side. This morning she had pulled it out for the first time. Knowing she might be gone much of the day, she'd filled up her regular water bottle and this one too. But she hadn't gotten around to drinking from it. It was filled with water, but new and untouched.

Mira showed it to the mother, who smiled and pointed to the blossoms, "Ahh, sakura, sakura," she said. She was bobbing her head as if Mira would surely understand, and amazingly she did. The mother was pointing out what Mira had missed—the flowers on the water bottle were Japanese cherry blossoms. The sight of them relaxed the mother, and Mira noticed even the child had stopped crying.

Next, Mira opened the bottle and poured water onto her hand then pointed to the scraped knees. She wanted to clean the dirt out of the skinned knees, and she hoped her pantomime was making that clear. The mother looked from the water to the knees and back, then she grinned and said, "Ahh." Quickly the mother spoke to her child, explaining with words and actions what was going to happen. When she was done speaking, her eyes met Mira's and she smiled.

As gently as possible, Mira poured water over the skinned knees, all the time marveling how she'd been thinking about water lately, yet hadn't considered its cleansing effect. The child winced but didn't cry out. "Good job. I'm almost done." Mira figured the child didn't understand her, but she hoped her tone of voice was soothing.

When the scrapes looked clean, Mira handed the mother a tissue and motioned for her to blot the cuts dry. She then showed the child the other item from her backpack—Hello Kitty band-aids. The child burst into a huge grin, tugging on her mother's arm until she turned to see what the excitement was about.

With a band-aid on each of the child's knees, Mira handed a few extra band-aids to the mother who bowed her head in a thank you. Then Mira noticed the water bottle sitting on the ground. She picked it up and handed it to the mother, trying in vain to explain that it was brand new.

A noise drew Mira's attention behind her. The child's father was rushing to their side, speaking rapidly and with clear concern. The three of them conversed back and forth with each other. When they finished, the father turned to Mira. "Thank you very much for helping my family."

"You're welcome." Mira again held out the water bottle. "I want you to have this water bottle. It's filled with water, but it is new. I haven't taken a drink from it. Please take it."

"Oh, no, no. You have already done so much."

"Please. I believe my husband gave it to me so I could give it away. I have another one already." She showed him her trusty water bottle. "It would make me happy if you took it."

He relented and the little girl's eyes lit up. "May we buy you dinner?" her father asked.

"Thank you, but I already have plans."

He nodded, but then reached inside the bag he was carrying with *The British Museum* written on the side. He pulled out a newly purchased umbrella and offered it to Mira. She broke into a wide grin. She'd been using Cordelia's brolly from the flat. Having one of her own would be nice, and this umbrella, given the circumstance, would mean even more.

"Thank you very much," she said, hugging the umbrella to her. "By the way, my name is Mira."

"Mira? Ahhh, mira," the mother said.

The father, attempting to interpret, said what sounded like, "Mira," again.

Puzzled, Mira glanced between the two of them while they seemed to repeat her name. The mother pantomimed looking into her hand, and Mira had an idea. She fished around in her bag until she found the pocket mirror Warren had given her. She showed it to the mother, who nodded vigorously, saying, "Hai, hai."

"Hai, yes, mira. In Japanese, your name means mirror." The way he said it, *Mira* and *mirror* sounded the same, but now she understood.

The daughter's name, Mira learned, was Meiko, and the mother and father were Yui and Haruto. Haruto's English was quite good, but even before he showed up, the lack of words hadn't gotten in their way too much.

Before they parted ways, they flagged a passer-by to take their pictures together and then exchanged contact information.

When Mira was once again on her way, she took the wrapping off the new umbrella even though there wasn't a cloud in the sky. She hadn't noticed the design before. It was an image of the Rosetta Stone.

LOOK

"The question is not what you look at; but what you see."

–Henry David Thoreau

CHAPTER 9

When Mira arrived at the DoubleTree, a new face was at the front desk. She hadn't bothered to ask Dylan for a room number and, much to her chagrin, she also had yet to get her last name. So, she sat down and texted Dylan. "Hey, I didn't tell you I was coming right away, but Surprise! I'm in the lobby."

It took only a minute for Dylan to respond. "Good because we decided we're all hungry. I'll be down in a few."

Mira sat back to wait and realized she was still holding the Rosetta Stone umbrella, had been clinging to it since leaving the museum. She opened her backpack to store it inside.

Her eye caught on the Hello Kitty band-aids. They came from a long-standing joke between her and Warren. When they got married and moved into their first apartment together, Mira brought along a half-used package of plain band-aids she'd had for some time. On one of their first trips to the store, Warren put a box of brightly-colored band-aids in their cart.

"What are those for? We've got band-aids at home."

"Yeah, but they're boring. These are more fun."

"But band-aids can't be …" she stopped, not sure what they couldn't be.

"What, babe?"

"Umm, I don't know. I guess I'm just used to plain old band-aids." She shrugged, not understanding her reluctance.

When they returned home, she pulled the box of band-aids out of the bag and the reason for her hesitation clicked. "Oh, my goodness, Warren. I know what my problem was." She was laughing.

"Your problem with what?"

"The band-aids. When I was little, Mom used to buy me princess band-aids and something like Power Rangers for my brother. One day, my dad cut his thumb right before work. We didn't have any plain band-aids, and he had to choose between princesses or superheroes. It wouldn't have been a big deal except he was heading into a meeting with top management as soon as he got to work." She laughed even more at the memory. "He was not pleased! Mortified, is more like it. From then on, Dad bought all our band-aids, and they were always plain."

"Wow. I didn't know you led such a deprived childhood. That's terrible." Warren sported a mock-serious expression.

"You know I had a great childhood," Mira said gruffly. "It was only band-aids."

Warren couldn't hold it in any longer and burst out laughing. "I know. I couldn't resist. Just kidding." But from then on, Warren bought all their band-aids, and they were never plain. If he wanted to cheer her up, he might buy her flowers, but just as likely, he'd buy her band-aids—with the latest cartoon characters emblazoned across them.

Mira had been so lost in her thoughts, she didn't see Dylan approach. "Hey! How are you? How's London treating you? You look great!"

"Thanks," Mira said. "It's been a good day."

"We explored the Tower of London today. So cool! Have you seen it yet?"

"Yes, and I agree." They chatted about the places they had both seen and some they hadn't while making their way up to Dylan's room.

"You'll have to excuse us. We make a pretty big group, so we have several rooms on this floor. Anyone could be in any one of the rooms at any given moment."

They entered a room in the middle of the hall. Before Mira had a chance to say a word, she was mobbed by three people she'd never met before.

"So good to meet you."

"Hi, Mira."

"Come in, come in."

All this was happening with a general jostling of position to hug Mira first. She didn't even know who she was hugging.

"Mom, Zita, Olivia, let her breathe, will you?" They laughed and moved back to allow her to enter the room. "As you can tell, you've won over my family before they've even met you. I'm also sure you can see they're the rather shy type."

"Yeah, I noticed that," Mira said with a smile.

"So, everyone, this is Mira, as you've already surmised. Otherwise, we'd have a very surprised hotel maid." They all laughed. "Mira, let me introduce you to part of my family. I'm sure the others will trickle in before long. This is my mom, Avelyn."

"Hello, Avelyn. I recognize you from the picture Dylan showed me on the plane. You must be an amazing woman. She spoke so highly of you. I'm impressed with how much Dylan looks like you and your husband. It's hard to believe she was adopted."

Avelyn smiled and blushed at the same time. She was a beautiful woman who had aged well. Mira would have pegged her for being in her 40s if not for the wisps of gray in her curly hair and the deep laugh lines around her eyes. "Dylan was always meant to be part of our family, but it's more about a shared heart than a shared look," Avelyn said while glancing at another one of her daughters.

Mira followed her gaze to the young Hispanic woman in a chair to her right. "I'm sorry. I didn't mean …"

"No worries, Mira," Dylan said, "This is one of my sisters, Zita. She just finished her second year of college." Then in a stage whisper, she added, "She's adopted too, but don't tell her. She doesn't know yet."

Zita smiled broadly. "Hi, Mira. I was adopted when I was eight."

Dylan perched on the arm of the chair Zita was sitting in and ruffled her hair. "Yeah, she was added to the family two years after I was—because it had gone so well with me, you know."

"And two years after that, Bin joined us," said Avelyn. "You'll meet him in a minute or two. He's around here somewhere. He's fourteen. He was four when we adopted him. He's of Korean nationality."

"Wow. Did you go to Korea to get him?"

"No. He'd been adopted from Korea by another family, but he had a hard time adjusting. They thought he might have learning disabilities. So, we ended up adopting him instead." She shrugged as if it were nothing.

"That's incredible." Mira was curious but hesitated to ask more, not wanting to be intrusive. But then she saw the inviting and open look on Avelyn's face, so she plowed ahead. "Was the language an issue?"

"No. He was initially adopted when he was 2½, so he picked up English quickly and promptly forgot most of his Korean. But he'd been in an orphanage with a lot of other children. He was adopted into a home as an only child. It left him feeling so lost and alone. We truly felt sorry for that mother and father. It was so heart-wrenching for them. Our other children were older than Bin, but I guess the slightly chaotic nature of a large family made him feel at home. From what I understand, the first time he slept through the night in America was his first night with us."

"He fit right in," Zita added. "Besides, I loved not being the youngest anymore." She turned to her mother and said something in Spanish. Then to Mira she said, "Excuse me. I'm going to round up the others."

Mira's laughter was met with puzzled expressions. "I'm sorry. Excuse me here means you burped. I learned that the hard way." They all laughed while Zita covered her mouth, but she was laughing too when she left the room.

As she did, Mira looked up at the last unknown female in the room, a woman with creamy brown skin, short black hair, and an intense stare. Seeing Mira's gaze, Dylan quickly said, "I can't believe I didn't introduce you to Olivia. She's the sister I talked about incessantly on the plane. She's almost a year younger than me, but with our birthdays being where they were, we ended up in the same grade."

"That had to be interesting," Mira said, raising her eyebrows.

Olivia's face relaxed and she giggled. "You have no idea."

"Well, when you get a new sister around your same age when you're ten, there are bound to be adjustments," Avelyn said. "But we managed. Didn't we?" Dylan and Olivia nodded and smiled while also making faces. Clearly it had been an adventure but one that appeared to have a pleasant conclusion.

A minute later, there was a knock on the door. Olivia got up to let in two more people. "Mira, this is our oldest brother Caleb, and this is his wife Tiana." Then she patted Tiana's belly. "And this," she squealed, "is my future nephew or niece." Tiana rolled her eyes but also beamed.

The pregnant belly gave Mira pause. She waited for the emotions to come—sadness, heartache, jealousy—but they didn't. She was genuinely happy for this sweet family. Fortunately, she didn't have time to rethink those emotions before three other people entered the room—Dylan's father ("You can call me Elijah") and two other brothers, Jeremy and the aforementioned Bin.

Lastly, Zita returned. "I found them all, but they were scattered everywhere. Caleb and Tiana were easy. They were in their room. Bin was playing video games in another room. I found him, but it took a while to convince him to come." She looked at her little brother with a mixture of love and annoyance. "And then Dad and Jeremy were off at the vending machines."

The boy who must be Jeremy shrugged. "I was hungry."

"We're getting ready to go to dinner," Avelyn said, turning to her husband for an explanation.

Elijah got a sheepish expression on his face. "He's a growing boy. You remember what I was like at his age, fresh out of high school." He shrugged too, and when he did, he looked just like his son.

Avelyn sighed. "Oh, come on then. Did you call the restaurant? We're bringing a small village. I don't want to surprise them."

Elijah immediately brightened. "Yes, I did, dear. We're all set."

It was a jumble of people grabbing shoes, bags, and an umbrella or two for the next several minutes. In the process, Dylan made quick introductions between her younger brothers and Mira, who was beginning to feel like family. However, she had one more question. "Dylan, this is embarrassing, but what is your last name?"

"Oh, gee. We're the Forests. You know, so many of us, that you can't see the forest for the trees. What about you?"

"Forest, I like that. My last name is Silverman—although I'm sure that's wishful thinking on some ancestor's part."

"Probably," Dylan said, smiling as they headed out the door.

The restaurant was a short distance down the street and around the corner from the hotel. They walked in ever-changing groups of twos and threes down the sidewalk. Mira once again heard Zita and her mother speaking Spanish to each other. "Dylan, did Zita come to your family knowing Spanish?"

"Yes, she was bilingual. None of us knew a lick of Spanish, but Mom didn't want her to lose it. So, she learned Spanish." Then in a whisper, she added, "She was terrible at first. Zita used to tell us how bad Mom's Spanish was, but she loved that Mom was trying. She's gotten a lot better. Although, I have no idea how she'd do with someone who isn't used to her accent and sometimes unique pronunciations."

They rounded the corner and could see the restaurant ahead, but Mira stopped. She was rounding a corner just like those sisters had that fateful day. Other than the difference in their looks, she and Dylan were talking like those sisters had. They had barely met, but a connection was already forming. That made her think of Cordelia, and it made her think of Kailani. She glanced at Avelyn and Zita, at Olivia and Tiana. Potential sisters were everywhere with a whole range of ages, and she was learning to find them, to reach out a hand.

Dylan noticed that Mira had stopped and came back to where she stood. "Are you okay?"

Mira had to wipe away a tear but answered heartily, "Yes, I am. I am definitely okay."

CHAPTER 10

When they arrived at the restaurant, it appeared it would be a few minutes before their table was ready. Mira excused herself and stepped outside.

Warren picked up after the first ring. "Hi, babe. How's it going?"

"It's going great! I wish you were here doing this with me, though."

"Oh?" His voice betrayed a note of disappointment.

"What? Don't you want to be here?"

"I'm sorry. You know it's not that. I would love to be with you. But I can't get you back until you're okay walking on your own. Wasn't that kind of the point of this?"

"You're right, and you have nothing to worry about. I'm doing great. And I'm actually finding sisters."

Just then, Dylan popped her head out. "Mira, they're ready for us."

Mira gave Dylan a thumbs up. "Hey, Warren. I need to go. Do you remember I told you about Dylan, who I met on the plane?"

"Yeah."

"Well, I found her! I'll have to explain later. But her family invited me to join them for dinner, and our table's ready. I'll talk to you later. I love you."

"I love you too, babe."

When she hung up, she found a smiling Dylan waiting patiently beside her. "Your husband?"

"Yes," Mira said, unable to conceal her smile. "Hey, I just remembered. I heard your dad loved the ring." By way of explanation, she added, "The guy at the front desk mentioned it."

Dylan shook her head. "He loved it almost too much. It was kind of embarrassing," she said, laughing, "but not really."

"What about your Mom? Did the whole speech and everything go okay?"

Dylan cast her eyes down and put her hands in her pockets. Instead of a response, she pulled the ruby slippers key chain out of her pocket.

"Oh, I see."

"I gave my dad the ring, and he was so happy and everyone was laughing. I just didn't know how to switch to a serious talk with my mom." She shrugged. "Now, I'm not sure how to start it."

"Well, there's no time like the present. Your whole family is in there right now." Mira tipped her head toward the restaurant door.

"Maybe. We'll see."

When they went inside, the family was seated not far away and motioned for Dylan and Mira to join them. There were ten of them once they were all seated around the table. It was a happy, slightly noisy gathering.

The restaurant was certainly fancier than *The Red Fox*. The food was good, but Mira liked the pub fare just as much. As they were finishing, Elijah asked for everyone's attention. "We're all having such a great time here talking to each other. I hope you don't mind me interrupting, but I want to say a word to everyone.

"This has been such a fantastic trip. I'm so grateful to all of you for coming together for the two of us to celebrate our anniversary. And, quite honestly, I'm amazed no one let slip the surprise to your mom."

Avelyn beamed. "I honestly had no idea. It was the best surprise ever!"

Elijah chuckled. "She was upset with me for proposing it just be the two of us. 'Bin's only 14 and Jeremy's 18. We can't just leave them,' she said," Avelyn gave him a mock dirty look. "At any rate, it all worked out in the end, didn't it?" He turned to his wife for confirmation, which she reluctantly gave.

"So, again, thank you all for making this work."

"That must have been something, pulling it all off," Mira said.

"Most of it wasn't too bad," Elijah responded. "The tricky part was getting Bin and Jeremy here on an earlier flight so they could surprise us, with Avelyn being none the wiser." Murmurs of agreement rippled around the table.

"How did you pull it off?"

Jeremy answered, "I supposedly arranged for Bin and myself to stay at a friend's house while Mom and Dad were gone. I told Mom that to make things easier we'd go over the day before they left."

Caleb picked up the story from there. "What really happened is we got into town, picked them up from the friend's house, and took them to the airport. They flew here with us."

"I still can't believe what you all did," Avelyn said. "This will be a memory I'll never forget. I love you all so much. What a wonderful fortieth anniversary."

"Mom?" Mira was surprised to see Dylan stand. "I told you and Dad about the ruby jewelry I left at home. And you saw the ring from Mira that I gave to Dad."

Murmurs of, "Yeah, everyone saw that," with ripples of laughter circled the table.

"Well, Mira gave me something else, something for you." Dylan retrieved the key chain from her pocket and passed it down the table to her mother.

"Oh! Ruby slippers. It's a different kind of ruby."

"Yes. Can you read what it says?"

Avelyn examined it and read, "You've always had the power, my dear, you just had to learn it for yourself."

"Mom, I know I was a difficult child. You loved me from the start, but I didn't trust that love. I figured, given enough time, you'd get tired of me and want to get rid of me too. I'm sure you knew that." Dylan paused to fiddle with her napkin and her water glass. Around the table it was silent, but Mira noticed every pair of eyes were intently on Dylan as if to say, "We know what you're trying to say, and we know you can say it. Keep trying."

When Dylan looked up, she was met with all those loving eyes. She glanced from one family member to the other. Wiping a tear from her eye, she spoke. "Mom, you knew I could be loved, that I could be saved and be a real part of this family long before I did. I can't believe it took me so long to figure that out for myself." She straightened up then continued, "But I did. I figured it out after I left, but it was because of you that I did. You let me have my wings. You let me fly away, but you never let me leave your heart. And that has changed me." She rested both hands on her heart.

Avelyn grinned while the tears flowed freely. "It doesn't seem possible," Dylan continued, "but you loved me enough for a whole childhood. Now, when I think back about the time before I met you, when I was being shuttled from foster home to foster home or even before that when I would try to hide from my drunk mom and her boyfriend, I still feel loved. It doesn't make any sense, I know. Some of those memories are horrific, but it's as if they happened to somebody else. They happened to a little girl who wasn't loved, and now, because I am, I'm someone else." She cast her eyes around the table. "You all loved me from the moment our paths crossed, including the newest to join our family." She grinned at her sister-in-law, Tiana, "but, I'm sure it's no surprise to any of you that Mom just did it best."

All heads were nodding. "Thank you, Dylan. I love you so much," Avelyn said. It was clear her heart was full and she had more she wanted to say, but the words wouldn't come as the tears flowed without restraint. Dylan moved to her mom's side, and they embraced long and hard.

Elijah wiped his own tears away. "You can see why I married her forty years ago. I'm not sure why she married me, but I'm guessing her equal simply didn't exist," he said.

Dylan eventually returned to her seat as the general buzz continued around the table. Mira patted her arm, smiling her approval.

Leaving the restaurant, Mira found herself surrounded by Dylan, Olivia, and Zita. "Where did you find those ruby slippers? That was perfect," said Olivia.

"My husband Warren found them. Who knew they'd come in so handy?"

"Well, I definitely owe you one," said Dylan.

Mira tipped her head to look at her. "Actually, we're even."

"How do you figure that?"

"Do you remember what you asked me when you were getting off the plane?"

"Umm, I haven't a clue."

"You asked me what my name meant, and I didn't have an answer for you. Because of your question, I looked it up. It means ocean."

"Okay," Dylan said, her eyebrows raised.

"At first, that just made me feel like one little, insignificant drop of water in a vast ocean. But now, I'm beginning to see how much power one drop of water can wield. Even your speech in there to your mom. That was amazing! I'm not trying to take credit for it, but one little thing, like a drop of water, or a nudge, can make a difference. And you posing that question to me made a difference. Thank you."

"You're welcome."

"Mira?" a voice said on the other side of her. She turned to see Zita had spoken to her. "Did you know that mira is the Spanish word for look?"

Mira was slow to respond while that thought sunk deep within her. "No, I didn't, not until now."

•   •   •

It was late by London time when Mira returned to the flat. She first thought, *I don't want to bother Warren when it's so late*, but she really did. Then she realized it wasn't late at all for him.

"Mira! Oh, babe, I'm so glad you called. You sounded so good before, I couldn't wait to find out what's up."

Mira told him about finding Dylan and meeting her family. "Warren, I feel like I turned a corner," then she laughed. "It really was while I was literally turning a corner. We were walking along the street, and ... I'm not sure how to describe it, but I suddenly felt like one of those sisters I saw back home. It's like the world has opened up to me, that I can make those connections I've been longing for." She was smiling at the memory. "This may sound cliché, but I feel like a new woman."

"Well …"

"What?"

"Babe, don't take this the wrong way, but what you sound like to me is the woman I married."

"What do you mean?"

"When I first met you, you were so vivacious and outgoing. This last year or so has been tough, and you've withdrawn into yourself. I think it happened gradually, so gradually that I'm not sure I recognized it until right now. But the sound of your voice brings it all back."

Mira wasn't sure how to respond, but as she pondered his words, they made sense. "I guess you're right. I … I haven't thought about who I was becoming for a long time."

"You know I'll love you through ups and downs, and I'll be with you along every journey, but I guess it's nice this is the journey you're on, isn't it?"

"Yes, I guess so," but it made her stop and think. She was heading down the right path, yet she was still far from her destination. Mira hoped she wouldn't disappoint Warren in the end, despite what he'd said. She tried to shake the thought. "I forgot to tell you about the Japanese family I met," she said, changing the topic.

Warren loved hearing about the reaction of the mother and daughter to the Japanese cherry blossoms on the water bottle and laughed about the Hello Kitty band-aids. "Who knew?" he said.

"I'm just glad I saw them and was able to help. It made my day up 'til that point. But then my day just got better."

"Well, I'm glad you stopped to look around. Not everybody does that anymore."

Look. She had looked, hadn't she? "You're right," she said, while still distracted by that word *look*.

"Well, you sound tired. I better let you go to bed. What are your plans for tomorrow?"

"Huh?"

"Your plans for tomorrow?"

"Oh, right. I don't have much in the morning, but I'm meeting Dylan's family in the afternoon. I don't know what we're doing. They were still debating where they wanted to go when I left, so I guess I'll find out tomorrow. They've temporarily adopted me, which I don't mind in the least."

"That sounds nice. I love you, babe."

"I love you too, Warren."

It was late and she was tired, but Mira wrestled with falling asleep. Her mind kept returning to her name and what it meant to look.

CHAPTER 11

When Mira awoke, she was still slightly groggy from her late night, and it took her longer than normal to sweep the last bits of dream from her mind. But rather than think of the day ahead, she was drawn to her conversation from the night before. What had Warren said? Something about it was good that she was looking and saw Meiko.

What could she make of the fact that her name meant mirror and look? She got up and scrounged through her backpack until she found the compact. Opening it, she stared at herself. What do you really see if you look hard enough?

Studying her reflection, Mira could see eyes that were slightly puffy from not enough sleep with smeared mascara since she'd forgotten to wash it off last night. But, other than that, she was seeing her familiar high cheekbones, her sweetheart-shaped lips, her slightly-pointed nose, with wisps of brown hair sneaking into the frame. Without a mirror, however, none of those things would be familiar. They were features she saw every morning yet somehow hadn't been seeing lately. She had been lost as if seeing her reflection in a cracked or hazy mirror.

Mira smiled, grateful for the clarity she'd been gaining. As she did so, creases appeared at the edges of her eyes. Over the years, she had often smiled with those eyes, cried with those eyes. She had first seen Warren with those eyes. What else had she seen?

She stood up straighter. That was the real question, wasn't it? What had those eyes seen? Or maybe it was what *could* they see? A mirror was helpful to see yourself, but did it help you look—look beyond yourself? By tilting the mirror slightly, she could see past her face to her hair, her ear, and eventually the room around her. But helpful as the mirror was, if she wasn't careful, it got in the way, narrowing or blocking her vision.

Mira dropped the mirror on the bed. She needed to get ready for the day, but thoughts kept swirling in her brain. She *had* looked around as she left the museum yesterday. If she hadn't been looking, she wouldn't have seen Meiko and her mother. But surely seeing meant more than that.

These thoughts were still on her mind as she finished her shower and threw clothes on. As a last touch, she looked in the bathroom mirror as she put her hair up in a ponytail and secured it with the red scrunchie. Stopping to examine her reflection again, Mira was startled by her phone.

She recognized Cordelia's voice as soon as she said, "Hullo, luv."

"Hey, Cordelia. What's up?"

"Well, one of my short-term tenants had to leave for home early, so he left me his theater tickets for tomorrow night since he couldn't use them. Would you like to see *Phantom of the Opera*?"

Mira squealed. "I would love that! But are you sure you don't want to see it with someone else?"

Cordelia laughed. "I convinced my boyfriend it's a love story, so he has no interest in going."

"Well, it's not your typical chick-flick material, but I'm not going to argue since his loss is my gain." She squealed again. "I'm so excited. How would you say that? I'm chuffed?"

"Oh, blimey. I'm not sure if I like that coming out of your mouth or not. But yes, you would be chuffed."

Mira could almost hear Cordelia's headshake and see her eye roll. The image of it made her laugh. "I'll remember a brolly if that makes you feel better."

"Oh, stop! And yes, bring your *umbrella*." And before Mira could squeal or laugh again, Cordelia added, "And would you tone it down? You sound so cheerful! That's not the Mira I've come to know."

Mira laughed again. "When you see me, you won't even recognize me."

"And how did that happen? A period of self-reflection?"

Mira glanced up at the mirror. "Yes and no. I think seeing myself and remembering who I was or who I am is allowing me to see others too. Does that make sense?"

"More than you know, luv. I believe we were put on this Earth to help other people, but a broken wrench can't do much to fix a leaky faucet now, can it?"

Mira nodded before realizing Cordelia couldn't see her. "You're right," but her mind had caught on something else. After they made arrangements for where and when to meet the next day, Mira hung up and made a beeline for Warren's bag.

In the bottom corner, still wrapped in tissue, she found what she was searching for. It was one of the silliest things Warren had included, which was saying something, and it still brought a smile to her face. But now it gave her pause as well. She examined it more closely then set it on the nightstand to give to Cordelia the next day.

.   .   .

Mira's morning was free from plans, so she decided to take another look around her neighborhood to see what she could "see."

As Cordelia had picked up on, until now and out of necessity, Mira had been concerned about herself, finding herself, becoming comfortable again in her own skin. She hated to admit it, but Warren was right. She had lost sight of who she was lately. It felt good to be rediscovering the old Mira.

Putting her hand on the doorknob, she took in a great cleansing breath and opened the door. Despite her grandiose plans, the first thing she saw was rain—and she hadn't grabbed her new brolly! She chuckled out loud. Maybe she needed to ease herself into this new, or old, person she was becoming.

Closing the door, she retreated to her bedroom and picked up the Rosetta Stone brolly. When she returned to the front door and opened it, she laughed again. The rain had, in that short time, stopped. A damp but shimmering world greeted her. The sun was shining, reflecting off every surface. Wet as it may be, it beckoned to her.

Gingerly, Mira stepped out into it. Which way should she go? She could head back to the park or maybe try exploring some side streets or local stores. What caught her attention gave her a different idea altogether. Kailani had just opened her front door.

Mira waited until she caught Kailani's eye. When she did, Mira gave her a small wave. Kailani hesitated, glancing back at the door that had closed behind her, then her face lit up with a large smile and she waved vigorously.

Mira walked down her steps and slowly along the street, stopping across from Kailani. She watched the child's face the whole time to see if she would be welcome. Kailani's smile grew bigger the closer Mira got.

Mindlessly, Mira fiddled with the red scrunchie in her hair. What was it Warren had said again when he'd brushed her hair back? That he wanted to see her face. But he saw more than that. He saw things about her personality, about who she was inside—as if those characteristics were evident in her very skin. That's the kind of "seeing" she needed to do too.

"How are you today, Kailani?" Mira asked, still standing across the street.

"I'm fine. How come you didn't come over here?"

At that, Mira bounded across the street. "I guess I wanted to make sure it was okay first."

Kailani smiled shyly. "It's fine. I don't mind."

"What about your mom? Is it okay with her?"

A shadow crossed Kailani's face, and she again turned to look behind her. Then she shrugged. "It's fine. My mum's just … well … she's just …" She finally added, "Really friendly too," although Mira was certain that's not what Kailani had intended to say.

Deciding not to press it, Mira said, "Okay. What's your mom's name?"

Kailani scrutinized Mira before answering. "Her name is Bibi."

"That's a nice name. Is it only you and your mom?"

Kailani hesitated and her eyes darted around the street. Then without a word, she turned and ran inside, slamming the door behind her.

Mira stared at the closed door. Out of the corner of her eye, she thought the curtain moved, but she couldn't be sure. She blew out a breath. "Well, that went well, didn't it?" she muttered to herself. And as she moved down the street, she realized that she'd blown it. She should have been busy looking instead of talking. She'd work on that next time— assuming there would be a next time.

Now not sure what to do with her time, Mira made her way to Regent's Park again. She took a different pathway this time and ended up near the lake where paddle boat rentals were available. Instead of renting one herself, she chose to sit on the ground and watch the others.

She pulled out her journal much like an artist would pull out a sketch pad. She had already filled pages and pages about her journey—both physical and personal. This time she concentrated on what was around her. Again, she wondered what she would see if she looked hard enough.

There's a small child across the way, a boy perhaps. He's not happy about something, but, from where I sit, I can't tell what. Moving closer simply to satisfy my curiosity doesn't feel appropriate, so I'll have to be content with what I can observe from here.

His mother is crouching down to talk to him at eye level, but he's stomping his foot and shaking his head. I can see his mother opening a tote to show him what's inside and motioning to a shady spot nearby, but he will not even meet her eye.

Now, after a few minutes of this, the mother stands up, shrugs, and walks over to the shady spot she indicated earlier. There's a subtlety to her movements—an apparent turning away but only slightly so her son is never out of sight even though her attention appears to be elsewhere. She's pulling out a large picnic blanket, shaking it out, and spreading it evenly on the ground. It's not time for lunch yet, so I wonder what's in her bag.

I don't have to wait long. She's brought toys along with an assortment of snacks—grapes, crackers, cheese, and juice, from what I can tell. Lastly, she pulls out a child's storybook which she is now apparently reading to herself.

While that mother may have never let her child out of her sights, I did, engrossed as I was in her very deliberate show. She hadn't turned more than a few pages of the book while nibbling on grapes when he made his way to the end of her blanket. He's quiet now with a thumb in his mouth. Gradually he moves into place where he can see the pictures on the page, edging closer and closer until he is sitting right next to his mother.

Without missing a beat, she shifts the book to be directly in front of him and wraps her free arm around her son, holding him close and safe.

Mira shook her head to clear her thoughts. How easy it would have been to judge that mother—because her child was throwing a tantrum or when she walked away from him. But, with time, a different picture emerged. When Mira eventually had children, would she be that measured and patient? She wasn't sure, but she hoped so.

Becoming stiff from sitting in the same position, Mira shifted. As she did, she realized something else about that mother. She had chosen a shady spot, not because it was too hot in the sun. She had chosen a spot that had stayed protected and dry during the recent short downpour. Mira had not. The seat of her pants was more than damp.

The way she saw it, she had two reasonable options. She could return to the flat and change, or she could walk around and hope the sun was kind enough to do her work for her. Fortunately, she was only wet and not muddy too.

She didn't want to head back, but she might need to anyway, depending on where she'd be meeting up with Dylan and her clan. She shot a quick text to Dylan. "Where are we going today? I'm assuming you've decided by now."

She was exiting the park when she got a text back. "The London Zoo. Is that okay with you?"

"Sure. I love zoos!" She was about to ask where it was when something made her stop. She turned around to face the park. An older man brushed past her. "Exc—, ... umm, sir, could you tell me where the London Zoo is?"

He stopped and turned. "Why, certainly. It's on the far side of the park. If you take this outer walk, you'll run right into it."

"Thank you." She thought she'd seen signs to that effect somewhere. She turned back to her phone and texted, "I'll meet you there. What time?"

The plan was to meet at 1:00, which gave Mira a couple free hours. Close by was the Sherlock Holmes museum. That would be fun along with a quick lunch. It also sounded better than walking back to change her clothes. With that, she'd hope for the best.

• • •

With the zoo coming into view, after her museum tour and lunch, Mira's heart skipped. She had always loved animals, but the fact she was meeting up with a whole family who had welcomed her completely overshadowed that. Who would have thought that so much could happen in less than a week?

She heard them before she saw them, the jumble of voices reaching out to her, pulling the corners of her mouth into an involuntary grin. "Mira!" Dylan shouted when they came into view. "I hope you haven't been waiting long."

"Not at all. Did everyone come?"

"Almost. Tiana was tired, but that's understandable with her pregnancy, and Caleb decided to stay back with his wife. The rest of us are here." Mira could see various family members coming up the walk. "Have you had lunch yet?"

"Yes, I just ate."

"We did too, but Jeremy and Bin are hungry again. So, I think they're going to make a beeline for a food court or restaurant or whatever they can find inside. Dad's either indulging them or encouraging them. I haven't figured out which yet."

Once inside the entrance, they split up to see their favorite animals (or food), meeting back up then splitting again in different groupings for the rest of the afternoon. After one such split, Mira found herself alone with Dylan's mom, Avelyn. They were both tired and had decided to sit out the next round of animal visits.

"I'm not as young as I used to be, much to my chagrin," Avelyn sighed. "But, Mira, you don't need to sit here to keep me company. I'm quite used to the clan running off without me."

"No problem. To be honest, I didn't get enough sleep last night. So, I'm grateful for the excuse to sit."

Avelyn raised her eyebrows. "Is everything all right?"

"Everything's fine. Once I got home, I called my husband, and then I had a hard time shutting my mind down to go to sleep."

"I understand." Avelyn patted Mira's leg. "Tell me about your husband. What's he like? He must be a real sweetheart to encourage you to take this dream trip of yours."

"He is," Mira said, lost in the thoughts of missing him before she continued. "We met in high school."

"High school sweethearts?"

She laughed in response. "Not exactly. We ran around in different crowds. I thought his crowd were snobs and he thought my crowd were prima donnas. Come to think of it, that was a pretty accurate view of most of them.

"It wasn't until the summer after our first year at college that we had more than a passing conversation. We'd come home and both found summer jobs at the same local bookstore. One day after work, we found ourselves both walking to a deli up the street. So, we decided to eat together. It turns out he had distanced himself from his group of high school friends and so had I—you know, because they were snobs and prima donnas."

"Let me guess, that was it? The start of something else?"

Mira nodded. "We talked until the deli closed for the night. We had no clue we'd been talking that long. It was the most incredible feeling. I went home and told my mom I'd met the man I was going to marry, even though, technically, we'd met a long time before that. Apparently, Warren felt the same about me."

"So, how did you manage school? When did you get married?"

"Those were the questions we had too. By the end of the summer, we had become inseparable. We even talked about getting married in the future. The most logical thing was to wait until we'd both graduated from college. But two months into my fall semester, I knew that would never work. I couldn't concentrate on my classes. If we hadn't become so close, so inseparable, it probably would have been fine. Given the circumstances, however, I was a basket case.

"We had some long conversations over the phone. In the end, Warren decided to transfer to the university I was attending. He was able to pull it off by the next semester."

"And when did you get married?"

"The following summer. It was lovely."

Avelyn again patted her leg. "I'm so pleased for you. How long have you been married now?"

"Six years." It had been six years, hadn't it? "It seems like only yesterday, but it also feels like we've been married for as long as I can remember." She grew silent then added softly, "I figured we'd have children by now." She hadn't meant for Avelyn to hear her, and for a moment she thought Avelyn hadn't.

But then she responded, "That's what I gathered, but I was trying not to assume."

"What do you mean? How could you know that?" She wasn't offended but curious.

"It's a subtle thing. I'd love to say I picked up on it because I've been around the block enough times to notice everything about people. But honestly, it's because I've been where you are."

"You have?"

"Think about it, Mira. We just celebrated our fortieth wedding anniversary. Yet my oldest child isn't even thirty. That could have been a choice but doesn't seem likely when you end up with five children, does it?"

"I didn't … I didn't realize." What she wanted to say was she didn't see.

"Of course, you have to be careful about assumptions, but …" She shrugged.

"What did you see with me? How did you know?"

"Tiana. It's how you reacted to Tiana and her pregnant belly. You hesitated before being happy for her. You appeared to be steeling yourself so as not to take it personally somehow."

"You saw all that? I mean, I did do that, but I didn't realize it was obvious."

"It wasn't obvious. I told you it was subtle. When my Elijah and I got married, we wanted children right away. Ten years later, we were still waiting. I thought you could plan when to have children. I'll admit, some people can, but that wasn't the case with us. I did get pregnant after a year or so, but then I had a miscarriage. That was followed by more waiting and more miscarriages. The doctors got involved, which honestly added stress to everything. In the end, I told Elijah I needed to take a break from it all.

"It was during that break that we decided to adopt. We had everything set to go when I found myself pregnant again. I was so worried I would miscarry again, but I didn't. We welcomed a healthy baby boy, our dear Caleb. That was the most incredible moment. Four years later, we were blessed to have Olivia. Six more years gave us Jeremy. Then, obviously, we adopted our last three."

She gave Mira a searching look that seemed to reach into the depths of her soul. "I don't tell you that story to pour salt in a wound. Yes, we ended up having children. I'm not going to promise you that it will end up that way for you. You certainly have a lot more medical options available now, but those are decisions for you and your husband. The real reason I tell you that story is to let you know you're not alone—not alone in the feelings you have. I recognized your look with my daughter-in-law because I've worn that look myself. I watched my friends have children— one baby, two babies, four babies—while I had none. I listened politely while they complained about those same children. And I held my tongue. Each time, I had to make the same decision you did yesterday. Can I be happy for you and what you have? Can I do so without it undoing me? And each time I could answer those questions with 'yes,' I knew I was winning. I was playing to the 'better angel of my nature,' to borrow from Abraham Lincoln."

Mira was speechless, but a tear started to wend its way down her cheek.

"Mira, I'm not saying you can't be sad, so don't get me wrong. I cried my rivers of tears, believe me. I'm just glad I didn't let it own me. I'm glad I could see beyond myself, at least some of the time."

They sat in silence for a long time, Avelyn's arm around Mira's shoulder. At last, Mira found her voice. "Avelyn, would you mind being my adopted sister?"

CHAPTER 12

By the time the others rejoined them, Mira and Avelyn were all smiles, swapping funny stories about their husbands. The family invited Mira to join them for dinner again, planning on taking the waterbus from the zoo to Little Venice to see what they could find there. But Mira declined. She wanted to go back to her flat and talk to Warren.

It wasn't a long walk back, and Mira took her time, taking in her surroundings. The rain came back, which made her grateful she'd brought along her brolly. Little drops of water splashed playfully around her, creating ripples in puddles, bending leaves, serenading her as they plop-plopped on the top of her umbrella.

The rain was steady but not heavy. Mira moved her umbrella aside, letting the drops collect on her hair and drip down to its tips. Once again, she was crying along with the heavens as new thoughts had entered her mind.

When she reached her front door, she glanced down the street for any signs of Kailani. With the current drizzle she wasn't surprised that Kailani wasn't anywhere in sight, and Mira was quite honestly relieved.

She changed into her warm, dry pajamas before plopping down on the couch, curling her feet up underneath her to get them warm. It was dinner time, Warren's lunchtime, and the perfect time to call him. Mira, however, didn't pick up her phone.

Dylan's mom was likely around the same age as her own mother would have been. She had died suddenly in a car accident only two years ago, a year after she and Warren had moved close by. They had already been talking about starting a family by then. But something changed in her when her mother passed away—only she hadn't put her finger on what until now.

She wanted to talk to Warren, but before she did, she took the time to write in her journal.

I cried today—more than once. They were sad tears and happy tears at the same time. I didn't know that was possible, but I guess it is. Avelyn, Dylan's mom, talked to me about her own struggles with infertility, but the talk was more about the emotions that accompany it than anything else. I believe that's what I've wanted to fix all along. Doctors can help us with the physical issues, and time will tell if we'll be successful in that department. The emotional side of things, though, is something else entirely. I can work on fixing that now. It's the main reason I've felt the need for sisters. Face it, men's emotional needs are different from women's. Much as Warren has wanted to, he just hasn't understood what my emotions are like. Making that connection today has already made this trip worth it.

In an odd way, I'm learning that I need to love myself and then I can love others. But reaching out to others and being willing to share some of myself is also what helps me. It's the classic chicken and the egg dilemma. Avelyn wouldn't have shared what she did if I wasn't willing to admit to my own situation. I whispered thoughts about wanting children, thinking she wouldn't hear. In reality, I'm quite certain I hoped she would hear. But I don't think I would have had the courage to whisper that if I hadn't begun finding myself again these last few days. I hope I can do for others what she did for me today. And it all starts with being very observant—from looking.

Something else struck me too—my mom. I've been desperate to have a child, with a fervor that didn't make sense. We've been trying for a year and a half now, a time frame that's not that unusual. I've often heard that a year is perfectly normal. Yet, I didn't act as if it was, and there's no way Warren could understand it because I didn't understand it! Despite what I said above about Warren not understanding because he's a man, I realize that's not the whole story.

Sitting on that bench talking to a woman who was old enough to be my mother made me realize I miss her; I miss my own mother. She's the "sister" I've been searching for more than anyone. She passed away before

I was ready, before I was a mother myself, before I could compare notes, ask for advice, or let Grandma spoil my kids. I feel cheated!

There, I said it. I feel cheated! And now I realize I was in a hurry to have a child of my own to have a mother-child relationship. If I couldn't have it with my mother, I'd have it with my child instead.

This doesn't change my desire for children. It just puts it in the right perspective. I'm glad we were already talking about having children when Mom passed away. Otherwise, I might question my motives.

This journal of mine—this sister journal—could fulfill another need I didn't know I had. Warren told me to write in it about the "sisters" I meet so I can then visit them often in these pages. Whether while on this trip or when I get home, I need to write my memories of my mother. Then I'll be able to visit her anytime I want. She'll be there for me through thick and thin—like when she was alive.

Mira would write more later, but she needed to make a phone call first. "Warren, do you have a few minutes to talk?"

"Sure, Mira. I always have time for you. It's my lunchtime anyway, but what's up?"

"I was thinking about my mom."

.   .   .

When she got off the phone, Mira decided to grab a quick "take-away" dinner, as it was called in London. She'd spotted an Indian restaurant a short distance away that she'd been wanting to try. Then she looked at herself and realized she'd already changed into pajamas. Throwing something together from the supplies she had sounded like less work than changing clothes.

When she had a warm grilled cheese in front of her, Mira reflected on her conversation with Warren. The feelings she was finally admitting to having made sense to both of them.

"Warren, I owe you an apology," she'd said. "I resented how you were dealing with things, with not getting pregnant. No doubt it's different for you than it is for me, but I was carrying around more baggage than we both realized. I took that out on you, and I shouldn't have."

"I appreciate the apology, but I'm not sure it's warranted. Neither of us realized what was going on, and you never lashed out at me or anything."

"I know, but this trip … everything that led up to it. I'm feeling bad about spending all this money when I was blowing things out of proportion."

"Are you kidding? Your feelings and needs were real—are real. Part of them just came from a different source than we both realized. That doesn't make them any less important or valid."

"You're right, I suppose."

"Of course I'm right," he chuckled. "But, seriously, Mira. If you hadn't been where you were today, you wouldn't have figured this out, would you?"

"You're right … again."

"I mean, maybe you would have eventually figured it out, but maybe not. It's taken breaking back out of your shell to even open up the possibility of learning these things." She was nodding to herself. "Mira, don't ever question your worth with me. The money for this trip is nothing. You, on the other hand, are everything to me. It's not just today, but you've had several days where I can hear the changes in your voice. I can feel you coming to life again—all because of this trip. I …" Mira could hear him getting choked up. "I am so proud of you. You've been trying to hide it, but I know how difficult this trip was to start with. Believe me, it was difficult for me too, but in different ways. You are so incredible, and I love you so much. Just keep getting out there, babe. You're rocking this!" His words had brought more tears to her eyes, but they were wholly happy tears this time.

After cleaning up her dinner dishes, Mira headed off to bed. The bed was comfortable, almost as if Warren had warmed it up for her.

CHAPTER 13

Saturday morning dawned bright and early for Mira. For once, she had concrete plans. First, she was going to wash some clothes. And then she planned to check out the Camden Lock Market. On a whim, she texted Dylan. "Heading to Camden Lock Market today. Any of you interested in joining me?"

It was only a minute before she got a text back. "Oooh! Me, me! Olivia's in too. We'll see who else wants to tag along. How about lunchtime? Then we can grab a bite to eat and shop!"

When they had finished arranging where and when to meet, Mira got busy with her laundry. Cordelia had shown her the washer in the kitchen and how it worked. When she'd asked about a dryer, Cordelia laughed. "You simply hang your clothes up to dry on their own. Why would we waste electricity doing something the air can do?"

While the wash was going, she made her way to the supermarket to restock her fridge and cupboards. She and the washer finished simultaneously. So, she pulled out wet clothes and draped them everywhere. Much of the flat looked like a backyard clothesline, but if it worked, who was she to argue. By the time she finished, it was time to head out.

Walking out the door, she shot Warren a quick text. "Love you, hubs." When they were first married, she called him hubby but then shortened it simply to hubs. He had always called her babe, but she'd gotten out of the habit on her end. It made her smile, and she was sure it would make him smile too.

Camden Lock Market was an experience. It wasn't like a shopping center, closer to a swap meet, but even that description didn't do it justice. Eclectic is the word that came to Mira's mind what with jewelry of all kinds, clothes not found in your typical department store, and unusual and varied gift shops. She discovered intriguing places that drew her in and a few that repelled her as well. It was amazing yet overwhelming.

"Boy am I glad to see you," she said when she first spotted Dylan. "I was beginning to worry this place would swallow me, and I don't know if that's a good thing or not."

Dylan laughed. "I understand what you mean."

"Where's Olivia? Did she change her mind?"

"No. All the women wanted to come. I mean, we're talking shopping, aren't we? But I left them in various food lines. I was sent on the scavenger hunt to find you."

"Oh, good, 'cause I'm starving. Let's go."

The food choices, however, were just as daunting as the shops. "I'm guessing I could essentially visit all kinds of foreign countries through their food just in this one spot," Mira said.

"I know, right? Mom's right over there. She wanted to try Indonesian street food, which honestly sounds amazing. Olivia was trying to find a Mexican joint, and I'm not sure where Tiana and Zita are."

When they'd all gathered with their various meals, the chatter never stopped. Zita was swapping some of her Peruvian street food with her mom's Indonesian, and Dylan kept offering everyone a taste of her falafel. Tiana seemed hungry enough to eat it all, but she always stopped to sniff it first. Dylan whispered, "She's not usually a picky eater, but since being pregnant, certain smells drive her nuts."

Avelyn overheard the comment and met Mira's eyes. Mira gave her a reassuring smile, relieved that she wasn't bothered by Tiana's pregnancy or any talk about it. However, so much had gone on in her head lately, that as conversations started in earnest between these women, Mira was content to sit back and observe the happenings rather than participate.

Avelyn was so clearly the mother, encouraging each of her daughters in turn. Tiana was a bit more reserved but smiled and blushed anytime anyone spoke to her. She relished being cocooned in the safety of this circle and in response often touched her belly in a similarly protective gesture. Dylan and Zita were the most talkative of the bunch, turning from one person to another so fast Mira wasn't sure how they kept any of their conversations straight.

But something was up with Olivia. When her mother looked in her direction or spoke to her, she was animated. When Zita turned her way, she always had a snappy comeback. Dylan often reached over to squeeze her hand or her shoulder, and Olivia always responded in kind. But when she didn't think anyone was watching, Olivia got a faraway look, lost somewhere in the dark recesses of her mind.

"Mira, you're so quiet. What are you thinking?" Zita said.

"Sorry. I'm busy looking." Zita's expression was puzzled. "It's your fault," Mira teased. "You told me my name means look. I'm practicing a little looking instead of talking."

Zita smiled and nodded. But Olivia quickly glanced her way, an unspoken question in her eyes, *Did you see me?*

Mira smiled at Olivia, trying to put her at ease. The expression Olivia returned was confusing. At first, Mira pegged it as scared or guilty, like a child that's been caught with her hand in the cookie jar, but then she wondered if it wasn't more pleading instead. But what was Olivia pleading for?

She didn't have an opportunity to answer that question. No sooner had this look passed between them then the others stood up ready to explore.

Several hours later, with an armful of interesting purchases, Mira bid the others goodbye. She needed to return home and prepare to meet Cordelia for the theater that evening.

When she walked in the door, ready to dump her purchases, she was greeted with the results of her earlier handiwork—clothes were draped everywhere. For the most part, they were even dry, much to her relief. She put them away and got ready for her evening.

.   .   .

Mira took the tube to meet Cordelia. While it sped to her destination, Mira idly fiddled with the gift she had for Cordelia. It was what Mira referred to as a USB drive, albeit an unusual one. Warren, however, liked calling it a memory stick. When she remembered that, it dawned on her why he had picked this in the first place. He often playfully teased her about her memory and organizational skills, knowing he had to rely on technology to accomplish the same thing. This was a tongue-in-cheek jab at both of them, with a bit of whimsy thrown in.

Mira and Cordelia had arranged to meet at a small café not far from the theater. Cordelia was already there when Mira slipped into the seat beside her where a plate of biscuits was waiting. "What a cute little place this is." She took a bite of one of the biscuits. "Ooh, that's good."

"Yes, this place is another one of my favorites."

"Your boyfriend's missing out, but I'm not complaining." Cordelia was uncharacteristically quiet, so Mira continued. "Before we head off to the theater, I have something I wanted to give you. You told me yesterday that a broken wrench couldn't fix a leaky faucet or something to that effect. So, I'd like you to have this." Mira handed her the memory stick. It was fashioned to look like a crescent wrench.

Cordelia laughed. "What is it? That's the funniest looking thing."

"It's my husband's idea of a memory stick. He bought me these sweet and funny gifts before I left, but, I admit, that was one of the silliest. I thought of it after you said what you did."

Cordelia opened it up to reveal it was indeed a USB drive. "Who would have thought? That's brilliant, luv!"

"You were right too. I've been working on fixing my own broken wrench so I can work on helping others. I loved your turn of phrase. How did you come up with that?"

Cordelia was again at a loss for words for a moment. Then she brushed it off with, "Oh, it's nothing. You know, we ought to get going," she added, although they had barely touched their biscuits.

·   ·   ·

The play was fantastic. Mira had never been to Broadway, but she'd seen a production of *Les Misérables* when it came to Chicago. She and Warren had loved it. Like that experience, the music of *Phantom of the Opera* filled her and left her speechless.

Leaving the theater, Mira said, "Thank you for inviting me. That was incredible. My husband Warren would have loved it too."

"I'm so glad you enjoyed it. I did too."

"Your boyfriend missed out, but I'm not sorry."

Cordelia stopped walking, upsetting the flow of people leaving the theater. She turned to Mira with a serious expression on her face. "Come here." She grabbed her arm, pulling her away from the crowd of people. They walked in silence for a short distance until Cordelia found a quiet and sparsely filled coffee shop. She had not said another word to her as they walked and even while they found an empty booth.

When Cordelia did speak, it was subdued. "I didn't have to convince my boyfriend that he wouldn't be interested in the play. I don't have a boyfriend."

Mira hadn't known what to expect, but this statement caught her off guard. "Really? Okay, but why …" Mira trailed off, not knowing what else to say.

Cordelia didn't respond right away. She reached into her pocket and pulled out the USB drive Mira had given her, twirling it in her fingers. "I was that broken wrench, and I'm so much better now, but old habits die hard. Sometimes it comes in handy to have an imaginary boyfriend, so I trot him out on occasion. It's not that I needed to when I was inviting you to join me, I'm afraid it was a bit of a reflex action. I'm sorry."

Mira was waiting for more of an explanation, but it didn't come. Instead, the serious expression on Cordelia's face vanished, being replaced by the one she usually wore. "Do you want to know what he looks like? The boyfriend? I mean, if you're going to conjure one up, he should be a right fine bloke, don't you think?"

Still confused, Mira said, "Okay," and tried to smile. While Cordelia described her rather well-built, handsome boyfriend, Mira marveled how looks could be deceiving. Just like a good-looking boyfriend who didn't exist and a USB drive that looked like a wrench, Cordelia presented as the happiest person alive without a care in the world.

CHAPTER 14

Mira had been going strong ever since she arrived in England. With the arrival of Sunday, she decided making it a true day of rest wasn't a bad idea. She slept in then lounged around in her pajamas for much of the morning.

Back behind the flat was a small outdoor space—a garden, as Cordelia called it. Mira hadn't even so much as stepped out there in the week she'd been in England. With a quiet day ahead and nice weather to boot, Mira decided to change that. She grabbed her journal and opened the back door.

It was a beautiful little garden. Mira might have called it a backyard with a patio, but the term garden was so much more inviting—homey or homely, as Cordelia would say. It conjured up memories of *The Secret Garden*, a favorite childhood book of her mother's.

The garden consisted of a small patio against the house that sported a couple chairs and a small barbecue. Potted plants dotted the edges. Beyond this was a small grassy patch enclosed by hedges and rose bushes covered in pink, red, white, and lavender blooms. Mira felt safe and protected here.

Setting her journal down on one of the seats, she strolled among the roses, drawing the blooms close to take in their heady aroma. The lavender roses, past their peak bloom, weren't as delicate and pretty as the others, but their powerful scent surprised her. She carefully plucked one and took it back with her to the patio to keep her company while she wrote.

I'm constantly amazed by the flood of emotions that have accompanied this trip. I came looking to find myself and to find sisters for myself, but I selfishly hadn't considered that to have sisters, one needs to be a sister. I can make excuses that I was so stuck where I was that I couldn't see out enough to recognize that fact, but in the end, it's still merely an excuse.

Just as I need others, they need me too. I wonder about Cordelia. I don't know what has led her to where she is, but bright as she is, clearly her path has woven through darker times. I like to imagine that this garden I'm sitting in was her secret garden, that it was a place of refuge during difficult times. There is a care to the placement of roses for beauty, combined with hedges for privacy that tell me my suspicions are not far off.

I see a power in Cordelia that is at once awe-inspiring and which also might be a facade. I have yet to learn who the real Cordelia is, although I imagine she's a complex combination of all that I see. I hope I can be a sister to her.

Olivia, Dylan's sister, also makes me wonder. I know she already has sisters—and a mother, but I get the sense that right now that's not enough. She's putting on a good face for them, but clearly something is bothering her, something she's hiding from the others. I don't want to intrude where I don't belong, but maybe she needs someone who's on the outside. Maybe, even, that inside group is part of the problem? I don't know. And I don't know if I can help, but I'm going to keep my eyes open, and maybe at some point I can.

Sitting here in this beautiful, peaceful garden, it's hard to contemplate how much this last week (has it only been a week?) has meant to me, how much it has changed me. I have to shake my head at what Warren must have been putting up with lately. Amazingly, I know he didn't kick me out of the house because he was sick of it, even though he would have been justified in my mind. He is very committed to me, to us. I am too, but I hadn't realized how much I was struggling to hold up my end of things. Gratefully, I think I'm learning to give and not just take.

I shouldn't be so hard on myself, though, because I suppose we all have moments in our lives where we can't do it on our own. Those are the times we hope the people we have chosen to surround ourselves with will help hold things up for us, keeping everything from collapsing down upon us.

Mira set her journal down, letting what she'd written sink in while basking in the quiet of the garden. Her mind wandered from thoughts of Warren to Dylan to Cordelia to Olivia to Avelyn to her mother, even to Kailani then back to Warren again. It was a nice little circle she was building, and most of them had been added to it in the last few days.

Reflecting on that past week, she pondered the week ahead. It promised to be interesting in its own right. After a few more days in London, she would be heading to Paris.

Thoughts of traveling elsewhere prompted her to pick up her phone to text Dylan. She remembered Dylan saying something about being in London a few more days. When were they leaving? Mira knew they could stay in touch, but the sudden notion that Dylan's whole family might soon be leaving London threatened to leave a gaping hole in Mira's heart.

Trying to sound casual and not panicked, Mira texted, "Hey, what are your plans? How much longer are you going to be in London?"

When Dylan didn't immediately text back, Mira knew it was time for a distraction. The garden was no longer the haven it had been only a few minutes before. She wished she could text or call Warren, but he was likely sleeping in since it was Sunday morning.

Collecting her journal, she headed inside, but she was only there briefly, making a beeline for the front door. A nice Sunday walk would do her good.

Closing the door behind her, she scanned her surroundings. The street that was usually quiet on weekdays was abuzz with lazy activity. More people than she had seen before had spilled outside, walking dogs or stopping to talk to neighbors with an unhurried air about them. Maybe they were around more than this, but Mira hadn't been around much herself to know.

She automatically glanced over at Kailani's stoop but saw no sign of the little girl or her mother. Where Mira had always turned right before, she decided to head out left to see what she might find.

Mira walked on for some time not caring where she went, only paying attention to her turns so she could find her way home. London offered so much to see, but this time it wasn't the famous landmarks she was noticing but rather the people.

She saw children chasing after an errant dog, two women having a chinwag while they tended their planter boxes, and a group of men gathered around an old classic car each loudly giving his opinion. She emerged from a mostly residential area to find a cluster of small shops, some old, some new, but each with its own character.

Across the street, an old bakery caught her eye. A variety of pastries filled its windows and merited a closer look. She started to cross the street when an elderly couple came out of the bakery. From their appearance, they must have been married for a half-century. He pushed open the door and held it for his wife as she exited, but then she leaned against the door holding it open so he could follow. Mira watched as he then juggled his purchases to free one hand so he could use it to hold his wife's hand. It was tender and sweet watching them shuffle down the sidewalk together.

On a whim, Mira approached them. "Excuse ... I mean, hello. I couldn't help noticing you coming out of the bakery. Would you like some help with your bags? I'd be happy to carry them for you."

The couple looked up, somewhat startled. "Where are you from?" the husband said gruffly.

Slightly taken aback, Mira said, "The United States. My name is Mira. I'm just visiting here a bit."

He eyed her with suspicion, but his wife piped up, "Oh, Harold, don't be a git. She's being nice, can't you tell?"

The wife's biting tone caught Mira off guard. Maybe this wasn't the happily ever after marriage she'd made it out to be, but then Harold surprised her even more by letting out the biggest laugh she'd ever heard. "I can't believe you called me that," he said.

Mira, now more confused than ever, stood stock still, not sure whether to continue to offer assistance or to run the other direction as quickly as possible.

"Now see what you've done, Harold. You've scared the poor young thing out of her wits. You really are a proper git, aren't you?"

Harold roared with laughter again but stopped suddenly when he saw Mira's face. "I'm sorry, lass. Could we make it up to you with a cuppa? We live just up the street a bit."

Other than regretting having offered any help in the first place, Mira wasn't sure how to feel—about this invitation or anything. Harold's wife said, "I'm sorry. I'm Madge. My husband's really quite harmless. We'd love to accept your offer of helping with our things. And once we get home, we'd love for you to have a spot of tea with us, if you're so inclined."

Madge's soft tone of voice should have put Mira at ease, but it didn't. It was such a drastic change of tone from how Madge had spoken to her husband that it left Mira feeling a bit dizzy. Unsure what else to do, she gathered up the bags of bakery items and proceeded to follow Madge and Harold home.

As they walked, Madge softly asked Mira, "So, what brings you to England? Busy being a tourist?"

"Yes … and no."

"Well, can't you make up your mind?"

Mira chuckled. "Yes, I can. It's just that I'm here because I needed a new outlook on life, a break, I guess. But, as long as I was going somewhere, it may as well be someplace with a lot of wonderful, touristy places to visit, right?"

"Hmm. I see. And does your husband mind?" She had raised one eyebrow. The question was a probing one.

"You noticed my wedding ring, I see. No, he does not. He's the one who suggested the trip. And to answer your next question, no, he wasn't trying to get rid of me. He was only trying to help." Madge seemed satisfied and fell back into silence.

"You know, Madge, that was pretty skillful. I don't usually tell people that much about myself in the first few minutes of meeting them."

Madge turned a twinkling eye on Mira. "Well, I'm not the one who started this, was I now?"

Open-mouthed, Mira stopped. "I … I …"

"Didn't know I'd be so cheeky, did you?" Madge added, then turned away, continuing down the street. Harold smiled at Mira, gave a small shrug, then continued to walk alongside his wife.

Holding their purchases, Mira felt she had no choice but to follow. Within a few steps, though, her annoyance had turned to amusement. These two were something else again. Cheeky probably didn't begin to cover it, yet she couldn't help but like them.

Once their purchases were safely inside, Madge insisted on Mira staying for tea. They made awkward small talk while sipping tea and snacking on their bakery purchases. When they finished, Madge gathered up the tea things and said, "Harold, you look knackered. Why don't you go have a kip? I'll take care of this."

When he had shuffled from the room, Madge sat down and put a hand on Mira's arm. "I owe you an apology and an explanation. I'm sorry. My husband doesn't like being old. The help you offered was nice, but it also makes him feel his age. So, I just had to call him a git."

This wasn't helping Mira's understanding, but, if nothing else, it seemed Madge needed someone to talk to. "Because ...," Mira encouraged.

"Well, you see, in his younger days, he used to call anyone he didn't like even a little bit a git. It drove me crazy. I must have told him a thousand times not to call anyone that. So, when he's feeling particularly old, I call him a git. He thinks it's the funniest thing when it's coming out of my mouth, but it also reminds him of a different time. It makes him feel young again." She leaned in and whispered, "He has serious memory issues now, so I could call him a git every day and he'd think it was the first time I ever called him that. It makes it even funnier for him that way. I know it's sad, but I look for excuses to call him a git as often as possible." Her eyes became watery, but Madge pulled herself up straighter and blinked away the tears before they had a chance to fall. "He's not himself anymore. He can pull up old memories and old habits, but anything recent simply doesn't stay. I love him, but it is a bit lonely these days." Then she added in a barely audible tone, "He really is a git for leaving me like this."

Sometimes there are just no words.

Mira leaned over and wrapped her arms around Madge. Neither let go for a long time.

By the time Mira was on her way again, she'd learned much more about Madge. She and Harold had two sons. One was a barrister who lived a couple hours away and came to visit as often as he could, which amounted to about once a month. He was married with three children of his own. He would bring them along some of the time, but Harold didn't usually remember who they were, so it made it confusing for the kids. "I love having them around. I mean, *I* know who they are. But Harold and I are a package deal right now. He's not comfortable being out of my sight for too long at a time except when I can get him to have a kip. It makes being a gran a bit tricky right now," Madge had said.

Their other son lived in London, but he was single and traveled extensively for business. They saw him even less. Mira didn't know how she could help, but she knew somehow she would find a way to stay in touch.

On her way back home, she only took a wrong turn once. Fortunately, she quickly recognized her mistake and backtracked until things were familiar again. Approaching her front steps, Mira glanced down the street. Kailani and her mother—Bibi, if she remembered correctly—were just coming out their front door.

At the same moment, her phone dinged. Dylan had texted back.

"We're leaving London on Tuesday to explore Bath, Stonehenge, Dover, etc. I'm so excited." Mira was happy for her, but her stomach dropped. She was going to miss them. Then she brightened as she read the rest of the text. "We'll be gone a week but back to London after that. What about you?"

"I'm heading to France and beyond on Wednesday, but I'm coming back to London in a couple weeks if you're still around."

"We're going to head up to Scotland sometime, but we'll be around."

Mira looked up from her phone just in time to see Kailani and Bibi disappearing down the street. She considered running after them but wasn't sure if she'd come across as a stalker by doing that.

She glanced back at her phone as a new text came in. "Tomorrow we're heading to the Victoria and Albert Museum, Hyde Park and Kensington Palace. Do you want to come?"

"Sure!"

"10 AM @ V&A. See you there."

.   .   .

That evening, Mira pulled out her laptop. She and Warren were going to have a video chat, and she couldn't wait. She had stopped by the bakery near Madge and Harold's place and grabbed an assortment of treats earlier. Some were so pretty in design that she had decided to save them until she could show them to Warren.

"Oh, babe. Those do look amazing! I'm surprised you were able to wait to show them to me."

"Well, I may or may not have purchased two of the best-looking ones, so don't read anything into the fact that there's only one of each now." She pretended to avert her eyes.

Warren laughed. "Okay. I was worried there for a minute."

Neither of them could wipe the smiles off their faces. It was so good to see each other even after only a week.

They talked for over an hour—about everything and nothing. Mira told him about Madge and Harold. Warren told her about his week at work. They talked about the food they'd eaten with Mira trying new things at the pub and Warren trying his hand cooking a few new dishes at home.

By the time they were done, a few more bakery items had found their way into Mira's stomach and Warren had polished off a bowl of popcorn. Neither wanted to disconnect, but Mira's yawns kept telling them both it was time.

With a residual smile, Mira climbed into bed.

.   .   .

The street in front of her is deserted, but she can smell the faint hint of roses from somewhere. In the distance, she hears the cry of a baby. Is she hungry? Is she hurt? Will no one help her?

She finds herself frantically pedaling down the road on a bicycle that must have simply materialized since she doesn't remember it being there before. But no mind, she must find the child. She pauses, breathing rapidly from her exertion, to listen, to learn which direction to turn. Only, to her utter dismay, the sound has disappeared. The scent of purple roses, however, is stronger.

The cries must have come from the other direction. She drops the bicycle and sprints back the way she came. People appear at her sides. "Can I help?" "What's wrong?" "Where are you going?" She ignores them, brushing them aside like errant hair in her eyes.

There! Up ahead is a commotion. If she can just reach it in time, but she has wasted her energy by having first gone the wrong direction. She gasps for air, reaching out, pushing herself to take one more step then another.

She's so exhausted and thirsty, but she only needs to take five more steps ... four more ... three ... two ...

Mira woke in a cold sweat. She wanted a drink of water but knew of no way to quench her thirst.

CHAPTER 15

Mira had a hard time getting out of bed in the morning. After waking up with such a start in the middle of the night, she hadn't gone back to sleep for quite some time. Now groggy, she was aware she'd need to hurry to meet the whole Forest family at 10:00.

Fixing her hair became a quick motion of pulling it back into a ponytail and securing it with the red scrunchie. A leftover bun from the bakery provided her breakfast, and with that she was on her way. She'd text Dylan along the way to let her know she was coming.

She shouldn't have worried. At 10:10, she found herself in front of the museum with no Forest family members in sight. They were later than she was. She heaved a sigh and sat down on the steps to wait for them.

But sitting and waiting wasn't a comfortable thing because her dream from the night before started to haunt her. Warren often had strange, elaborate dreams that he relayed to her the next morning. But Mira didn't typically remember her dreams. If she awoke in the middle of a dream, memories of it would stay with her only long enough to dance before her eyes like wispy hints of clouds before being carried away on her next exhaled breath.

She'd heard that dreams could be your mind's way of working through problems, but what could she possibly be working through? Was the dream about her desire for a baby? With what she was focusing on lately, that didn't seem likely. Or dreams could be manifestations of your innermost thoughts. Again, she couldn't make the connection. She'd just as soon forget the whole thing, but try as she might, her mind kept hanging on, trying to understand what she'd seen.

A voice pulled her out of herself. "Hey, girl. What're you doing here?" She lifted her head to see Olivia standing over her.

"Oh, you know, trying to attach myself to some poor soul so I don't have to visit the museum by myself."

"Well, if you're going to make a habit of it, I guess that's all right," Olivia said with a smile. She reached out a hand to pull Mira up from her seat on the stairs.

When standing, Mira found herself a couple steps higher than Olivia. Over Olivia's shoulder, she could see the rest of the Forest clan gathered at the base of the stairs. "Well, it looks like they're waiting for us. I guess we should join them," Mira said.

"Oh, do we have to?" Olivia said. It came off light-hearted, but Mira wasn't sure it was. She was beginning to wonder if there was more of a sibling rivalry than anyone had let on. However, before she could respond in any way, Olivia had turned to join the others.

The Victoria and Albert Museum had something for everyone. Mira hadn't been sure what to expect from a museum of art and design, but the exhibits intrigued her. Bin and his dad, Elijah, were particularly fond of the exhibits from Japan and the Middle East. Zita was drawn to the sculptures, Olivia the tapestries, Avelyn to the furniture, while Caleb and Tiana got lost admiring the stained glass. Jeremy seemed mildly interested in everything, without much of a favorite, until he saw a café.

Dylan and Mira wandered away from the pack, discovering the illuminated manuscripts. "Wow, can you imagine how long it would take to produce a book if you had to hand copy it? Let alone add the decorative flourishes," Dylan said.

"It would be incredible to read something like that."

"I agree. But I'll take what we have if it means I can read lots of books."

"Or any books at all," Mira added. "No wonder ordinary people weren't taught to read. If you couldn't afford to own even a single book, why bother reading, or more accurately, why would someone take the time to teach you."

"I don't know what I'd do without books," Dylan said, nodding her agreement. "Hey, did you finish that book you were reading on the plane?"

Mira laughed. "You'd think I would have by now, huh? But I honestly haven't thought about it since. My head's been too full of other things. Maybe I'll pick it up again on my train ride to Paris." She said it, but she doubted it. There were too many interesting people to meet with too little time to do so.

"Look at this one," Dylan said. It wasn't a single page like some but a whole book propped open under the glass. "It's a Bible."

Something pricked at the back of Mira's mind—a story about dreams. It was about Joseph who was sold into Egypt. He interpreted the dreams of two men in prison then was asked to interpret Pharaoh's dream.

"Hey, Dylan. I had a weird dream last night. Do you ... do you ever find your dreams mean something?"

Dylan tipped her head to the side, thinking. "Well, kind of. If a dream keeps bugging me it's usually because I have unfinished business. Once I figure out what I've left hanging, then the dream stops bothering me." She shrugged. "But that's just me."

"I hadn't thought of that," Mira mused.

Jeremy and Zita surprised them by bursting into the room. "We were talking to someone in the other room. There's a natural history museum and a science museum across the street. Do you want to go check them out?"

Dylan and Mira looked at each other, shrugged in unison, and said, "Sure, why not?" But as they left the gallery to join the others, Mira kept pondering unfinished business.

.   .   .

Both museums were fascinating. As their group wandered from exhibit to exhibit, Mira wavered between two thoughts. First, Warren would love this. Who doesn't enjoy dinosaurs? And that barely scratched the surface of the two museums. Secondly, she kept asking herself if she had any unfinished business.

It wasn't until she was sifting through options in the gift shop that the obvious hit her. She was searching for something goofy to take home to Warren, like amber candy with a bug inside or a build-your-own-dinosaur puzzle, when she kept getting jostled by giggling children. They were everywhere. Some clung to their parents, others were busy examining toys or candy or activity kits, while some were wandering around with big eyes, hardly knowing which things were their favorites.

It was Kailani! Kailani was her unfinished business—how she smiled but didn't giggle. Mira had never seen her with a friend. Something was off and Mira knew it, and she hadn't done anything about it. She had seen Bibi, Kailani's mum, yesterday, only she'd let excuses get in the way of trying to talk to her. No wonder she dreamed what she did last night. She needed to help Kailani, but she'd failed to do so.

Mira glanced up and caught sight of the Forests. Surely others needed her help too. She knew something was up with Olivia. And she hadn't forgotten about Cordelia or Madge and Harold. But a child needing help struck her with more urgency. A child is rarely capable of changing her own circumstances.

That could be true with adults to varying degrees, of course. It's not as if Madge could give her husband his memory back. But, then again, she was in a way. She had found a way for him to laugh every day, to feel young again—the old git.

While other adults still needed her, and, for that matter, she still needed them, it was different with Kailani. Why hadn't she seen that before? But what to do? What *could* she do?

She picked up the few items she was considering for Warren. Then she sorted among the options for children. A nearby mother who was shepherding her children through the store caught Mira's eye. Approaching her, she said, "If you don't mind my bothering you, I'm trying to find something for an eight-year-old girl. Do you have any suggestions?"

The mother turned to see who had spoken. "Oh, not at all. Lizzy," she said, turning to her daughter, "what do you think an eight-year-old might like?"

Lizzy, it turned out, was ten and felt quite honored to be the expert in the situation. She had a younger brother, but she said, "Will doesn't know what girls like yet," with an air of great understanding and condescension. Eventually, Lizzy suggested a stuffed blue whale, "not life-size," she reminded them, and a stone bracelet, "not real jewels but still pretty," she added.

"Thank you, Lizzy. If it's all right with your mother, could I buy you something?" Lizzy turned with big eyes to her mother who nodded consent. "And do you think you might help your brother pick out something too?" Lizzy's face fell, not feeling special anymore. So, Mira quickly added, "You're very good at picking out things for others." Lizzy's eyes lit up. She liked being the expert shopper. With great gusto, she found a bracelet for herself and a book about dinosaurs that Will adored.

Mira completed her purchases and sent a smiling Lizzy and Will on their way. Making her way out of the gift shop, she caught up with Dylan and the others. "Were you all waiting for me?"

"Partly, but Jeremy's not back yet. He's gone hunting for food." At the mention of food, they all started to fidget. They'd grabbed a quick lunch at a café at the Victoria and Albert Museum, but that was hours ago now.

"Hey, if you don't mind coming a little farther toward my flat, I know a great pub. We could grab an early dinner. That is if you don't mind shifting plans. We haven't explored Hyde Park or Kensington Palace yet."

"We already shifted plans anyway," Zita said. "We hadn't planned on visiting these museums, which turned out to be a great call. So, to me, a nice pub sounds like another great call. My vote's yes."

"You know, since we're leaving for Bath tomorrow morning, we should pack up tonight. So, an early dinner would be a good idea," Avelyn said.

She was met with a general murmur of agreement, and Tiana, rubbing her belly, added, "Food sounds good to me. At any rate, I'm done walking around."

No one was more enthusiastic, however, than Jeremy when he rejoined them and was informed of their change of plans. "Yes!" he said, with an added fist pump.

"Oh, and Jeremy, their portions are large," Mira said.

"Mira, I love you!" Jeremy said, to everyone's laughter.

Since *The Red Fox* was just around the corner from Mira's flat, the whole group made their way to the flat first. "I'm going to dump my bags on my bed. The bathroom is that way if anyone's interested. Feel free to check out the garden in the back. I'll be right back," Mira said, pointing and directing people as she did so.

When she returned, Tiana was sitting in a chair with Caleb rubbing her feet. Olivia was on the couch with her head thrown back and her eyes closed. No one else was in sight. Mira sat down on the opposite end of the couch as Olivia, who opened her eyes. "Hi, Mira."

"They scattered fast, didn't they?"

"Yep. It's only us four left, a small group by comparison. If I overheard right, Mom and Dad love your little backyard, but it doesn't have enough room for a football game according to Bin and Jeremy. I'm not sure where Zita is, and I think Dylan's in the bathroom. I hope we haven't overwhelmed you."

"Maybe a little, but I kind of like it. Do you all get together often?"

"Not as often as you might think," Caleb said. "Once we started leaving for college and then jobs, it became more of a challenge."

"But this has been so fun," Tiana said, "that we're going to try to make it happen more often. Don't tell Mom yet, but we're planning on moving closer after the baby's born."

"That's great. What do you all do? Do you have jobs that you can transfer?"

"Well, I'm a high school math teacher. There's a private school near Mom and Dad's that's been begging me to come. It would be a pay increase too. We're just hammering out the details," said Caleb.

"That's great!"

"Tiana, what about you?"

"I'm a nurse. I'm going to take some time off once the baby's born, but I should be able to find work without too much trouble when I'm ready." She smiled down at her husband as he continued to rub her feet.

"Olivia, what about you?"

"Umm," Olivia said, appearing tongue-tied.

"Don't let her fool you," Caleb said. "She may not want to brag, but she's the smartest of the bunch. She graduated a couple years ago in chemistry, and she's had a good job ever since. Mama Forest didn't raise no dumb bunnies."

"Yes, and Zita is studying psychology. She wants to be a counselor and use her bilingual skills with that," Oliva was quick to add.

Mira started to form another question, but Olivia jumped in before she had a chance. "Jeremy is heading off to college with no clue as to what he wants to do. He's good at just about everything though."

"Yeah, his problem is going to be focusing enough. As you can tell, he loves eating, but that love extends to basketball, dating, playing guitar, you name it," Caleb added. "We all wish we were as talented as he is, but none of us wants to be him either."

"So, what do you do, Mira?" Tiana asked.

"I'm an accountant. I like it enough, but I'm not sure how I got there because I appreciate having creative outlets."

"Like what?" Olivia had perked up.

"Well, when I'm home, Warren and I have been cooking and baking a lot. We're not great at it, but we're not bad either." She saw her journal sitting on a side table where she'd set it yesterday. "I'd kind of abandoned it for a while, but I've always loved to write too. This trip is meant to reignite that."

"And has it?" Olivia said.

Mira nodded. "It's beginning to."

Olivia reached over and surprised Mira by grabbing her arm. "I need to—" Olivia started but abruptly stopped when most of the family burst into the room.

"What a great little place you've got here to stay," said Elijah. "It's as if you're a member of the community. I heard a neighbor of yours. Tried to say, 'Hi,' to him, but he couldn't see me over the hedge, so he didn't answer. But anyway, what a wonderful place."

"Too bad there's not a basketball hoop or something back there," added Jeremy.

"Yep," Bin said. "But other than that, pretty cool."

By the time everyone had had a turn in the bathroom, it was close to a normal dinner time after all. Mira had tried during that time to catch Olivia alone, but with so many people in a one-bedroom flat, it wasn't possible. So, whatever Olivia needed remained unsaid.

The rest of the evening was a delightful jumble. When they entered the pub, Bill came over immediately. "Cordelia's friend! And ... *her* friends." As more of the family filed in the door, his smile got wider. "And her friends' friends, it appears. Usually, I'd say, seat yourself, seat yourself. But, let me take care of that. Let me take care of that."

Since it was the top of the dinner hour, the pub wasn't too full yet. So, before long, three tables had been pushed together and the chattering group was seated around them. "I've had bangers and mash and fish and chips so far here. Both are delicious, but remember, I said the portions are quite large."

Jeremy said, "Good!" while the others decided to order a few dishes to share.

Once they got their food, Bill came over to check on them. "How are you all doing? How's the food? Is there anything you need?"

"It's delicious."

"We love it."

Jeremy's mouth was too full to say anything, but he gave an enthusiastic thumbs up.

Bill leaned closer to Mira. "How is Cordelia? Is she okay?"

"Yes. Well, I think so."

He simply nodded and walked away. Mira made a mental note to spend some time with Cordelia before she left town.

• • •

The family, with the exception of Caleb and Tiana who grabbed a cab to head back, decided to walk with Mira to her flat. From there, they would hop on public transportation to make it back to their hotel. It wasn't turning out to be as early of a night as Avelyn had hoped, but no one seemed to mind. The night was clear with a slight cool breeze but rather pleasant for walking.

Spreading out on the sidewalk, Mira grabbed Olivia's arm and purposely hung back. "You started to say something to me at my flat. What was it?"

Olivia hesitated, staring at the group in front of them. "I just can't bear to disappoint them," was all she said.

"What are you talking about?"

Olivia stared at Mira, indecision etched across her face. "It's really nothing. Don't worry about it." Then she hurried to catch up with the others. But, as with most people, telling Mira not to worry usually had the opposite effect.

CHAPTER 16

When morning came, Mira wished she'd been able to talk to Warren more the previous night. By the time the others left, she was exhausted, especially given her poor night's sleep leading into the day. She'd dashed off a quick text. "Hey, hubs, I love you. I'm heading to bed, but I'll call tomorrow for sure."

"Love you too, babe. Sleep tight. Don't let the bedbugs bite."

Thankfully, she had slept well and awoke with a newfound determination. This was her last full day in England for a while, so she wanted to make the most of it. While most might view that as motivation for doing some last-minute sightseeing, Mira wanted to work on her unfinished business. She realized too that there was no reason not to attempt killing two birds with one stone.

"Cordelia, how are you doing?"

"Smashing, luv. We need to meet up, don't we? You're leaving tomorrow, right?" Mira had arranged to rent the same flat when she returned to the U.K., and Cordelia had been kind enough to offer to store some of Mira's belongings while she was gone.

"Yes, well, I mean, no, that wasn't why I called."

"Then why did you ring me up?"

"I need some advice, and I was wondering if you might be willing to help."

Cordelia's morning was busy, but she agreed to pop by in the early afternoon. "We can work out what you want stored at the same time if that works for you?" It did.

Mira decided to spend her morning making sure everything was ready for her trip. She wanted to travel light, so she picked one suitcase to take. Everything else could wait for her in London. With limited space, she decided to leave the bag from Warren behind, but she couldn't bear not taking something of him with her, so she grabbed a few small items to stow in a side pocket. The whole process didn't take her long since she'd kept her things organized while she'd been there.

With her leftover time, she sat in the garden and wrote memories of her mother in her journal. When the warmth of the day caught up with her, she dozed in her chair while the fragrance of roses danced over her. Only when her stomach reminded her of lunchtime did she move back into the flat.

After lunch, while waiting for Cordelia to arrive, Mira texted Dylan. "Hey, hope you guys have fun. See you in a couple weeks."

"Thanks. You too."

Then before she could have second thoughts, and hoping she wasn't betraying a trust, she texted, "Something's up with Olivia. I don't know what. I know she's your sister, but she's hiding something from the family. She started to talk to me yesterday, said she didn't want to disappoint you all, but then wouldn't tell me what she was talking about. Just thought if you knew, you could keep an eye out."

"Thanks! She's not as cheerful as she usually is, but I figured it was jetlag. TBH after the first couple days, I didn't really notice. I should have. I'll keep an eye on her."

Feeling better on that front, Mira pulled out the presents she had bought for Kailani. She had no illusions that she could solve whatever problems Kailani had in one day, but she was at least hoping to find out more about what those problems might be. She debated about giving her both the stuffed blue whale and the stone bracelet but decided to save one for later.

Once Cordelia arrived, they first went over what bags of Mira's were staying behind, which Cordelia promised to keep safe until her return. Then Mira asked if they could talk for a bit. "I mentioned to you before about a little girl I met who lives across the street. Her name's Kailani. She told me her mom's name is Bibi, whom I haven't met yet, but I'd like to."

"Why? And what do you need my help with?"

"Well, something isn't right. I don't know what. And I figured since you live here, you're British ..."

"That maybe I'd have a better handle on it?"

"Something like that."

"Do you think her mother is abusive?"

"I hope not, but who knows? Kailani casts nervous glances in her mom's direction, but that's not enough to accuse anyone. The last thing I want to do is make things worse."

Cordelia nodded but remained silent, thinking.

"I bought this stuffed animal for Kailani at the Natural History Museum yesterday. I thought that might help me be able to talk to her, but I don't honestly know."

"Well, I don't know either, but we may as well try. Let's go see if they're home."

Mira and Cordelia approached Kailani's building cautiously, neither knowing what to expect. Shortly after knocking on the door to her flat, it slowly opened.

"Hi, Kailani," Mira said, bending down to be at her eye level. "Is your mum home? I have a present for you, but I want to make sure it's okay with your mum first."

Kailani didn't answer. She peered past Mira to Cordelia standing behind her. Seeing the movement of her eyes, Mira said, "This is my friend Cordelia. She owns the flat I'm staying in. Is it okay that she came with me?"

Kailani's eyes swept over Cordelia, then she turned away, shutting the door in the process. Cordelia and Mira exchanged puzzled expressions and shrugged. But a moment later, the door opened again, this time to reveal Bibi with Kailani behind her. Bibi had passed on many of her features to her daughter. They both had large distinctive eyes, a small nose, and full lips. But Bibi's hair was darker than Kailani's blond hair—light brown with wisps of premature gray.

"What do you want?" she said, warily.

"Hi. My name's Mira. I'm visiting from the United States. I'm staying across the street. This is Cordelia. She owns the flat I'm living in." Bibi's eyes narrowed, but she didn't say anything, so Mira plunged on. "I met your sweet little girl when I first got here. So, yesterday, when I was at a museum, I bought this for her. I wanted to make sure it was okay that I gave it to her."

Bibi glanced from Mira to Cordelia, her expression remaining unchanged. Then, suddenly, she started violently coughing. Mira could see Kailani's eyes grow wide. She ran to retrieve a glass of water for her mother, but Bibi waved it away as she continued to cough.

Leaving the door swinging open, Kailani helped her mother to a nearby couch as her coughing began to subside. The two women in the hallway looked at each other and cautiously entered the flat.

"Can we help with anything?" Cordelia said.

Bibi's head came up, her eyes ablaze. "No! Just go away!"

Shocked, neither woman moved. "I'm sorry," Mira finally said. "Would it be all right if I left this gift for Kailani?"

"We don't need your charity," Bibi spat.

With a calmer voice than Mira felt, she said, "I'm sorry. I think there's been a misunderstanding. When I first got here, Kailani helped me. I was feeling rather insignificant." Mira moved to sit down, even though she hadn't been invited. She didn't want to be standing over Bibi. "Your daughter helped put things in perspective for me. It literally changed me. What she said helped convince me to stay here in London instead of running home. This has been a transformative experience, and I would have missed it if it wasn't for Kailani." She smiled at the child who beamed in response. "So, this gift is a thank you."

Bibi visibly relaxed. She nodded at Mira. Mira decided that meant the present was okay and handed Kailani the gift she had wrapped in tissue paper from Warren's bag.

Kailani gingerly took the gift and unwrapped it. When the blue whale emerged, she broke into a grin and hugged it tightly.

While she'd been unwrapping it, Mira tried to discreetly look around. Was there anything she could learn from what surrounded her? The flat was ordinary enough on one scale—the furniture was older, some of it in various states of disrepair, some even broken. But the walls were lovely, covered with paintings and prints. A large watercolor hung above the couch. It was of a mother and child, almost as if it were Bibi and Kailani.

"Don't forget your manners, child," Bibi said, coughing again.

Kailani watched her mother carefully, but when the coughing stopped, she turned and said, "Thank you, Mira. Thank you very much."

"That's better," Bibi said, gently stroking her daughter's hair.

Silence fell on them all. Cordelia found a seat and faced Bibi. "May we please help you? That cough can't mean anything good."

Bibi's eyes grew wide with fear. "No. You don't understand. I'm fine. Really, I'm fine." Turning to Mira, she said, "Thank you for the gift. Now, I must ask you to leave." She stood up abruptly and ushered them to the door. Kailani followed, clinging to her mother.

Not sure what else to do, Cordelia and Mira walked to the door, bid their goodbyes, and left. The door shut behind them, but they could distinctly hear the sounds of coughing starting up again.

Walking back to the flat, Mira said, "What do you make of that?"

"I don't know, but I'm going to find out," Cordelia said. She was her energetic self, but a fierceness was present that hadn't been there before.

CHAPTER 17

Paris was amazing. Mira had been there for three days, taking in as many sights as she could each day. The Louvre was as incredible as she had been led to believe it would be, and she loved seeing the city from the Eiffel Tower, even if the wait was long to ascend it. She had perused the city's museums and cathedrals and lingered in its famous shopping areas. The feel of the city, the food, the culture, everything appealed to her. She had one more day to spend in the City of Light before embarking on a whirlwind trip stopping in Brussels, Amsterdam, Munich, and finally on to Italy. After being gone from London for two and a half weeks, she'd fly back there from Rome. It was ambitious but would give her a little taste of several places and cultures.

The only thing she missed in Paris was having a common language. She hadn't forgotten how things had changed for her in London, and she kept an ever-vigilant eye out for people, writing about them in her journal.

At first, what she saw seemed ordinary—people buying groceries or hurrying to work, children laughing and frolicking in the park, subway riders avoiding eye contact with others. But the more she looked, the more she saw. She watched a mother bend down to listen as her youngster told an animated story, nodding in all the right places. She saw a young man give up his seat on a bus to an elderly gentleman. There was a baker who purposely threw crumbs out his back door to a flock of waiting birds. The world could be a wonderfully kind place—if you took the time to notice.

Of course, there were grumpy and rude people too. But, surely, they had a story too. It made Mira think about Bibi. Cordelia had texted her a couple times already. She was doing a little background on Bibi, her flat, anything she could find. She hoped to have something to tell Mira when she got back to London. Things were in good hands with Cordelia, but it was personal with Kailani. Mira desperately wanted to help her.

Why was Bibi so upset when they were simply trying to help? She puzzled over this but came to no good conclusion, knowing things weren't always as they seemed. "Thanks for checking on things," Mira texted to Cordelia. "Keep me posted."

Much as Mira was enjoying Paris, everything reminded her of Kailani. Her first day there, she had discovered a fantastic bakery only a short distance off the beaten path and not far from her hotel. After sampling a pastry, her first thought was, "I'll bet Kailani would love these!" That thought was quickly followed by, "My mother would have too, and so would Cordelia and Dylan, and for that matter, Dylan's whole family … especially Jeremy!"

Now, on her third day in Paris, she was visiting the same bakery for the third time. The baker greeted her with a smile. He spoke some English, and simply said, "Again?"

"Oui. Très bien."

He smiled and pulled out a box for her purchases. A short time later, as she emerged with more pastries than anyone could eat in one day, she spotted a group of boys darting in and around the tables of a nearby sidewalk café. At first glance, she wondered if they were pickpockets darting away, and she instinctively put a hand on her waist over her hidden money belt. Then she saw they were chasing a little kitten.

Certain they were tormenting the poor creature, she moved swiftly in their direction to intervene. But as she got closer, she recognized that they were calling and whistling to the kitten to come. The youngest little boy was distraught, with a tear-stained face. An older boy put his arm around the child and said something to him that sounded comforting.

It appeared that the kitten had hidden somewhere among the potted plants and shrubs in the shadows under the awning of the café, but the boys were having difficulty locating it. Mira approached slowly. She had heard that pickpockets liked to create a diversion to enable an accomplice to do the actual pickpocketing, but she was pretty sure what she was seeing wasn't a diversion. The real reason she approached slowly was not to scare the boys.

When they noticed her presence, she tipped her head and smiled. She had a small cross-body bag to hold a few items for her day. She reached inside it and pulled out a small flashlight. It was one of the things Warren had given her when she left. She showed it to the boys, then turned it on, shining it into the nearby bushes. They quickly understood and enthusiastically nodded their approval.

Before long they were all gathered around the bushes following the beam of the flashlight to see if it would expose a paw or a whisker. Mira passed the flashlight among the boys as they tried to search from different angles. At last, they spotted the kitten, but as soon as they did, it just retreated farther into the bushes.

"Aah! I have an idea," Mira said. They turned at the sound of her voice, but none of them understood her words. She motioned for the black-haired boy who was currently holding the flashlight to hand it back to her. He did so with a puzzled expression on his face.

Mira shone the flashlight where they knew the kitten to be, then she slowly withdrew it, painting circles with it in the shadows while she did so. The kitten didn't budge, so she repeated her light dance, drawing faster and more elaborate circles and designs as she did so. The kitten's nose cautiously emerged. The boys quickly caught on and silently begged to have a turn.

By the time the youngest boy, the apparent owner of the cat, was having his turn, the kitten was dancing on the shaded pavement in front of them, trying in vain to catch the light. When his turn was over, the small boy scooped up his pet and gave him a big hug. The kitten responded by licking his face.

While holding his cat securely with one hand, the small boy held out his other, offering the flashlight back to Mira. She shook her head and pressed the flashlight more securely into his palm. "You keep it—for the cat," she said, indicating the furball in his arms. He beamed.

Mira straightened up, smiling. She spotted her box of pastries where she had hastily deposited it on a nearby table. She opened it, exposing the contents and offering them to the group of youngsters. "Merci, merci," they shouted in unison. In a flash, all the pastries were gone as the boys disappeared in a blur down the street.

Smiling, she returned to the bakery. "I'm sorry, but I need more," she said, shrugging.

The owner said, "All gone?"

"Oui, some boys," she said, pointing down the street as if they were still visible.

The baker raised an angry fist. He muttered something in French.

Mira laughed. "No, uh, non. I … gave them the pastries." She touched her chest then extended her hands out, a movement she hoped conveyed her meaning.

The baker stared at her for a moment then his face split into a grin. "Oui, oui." He filled up a box for her again, although she wisely indicated he should start with a smaller box this time around. When she had finished choosing—mostly her favorite eclairs, he handed her the box and refused payment. "Enjoy," he said in accented English.

Mira nibbled on an eclair as she made her way back up the side street toward the wider avenues that were home to some of the major tourist attractions. She was just emerging between two buildings when a disturbing scene assaulted her senses.

People, drenched in sweat, scurried past her, alarm etched on their faces. In chaotic commotion, they ran in conflicting directions. The sound of their voices wasn't the familiar lyrical French but a rough sandpaper sound, that hurt when it touched her ears. Then an acrid odor reached her, and she instinctively covered her nose against the smell of fear.

"What's happening? What's wrong?" Whether anyone understood her or had answers, she couldn't tell, only a cacophony of unknown French whirling around her.

Pinned to the side of a building by the crowd, Mira scanned the faces, seeing nothing but terror and confusion. A mass of people moving like a storm-filled river surged toward her, an elderly gentleman carried on their wake. She locked eyes with him, his terrified expression screaming, pleading for help. She lunged for his hand, attempting to pull him free.

Their fingers touched, and he grasped her hand tightly. She tugged, but nothing happened. She tugged again, and then everything happened—the man flying at her as the ground violently shook.

Simultaneously, a sound she couldn't place hit her ears, ricocheting off the sides of the buildings encircling them.

. . .

Mira flicked open her eyes to see rubble-littered pavement in front of her. She lay on the sidewalk, yet couldn't remember how she'd gotten there. Dust billowed around the scene, obscuring her view, giving it a sepia, other-worldly feel. She tried sitting up to get a better view, but the pounding in her head violently objected. Instead, she rolled to the side. People littered the ground, hands and legs all a jumble. With a start, she spotted a familiar hand a short distance away, that of an old man. It had been warm in her fingers only moments before. She crawled toward it. The man lay on his face, arms outstretched, but his clothes looked pockmarked as if made of polka dots that had individually exploded, leaving red dots behind. She strained to touch his fingers. Inching forward with her last ounce of energy, she clasped his hand in hers before collapsing on the street next to him. Sirens assaulted her ears as she felt the hand in hers grow cold. From all directions came screams. As she lost consciousness, she recognized one of the screams as her own.

WONDER

"He who can no longer pause to wonder and stand rapt in awe, is as good as dead: his eyes are closed."

—*Albert Einstein*

CHAPTER 18

When Mira opened her eyes, how much time had passed eluded her. The room was dark, dark like she felt, only she couldn't remember why. Her eyes adjusting, she could discern shapes around her—a chair with something draped over it, behind the chair a wall with two pictures covered in glass. She couldn't make out the images, but a small amount of light was coming from somewhere that reflected off the glass surfaces. Mira twisted around to see a window with the shades drawn. It appeared to be daytime as light was seeping in around the edges of the blinds.

Straightening in the bed she found herself on, a stab of pain shot down the length of her body, and she let out an involuntary gasp. It must have been louder than she'd thought because a minute later a door opened and an unfamiliar face peeked in.

A woman, Mira assumed she was a nurse, approached her bed, smiling. She spoke French, but Mira shook her head, immediately regretting the movement as her head pounded inside her skull.

The nurse said something and abruptly left the room while Mira cradled her head. Where was she? What had happened? She wondered where her things were. She needed to call Warren, but where was her phone? In the dim light, she couldn't tell if her belongings draped the chair or something else did. Turning the light on would help, but her pounding head told her the room was dimmed on purpose.

A few minutes later, two new people entered her room, a man and a woman. They were both clearly medical professionals, most likely doctors. They began to poke and prod her, speaking rapid French as they did so.

She tried to shake them off, to get them to realize she didn't understand what had happened, but they largely ignored her attempts at communication. In desperation, she yelled, "Non!" They jumped back, startled. The effort had cost her, as her head felt like it would explode. "Non," she repeated, more softly this time. "I don't speak French. English? Does anyone speak English? I need to know what happened."

The man turned and spoke to his colleague in French. She quickly left the room. The doctor who remained eyed her cautiously but didn't attempt to examine her anymore. She was grateful for this brief respite.

A short time later, the woman returned with a young woman trailing behind her. This woman, however, was wearing no medical gear. She was dressed in a skirt and blouse as if she'd just stepped out of an office building. Her short, mousey hair fell in lazy waves around her face, and she had a subtle yet commanding presence.

"Hello, how are you?" Her English carried a wonderful French lilt as if the words were written in curlicues in the air. Mira immediately relaxed.

"I've been better. Where am I? What happened?"

"You are in a hospital in Paris. A bomb was set off by a terrorist a short distance from where you were found. I am Aissa Caron, and these are doctors Laurent and Martin," she said, indicating the man and woman in turn. "They want to ask you a few questions." Aissa laid a hand on hers and smiled.

"Okay."

"First, are you Mira Silverman?"

"Yes, how did you—"

The woman tipped her head toward the chair. "Your identification was found on you."

Mira stiffened. She had just survived a terrorist attack, but the idea that someone had gone through her things without her permission upset her much more. A terrorist attack seemed so unlikely and remote that its reality didn't register in her mind. It couldn't possibly be real. Her purse, her money belt, her things, however, were real. They were hers. "Why did you go through my things?" she asked, seething.

Aissa glanced at the doctors for guidance then back to Mira. "I'm sorry. We needed to know who you were, in case, ... well, so we could take care of you."

"What? In case I *died*?!"

Dr. Martin spoke to Aissa who interpreted. "The doctors believe you are fine, but when you first came in, you were covered with a lot of blood. It was not at first obvious that you would be okay." She paused while Dr. Martin spoke again. "It turns out you had several cuts and bruises but no major injuries." Mira started to relax until Aissa added, "Most of the blood was not your own."

It was said as if this would make Mira feel better, but how could it? "An old man was beside me on the ground. Is he okay? Was it his blood?"

The three talked together softly, then Aissa said, "Yes, we assume it was his blood." She said it gently, and Mira knew she didn't need an answer to her first question. He was not okay. He was dead. He had died right beside her, while she'd been holding his hand. And she had managed to escape with only bumps and bruises—and a terrible headache and heartache that threatened never to leave.

She slumped back onto the bed, all fight gone from her. She no longer resisted as the doctors both examined her, peppering her with questions through the interpreter. Mira answered what was asked but offered nothing more. She did learn she had "suffered a terrible shock," as if that was a surprise, and that "she had been asleep for two days." This news finally elicited a reaction.

"Two days! My husband, he'll be so worried. I need to call my husband!"

Aissa put a hand on her arm. "It's okay. The name of your hotel was in your things. We contacted them, and they contacted your husband and told him you're okay. He's trying to get an emergency passport to come join you."

"No!"

Aissa recoiled. Mira hadn't meant it to come out so forcefully, but this place, this country suddenly seemed to be the most unsafe place on earth. She loved Warren with all her heart. The last place she wanted him to be was here in France. Mira noticed the shock in Aissa's eyes. "It's that, well, ... he can't come here. It's not safe."

Aissa replaced her hand on Mira's arm. For a minute, Mira thought she was going to say, "There, there," as if she was a toddler having a tantrum. Instead, she said nothing, and that nothing was what she needed. Mira's breathing soon returned to normal and her hands stopped shaking, although her mind was still reeling.

The doctors finished up their examination and spoke to Aissa. She turned to Mira. "They both say you are in good health, but they want you to stay for a few more days. They are hoping your headaches will be gone by then or greatly reduced."

She started to nod her head, but it's pounding echoed the doctors' wishes. "Okay," she conceded.

Aissa saw the doctors out then returned to Mira's side. "Your hotel is holding your things for you, but they will send them over if you want. Also, your American Embassy has been asking about you, offering to help in any way they can."

It seemed odd to Mira that "her" embassy should care what happened to her. She was not a diplomat or a politician. She was merely an ordinary, average American. But then again, terrorist attacks were anything but ordinary.

"One more thing," Aissa said on her way out, "the police want to speak with you, to take your statement. They have asked to be informed as soon as you are awake and can talk. I imagine the nurse has already contacted them, but I can be 'unavailable' for interpreting for the remainder of the day if you like?"

Mira settled her head into her pillow and closed her eyes. "Thank you. That would be very nice. I don't think I'm ready to make a statement."

"I can't hold them off long. Do you think you can handle talking to them tomorrow?"

With a sigh, Mira opened her eyes, immediately noticing the concern etched on Aissa's face. "Yes, I suppose. Will you be here?"

Aissa beamed in response. "Of course I will. And between now and then you should think about questions you want to ask them." She winked. "You will only have the one chance, but you are in a unique situation. If we ask your questions first, they will likely be willing to answer. Correct? Especially if I politely explain it is a condition of your cooperation."

Mira almost smiled. "But won't I come across as a rude American that way?"

Aissa shrugged. "Paris is the city that wronged you. I don't see how you could be considered the rude one." She winked one last time then made sure to quietly close the door behind her.

.   .   .

It took Mira a few hours to pull herself together enough to call Warren even though she wanted nothing more than to hear his voice. When she did, the call was emotionally charged.

"Mira, I already have a plane ticket. I'll be leaving Wednesday if we can get the passport squared away. The airline has been so helpful. The terrorist attack has been all over the news. You were one of three Americans hurt in the blast. So, it's not hard to convince the airlines that I'm telling the truth. I'm just glad you're doing okay."

Other than asking about the old man, Mira hadn't considered how this violence had affected anyone else. The guilt of her selfishness churned her stomach. "Warren, what happened? I don't know anything about the attack."

"Oh, I figured you'd know everything—more than the rest of us."

"I haven't even been conscious. Why would I know anything?" She was angry—not at Warren, but he was there, and she lashed out.

"I'm sorry. You're right. It was a lone terrorist, a radical Muslim. He started yelling and ranting as he walked through the streets of Paris. That sent people running in all directions. When the police started closing in on him, he set off the bomb. It killed him, so they've been going through his things to find out what connections he might have had."

The irony that they were going through his things like they had gone through Mira's made her skin crawl. She may be innocent, but she felt like just another body to them. She knew by the care they were taking with her that she was being unfair, but she didn't care.

"Are you there, babe?"

"Yes." She hesitated. "Was anyone else … was … I know an old man died. Was there anyone else?"

"Yes," Warren said, softly. "Twenty people died, and many more were injured. How did you know about the old man?"

"He … he was getting carried away in the crowd. He wanted to get out of it, so he reached out to me, and I tried to pull him free." Tears coursed down her face. She couldn't say it, but would he still be alive if she hadn't pulled him toward her? Would he have been safer in the cushioning support of a hundred bodies instead of with her on the sidewalk? "Do you know his name?" It came out as a whisper.

"The news mentioned an older man. That must be who you're talking about. Let me look it up." Mira was quiet while she waited for his answer. "Babe, I found it. His name was Marcel. Marcel DuBois."

Mira began to weep. "Did he have a family?"

"I don't know. The article didn't say."

Mira knew Warren could hear her sobs over the phone. And she was incredibly grateful he didn't try to quiet them. He simply listened as she grieved. "Warren, if one day we have a little boy, I want to name him Marcel. We could call him Marc."

"I like that," Warren said, and Mira could hear the soft hitch in his voice. "Babe," he said softly, "I can't wait to hold you. This has been the most terrifying thing I've ever experienced. I can't even begin to imagine what it's been for you." He sniffed. "I was so afraid I would lose you."

The push-pull of wanting him near and wanting him safe nearly tore Mira apart. "Warren, you can't come."

"Mira, I told you, we're working it all out. I should have my passport in a few days."

"No. You don't understand. You can't come. I know you came close to losing me, but that means I came close to losing you too—to us losing each other. I've been through this attack, and I survived. But you haven't survived yet. You can't come here. It's not safe."

"Mira, you're not making any sense. The attack is over. All that matters is that we're together."

"No, Warren. I don't know how to get you to understand. It's like I'm standing on the opposite side of a minefield. I've made it through. I'm safe. But if you touch down in France, it'll be like you're just starting to walk across that minefield. You're not safe, not yet. Warren, I can't lose you. You're my anchor back home. Because of you being where you are,

I know I always have a safe place to run. You *are* home. And as long as you're there in our home, I have that safe anchor." When he didn't respond, she said, "Please try to understand. I want your arms around me more than you know, but not here. Here isn't safe."

"Okay. Then come home. Are you okay to travel?"

"Not yet. I'm having bad headaches, so the doctors want to keep an eye on me for a few more days."

Mira could hear Warren blowing out an air of frustration. "Look. I need to be with you—here, there, I don't care. But this is nuts, babe."

The truth was Mira wanted to be with Warren too. However, as much as she was frightened about him coming to France, the idea of flying home early filled her with dread. She had left many of her belongings in London, but more importantly, she had left unfinished business in London. Contemplating possible solutions was clouding her mind and aggravating her headache.

"I'll make a deal with you," Mira said. "Go ahead with your plans to come here—the passport, the flight, everything. Just don't get on that flight until we both agree it's the right thing to do. Okay?"

"All right. And what about you coming home? What about that?"

"I can only process one thing at a time right now. It's still on the table, but it's a moot point until the doctors release me. We'll keep talking about it, okay?"

"Okay. Fair enough." He probably still thought she was being irrational, but giving her the benefit of the doubt right now seemed reasonable—given what she'd been through. "I love you, babe."

"I love you too, hubs."

They talked on until Mira's head hurt too much to concentrate. Reluctantly, they hung up, vowing to talk the next day.

CHAPTER 19

The next few days came and went as if like ocean waves, the passage of time sometimes undulating slowly and rhythmically and other times crashing suddenly and rapidly upon her. Monday morning's police visit hit Mira like a splash of cold water, but Aissa's presence helped mitigate the chill.

Before the two police officers had a chance to open their mouths, Aissa moved between them and Mira, speaking to them in French. The words themselves came out with the typical French cadence, but the tone was unmistakable. Aissa was in charge, and she took it as a duty to protect Mira.

When Aissa moved aside, the police officers were looking down and fidgeting, completely cowed. With a wink, Aissa said, "What would you like to know? I'll ask them."

"Why?" It was the biggest question she had, probably anyone had.

The interpreted response didn't answer her question, but she hadn't expected it to. "The man with the bomb, Faisal Tariq, was radicalized in a camp a year ago. He was the only bomber, but they have traced his contacts, those who supplied and supported him. Twelve have been arrested. The others fled the country; alerts are out for them."

Mira sighed, digesting the information.

"I can press for more details if you want," Aissa said. "They tell me little else is known, but I believe that is not the case. I am certain they know more but do not wish to divulge it for the sake of the ongoing investigation."

Mira shook her head but wasn't at all sure she'd learned enough. She mentally shifted gears, but it took a moment before she was able to form her words. "What can they tell me about Marcel DuBois? I believe he is the gentleman who died with his hand in mine."

After a short exchange, Aissa said, "Yes. That was his name. He was dead on the scene. You would not let go of his hand, although I don't believe you remember that. Once they pried you loose, you lost consciousness and were brought here."

Mira wiped away a tear. "Did he have a family?"

Surprisingly, the police were prepared for this question. After Aissa interpreted it to them, the younger police officer, a man in his thirties, stepped forward and handed a photograph to Mira. A smiling couple stared back at her with a small boy perched on his father's shoulders and a baby girl in her mother's arms. The officer turned the photo over to show her a handwritten note on the back.

My papa was a good man, a good father and grandfather. Thank you for holding his hand as he died. It brings us much peace that he was not alone. It is comforting to know there is still goodness in the world.

Our love and gratitude to you.

Nicolette

Aissa wiped her eyes as she read over Mira's shoulder. "S'il vous plaît," the younger officer said, touching Aissa's arm. He spoke briefly to her in French.

"He tells me Marcel's wife died a year and a half ago. They had been married for forty years. Nicolette was their daughter. The picture is of her and her family."

Mira noticed the room had gone quiet except for an occasional sniffle. Holding the picture, her hands shook slightly. *How could someone be filled with so much anger that they would do such a thing as this? Take a grandfather away from those he loved?*

The rest of the room faded around her as her thoughts focused on Faisal Tariq. An unfamiliar sensation was brewing in the pit of her stomach. It felt like bile, threatening to make her physically sick if she allowed it to stay. It was dark and ugly, and she didn't like it. It was hate—

pure, black hatred. However, she found it was sitting in a doorway, not yet invited in.

Mira lifted her eyes to Aissa and saw tears trickling down her cheeks. She turned to the police officers. Surely their jobs made them cynical, but astonishingly, tears pooled at the corners of their eyes as well.

Bringing the photo up to her face, she made a decision. Anger was not her way. She would not welcome in the hatred. Those emotions belonged to a terrorist who had ended his life and the lives of others because of it. She felt an odd sense of pity for him. How empty his life must have been.

But her life was not! It was full and wonderful. Maybe not at this moment. Maybe not in this situation, but it had been, and it could be again. She had a fair amount of trauma to process. However, she saw no need to complicate that further by adopting the destructive emotions of another. After this moment, she would not give that evil man another thought.

"Merci," she said to the officers, holding up the photograph. "Aissa, would you ask them to tell Nicolette thank you for me. She has healed a wound that could not be fixed any other way."

After the officers had collected her statement and left, Mira collapsed back onto the bed, completely spent. Aissa quietly backed out of the room. As Mira gave in to her exhaustion, she distinctly heard Aissa speaking in sharp tones to the nurses out in the hallway. "She's ordering them to leave me alone," she muttered to herself before falling into a dreamless sleep.

■　　■　　■

After Monday's police visit, Mira's biggest marker of change was the gradually increasing light allowed into her room. At first, the blinds were turned to let more daylight in, then fully raised so she could be bathed in it, although it didn't bring any warmth with it like sun is supposed to do. Finally, the lights in her room were turned off and on as needed by the many medical personnel who felt it their duty to check on her every half an hour, day or night—when Aissa wasn't around to chase them off.

Aissa came regularly and was the one person Mira looked forward to seeing. With her help, the hotel had sent over Mira's things. She didn't physically need them since she was wearing a hospital gown and any toiletries she needed were provided, but emotionally she did. She didn't want a part of her to be here and a part of her to be there—close to where it happened.

Other than Aissa and her many doctors and nurses, she had no visitors. Reportedly, others wanted to visit her—people from the American embassy and various media types, but Aissa made sure Mira was given the privilege of accepting or declining their visits. She declined them all—except one.

On Tuesday morning, Aissa entered her room. "I have the most unusual visitor for you today. It is a man who claims you will know him. He says he is a baker."

Mira sat up and grinned. "Does he have a small mustache but is mostly bald?"

"Yes, that's him. So, you do know him?"

"Yes! He's my friend. Please let him come in. I'd love to see him."

"Do you want me to stay or does he speak English?"

"He speaks very little English, and as you already know, I speak very little French. But it won't matter." Then she had another thought. "Actually, will you stay? I'd like to speak to him, you know, more than I've been able to."

"Of course." Aissa left but soon returned with Mira's favorite baker. He came in with a familiar-looking box. He beamed as he handed it to her.

Mira opened the lid to see an assortment of beautiful pastries, filling the box to near overflowing. Her obvious favorites were there, having chosen them many times, but others were elaborate delicacies she hadn't seen before. Her heart gave a small start at the sight of the eclairs, but she hastily recovered. When she gazed up into the gentle baker's face, her eyes were shining. Her voice choked as she said, "Merci!" and touched her hand to her heart.

He leaned forward over the pastry box in her lap to kiss her on each cheek. She threw her arms around him. He stiffened in surprise then responded by gently patting her on the back. When Mira released him, both sets of eyes were wet.

Up until this time, Aissa had hung in the background. Now she stepped forward. "Is there anything you'd like to say to him?"

Mira nodded, although she wasn't sure what to say. When she hesitated, the baker turned to Aissa, speaking in rapid French. When he was done, Aissa smiled and said, "He wants you to know that he is sorry this happened to you in the city that he loves. Paris is better than this. He also said his wife, who rarely bakes anymore, insisted on making you some special macarons, and he talked to other bakers he is friends with. All of them made something for you."

The baker tugged on Aissa's arm, telling her something else. "He also says to eat up because he will be back with more tomorrow."

Mira laughed. "Merci! I'll have to share them with everyone then." When Aissa was done interpreting, the baker beamed.

"Would you ask him his name, please?"

When Aissa interpreted the request, the baker turned to Mira himself. "Jean LeClaire." He pointed at Mira then shrugged with his palms up.

"Mira Silverman."

They nodded in unison. No more words were necessary. They kissed each other on the cheeks, and then he was gone and Aissa with him.

Mira stared into the box wondering where to begin. She withdrew two pastries and broke off pieces of several others to sample. Then she rang for her nurse and pantomimed that she should take the box and share its contents.

The pastries reminded her of Kailani, of how much she had wanted to share them with her when she'd first come across the bakery. The other reminder was all too real. She'd been nibbling on pastries just before ... just before everything fell apart. Jean had been kind enough to include her favorite eclairs in the box he'd packed—the same eclairs he had packed for her that fateful day. She didn't know if she'd ever be able to eat them again. Before calling the nurse to come take the box away, Mira had buried them under the other pastries so she couldn't see them.

Lost in these reflections, the sound of her phone buzzing on the table beside her made her jump. It was a text message, likely from Cordelia or Dylan. It was too early in the morning for Warren to be up.

When she'd first retrieved her phone so she should call Warren, she had 29 text messages waiting along with dozens of missed calls. Fourteen of the texts were from Warren, six each from Cordelia and Dylan, one from her Paris hotel, one about her Brussels' hotel reservation, and the other was a random offer for pizza. She initially ignored them all.

Eventually, she canceled her hotel reservations for places she clearly would never reach in time—Brussels, Amsterdam, and Munich. After another day had passed with more increasingly panicked texts from both Dylan and Cordelia, she texted back that she was fine and would be in touch soon.

Soon had probably come and gone. Mira picked up her phone to read the latest text. It was from Dylan. "Hey, girl. What's up? Things are so boring without you. Zita made me say that. I think she prefers your company to mine. Seriously, talk to me. You're not answering your phone or your texts. You say you're fine, but I read the papers. You were there. I need to hear how you are from your own lips."

As Mira was reading it, a follow-up text came. "If you don't call me right away, I'm coming to Paris to track you down, and Olivia is coming with me. We outnumber you, you know. And if that doesn't work, Mom's threatening to come. You don't want that!"

She couldn't help but crack a smile and was relieved to have a distraction from going down a particularly terrifying memory lane. She dialed Dylan's number before she could change her mind.

"Mira? Oh, wow, I can't believe that threat actually worked. Thank goodness!"

"Hi, Dylan. I'm calling on one condition. I don't want to talk about it, okay?"

"Okay, okay, as long as you tell me *honestly* how you're doing. Are you still in the hospital? What's up? We've been worried sick despite your, 'I'm fine,' text."

"I *am* fine, really. I'm still in the hospital because I've had a lot of headaches and I'm sore with bumps and bruises, but that's it. The doctors are being overly cautious if you ask me. The headaches are getting better. The bruises have bloomed so they look terrible, but they're actually starting to feel better. Quite honestly, I'm being spoiled." She glanced over at the pastries still waiting for her. "So, enough about me. What are you guys up to?"

Dylan's hesitation to shift topics was obvious in her stammering reply, but she respected Mira's wishes and told her about the places they'd been and the things they'd seen. Mira listened with half an ear. Sightseeing seemed like a world away to her, and she couldn't bring herself to care. But soon Dylan's cheerful, familiar voice calmed her troubled heart, almost lulling her to sleep.

"You sound tired, so I'll let you go, but only if you promise to call me tomorrow."

"Okay. I promise," Mira said, finding the notion of a conversation the next day, thankfully, a pleasant one.

She rolled over after hanging up, intent on having the nap that had been coming on, but the phone call had left her troubled. Dylan, while concerned, was going about her life. Dylan was living a normal life. *Can I ever live a normal life again?* Mira wondered.

More than anything, she wanted Warren to put his arms around her and tell her that everything was going to be okay. She wanted him to kiss her and hold her tight. She wanted to curl up on the couch with him and watch a sappy movie and cry as if those people were real. She wanted her old life back … or did she?

Warren with her, yes, she wanted that, but she didn't want to go back to how she was before this trip. She was miserable, and now she was … She didn't know what she was. She had learned to believe in herself, but now she was afraid of her own shadow. She'd been looking and seeing others, reaching out to help them, but now she couldn't even pay attention to what was going on in Dylan's life, let alone care about it.

Who am I, after all? Mira began to cry and do something she hadn't done in a very long time—pray. She couldn't remember how long it had been or why she'd stopped—probably when she didn't get pregnant as soon as she had hoped, even after desperate pleading. Or maybe it was when her mother was taken from her so unfairly. Whatever the reason, she began to plead for help and understanding, for relief, direction, for hope.

She was interrupted by a knock at her door, and Aissa poked her head in. "I was going to head out to lunch. I wondered if you wanted me to bring you something other than hospital food."

"That would be fantastic. Thank you."

"What would you like? Soup? Sandwich?"

"A sandwich on any type of French bread would be great. Just surprise me."

"Okay. I'll be back soon with something tasty."

As the door started to close, Mira thought of something else. "Aissa, could I ask you a question?"

She came back into the room. "Sure."

"What does Mira mean in French?"

Aissa shook her head. "I'm sorry. It doesn't have any meaning in French."

Mira's face fell. That wasn't what she was hoping for, but it was, unfortunately, how she felt. She was meaningless. Her life was meaningless. She noticed Aissa staring at her. "Well, thanks anyway. That was it."

Slightly puzzled, Aissa said, "Okay," and turned to leave. Touching the handle of the door, she paused and swiveled to face Mira. "I studied Latin in school. Mira does mean something in Latin."

"It does?" Mira said, hopeful.

"Yes, if I recall right, it means wonder or wonderful."

Mira caught her breath. She could live with that.

CHAPTER 20

After talking to Dylan, the guilt of shutting Cordelia out as well got to her. She "rang her up," as Cordelia would say. Cordelia was in the middle of something, but she refused to let Mira go until she had been assured that she was on the mend.

"Anything you need, you just let me know, okay?"

"Is your flat available to rent sooner than I'd planned if I came back to London now?"

Cordelia hesitated. "Someone's there right now, but I can find you a place, no problem. Just give me the word."

This news was unsettling. Mira had thought a nice place to recuperate before attempting the long flight home might be the comfortable, familiar flat of Cordelia's in London. Maybe she could even find ways to reach out to Kailani before she left for home. Staying somewhere else didn't fit in her plans.

"Mira? Are you there?"

"Umm … yeah, I'm here. It's … never mind, it's okay."

"Wait, I'll have those tenants move. I can offer them a nicer place. I'll make it happen, just let me know when you need it so I can get it cleaned up for you."

"No. It's all right. I'll be fine. I'll … I'll be in touch."

Cordelia was not convinced and tried to argue with her, but Aissa returned at that moment with sandwiches. So Mira made her excuses and hung up.

The food looked and smelled delicious. Aissa had not only brought a flaky croissant piled high with meat and cheese, she'd brought fresh fruit too. Mira was hungry, but the phone call had put her on edge, forcing her to process options which made her head hurt. "Would you mind opening the blinds and turning off the light?" she said, cradling her head.

"Sure." Aissa complied then quietly slipped out of the room.

After a nice lunch and an even nicer nap, Mira was feeling much better. She was eager to call Warren again. They'd been having wonderful, long conversations every day, sometimes multiple times a day. Mira had questioned if all the time on the phone was creating a problem at work for him, but Warren dismissed her concerns. "They understand, and besides, when I take too much time out of my day, I just use a few hours of my vacation time."

It was midafternoon by now, but Paris was one hour ahead of London, which meant if she called Warren now, he'd just be settling in to work. She should probably wait. Mira still didn't want him to come to Europe. She knew her fears for him were irrational, but she clung to them anyway.

She had decided, however, that she would go home as soon as she felt she could handle the flight. She still had frequent headaches, but they weren't as severe as they had initially been, so she was hoping to be released from the hospital tomorrow—a pleasant and terrifying idea.

Mira got out of bed and cautiously turned on the light. Her head did not object. She caught sight of the pile of things in and around the lone chair in the room—her things in disarray. Taking back a small piece of control, Mira set about to organize what was there.

The inside of her suitcase was still neat, the way she always kept it, but the various bags the hotel had filled with items she had spread around her hotel room were another matter. Her cross-body bag that she'd been wearing was also a mess. She tried not to think about who might have been the one assigned to go through her things to learn who she was.

It was likely that her driver's license or passport had been their means of identification. Her name as listed was Mira Wilkens Silverman. Mira—a name that also meant wonder. How could she possibly be filled with wonder at a time like this? She sat down in front of her pile of things to ponder that thought.

"Well, first thing—I didn't die when I so easily could have," she said out loud to herself. But that idea made her shiver as she thought about those who did die, especially Marcel. Why him and not her? If she was going to move forward, she'd have to do better than that.

She resumed her repacking and rearranging with vigor. When she came across her journal, she stuffed it underneath her clothes in the corner of her suitcase. She hadn't written in it since the attack, and she wasn't about to start again now.

Mira lingered over the things she'd brought with her from Warren's bag just long enough to make her homesick for him. Finding that unproductive, she stored them in a side pocket and continued with the other items strewn around her.

When she finished with her suitcase and the things gathered from her hotel room, she moved to her bag and money belt. The money belt was surprisingly neat, so she carefully set that aside to more thoroughly examine her cross-body bag. It was a jumble, so she dumped out the entire contents in her lap then set about replacing them one by one in a neater fashion. When she came to her camera, she set that aside until everything else was properly stored.

Mira was tired of the bed, but it was the most comfortable seat in the room. So, she took her camera with her back to the bed. She had taken a lot of pictures since she'd left home and was soon scrolling through them while smiling and laughing at the recent memories.

She had pictures of the bright red bus from her tour of London and the open-air top level. Big Ben and Buckingham Palace, swans and trees from Regent's Park, boats and people and buildings, new friends and strangers were there. She had a great shot of Jeremy and Bin outside a monkey enclosure, acting more monkey-like than the inhabitants within. Elijah and Avelyn were embracing in one while Madge and Harold were sitting side by side in another and still another showed Caleb cradling Tiana and her baby bump when he thought no one was looking.

Without considering the time, Mira picked up her phone and called Warren. He didn't answer until the third ring and then sounded surprised yet pleased to hear from her.

"Is it okay that I called?" She was suddenly hesitant.

"Of course it is. I was just in my usual morning meeting, so I had to step out before I could answer, but it's totally fine. You know I always love to hear your voice."

Mira beamed. She felt the same way. "I could call you back?" she suggested.

"No way! You're not weaseling out of this that easily."

"Good! I was hoping you'd say that. I've been going through the pictures on my camera. I can't wait to show them to you and tell you the stories behind them. I know I've told you a lot, but it feels like there's so much more to share. I can't wait to come home."

"So, you're coming home?" He sounded hopeful.

"Yes. I still can't picture you coming here. Every time I try, I almost have a panic attack at the thought. Is it okay if you don't come?"

"Well, I kind of liked the idea of rushing over there to be your knight in shining armor, but, yeah, it's okay. I got my passport yesterday and my plane ticket is for tomorrow, but if you're sure … I mean, to be honest, when you first told me you didn't want me to come, it kind of hurt. But the more I thought about it, the more I could understand where you were coming from. It didn't make sense, and yet, it did. So, I figured this is where we'd end up. I've already talked with the airline. They'll refund my ticket if I want."

Mira let out a breath she hadn't realized she'd been holding. "I'm glad you feel that way. I didn't want you to take it the wrong way."

"So … when are you coming home?" His tone was eager.

"I haven't been released yet. The doctors are coming tomorrow morning, and I'm hoping they'll decide I'm ready. My headaches are getting better every day, but I'm still a little hesitant about such a long flight."

"Which means …"

"What if I waited a couple days after being released before hopping on a plane?"

He sighed. "Okay. For a minute there, I thought you were going to say a couple weeks. So, given that, a couple days doesn't sound so bad. I know better than to say it, but you know …"

"Yes. You'll happily come sweep me off my feet to carry me home. All I need to do is ask."

"Yeah, that about sums it up."

"I love you, hubs. You're so good to me."

"I try. I love you too, babe."

"The only problem, though, is where to spend those few days recuperating. Every time I try to figure it out it gives me a headache. I talked to Cordelia about the London flat, but it's not available. I wasn't due back yet, and someone else is using it. I don't want to go back to my Paris hotel. It's ... it's close to where ... you know. So, now what?"

"Why not find a different hotel in Paris? One on the other side of town?"

"Oh, that seems obvious, doesn't it?" It did make sense, but Mira didn't know how to tell him about the other mixed emotions she was having. She couldn't explain how much she wanted to go back to London, to that familiar flat, while at the same time not wanting to inconvenience Cordelia or her other tenants. "Thanks, Warren," she said instead. He was being so understanding about not coming to Europe himself, that Mira didn't want to push it. The whole thing was making her feel like a selfish child who had to have her way.

She changed the topic to avoid having to deal with the feelings that confused her. "In the meantime, I'm going to send you more pictures. Watch out, you're going to get a flood of them."

"I'm okay with that. So far, you've sent me pictures of things you've seen but not the people you've met. But since you've told me so much about them, I'm wondering if I can match people to their photos."

"I haven't sent you pictures of people?"

"Nope."

"Hmm. I guess I must have wanted to save them until I could show you in person and talk about them." She paused. "I wonder ... well, I wonder if I was keeping them to myself, like they're my new sisters and I wasn't willing to share them with anyone yet. Wow, am I that kind of person?"

Warren laughed. "You have nothing to worry about. You've been telling me all about the people you've met. But I do think it's new territory for you. I'm guessing you want to make sure the friendships are real, that you're not going to lose them before you share their pictures."

"You scare me sometimes. It's like you know me better than I know myself. I hadn't thought of that, but once you said it, I'm pretty sure you're right." She let out a breath. "Okay, no more fears. I'll send you the pics today. I've got so many people to share with you. And I'm not sure I've sent you all the pictures of the sights either." She scrolled through the photos while she was talking, checking with him to see what she had already shared and what she hadn't.

"It's incredible all the things you've seen and the people you've met. I can't believe it. It's wonderful!"

"Yeah," she said slowly. "It is wonderful, isn't it?"

"Yes."

"My only regret is Kailani. I can keep in touch with everyone else, but I don't know what to do about Kailani. Here, I'm going to have to find her picture. I want to send that to you first." But no matter how much she searched, it wasn't there.

"I can't find her picture, Warren. It's not here! I ... no, of course, it isn't. When would I have taken her picture? I only talked to her for a few minutes here and there, and I didn't want to take her picture without her mother's permission ..." The anguish of it hit her. "I don't have her picture, Warren. I don't have it."

"Well ... let me think. What about Cordelia? Could she get a picture for you?"

"Yes, I suppose so. It's just ... yeah, I'm sure that would be fine," she said, the disappointment evident in her voice.

"Mira, would you let me have Cordelia's number? I'll talk to her. Let me do that. Please? And could I have Dylan's number too?"

"Okay." She mechanically passed along the information.

"Hey, cheer up, babe. I'm not there, but I can still help take care of you. Do you want me to find a Paris hotel for you? Or I could send you back to London on the train. Would you be comfortable with that?"

"Sure."

"Okay. I'll take care of all the arrangements. Is there anything else you need me to do? Did you cancel your reservations around Europe yet?"

"I canceled most of them. I can handle the rest."

"I know. You've been handling things really well, but I think Kailani is threatening to be your last straw. So, let me do this for you. Please?"

"Okay. I've canceled everything except Rome."

"I'll take care of it. I've got your itinerary. I'm going to make some phone calls and call you back. Is that okay?"

He was treating her with kid gloves, and she knew it. But she'd lost the energy to fight it or even care. What he was doing was what she needed. She just didn't want to need it. "Okay," she finally said and hung up.

Freed from having to make decisions about logistics, Mira determined to rise and not sink under the strain. She picked up her camera and slowly examined her pictures. They were beautiful, whether it was the architecture of a building or the graceful bend in a tree. The skies were sometimes clear and sometimes angry. The colors were bright or soft. She stared at the faces of people who had come to mean something to her. Gradually, the tension began to leave her body. One by one, picture by picture, a sense of awe and wonder flowed then overtook her.

CHAPTER 21

Wednesday dawned with the full morning sun flooding her room. Mira had forgotten that she'd thrown the blinds open the day before to take in the wonders of what lay outside her window. Even though other structures partially obstructed her view, she'd found the brickwork on the neighboring buildings to be amazingly intricate. She could only imagine how long ago they had been constructed and what the builders' lives might have been like. A little slice of Paris was visible where the buildings parted. It was like watching an animated postcard as people ducked in and out of stereotypical Paris stores and cafés.

Closer to her window, she had spied a couple of pigeons nesting on a nearby ledge. They were likely a breeding pair, with one being slightly larger than the other. She named them One and Two for simplicity but kept mixing up which was which, her headache-addled brain confusing which name she'd given the larger bird. This didn't, however, stop her from calling to them and telling them her life story. She had "conversed" with them for much of the previous afternoon.

When the morning light woke her, she hurried to the window to see if her friends were still there, but they were not. "Serves you right for …" but she could think of nothing that it served them right for.

She climbed back into bed, anxious for the day to begin in earnest. Warren had not called back yesterday, although he had texted her several times. He said things were a little complicated but that he was taking care of everything, so not to worry. One of her doctors was supposed to show up to check on her progress, and she kept hoping that Jean the baker would indeed return as promised.

With all these things to anticipate, the arrival of her breakfast had not been one of them. She was beginning to suspect that as a foreigner injured on their native soil, she had been given great privilege at the hospital initially, as evidenced by the multiple doctors, the interpreter, constantly vigilant staff, and delicious food. Lately, however, the doctors were less attentive (she was getting better, after all), the staff less responsive, and the food now met the best of hospital food expectations.

The tray with watery oatmeal, gelatin, and a hard-boiled egg didn't remotely appeal to her, and she nibbled it merely out of boredom. This attempt to eat was interrupted when a doctor entered her room, one she had never met before. Thankfully Aissa accompanied him.

"Good morning, Mira," Aissa said. "This is Dr. Lambeau. He's been tasked with determining if you are ready to be discharged."

The examination was over before she knew it, and Dr. Lambeau had left before Aissa could interpret his last message. Clearly, Mira would not get a chance to ask him questions even though she had answered every one of his.

"He says you are doing well. He only wishes your headaches had stopped, but the fact that they are lessening is a good sign. You are to be discharged tomorrow morning."

"Tomorrow? Why not today?"

"He did not say. I'm sorry."

Deflated, Mira let out a sigh. "Okay. After breakfast tomorrow then?"

"Yes. All the paperwork will be ready to go. Do you have someplace to go?"

Did she? She didn't know but assumed she did. "My husband, I think, is taking care of that."

After Aissa left, the day gave new meaning to moving slow as molasses—wet concrete seemed more like it. Mira had been reluctant to talk to Cordelia and Dylan before, but the mindless waiting prompted her to pick up her phone and start dialing. She reached both of them, but the conversations were short as both were in the middle of something.

Hospital policy dictated she remain in a hospital gown, but Mira decided to ignore that. What were they going to do? Throw her out? After a shower and slipping into her own clothes, she felt much better, even felt a bit of control slipping her way.

Just before lunch, her pigeons returned. "Hey, One, Two, where have you been?" When they didn't even so much as look in her direction, she added, "It must be the English. I'm sure you'd respond if I spoke in French."

"Well, you never know," said a familiar voice.

Mira turned with delight to see Aissa once more entering her room, and right behind her was a smiling Jean LeClaire with an even larger pastry box than before. She was grateful for the shower and the fresh clothes she'd put on.

"Jean!" she said, running to him and throwing her arms around him.

When she let go, he was blushing. After kissing her on each cheek, he turned and spoke to Aissa. Mira caught the word *amour.*

"He says you should not tug at his heart so. He has a wife, you know."

Mira laughed. "And I have a husband."

He was still beaming when he opened the box to reveal its contents. Eclairs were sitting prominently on top. Mira shuddered and winced slightly. Noticing, Jean said something in French.

"He wants to know if something is wrong," Aissa said.

"No, no," Mira started, but she could tell by the pained expression on the baker's face that she needed to explain, to be honest. "Aissa, please tell him not to worry. The eclairs are my favorite, but I was eating one when … when the bomb exploded. They are hard for me to look at now. I'm sorry."

When Aissa finished interpreting, Jean's face clouded with dismay. Mira took the box from him, set it on the bed, then embraced him. He at first resisted, then gave in and held her tightly while she cried on his shoulder.

When she pulled back, his eyes too were wet. Jean stared intently at Mira, patted his chest, and said, "Papa." He touched her then himself again and repeated, "Papa."

Tears streamed unrestrained down her cheeks. "Papa," was all she could say.

She bid him farewell with the assurance that tomorrow, once she was discharged, she would come to him instead of the other way around.

Alone in her room, she once again opened the box of pastries. The eclairs were still sitting on top. They still evoked unpleasant memories, but that wasn't all this time. Mira reached into the box to lift one out. She stared at it for a long time, struggling with competing emotions. Finally, she declared, "I'm going to call these 'Papa's eclairs' from now on." She tentatively took a small bite. To her delight and amazement, it tasted delicious. This time she shared all the pastries with the hospital staff— except the eclairs.

•

It wasn't until 2:30 in the afternoon that she got a call from Warren. "Hey, I wondered if you'd forgotten about me," she teased.

"Sorry about that. I didn't get everything squared away until late your time. I didn't want to wake you. At least, I was hoping you were sleeping. I'm getting ready to head out to work, but I wanted to call you first."

"I'm glad you did. I love hearing the sound of your voice."

"Good. Are you sitting down?"

"Umm … of course I'm sitting down. What's up?"

"Well, don't be mad at me, but I made some arrangements."

"Why would I be mad about you making arrangements? That's what you were going to do anyway, right? So … what exactly did you do?" In her mind, she tried to explore the possibilities but drew a blank.

"Well, the choice is yours, but I suggest you finish out your trip. Don't come home yet."

"What? Really? You'd be okay with that?"

"Yes."

"But why? Why stay? And why are you okay with it?"

"You mentioned Kailani yesterday. You told me before that she was a piece of unfinished business. I know she still is. And I think you are your own unfinished business too. This is a setback, to be sure, but I don't believe what happened is a complete undoing of what you've gained. It would be good for you to be able to finish what you started."

"You mean it?"

"Yes, I do."

"But … do you think I can?"

"I know you can. I even greased the wheels for you."

"What does that mean?"

"Well, you'd already canceled your plans for Belgium through Germany, and maybe doing all of that would be too ambitious when you're trying to recover anyway. Italy, however, might be a nice treat. So, I talked to Dylan. She and Olivia would love to meet you there. If you want, I found a flight from Paris to Rome, and Dylan and Olivia can catch a flight from London. The three of you can spend a week together. Then you can fly back to London, almost on schedule with your original plans. Cordelia's flat will be ready and waiting—right down the street from Kailani. What do you think?"

"I don't even know what to say. That sounds … incredible!"

"Good. I was hoping you'd feel that way. I found an apartment to rent in the heart of Rome that will fit the three of you. I figured that would be nicer than a hotel room. Everyone is in on the plan, just waiting to hear back from me that it's a go."

"Oh, it is definitely a go!" She giggled with excitement. "But Warren, how are you okay with this?"

He chuckled. "Well, I know you'll enjoy having Dylan and Olivia with you, but they're actually my spies. I made them promise within an inch of their lives to watch out for you and take care of you. So, if they smother you a bit, that's my fault. Don't take it out on them, okay?"

Mira shook her head and laughed. "All right. I understand now. I'm guessing you've placed Cordelia under the same obligation?"

"Boy, it's almost as if you know me or something."

"Just so you know, I'm rolling my eyes at you right now."

"Yep. I was already imagining that. So, way ahead of you, babe."

"I love you, you know."

"I love you too, Mira. But no more delays and no more surprises. Deal?"

"Deal."

"And when you get back to London, make sure you get a picture of Kailani. I want to at least see what all this fuss has been about, all right?"

"Way ahead of you this time, hubs. I was already planning on it."

CHAPTER 22

Thursday morning—it had arrived. Mira had been in the hospital just under a week, and she was ready to be done with it. She woke early, took a shower, changed her clothes, and sat in the chair instead of the bed waiting for her discharge papers.

Her pigeon friends, One and Two, had, to her delight, visited her first thing that morning. She'd had a nice long conversation with them, and they even lifted their heads in her direction occasionally while she spoke. It was promising to be a good day.

Aissa arrived at nine, shortly after Mira had finished nibbling at her grayish-colored breakfast. "Yay! You're here. Does that mean I can go?"

"Wow. Eager to get rid of me, are you? I planned on pestering you for at least an hour before allowing you to leave."

Mira smiled. "Well, if you can break away, I'd love to take you with me to Jean's bakery. I imagine that could take an hour? Are you up for it?"

"Well, if you insist," Aissa said with a wide grin on her face. "And I suppose if you're ready, we may as well go now."

"Almost. I have something I want to give you first." Mira produced one of the items from Warren's bag that she had pulled out that morning. She handed the tissue-wrapped item to Aissa.

Aissa's eyes sparkled with delight. "Thank you. It was unnecessary, but thank you." Carefully unwrapping the gift, she discovered a pair of large hoop earrings inside.

"I usually wear smaller earrings, maybe an occasional dangly earring," Mira said. "But my husband is always kidding me that if I wore large hoop earrings, he'd be able to recognize me in a crowd." She rolled her eyes. "As if he wouldn't recognize me." She shook her head but smiled. "Anyway, I saw this pair of earrings this morning. They're new. I've never worn them. But they seem better suited to you. You automatically stand out in a crowd. You light up this room every time you enter. I can't believe how kind you've been to me, a friend in the midst of everything going on—running interference, standing up for me, protecting me, even grabbing me lunch, going beyond what your job entails. That makes you stand out. You've been a constant for me here, and I appreciate it so much."

Aissa was taken by surprise but beamed, and for the first time, she was speechless.

.　　.　　.

It only took a few minutes to collect Mira's things—the suitcase and her cross-body bag. She'd already strapped on her money belt under her shirt that morning. She would be flying to Rome later that day. Warren had sent the flight information and ticket to her phone, so she was set to go. At the last minute, she grabbed a packet of pocket tissues Warren had given her in his bag. She wasn't sure what her emotions would be like today, and she wanted to be prepared.

Stepping out the front door of the hospital was a new experience for Mira. She hadn't seen what the hospital looked like from the outside before and, other than the view from her window, knew nothing about the surrounding environment. She swung her head left and right, trying to register what she was seeing yet registering none of it. Her only thought was she'd been unconscious the last time she was outside this building, when she'd entered it.

Breaths coming in ragged gasps, Mira froze at the top step. She had been safe here. She had been comfortable. It had become her home. She had two competing urges—run back inside or race to the airport and fly home to Warren.

Aissa stopped when she noticed Mira wasn't following her anymore. Retreating up the steps, she caught sight of Mira's face and gently touched her arm. "It's okay. I'm here. Mira, look at me."

Mira had no idea if Aissa understood what was going through her head or not, but she was there, standing beside her. One step at a time, she told herself. One step. Gradually, while Aissa never left her side, Mira made it down the steps and to the curb where a taxi was waiting.

She had to consciously slow her breathing, telling herself to be calm. Everything was going to be okay. As her suitcase was loaded into the trunk, Mira waited in the back seat, shaking slightly. In desperation, she prayed again, pleading for help, pleading not to be afraid. She felt Aissa slide in beside her and, almost as an afterthought, added one last thing to her prayer—gratitude for this newest sister.

Opening her eyes, Aissa smiled at her. They talked little on the way to the bakery. Mira instead gazed out her window, watching the streets of Paris glide by. She spotted a little family walking—mother and father on either side of a small boy. They were holding his hands, and every few steps they swung him up in the air to his delight. She saw colorful awnings of sidewalk cafés with small round tables cheerfully arranged out front and narrow cobblestone streets, the buildings rising on both sides. She spied window after window, some with brightly colored shutters, others with flower beds, and some with both. A feeling of wonder spread over her. There was so much to be grateful for, so much to enjoy. She didn't want what had happened to her to define her or her visit to Paris. She could gather up all these sights like a large bouquet. Her predominant memories of Paris could be positive if she let them. And with this thought, her heart felt better.

They approached the bakery from the opposite direction she had walked from her hotel, for which Mira was grateful. She was determined to shed her anxious feelings, but there was no need to test that resolve.

When they climbed out of the taxi, Aissa asked the driver to stay and wait for them. "I'll see you off to the airport when we're done here if you don't mind."

"Thank you," Mira said, relieved.

Opening the door to the bakery, the wonderful aroma of freshly baked bread greeted them followed by a hint of sweet pastries and fruit filling. Jean had been expecting them and rushed forward to greet Mira, kissing her on either cheek.

"Papa," she said, returning the kisses.

Jean turned and motioned for a woman to join him. "Ma femme, Monique," he said. Jean's wife then smiled at Mira, putting her hands on either side of her face. She said something in rapid French then kissed her on both cheeks too.

Aissa didn't even bother to interpret as Jean paraded Mira around the bakery, introducing her to employees and customers alike. Partway through these introductions, the bakery door opened. Jean glanced over and said, "Ahh." He smiled at Mira and turned her around to see the group of boys she had helped with their kitten.

The boys gathered around her, all chattering at once with words she could not understand. Aissa interpreted, "They say thank you for helping them with the kitten. They haven't lost him again, you'll be happy to know."

Jean sidled up to them, whispering to Aissa. She laughed. "He said to tell you to be careful because even though they really did have a lost kitten last week, they're actually active pickpockets."

Mira spun, wide-eyed to Jean for confirmation. He nodded with a twinkle in his eye. She reacted by holding her bag more tightly against her body.

When Mira and the boys had said their thanks and their goodbyes, Jean ushered her back to the pastry counter. "Anything," he said, sweeping his arms out to indicate the entire array. It was then that she noticed an empty section. Where the eclairs usually sat, it was empty.

"For me? You didn't make eclairs today because I was coming?"

When this was interpreted, Jean gently nodded. He patted his chest, and quietly said, "Papa." Mira pulled him into an embrace, so touched by his kindness.

Aissa laughed. "Mira, hugging is not something we French do. You keep making the poor man uncomfortable. And now his wife is going to be jealous."

But Jean brushed Aissa's comments aside with a wave of his hand and returned Mira's embrace. When she let him go, Mira discovered tears pouring down his face. His wife behind him was similarly crying. Mira reached into her bag, pulling out the pocket tissues. She handed them to Jean. Then she touched both hands to her heart. "Papa."

Mira left with more pastries than she could possibly eat, especially since she would be boarding a plane in a short while. The group of young pickpockets was waiting nearby when she emerged from the bakery. She offered a pastry to the taxi driver, Aissa, and took one for herself. She then called the smallest boy over and handed him the box to share with his friends and fellow thieves.

Before he returned to his friends, he said something to Aissa then ran off. "He said to tell you thanks for helping him get his kitten back, but that you shouldn't help anyone at the airport. It's probably a distraction so someone else can steal from you."

Mira smiled. "Who knew I'd be having a pickpocket give me advice."

With still time before her flight, Aissa directed the taxi driver to take a circuitous route around the city before heading to the airport. Mira would be able to see the sights of Paris one last time. "Aissa, are you sure you have time?"

She shrugged in response. "If anyone asks where I've been, I'll tell them I'm just making right what our city did wrong. No one should leave Paris with the last memories of it being what you experienced. We're much better than that."

It was a wonderful blessing to be able to see the Eiffel Tower, the Arc de Triomphe, and other sights again, to roll down the window and listen to the sounds of the City of Light. The taxi driver pulled over several times so she could take more pictures, and however briefly, make more memories.

She planned to sandwich her earlier photos with these, crushing the middle memories down to size. She wouldn't forget what happened. It was a part of her now. But this way she could also see all the good that happened on either side of it—the sights, of course, but also the people.

Getting to her flight at the airport was smoother than she expected. She smiled, remembering the little pickpocket's warning, and felt safer because of it.

Before she stowed her bag, she unzipped it, digging around until her fingers hit what she was searching for. It was to be a short flight, but she would use the time to her advantage.

Once seated and buckled in, she opened her journal for the first time in many days and wrote:

My name means wonder or wonderful in Latin—what an interesting and amazing concept. I am learning that to see the world with wonder or to recognize the wonderful things that exist within it is a choice. That hasn't been an easy choice in the days since I last wrote, and it's a choice I have to remind myself to make—sometimes successfully and other times less so.

Evil exists in the world. I ran into it headlong a few days ago. I haven't wanted to talk about this and certainly not write about it, but my journey, my story would be incomplete without it. A terrorist set off a bomb in Paris, killing himself and twenty other people. One of those people, Marcel DuBois, had his hand in mine when the blast hit. I held that same hand as he died. For some reason, fate chose him and not me, although I have no idea why. I was fortunate because I was only thrown to the ground and suffered minor injuries—physically. Emotionally is another story. I have good moments and moments where I shrink in fear from even the things that are good, not always certain I can trust my own judgment.

It's the people around me that give me hope for society as a whole. Even though a person did this despicable act, I've met people like Aissa, my interpreter and friend. I got to know, on a more personal level, the baker Jean LeClaire (my honorary papa) and his wife Monique. I've even learned that a group of pickpocket boys are, at their heart, still boys. They need love as much as anyone—and respond to it.

Warren. How do I even begin to describe what Warren has done for me? He just defined unselfishness in ways I had not conceived of before. I'll write about the results of that in the coming days because he has made it possible for me to write again. He has given me back myself, once again.

CHAPTER 23

The flight to Rome was only about two hours. She breathed in the air when she walked off the plane as if it would be different from Paris air and could give her new life. Moving through the airport, Mira's eyes drifted upward to a large, intentional crack in the expansive ceiling, forming an enormous skylight. The blue heavens beyond were comforting.

She needed to catch a taxi to take her into the heart of Rome, inside the old walls to where the apartment Warren had booked was waiting. Hopefully, the landlord would be waiting as well.

With the help of a phrasebook and the written address of her destination which she handed the driver, they were soon on their way. Italy had such a different feel to it, but she couldn't exactly pinpoint why to start with. Gradually as they passed numerous buildings and groups of people, she began to understand. It felt like the laid-back little brother of Paris. Both places had multi-story buildings rising from the streets, often with ornate balconies punctuating the exteriors. But where Paris might be white and elegant, Rome was the color of a beautiful red clay, stately yet like a well-loved vase. She had often felt the need to dress up in Paris. Here she felt she could dress down, in fact, would fit in better if she did.

When the taxi driver dropped her off with her things, she couldn't believe what she saw in front of her. The entrance to her rental had an arched entryway that looked hundreds of years old. Great urns with plants graced either side. But it was what she saw when she turned her back to the entrance that caught her breath. Warren had found a place just down the street from the Colosseum! Its massive form was partially visible where the street opened up a short distance away.

People, most with dark hair, moved up and down the street, speaking with their hands as much as their lips. She felt as if she'd walked in on a summer party, the warm air adding to this mystique.

"Are you Mira?" a heavily-accented voice said behind her.

She whipped around to be met by a handsome Italian who was smiling at her. She loved her husband, but the eye candy was not to be ignored. Blushing and embarrassed, she said, "Yes. That's me."

"I am Francesco. Shall I show you the apartment?"

"Yes, please." She followed as he led the way inside. No sooner had she taken a few steps when her jaw dropped at the sight facing her. Hidden away in the middle of the building was a private courtyard. Archways led to it from two sides. In the center of the courtyard stood a fountain, water rising from the mouth of a large fish, gracefully falling into the waiting pool below. Lush plants surrounded the inner walls.

Mira stood transfixed until Francesco lightly touched her arm. "The apartment is this way, but you may visit the courtyard anytime you wish."

She nodded, unable to speak, then followed him up two flights of stairs to the apartment. It had two bedrooms and a sofa bed, so each of them would have their own space. Since Mira was first, she gravitated to the smaller bedroom that had a balcony overlooking the street.

When he finished with the brief tour, he pointed out several restaurants from the balcony that she might enjoy and gave her directions to the nearest metro stop. It wasn't necessary to point the way to the Colosseum.

Dylan and Olivia arrived two hours later. They texted when they were near so Mira could meet them at the entrance.

She squealed when they stepped out of the taxi, racing to embrace them both. "I'm so glad you're here!"

"Same! The whole family wanted to come, but we told them they weren't invited." Dylan laughed.

"We didn't want to overwhelm you," said Olivia. Then with a twinkle in her eye, she added, "Two of us can be enough to handle."

"I think I can manage." It felt good to smile and to be in the company of friends. "Hey, wait 'til you see this place. You're going to love it!"

They were in awe of it as much as Mira was. When Dylan closed her mouth enough that she could speak, she said, "I can't believe we're staying here. This is incredible!"

"I agree," added Olivia. "I mean there are awesome sights to see, but I kind of just want to stay here, you know what I mean?"

"I felt the same way, but then I went to the market down the street to buy supplies. It was delightful. I loved Paris—well, mostly, and, of course, I love London. I can tell I'm going to love Rome too. Each place has its own charm. I'm glad I don't have to pick a favorite."

It was difficult to choose where to eat dinner that night because so many good options existed. They ended up at a seafood restaurant that appeared popular but not so busy that they wouldn't be able to eat soon. While they waited for their food to come, Mira texted Warren. "It's been a great day. Not too many headaches. And even though I had moments where I was terrified of the world, the people around me made it okay. I know you're not physically here with me, but you are with me in so many ways—in everything you arranged for me. I love you."

He immediately texted back. "I love you too, babe."

"The three of us are out for dinner just waiting for our food. The place you rented for us is fantastic, lots of Roman charm. I'll call when I can."

The food arrived shortly afterward. Mira had ordered a linguine seafood dish, Dylan a seafood stew, and Olivia, being adventurous, ordered something in Italian. When it arrived, she found it to be an entire cod in a broth, surrounded with clams, olives, and tomatoes.

It had been a long day, and they were hungry. As a result, they ate with abandon, sopping up the last of their meals with traditional hearty Italian bread. When they weren't eating, they were talking. They had seen different sights since they had last been together in London, but their talk centered more on their lives, their hopes, their dreams, even their disappointments.

A few times Olivia deftly changed the topic or steered the conversation away from herself, and this did not go unnoticed by either of the other two. Gently they would redirect the conversation back to Olivia, but they repeatedly found a wall they could not penetrate.

Walking back to their apartment after dinner, Mira kept pondering on Olivia, wondering what was going on. Then something else hit her. She had been so concerned about Olivia that all during dinner she hadn't thought once about the attack in Paris. It's not that she was grateful Olivia had a problem, but focusing outward was a positive step forward.

The three of them talked well into the night, but when the yawns became too prevalent to ignore, they reluctantly went off to bed. Mira climbed into the comfortable bed and promptly fell asleep.

.   .   .

It's noon, she can tell because the sun is directly overhead, but the light it casts is dim, like a dying bulb in a ceiling fixture. She shivers, cold as if she were standing in the shade on a winter's day—even though neither of those conditions seems to be true. People are moving swiftly around her, brushing past, bumping against her, yet completely unaware of her existence.

She reaches out to tap someone on the shoulder but is immediately rebuffed, shrugged off with nary a word. Rooted to this one spot, she finds she is able only to turn in place. Spinning around, she yearns to make eye contact with someone, anyone. Desperate, she calls out, but no one hears since no sound has escaped her lips.

A tug pulls on her arm. Glancing down, a small child is grabbing hold of her hand, and she is smiling. At once, the sun releases a single ray of light which engulfs the child.

She reaches down to scoop the child up in her arms, but in that same moment, the ground beneath her cracks in every direction. Abruptly, the child is ripped from her arms and is gone. She alone remains on the only piece of land still standing, in the middle of a sea of rubble and despair.

.   .   .

With a loud gasp, Mira woke, shaking all over. She tried to pull the covers up around her, but they did nothing to stop her shaking. She sat shivering on the bed for several minutes, finally doing the only thing she could think of—in earnest, she prayed for help. Then climbing out of bed, she grabbed a throw blanket and wrapped it around her shoulders. The curtains in front of the balcony were faintly lit by the lights from the city outside. Mira crossed to them and tentatively pulled them aside.

It was the middle of the night, but the street lights were aglow. She cautiously lifted the latch and opened the balcony door, letting the warmth and the summer fragrances entice her to step outside. She sat in one of the two chairs on the balcony and pulled her feet up to rest on the other.

The night transformed the street below. No longer a bustling corridor, it was a lazy, serene promenade. A young couple strolled by, hand in hand, talking softly. Occasionally she could hear the soft tinkle of one of them laugh. A cat crouched nearby behind a potted plant, but the couple was oblivious to its presence.

A slight breeze ruffled Mira's hair, bringing with it a floral scent, possibly jasmine. She relaxed her hold on the blanket, letting the night air warm her instead. It was an incredible world around her. Why couldn't she let that be enough?

She stepped back inside long enough to grab her phone before returning to her perch on the balcony. Could her name really mean wonder? She had moments where she felt full of wonder, but they seemed so easily chased away.

Googling "Mira wonderful," she scanned the results. One stood out to her. A star in the constellation Orion was called Omicron Ceti, but its proper name was Mira and had been known as Mira the Wonderful by early astronomers. *It is a curious star that varies in brilliance from time to time. At its brightest, it is visible to the naked eye, but otherwise, it is not. Because of this, it was called Mira the Wonderful, or a star that aroused wonder.*

A new level of meaning settled in her mind. It was true that she had much to be grateful for; a whole world of wonder existed for her to appreciate. Certainly, there were times where that helped. But maybe, just maybe, she wasn't going to feel that way every second of every day. And maybe, just maybe, that was okay.

What she'd experienced in Paris was real. "I could have died," she whispered to herself. "I could have died, but I didn't." Because she survived, didn't she have an obligation to grab hold of life? Pondering the Latin meaning of her name made her think of one of the only other things she knew in Latin: *carpe diem*—seize the day! Yes, she could do that ... if she also remembered the message of her star. She didn't have to be good at it all the time.

She shuddered, remembering her dream, but she also glanced around her, even leaning back to gaze up into the night sky. Because of the interference of city lights, few stars were visible, but some stars could still be seen twinkling in the heavens. The terror of her night dream was juxtaposed against the majesty of the stars above. Both good and bad could exist at the same time, both difficult and easy, both happy and sad. Mira could recognize both and then choose which to dwell on.

She did some quick calculations to figure out what time it was for Warren. He was seven hours behind her. Her phone said it was 3:12 AM which meant it was 8:12 PM back home. She eagerly dialed Warren.

"Mira? Are you okay? Isn't it the middle of the night?"

She tried to answer softly so as not to disturb Dylan and Olivia or anyone else for that matter, with the result that Warren couldn't hear her.

"What? Are you there? Are you okay?" His voice sounded frantic.

"Yes, I'm here. I'm fine, better than fine, actually." She could hear his sigh of relief. "I'm sorry for scaring you. I ... I had a nightmare that woke me up, but now I'm sitting on a balcony enjoying the streets of Rome from above and the night sky from below. It's the most wondrous thing, and I wanted to share it with you."

"I'd love to say I'm glad you called. I'll probably feel that way in a minute, but quite frankly, you scared me."

"Yeah, I didn't think about how a phone call might come across. I'm sorry."

"It's okay. I'd forgotten how spontaneous you used to be. So, let's back up. What did you want to share with me?"

"Rome. Simply put, Rome. I'm on this little balcony by myself, and I can see so much. There's a cat below that doesn't know I'm here, but it's hunting for sure. It crouches then slinks forward then crouches again. I saw a couple walk past a few minutes ago. Now I see an old drunk staggering by. He stops to lean against the building every few steps. Then he takes another swig from a bottle before trying to take a few more steps. I see him and I feel sad for him, maybe because I don't just see him as a drunk. He's a person. I wonder what his life has been like. What led him down this path? I may never know, but asking the questions ... I don't know how to describe it, Warren, but I feel alive. It's like I understand that one person can feel both dead inside and alive inside—maybe not at the same moment, but in the same lifetime, even in the same day or week."

"You are something else again, babe. It's the wee hours of the morning over there, and you're busy having an epiphany. You blow me away sometimes."

She laughed airily. "I surprise myself sometimes, hubs."

"What else do you see? I like seeing things through your eyes."

She told him about the stars overhead and about Mira the Wonderful. She told him about the apartment behind her that he'd rented for them. When the baker down the street entered his shop early, presumably to start the day's baking, she described his appearance, down to his jolly belly that probably meant he sampled what he baked.

They talked until Mira's phone battery started to peter out, and she realized with a yawn that she needed more sleep if she was going to attempt to keep up with Dylan and Olivia while sightseeing. Reluctantly, they said goodbye. Mira once again climbed into bed, but this time she slept undisturbed until the morning light streamed in through the balcony doors.

CHAPTER 24

Mira was understandably a bit bleary-eyed when the three of them gathered around the kitchen table. However, Dylan and Olivia's excitement was contagious, and she was soon as perky and eager for the day as they were.

Based on a recommendation from Francesco, Mira had arranged for a local tour guide to show them around. Gia arrived in the street below promptly at 9:00. She had dark hair and expressive dark eyes and looked to be in her 40s. According to Francesco, she was a native Italian but spoke perfect English.

"Since it is close, why not start with the Colosseum? Va bene? Okay?" Gia's words were clipped, almost exaggerated in their diction. The women easily understood her, and the underlying Italian flavor her accent added made the words delightful to listen to.

No one had any objections to Gia's suggestion, and they eagerly followed her to wherever she wanted to take them. The day passed in a flash as Gia navigated them through the crowds to visit the Colosseum, Roman Forum, Pantheon, Trevi fountain, and the Spanish steps. It was a whirlwind adventure that left them in awe.

"I've seen pictures of these things all my life, but seeing them for real is a completely different experience," said Olivia.

"I know," agreed Dylan.

They were sitting at a charming café, having chosen the seats outside so they could watch Rome swirl around them while they reviewed their day. All three were rubbing their feet. Each had taken a myriad of pictures—selfies, scenic views, ancient structures, and group shots Gia snapped in front of every place they visited.

"Thank goodness we have photographic proof of where we've been. I wouldn't even believe it myself if we didn't," Mira said, scrolling through her pictures. She had enjoyed the day more than she'd thought possible.

"I'm tired, but it has been a fantastic day," Olivia said. "Mira, what about you?"

She smiled to herself before responding. "I am very tired. But I feel better about life if that makes sense."

"What do you mean?"

"I've realized that it's okay to struggle, to have a bad day. What happened in Paris was terrifying, but I don't need to wallow in it. I'm still working hard to let go of the fear and nervousness that came with that, but, at the same time, I don't need to be hard on myself for not being perfect at it. Strangely, feeling okay about being down has helped me not be. A burden has been lifted." She paused letting her own words sink in. "And then, today ... today was incredible. I can't wait to share all this with Warren."

"You're really doing okay?" asked Dylan. "You're not just saying that and lying to us, are you?"

Mira laughed. "No, I'm not just saying that, and I've definitely had my moments. Any time we saw a large crowd pushing forward, I had to catch my breath. It reminded me so much of the crowd that was running away from that madman. But then I'd look at the two of you, at Gia, and I knew the situation was different."

"That explains why you grabbed my arm a few times. I thought you were trying to steady yourself or something."

"I was steadying myself, just not physically."

"Well, you'll have to write about that in your journal," Dylan said.

"What? How did you ..."

"You told me about your journal, girl. It's not only about other people—it's about you too, isn't it?"

"Yeah, it is, but I didn't realize you knew that."

"Of course we did," Olivia said. "Now, what kind of sisters would we be if we didn't know what was going on in your head?"

Mira laughed. "All right. I'll make sure it makes it into my journal." She threw her hands up. "Is this what sisters do? Nag you?"

"You've got that right," Dylan said, while Olivia nodded her agreement.

"So, Olivia, if sisters know what's going on, what's going on with you? You keep dancing around something every time we talk. What's up?"

It grew unusually quiet while Dylan and Mira waited for a response. "It's complicated. I ..."

Gia walked up at that very moment. She'd gone off to secure tickets for the following day's adventures, promising to meet them at the café to review their plans. "Buongiorno. How are you after our full day? Are you ready for another one tomorrow?"

Dylan and Mira were still staring at Olivia who broke the silence to address Gia. "You bet we are."

"I'm sorry. Did I interrupt?"

"Nope," Olivia was quick to respond. "We were just chatting. All we've had are drinks so far. Would you like to join us for dinner? We'd love the company."

They were happy to have Gia join them, but Dylan and Mira exchanged meaningful glances, knowing what Olivia had done. But she couldn't avoid them forever.

Gia helped them read the menu, and they were soon enjoying their various pasta dishes. "This is delicious, Gia. Do you come here a lot?"

"Yes. I love bringing tourists here. Then I get to eat a nice dinner too."

"How long have you been a tour guide?"

"Twelve years. I love it. You meet so many interesting people."

A waiter approached their table, but not the waiter who had taken their order earlier. He was young and spoke in strongly-accented English, but they could understand him. "Is everything okay with your meal?"

"Yes," "Of course," "Absolutely," they all said at once.

"Very good." Then to their surprise, the young waiter leaned down and kissed Gia on the cheek, then walked away. Gia was smiling but did not blush.

"Wow, you must come here a lot," Dylan said.

"Not often enough," Gia said. Then laughing, she added, "That was my son, Salvatore. He just started working here ... with his father." She smiled mischievously then motioned one of the waiters over and whispered in his ear.

A minute later, a handsome, middle-aged Italian man approached their table. He swooped down and kissed Gia on the lips, then turned his attention to the rest of them. "Welcome to Rome. Is your food good?"

"Yes, very good," Mira said while the others murmured agreement.

"This is my husband, Angelo. And this delightful place is our restaurant." Gia's smile radiated with pride. "And, Angelo, this is Mira, Olivia, and Dylan. They are from the United States."

"Very nice to meet you. I hope Gia takes good care of you?" They nodded. "Now, excuse me," Angelo said. He spoke Italian to his wife, kissed her again, and returned inside the restaurant.

"We have a daughter too. She is in school at the university right now. Her name is Gabriella."

They had known no more about Gia before this than that she was friendly and spoke excellent English. That had changed in a moment. Suddenly, she was no longer a tour guide but a real person like themselves.

"I do not usually introduce my family, but Salvatore recently turned fifteen and began working here. He loves to greet me when I come." She was beaming.

"He seems like a fine, young man. You must be proud."

"Yes, I am." Her face darkened briefly. "But it was not always so. He had friends that were constantly in trouble. We are so busy with the restaurant and the tours that we could not keep an eye on him all the time. It greatly worried us."

"What turned him around?"

"One of his friends mixed alcohol and drugs and nearly died. It scared Salvatore, but he would not listen to us to get away from those friends. His sister Gabriella is the one who finally got through to him. She took him to her university and showed him where the drug addicts hung out and what they were like. Then she introduced him to her friends. The difference was apparently startling. She helped him see what we could not get him to understand, that he had a choice, and that being young didn't have to equal being stupid."

They didn't know how to respond, but Gia didn't seem to expect a response. "It has been almost a year now. He has made different friends, and he is happy again, and, best of all, he is a momma's boy again." Salvatore came outside bearing a customer's order, and she smiled sweetly while she watched him. "Thankfully the depths of darkness and despair do not need to be permanent."

Gia soon changed the topic, and they passed their meal in animated conversation, punctuated by frequent visits from Salvatore and Angelo, bringing more bread or anything else they might want. Olivia wanted to know all about the café, and the women listened with interest about the up and down world of the restaurant business in the heart of Italy.

They finally parted company, very full and satisfied, taking a round loaf of Italian bread that Angelo pressed into their hands home with them. Worn out from the day, they changed into pajamas, completely forgetting to press Olivia for more information. Deciding to write in her journal another day, Mira sent a brief text to Warren and fell into bed.

.   .   .

Saturday in Rome was busier than they had expected, but Gia assured them there was still plenty of time to see what they wanted to see. Much to their delight, Salvatore joined them.

"My mother wants me to work on my English, so I can be a tour guide like her. But my father wants me to work on my cooking skills, so I can take over the restaurant someday," Salvatore told them as they wrapped up their morning.

"But what do you want to do?" Olivia asked. "Do you like those choices?"

Mira and Dylan glanced at Gia to see if she took these to be impertinent questions, but she just wore a bemused smile. "You may speak freely, Salvatore," his mother said.

He laughed. "My mamma knows how I will answer this. I want to get better at my English *and* better at cooking because I want to have a taco truck like in America to serve tourists."

Mira and Dylan smiled and chuckled, but Olivia did neither. She ruffled his hair as if he was a much younger child and said, "If that is what you want to do, don't let anyone talk you out of it."

It was Gia's turn to laugh. "I have told him that as long as he stays away from drugs and drug addicts, I will help him be anything he wants to be. Last week he wanted to be an oceanographer. The week before he wanted to run a zoo. There is no one right answer for this child of mine. And maybe he will become all of these things."

Salvatore beamed at his mother. "Maybe I'll be an Italian movie star or move to Hollywood and become an American heartthrob."

"Well, from what I've heard about you and seen of you this morning, I wouldn't put it past you," Olivia said, smiling. "I'm sure you can do whatever you put your mind to." The others enthusiastically agreed, and Salvatore's grin grew wider.

"Thank you. I must go help at the restaurant, but I enjoyed the morning."

"I'm sure we'll see you again. I mean, we need to eat dinner somewhere, don't we?" Olivia said while the others smiled their agreement.

When he had gone, Olivia addressed Gia. "I hope I didn't intrude where I shouldn't have. I'm sorry. I didn't mean anything by it."

"Please do not apologize. You have helped me."

"How?"

"Salvatore is a strong, independent child. He loves me, but he doesn't like to listen to me. So, I listen to his ideas, and I encourage him. I tell him he can do these things. But ... that is not always enough. He fears that I am ... that I am different because I am his mother."

"That you are biased?"

"Yes, biased. That is the word. You have all expressed confidence in him. He will not forget. So, I thank you for helping me by helping my son."

After that, Gia refused payment for the day and insisted on taking them to her favorite out-of-the-way shops. They bought gifts for family members left behind in London and many other items for themselves that caught their eyes.

Mira collapsed into a chair outside a shop where Olivia and Dylan were still ogling and debating over purchases. She was exhausted. Gia soon joined her.

"Are you okay?"

"I am. Mostly, anyway. I had a difficult experience just over a week ago. Rome, and you, have been so amazing. I am constantly in awe at how lucky I am to be here—in Rome, but also here, alive. It's an overwhelming feeling sometimes."

"That is not a carefree thought. You are not like my usual tourists."

Mira laughed. "You're not the first to notice that." She was reminded of Cordelia. "Honestly, I never have been. I came to Europe to find myself and to find other women I could call sisters. I've found more than I bargained for—in good ways and bad." She sat back and sighed. "I'm learning to let the good win out, or at least trying to, but sometimes that takes a lot of effort."

"So, you are tired?"

"Yes, I am tired. But that's okay too. I know this will take time."

Gia patted her arm. "You will make a good mother one day. Learning that things take time. Learning to be patient. Those are important."

It was a reminder again of the whole infertility concern that had been the last straw, prompting this trip. Would she be a mother someday? She hoped so. But for once, she allowed herself to consider an alternative, that maybe if she didn't have a child of her own, it wouldn't be a personal failure. If her body didn't work the way it was intended to or if Warren's didn't, for that matter, it wasn't anybody's fault. It just was.

"You are crying? Have I said something wrong?"

Mira touched her hands to her face to discover she was indeed crying. "No. You have said nothing wrong. But would you mind being my adopted sister? It turns out all of us can use all the sisters that we can find."

"I'm not sure how good a sister I can be from Italy to you in the United States, but I like the idea. I would be happy to be your sister." She grabbed Mira's face in both of her hands and gave her air kisses on the left and right.

"Hey, what are you two up to out here?" Dylan asked a few minutes later when she came across Gia and Mira swapping stories and laughing.

Olivia was right on her heels. "Yeah. What's up? Why weren't we invited to the party?"

"Oh, but you are invited," Mira said. "Meet the newest one of my 'sisters.'"

"Well, in that case, it's okay," said Dylan. "As long as you know I was her first sister."

. . .

That night at the restaurant, Gia introduced them to the entire staff and even gave them a tour of the kitchen. Dinner, her husband Angelo insisted, would be something special that he would prepare himself especially for them—for family.

They laughed with delight when a pizza was brought out for each of them. "This is pizza bianca, a white pizza," Gia explained. A variety of wonderful smelling cheeses covered the top of each pizza, but the traditional marinara sauce the women were used to was missing. "The flavor of what is on top is the important thing. You do not need a sauce for such a pizza."

Gia was right. The pizza was delicious. They didn't miss the sauce one bit. Mira took in the happy group around her. Yes, she wanted a child, but if it didn't happen, if that particular part of her life went missing, the rest of life could still be wonderful.

CHAPTER 25

Sunday morning Mira awoke before the others. She took the time to catch up in her journal and discovered just how much there was to write. After covering the events of late, she added some newfound insights.

Sometimes the most mundane thing can end up being the most profound. I've walked all over great historic sites in Rome, places I can't believe I'm seeing with my own eyes, and they've filled me with wonder. But when I leave, what I'll take with me of them is a static image—impressive, but not alive, although historians would likely disagree.

On the other hand, seeing Dylan's eyes light up when she saw the Pantheon and watching Olivia point out the intricate detail in the Trevi fountain are moments I will replay in my mind again and again. It's people that inspire awe in me. In a way, that's where the historians and I would probably agree. What they "see" when they look at a historic site, I imagine, is the events of the past being played out by people long since dead. In that sense, stone and building live and breathe. I just happen to prefer the people who are still living.

But there's more to it than that. I love the tender moments where people connect, where they care for one another. Watching Salvatore greet his mother at the restaurant thrills me every time I see it with its expression of love, concern, desires for the future, and even anguish for mistakes made that pass between them in unspoken ways whenever they are near. It has a depth to it that a building can never hold for me. It speaks of those human emotions and interactions that have existed for all of time—long before a Pantheon was even conceived. Those emotions pull my heart in so many directions as if it's swaying to some beautiful music.

I want a child, children, actually. I want them more than words can express. But I've come to an understanding with my inner self. If I cannot conceive, it won't be the end of the world. Warren and I will get through it. We may decide to adopt. We may not. But billions of people exist in the world. Surely, we can reach out and help some of them. I want to pull on someone's heartstrings like Salvatore does on his mother's or like the experience of being in Rome does for Dylan and Olivia. And when I pull on someone else's heartstrings, I know they'll pull on my own in return.

Whether we have children of our own or not, these are things I want to do with the rest of my life. These are things I will do the rest of my life.

Mira closed her journal and held it close. She could feel her heart beating against the leather binding. Feelings had poured out onto the page that were new and exciting and scary. Much of what she'd written in those last few paragraphs hadn't been completely formulated in her head until she'd committed them to the page. She wanted to call Warren and share them with him, but the time difference made that thought impractical. It would have to wait, but she was learning that she could wait.

Mira wandered into the living area of the apartment. Olivia was stretched out on the hide-a-bed, deep in slumber, and she could hear a wheezy snore coming from the other bedroom. Quietly as possible, she grabbed some bread from the loaf Angelo had given them along with an apple and some figs.

Taking this breakfast with her, Mira made herself at home on the balcony. She took her journal with her so she could write more stories about her mother. Seeing Salvatore and Gia together had reminded her of times with her mother she didn't want to forget. They weren't grandiose events just quiet moments. On the weekends, her mother would make her a special breakfast, like cinnamon French toast or applesauce filled crepes, but not until 10:30 so Mira could sleep in. She remembered her mother reading to her, even when she got older, although she'd never admitted that to her friends.

Writing these things down prompted other simple memories like the quiet, peaceful walks they took together, observing and identifying the birds they spotted along the way. These were everyday memories, but they were ones that would slip away if she didn't record them. Writing them down, she noticed, was adding to her sense of feeling whole.

After a while, she put down her pen to observe the people below her. Occasionally, someone would look up her way and notice her watching the crowd below, but mostly people were oblivious to her presence.

Her favorite to watch were the children. They were genuine. One little girl passed by with her parents. She was not happy and was making sure everyone knew it, stomping loudly with her arms folded across her chest defiantly. Each parent took a turn trying to placate the child, but she was having none of it. The trio sat down on a bench, the youngster moving to one end as far away from her parents as possible. By now, however, both parents were ignoring the tantrum, appearing to carry on a pleasant conversation instead.

At that moment, a teenage boy walked by with his dog. The unhappy girl leaped off her bench to approach the dog. An exchange occurred, apparently the child asking if she could pet the dog, which was granted. The parents watched silently while their daughter's entire demeanor changed.

The teenager patiently waited while his dog ate up the attention, wagging its tail, and generously licking the girl as payment. When the dog and its owner finally moved on, the girl jumped up and down, waving to them for as long as she could see them. Turning around, she saw her parents watching. She balled her fists, ready to stomp back to the bench, then her hands relaxed, she shrugged and skipped back to join them on the bench, snuggling up close this time.

The sudden shift in the child's temperament was real and interesting to watch, but the kindness of the teenager did not escape Mira's attention either. He likely had no idea the impact of his patience, but he spent the time regardless.

Other children passed before her—some kind and thoughtful of a sibling, some picking on another child, some clumsy, some careful. The scene they created in front of her was fascinating. She was being allowed a small glimpse into the lives of everyday people and families, and the glimpse made her smile and filled her with hope for the future—theirs and hers.

"Oh, there you are." It was Dylan. "We thought you might still be asleep, but your bedroom door was ajar, and we could see your bed was empty. Glad you're here."

"And that you didn't run away," added Olivia.

Mira turned to see if she was serious but was met with a smile instead. "Thanks for the concern there. It was so heartfelt."

"Well, I'm glad it doesn't need to be," Dylan said, seriously. "Warren figured you would be okay soon enough, but that doesn't mean he didn't make me swear up and down to take care of you. I'm sure he'd never forgive me if I let something happen to you. And he's never even met me."

"Yep, but now he's going to owe us one instead. I mean, can you imagine having to fly to Italy just so we could babysit his wife? The unmitigated gall of such a request!" Olivia said.

"Boy, you two really know how to sacrifice for a friend don't you?"

"Oh, I'd never do this for a friend, but a sister ... Well, when you're family, sometimes you frankly have to do unpleasant things."

"Well, thanks for the sentiment ... I guess." Mira stood up, giving them each a hug. "Let's go back inside, shall we? To see just how little we can do with our day."

It was Sunday, and Olivia was getting her wish to stay home in their amazing apartment. They all needed a day to unwind and rest, and besides, the Vatican with the Sistine Chapel, which they had yet to visit, was closed on Sundays. It was just the excuse they needed.

Gathering around the kitchen table, the three of them laid out the agenda for their remaining days in Italy. After consulting with Gia the day before, they had decided to take two day trips, one to a hill town nearby called Orvieto and another to Florence. Orvieto was a couple hours away but would give them a different feel from Rome. Florence was farther away, but they could get there faster, in about an hour and a half, thanks to a fast train and Florence's popularity. It would make for some long days, but they'd agreed it would be worth it.

After only a little discussion, the three decided Monday they would tackle Orvieto, Tuesday the Vatican and St. Paul's Cathedral, and Wednesday Florence. With both sadness and eagerness, they would head back to London on Thursday. Having a lazy day before that all began felt wonderfully indulgent.

"So, did you write in your journal yet?" Dylan asked once they'd dispensed with travel arrangements.

"Yes, I did," Mira said, rolling her eyes. "I thought you were going to be my sister and not my mother."

"Hey, that's the beauty of being sisters. We can nag when we want and then totally not give a care the rest of the time. We're not obligated like mothers are." She made a show of shrugging. "Remember, you picked us."

"Yep. And now you're stuck with us," Olivia said.

"Boy, you're even ganging up on me. I can't believe it. You know, I found another sister in Paris. Her name's Aissa. She wouldn't give me such grief."

Olivia adopted an expression of mock surprise. "What? We have another sister in Paris, and you didn't even tell us?"

"What other family secrets are you hiding?" Dylan said. "I'm not sure we can trust her, Olivia."

"Are there others?" Olivia said.

"No. Well, maybe. You know about Cordelia, right?"

"Yes, but we never met her. You're going to have to fix that when we get back to London. Anyone else you're forgetting?"

"Hmm. I met a couple named Madge and Harold. You'd like them. And there's Kailani and her mum, Bibi. I almost forgot about the Japanese family, although I'm not sure we're anywhere near family status. And I guess technically I'd have to include my adopted papa in Paris. He's a baker named Jean, and there's his wife, Monique, but I don't know her too well."

With all the joking they'd been doing, Mira was surprised to be met by silence. She looked at Dylan and Olivia, puzzled. "What?"

Quietly, Olivia said, "How do you do it?"

"Do what?"

"Meet all these people? Connect with them? How is it that you draw people to you so easily?"

The question caught Mira by surprise. "I don't know. I didn't know that I did."

"Of course you do," said Olivia. "But how?" Mira was at a loss for words.

"Well, I know," said Dylan. "You're real."

"What do you mean? Of course I'm real. Who isn't?"

Dylan shook her head. "See, that's part of it too. You don't realize that other people play games, that they're catty because you don't and you're not. You can't even conceive of people who do that. You're just you. You care and you're kind. Do you think I didn't realize you would have rather read your book on the plane?"

"I ... I ... you could tell?"

"Yes, I could. You would not be a good poker player, Mira. It was written all over your face. I was so nervous that I really needed to talk to someone. So, selfishly, I ignored what you wanted and went after what I wanted." She looked Mira directly in the eye. "It costs me to admit that. I don't like acknowledging my own selfishness."

"Hey, it's okay. I did want to read my book, but I liked your story. Pretty quickly I preferred our conversation to the book."

"You see? That's my point. You started to care about me, I could tell. That meant a lot, but I still feel bad about how that conversation started."

Olivia stepped up behind Dylan and rubbed her shoulders. "We still love you, sis." She turned to Mira. "Dylan told me about you before you ever found her again. She said you listened even though you didn't want to at first. But then you took a real interest in her concerns. You may have given Dylan some anniversary presents for our parents, but those were really gifts you gave Dylan. It's not often a complete stranger helps you out of a jam."

Mira was speechless, a solitary tear trickling down her cheek. She did the only thing she felt capable of. She embraced the two women in front of her—her sisters.

When they'd all dried their eyes, Olivia got up with a suddenness that surprised them. "I'm going to treat you both to lunch. Stay here. I'll be right back." She grabbed her bag and was gone before the others could say a word.

Olivia came back a short time later, and, as promised, she had her arms full with the makings of a fantastic lunch. "I grabbed bread from the bakery down the street, meat and cheese from the deli, and the rest came from the market." The rest included various beverages and fruits. "I wanted to get some gelato from the vendor down the street, but I figured it would melt before we got to dessert. So, we're just going to have to walk down there later and buy it when we're ready."

"Wow. I'm impressed. This is fantastic," Mira said.

"Yeah," Olivia said, but for some reason, she was staring at her shoes.

"What's wrong?" Mira said.

"All that talk before—about you being so genuine, and then Dylan getting all sappy and apologizing for being selfish ..."

Mira and Dylan exchanged glances, not sure where this was headed. "What's wrong?" Dylan gently prodded.

"I need to be straight with you and tell you what's going on. I haven't wanted to, but then ... well, you're being too nice and honest. It's making me look bad."

"I feel like I'm supposed to say 'sorry' but then again not," Mira said.

Olivia laughed, and it broke the tension. "Okay. I'll tell you everything while we eat. I'm starving, and this stuff looks and smells amazing."

While they made sandwiches out of the bread and fixings, Olivia started her story. "I met this guy a year ago. His name's Asher."

"A year ago? Why didn't you tell us?" Dylan said.

"Well, I don't know. I guess to start with, his name is Asher."

"Um, what's wrong with that? I take it he's Jewish? Do you think we care?"

"Yes, he is Jewish."

"So? What's the big deal with that? You know that doesn't matter to us, don't you?"

"I guess I do, but I told a few of my friends and they weren't okay with it."

"Then get better friends," Dylan said bluntly.

Olivia laughed. "You make a good point. I have kind of distanced myself from the friends who weren't supportive."

"So, what's he like? How serious are you?" Mira asked.

"Is that why you've been so cagey lately?" Dylan said.

"Okay, one question at a time. We're quite serious. He's very handsome—I'll show you pictures when I finish, okay. But let me tell you the rest because there is more to it."

"All right. We're listening."

"I met him about a year ago like I said. At first, I wasn't sure if anything would come of it, so I didn't say anything. You know how Mom gets. I've had boyfriends before, and she starts planning the wedding two weeks in."

Dylan rolled her eyes. "She's right, Mira. We love Mom, but she's a sucker for romantic weddings—can't wait to plan all of ours."

"Yeah. So, I hesitated saying anything. Then my friends flipped out about the whole Jewish thing. I hadn't even considered that being an issue, but they made me worry that it was or might be—not for me, but with others. Anyway, I'm not saying it was right, but I decided to keep things secret after that. Then when things started getting more serious, I didn't know how to bring it up. I figured I'd get the reaction you just gave me—wondering why I hadn't said anything before. The longer I waited the worse that got, but I wasn't sure what to do about it."

She took a deep breath before continuing. "And then there's the whole quitting my job thing."

"Quitting your job thing?" Dylan said slowly with a slight edge to her voice.

When Olivia hesitated before continuing, Mira said, "Go ahead and tell us. We're still listening."

"Okay," Olivia said, but she was nervously twisting a napkin in her hands. They had stopped eating, waiting for Olivia to finish. In a rush, she said, "I know I have this great job. I'm using my degree and all that. But Asher and I want to get married and then open a bakery. So, I'm going to quit my job and he's going to quit his job, and we're going to do it."

"Whoa! Or wow, just wow!" Dylan said.

"I know. Dad's going to flip out that I'm throwing my education away. He's going to think I'm being foolish, and the worst part is he'll blame Asher."

"Well, playing the devil's advocate here," Mira chimed in, "I'm guessing if Asher hadn't shown up, you wouldn't be opening a bakery. Am I right?"

Olivia, looking downcast, simply nodded.

"But now, are you passionate about owning a bakery?"

Olivia perked up. "Yes, I am."

"Well, that makes it easy then," Mira said.

"What are you talking about? What's easy about any of this?"

"You're happy, right? With Asher, with the bakery idea?"

"Yes. I've never felt this way before about anyone or anything."

"Then do it. The whole thing is a package deal. Tell your family you have wonderful news. You're going to marry the man you love and together you have a new dream," Mira said.

"But ... but ..."

"You're questioning your own dream?"

"No. It's just that it isn't that simple. Mom and Dad are going to freak out about everything."

"Olivia," Mira said calmly, staring her straight in the eye. "It isn't the ideal situation. Such things rarely exist. But it's good, isn't it? It's better than good. So, grab hold of it, even if it's not perfect. Do you really think your parents won't come around? You know they will, but even if they don't, you have to do what you feel is best for you—for Asher and you together."

"She's right, Olivia. It's kind of shocking, but it is good. Just tell Mom and Dad. And for heaven's sake, introduce us to him, will you? I want to meet him. I'm sure everyone will want to meet him. Especially if he'll be partly responsible for all our baked goods from now on."

Olivia visibly relaxed. "You're right. I need to just tell them."

"Now, where was this picture you promised to show us? I want to see who my future nieces and nephews might take after."

Olivia whipped out her phone to show them. "He *is* good looking," said Dylan. "Does he have a brother?"

Olivia laughed. "As a matter of fact, he does, but they're polar opposites. Levi is measured where Asher is spontaneous. Asher's creative; Levi's studious—so different from each other, but they get along quite well."

"The important thing is whether Levi is as handsome as his brother. The rest, well, the rest of him sounds nice too."

"Yes, he's handsome. I'll introduce you, okay, but don't start planning your wedding yet. Geez, you're worse than Mom."

"So, where did you want to open this bakery?"

"Well, that's the best part. We plan on moving closer to Mom and Dad and opening our shop the next town over from them in Ohio. It has a young population, and our market research tells us that's who we should be targeting anyway."

"That sounds fantastic. I bet if you lead with, 'Hey, Mom and Dad, I'm going to move closer to home,' they won't even hear the rest, they'll be so ecstatic."

"You're probably right."

"Olivia, I just put two and two together. You were asking Gia and Angelo about the restaurant business on purpose, weren't you?"

Olivia smiled. "It was fascinating. It almost made me want to switch from a bakery to a full-blown restaurant. But we plan on having a small café as part of the bakery anyway."

They spent the afternoon talking about Olivia and her plans—while they finished eating, on their way to get gelatos, while they ate gelatos, and pretty much all the rest of the time too. In the evening, they decided on a whim to video chat with Asher and welcome him to the family. He was surprised and a bit overwhelmed with the enthusiasm of Dylan and Mira, but once he got over his shock, he was genuinely pleased. The one thing they needed to explain multiple times, however, was the presence of this previously unknown sister named Mira.

After a bit, Mira excused herself so she could video chat with Warren. "You won't believe what Olivia told us today. She's getting married! And she's going to leave her job and open a bakery."

After she'd gone over the details and how Olivia's revelation came about, something struck Mira. "You know, hubs, this morning I couldn't wait to call and tell you about myself and what I've learned. I can't believe I forgot about that until now."

"I suppose that's a good thing, isn't it? A sign that you're healing— from Paris, from the issues before you left."

"You're right. I know Olivia's still worried about telling her parents, and I feel for her. But I'm not carrying the weight of it either. I feel like whatever I can do to help, that's what I want to do. But I'm not overwhelmed by that thought either."

"That's a good thing, babe. So, what was it you learned that you wanted to share with me?"

"It's simple and yet profound—for me, at least. I'm learning that the ideal is overrated, or more accurately, it's unlikely to be. But that doesn't mean I can't be grateful or in awe of what does exist. Warren, it's quite likely that we'll be able to have children. Medical science helps people achieve that dream all the time, so why not us too. But it's okay if it doesn't happen. I still have an amazing life. You're incredible, and these women I'm meeting are bringing a richness into my life. I feel so blessed."

"Talk about burying the lead, Mira. Those aren't words I ever thought you'd say. And, to be honest, I hadn't thought of it that way. To me, it's more like this is the next step for us, having a family. So, I haven't considered what would happen if we somehow missed that step. I mean we could adopt, couldn't we?"

"Of course we could. I'm not giving up on having a family one way or another, but if, for some reason, it doesn't work out, I'm okay with that. I'll get over it and refocus my efforts elsewhere."

"Honestly, that's new territory for me, but it makes sense. It sounds … well, it sounds healthy."

"Warren, there's more. I want to help people. I hadn't put it into words until right now, but with Olivia leaving her job to follow a dream … well, I need to get out of the accounting office. There I'm helping a business' bottom line. I need to help people more directly. It makes me feel alive. I hope I'll be helping our own children, but with or without that, I want to help people. I don't even know in what capacity yet, but I have to do this, hubs. I have to do this."

"That, babe, sounds like a wonderful idea."

CHAPTER 26

The next few days flew by. Orvieto was a delightful change of pace. The Sistine Chapel blew them away with its magnitude. And Florence brought them face to face with paintings and sculptures they'd heard about their whole lives but never dreamed they'd see in person. Riding the train back to Rome, the three of them collapsed in happy exhaustion.

Drawing near the station, Mira sat up with a start. "What are we going to do for Gia?"

"What about Gia?" Dylan mumbled, tiredly.

"I want to give her something before we leave, but I hadn't thought about it until right now, and we're leaving tomorrow.

"We'll think of something. Our flight isn't 'til late afternoon tomorrow," Dylan said, closing her eyes.

But Mira couldn't let it rest. She wanted to give Gia the perfect gift, but she couldn't think of what that might be. Olivia startled her by touching her arm.

"I can tell it means a lot to you. I'll help. What kind of gift did you have in mind?"

"Something small yet with some personal significance."

They both brainstormed until it was time to disembark, but no ideas had come to them. "I'm sure you'll come up with something," Olivia said.

It was nine o'clock when they made it back to their apartment in Rome. They deposited their purchases and guidebooks before contemplating a nearly empty fridge. They had only snacked on the way home and were hungry. "I bet we could get something from Angelo and Gia's place," Olivia said.

No one needed any further prodding. They were out the door in a flash. Mira decided to phone Gia before they got there in case the place was full. They'd noticed Romans often ate later than they were used to in the United States.

Gia laughed in answer to Mira's question. "Yes, we're busy. It's a beautiful night to be out eating fine food. But I will always make room for you, even if we seat you in the kitchen."

"Olivia would probably prefer that actually."

"Would she? Why?"

"I'll let her explain. We'll be there in a few minutes."

When they arrived at the restaurant, Gia greeted them. "Welcome back! How was Florence?"

"It was lovely. I can't believe what we saw. Did you keep yourself busy while we were away?" Mira said.

"Yes. I took a charming couple around the city all day long. They're sitting right over there," she said, discretely pointing to a far table.

"That's quite the little scam you've got going, isn't it? Take people around then say, 'Hey, there's this restaurant I know of that's very good.'"

Gia's eyes twinkled. "Well, they're paying me to show them the best. Are you saying I lied about the restaurant? That the food here is not delicious?"

Mira laughed. "You got me there."

"So, I'm curious," Gia said. "Why would Olivia want to be in the kitchen?"

Once Olivia explained her future plans, Gia kissed her on each cheek. "Perfetto! You are a wonderful child! Angelo will be so proud. Come, come, I'll take you to the kitchen, and you can ask anything you like. I'll find Salvatore. He can interpret for you." Bustling Olivia off to the kitchen, she called over her shoulder. "You two may sit at that empty table. I saved it for you. Don't worry about menus. I'll send out something you'll like."

Mira and Dylan did as they were told, and before long Gia came out to join them. "I don't work in the restaurant much myself anymore, especially on days I take tourists around, but everyone knows who I am," she said with a wink. "The kitchen staff are showing Olivia all their secrets."

Their food, full plates of rigatoni carbonara, arrived shortly. It was delicious. They were hungrier than they had even imagined, and the creamy pasta was soon gone, along with the crusty bread that had come with it.

They talked well into the night as the diners gradually disappeared around them. All this time passed without any sign of Olivia. Even after the restaurant closed, Gia, Dylan, and Mira continued to talk, not even wondering about their sister.

Salvatore eventually joined them as did Angelo soon afterward. When questioned about Olivia, Salvatore responded, "She …" He paused then spoke in Italian to his mother.

"Insists," Gia said.

"Yes, she insists on helping clean up," Salvatore said, winking.

"She is tired. You have a long day," Angelo told them, "but she wants to do everything. She works very hard." He added something to his wife in Italian.

Gia laughed. "He said that she is so excited about everything and eager to learn that she's making everyone else look bad. The staff doesn't know whether to admire her or throw her out."

Olivia finally emerged with the last worker who was turning off the lights as he went. Her face shone with perspiration and exhilaration. "That was the absolute best! I can't wait to tell Asher about it." Turning to Angelo and Salvatore, she said, "Grazie! Grazie!"

She talked non-stop their entire way home, recounting every detail of how the kitchen filled orders and prepared food, what they made ahead of time and what was done at the moment, even the rhythm of cleaning. As soon as they entered the apartment, Olivia tore away to video chat with Asher.

"Well, I don't know about you, but I enjoyed seeing Michelangelo's David today, but I'm guessing Olivia's forgotten we even went to Florence," Dylan said.

"I think you're right. Who knew a restaurant would be the highlight of her trip to Italy?"

Mira was tired but took the time to write in her journal and briefly call Warren before climbing into bed. Setting her phone on the bedside table, she noticed a text from Cordelia. "I've got the flat ready for you tomorrow. Looking forward to seeing you. And I've got things to tell you about Bibi."

Mira sat back up, wondering what that meant. She started to text Cordelia back to ask for more details when she noticed the text had come in a few hours before. The current time was 1:30 in the morning. With a sigh, she realized her curiosity would have to wait, and she was too tired to fight that thought.

Snuggling down in bed, she could still hear Olivia talking excitedly to Asher from the other room. Rolling over to go to sleep, she had one last thought. *What can I possibly give to Gia?*

.   .   .

Morning came far too quickly for the three of them after staying up so late the night before, especially Olivia who had talked with Asher for a long time after Mira was sound asleep. It was a challenge to slog through packing their things for the flight later that day—made worse by the fact that they were reluctant to leave a place that had come to mean so much to them.

They had promised to meet Gia at the restaurant for an early lunch before heading to the airport. Angelo insisted on feeding them, but they convinced him to let them have sandwiches instead of a more elaborate meal. He reluctantly agreed.

Sitting outside with Gia waiting for their food, the group fell silent. They'd always had so much to say and share with each other, but parting took the wind out of their sails.

Knowing there wouldn't be a better time, Mira pulled an item out of her bag. She had finally found a gift. It wasn't perfect by any stretch, and it wasn't even for Gia, but it would have to be enough. "Is Salvatore around?"

"He was still sleeping when I left this morning, but he's due in to help in the kitchen soon. Would you like me to call him?"

"No. I'll wait until he's here. I just have something to give him—a small trinket only."

"Ahh, you are so kind. It isn't often that someone finds a place in our hearts so easily, but you three have. We meet new people all the time, and I like people, but you ... well, you like me too."

They all smiled, too choked up to use their voices.

"It's too bad you couldn't meet our daughter, but maybe if you come again?"

Olivia opened her mouth to say something, but just then Salvatore walked up to his mother and kissed her on the cheek. "Hello, Mira, Olivia, Dylan," he said, indicating them each in turn. "Are you going back to London today?"

"Yes, we are."

Mira had regained her composure with the appearance of the bright-eyed teenager. "Salvatore, I have a silly little gift for you. It's something my husband sent me off to Europe with." She took the tissue wrapping off the item in her hands, instantly regretting her decision. It was cheesy, and she was giving it to a teenage boy. But he had seen it before she could put it back.

"May I see it? It is a pen?"

She nodded, embarrassed. "It's a four-color pen." The bottom half of it was blue, and the top was white where four colored tabs in red, blue, green, and black could be depressed to produce a pen with that color ink. Mira demonstrated how it worked before handing it to Salvatore.

"I had a pen like this when I was young. Do you remember, Mamma?"

"Yes, back when you were friends with Antonio and Matteo," she said, with a wistful smile. "They were good boys."

Salvatore didn't hear her. He was happily playing with the pen like a young schoolboy. "It was always fun." He grinned at Mira. "I played with it more than I wrote."

Mira laughed. "I'm pretty sure that's why my husband gave it to me in the first place. My friends had them when I was in elementary school. And one semester in college when we were buying books, I saw one in the bookstore. It's like I was a child again and had to buy it. But it drove Warren nuts because when we were studying in the library, I would absent-mindedly click it up and down. I'm not sure if it was the noise that bothered him or that he was embarrassed that I was likely disturbing everyone around us."

Mira's mind flooded back to the memories she hadn't recalled in a long time. "He started a game of 'losing' my pen on a regular basis then made a show of finding it. 'Oh, Mira, look what I found in the recycling bin. I don't think this pen's recyclable. You'd better take it back,' or 'Babe, why did you put your pen in the freezer? Is it in time-out? That seems a little cruel for just making noise in the library.'" She rolled her eyes while smiling. "Anyway, I'm sure you don't care about my stories." But she was wrong about that. Everyone around the table was smiling.

Embarrassed for a different reason now, she plunged on. "The point is, I wanted to give it to you because of how you talked about the taco truck. You have so many possibilities in front of you. You can pick the red path or the blue path or whichever path you want. There are four colors or four choices in this pen, but they're all held together in one case. That case is your family—your mom, your dad, your sister. They're the constant parts of your life, and they will help you bring everything together. They will always be there for you." She shrugged. "I know, it's a little sappy, but it's from the heart."

Salvatore wrinkled his brow. "Sappy? What does that mean?" He turned to his mother who explained in Italian. Salvatore's face relaxed into a wide grin. "You are like my sister, Gabriella. She would give me a gift like this, something sappy. Thank you. Grazie."

"You're welcome. I think I like your sister."

"Yes, you would like her very much. And, also, I don't want to own a taco truck anymore. I want to be a cruise director on the large cruise ships full of tourists that come ashore up and down Italy. I could start with cooking and interpreting and work my way up." He paused, struck with a sudden idea. "Maybe I'll be the captain instead. Yes, I like that ..." He walked away mumbling to himself, soon resorting to his native Italian as he made his way inside the restaurant.

They burst out laughing once the door closed behind him. "He is adorable, but don't tell him that. I doubt a teenage boy wants to be considered 'adorable,'" Mira said.

Gia beamed. "He's such a good boy now. I am so grateful."

Olivia cleared her throat. "Gia, I have a present for you, if you want it that is." All eyes turned to her, surprised.

"I didn't know you had a present," Mira said, pleased.

"It's from Asher and me. We were talking about it last night. Gia, Asher and I want to come to Rome on our honeymoon. We'd like to have you show us the sights for a few days. Then, if it's okay with you, we want to help at the restaurant. We may be planning a bakery, but it will have a deli as part of it, and we'd like to learn from your experience, if you don't mind. We would be happy to pay you for the opportunity."

"Oh! Perfetto! Benissimo! That sounds wonderful!" Gia jumped up and grabbed Olivia's face, kissing her on both cheeks. "You can meet our daughter too while you are here!"

Olivia was pleased with Gia's response. "I know that sounds like more of a present for us than for you, but there is something else we wanted to do for you. After spending time in your kitchen, we would love to stay even longer, doing anything needed—washing dishes, scrubbing floors, anything. Then maybe ..." Olivia hesitated, picking up Gia's hands in hers, "maybe you could take a vacation. Your workers know how to make all the food—we wouldn't try to do that. But Salvatore told me you haven't taken a day off in a very, very long time. Maybe you're due?"

It was fortunate that Olivia was holding on to Gia's hands because they began to shake almost uncontrollably. She was staring at Olivia without blinking. "You would do that for us?"

"Yes. Of course." Olivia said. Then the floodgates opened and both women were crying in each other's arms.

"I accept," Gia said when they had composed themselves. "I will talk to Angelo, and I'm sure he will agree. But I know he will insist on one condition. You will not pay for this opportunity. We will pay you. It may not be much, but we will pay you."

"We'll have to negotiate that one, but I'm sure we'll find a compromise somewhere."

"Also, you must stay long enough to learn what you need to learn. I can find you a cheap place to rent. Maybe six months?" Then she added with a twinkle, "Or long enough that you decide to open an Italian restaurant instead."

By the time Angelo had loudly proclaimed his approval of Olivia and Asher's proposal, along with the conditions Gia had predicted he would insist upon, they had to hurry their goodbyes to make it to the airport in time. Hugs, kisses, tears, and laughter enveloped them as they reluctantly bid farewell.

. . .

As the three of them settled into their seats prior to takeoff, Mira put her head back and closed her eyes. She was tired but happy. She silently said a prayer for help with Bibi and Kailani, whatever form that might take. Then without hesitation, she began to fill her prayer with gratitude—for the "perfect" gift Olivia had offered, for Gia's entire family, for Olivia and Dylan, for the many things she'd seen and the experiences she'd had, for Warren. She was grateful for the preservation of her life and the diminishing nature of her headaches. The list grew and grew in her mind. Mira didn't know when her prayers had changed from ones of pleading to primarily ones of thanks, but they had. And there was something else she hadn't noticed before—for the first time in a very long time, she was at peace.

PEACE

"Peace. It does not mean to be in a place where there is no noise, trouble, or hard work. It means to be in the midst of those things and still be calm in your heart."

—Unknown

"Peace I leave with you, my peace I give unto you: not as the world giveth, give I unto you.
Let not your heart be troubled, neither let it be afraid."

—John 14:27

CHAPTER 27

Mira had a better idea this time around when, after her arrival time, to have Cordelia meet her, but even so, the cabbie dropped her off at the flat slightly ahead of schedule. Sitting on the front steps waiting for Cordelia, she studied her surroundings. It wasn't home, but it was as close as she could come at the moment. The street was familiar and inviting, the steps she was sitting on like an old friend. She glanced down the street toward Kailani's, but not so much as a single blind fluttered. A cloud passed over her mind—concern, worry, and so many unanswered questions.

Allowing that chink to dampen her mood was like opening the floodgates to all kinds of negative thoughts. She was once again on the streets of Paris—not at the baker's, not with friends, but in that split second before the blast and only seconds later when she identified her own screams. She had lived a whole lifetime in the two short weeks since she was last on this street. A shudder cascaded down her body and darkness threatened to overtake her.

Fearing the emotions beginning to consume her, she forced her mind to move past the attack. She pictured Aissa and Jean, or Papa. She pictured her visit to his shop, his wife, the boys, and the carefree drive with Aissa around the sights of Paris before leaving. With relief, the shudder passed as happier memories pushed the fear aside. She detected a small headache, but that was all. Breathing deeply, she smiled.

Opening her phone, she texted Warren. "Back in London. I'll call you tonight. Love you!"

Next, she pulled up her email. Aissa had given Mira her email address. They had exchanged short emails along the lines of *I made it safely to*

Rome, and I'm glad you're there safely. Mira had just enough time before Cordelia was due to appear to send her a proper email, if there was such a thing.

Aissa,

I'm back in London—all in one piece. It's a lovely place, but so was Paris and Rome. I don't hold anything against your city, and I hope to return one day. Such a return would be even better if you were around and I could see you again.

I know I tried to tell you thank you and explain what you meant to me, but I don't think I adequately did. You were the first bright spot after what happened. "Papa," was there, but his entrance into my life as more than simply the baker will always be tied to you. I can't think of him without thinking of you—ushering him in, interpreting where needed, returning to his bakery with me. You were stable and steady at a time when nothing else seemed so. I appreciated the care of those around me, but it was different with you. I knew in your eyes I wasn't simply a client or a patient. You were my friend, and that provided the best healing of all.

Mira heard a familiar and cheerful, "Hullo!" She lifted her head to see Cordelia coming up the walk toward her. She raised a finger to indicate just a minute and quickly finished her email.

I've got to run, but once again—thank you! Those two words will never be enough, but they're the best I've got. Please stay in touch! Thank you! Thank you! Thank you!

Your friend,

Mira

Mira felt herself cast in shadow as Cordelia moved in front of her. "Hey, you're blocking my sun," she said, teasing.

"Wow, and here I thought you'd be happy to see me." The typical twinkle in Cordelia's eyes appeared even more pronounced.

"You are a welcome sight … even if you are blocking my sun."

Cordelia, her usual bouncy self, helped Mira in with her things in no time. Mira's belongings that she'd left behind were already neatly waiting for her inside.

"Mira, I really would have moved those other renters somewhere else so you could have come back sooner. You just had to say the word."

"I know. It was tempting, but Warren was right. It helped me feel normal to act like a tourist and see parts of Italy, to salvage some of the original plans."

Cordelia uncharacteristically put a hand on Mira's arm and was surprisingly quiet and still. It was a touch that conveyed what words could not—that Cordelia was sorry Mira had experienced something so devastating and horrific, that she was there for her, that she wanted to help carry the burden of her experiences even though she knew she couldn't.

In a rush of emotion and gratitude, Mira surprised Cordelia by grabbing her in a huge embrace. Tears pooled at the corners of her eyes, but they were happy tears, for the most part. When she finally let go, Cordelia needed to wipe her eyes too.

"You should know by now that the British are not the touching, hugging type. But given the situation, I suppose you're excused." Cordelia was attempting a stern look, but failing at it.

"Sorry, I guess." Mira shrugged. "You know, I'm doing quite well, given the circumstances. What happened has just fueled in me a greater desire to help other people. I don't want to wish my life away, always waiting for something to make me happy. I imagine I'll always have plans for the future, but I want to make the most of the here and now too."

Cordelia was quiet, turning to view the flat in quiet contemplation. She surprised Mira by standing and walking out to the garden. Mira followed silently. Cordelia was wandering about the flowers and bushes, reaching out to touch the tender leaves or gently leaning in to take in their fragrance. Mira pulled up a couple chairs, sitting in one, waiting for Cordelia.

When Cordelia had finished circling the small yard, she sat in the chair Mira had set for her. "I'm sorry. Sometimes I bury the memories of my own journey that brought me to that same understanding. I had to learn to be happy in my circumstances, whatever they were—even while trying to change them."

"You were in a bad relationship, weren't you?"

Cordelia abruptly turned to Mira. "How did you know?"

"Was it abusive?"

Cordelia stared straight ahead while fidgeting with her fingers. It was answer enough.

Mira continued, "To answer your question, I wasn't sure, but it made sense. It's the way you talked about this flat. It was clearly more than just a place to live for you. I saw you pause when looking at the deadbolt one day. That was probably your biggest give away. I wondered why a deadbolt would be so important to you ... unless you had been concerned for your safety."

Cordelia continued to silently gaze around her garden. When she spoke, her voice was uncharacteristically soft. "This place was the first safe place I had in a long time. I had a terrible boyfriend who became my even worse husband. I kept making excuses for him. He'll be nicer when he's not dealing with the stress of school. He'll do better if he can just get more sleep or not drink as much or have a better job or ... he won't need to hurt me if I just learn to be a better wife." She stopped while the tears wet her cheeks, but she didn't wipe them away.

"When did you accept the truth?" Mira said quietly.

Without looking at Mira, Cordelia spoke to her garden. "I got pregnant. I wasn't sure if I was happy or sad about it. I wanted a child, but I didn't want that child to have such a father. I couldn't bear the idea of an abortion. I considered leaving for the sake of the child or possibly giving the baby up for adoption." She paused, working to control her emotions. Then facing Mira, she said, "The choice got made for me. He didn't know I was pregnant, but he wasn't happy that I was sleeping so long, that I was lethargic when tending to him, to his every whim. He beat me so badly that I lost the baby and nearly lost my life."

She chuckled ruefully. "Yet, even in the hospital, I was loyal." Her tone was full of disgust. "I was going to go back to him. The nurses and doctors knew I'd been beaten, but they couldn't do anything to him without my cooperation, and I was unwilling to give it. It was right dreadful." She shook her head at the memory.

Mira put a hand on Cordelia's arm for support. "I'm sorry. I can't even imagine."

"No, I don't suppose you can. Your Warren's a nice bloke. He called me, you know, more than once. Wanted to make sure we had everything set up for your return to England. Made me promise to call him if you weren't tickety-boo. I worried for half a second that maybe he was a bit too controlling, but then I realized I was seeing things through my own experiences." She patted the top of Mira's hand. "He's blinding, luv. Don't ever let him go."

"I won't," Mira said. "I'm just sorry your experience was so different from mine. What happened? Did you go home with him?"

"No. I met Bill instead."

"Someone nice?"

"Yes, but not what you think. You remember Bill, don't you? Bill who owns the pub."

"Oh, right. He's more your father's age instead of ... well, you know. So ...?"

"His wife was in the bed next to mine. She had cancer in her bones. It made them brittle. They were long past fighting the cancer, but the doctors did try to help when she broke bones. It didn't take a fall or anything. She might just twist wrong and, next thing you know, her bone would snap.

"Bill was so sweet with her. Her name was Irina. She was such a lovely woman, inside and out. She would talk to me in those few moments where her pain meds made it so she could and before the same meds knocked her out. Mostly she slept, and mostly Bill was there, sitting beside her, brushing her hair, holding her hand.

"He noticed that my husband rarely came and that when he did ... well, he noticed that I bristled. He started talking to me. He told me I deserved better than that bloody tosser. He was absolutely gutted that I was planning on going back home to him. Anytime his wife was asleep, he'd talk to me. I told him about the baby I'd lost. I hadn't even told my husband about it.

"That was the last straw with Bill. After that, he wouldn't leave me alone in my hospital room. If he had to leave, he'd get one of his blokes to stay in the room. They always sat near Irina, but he told me they were there for me if I needed them, for anything. They were nice to me too.

"For the first time in a long time, I realized I was a good person just for being me." She paused and looked at Mira. "Do you remember that broken wrench I talked about? That gave you the idea to give me that wrench memory stick?" Mira nodded. "Well, Bill's the one who told me that. He told me I needed to heal myself and not just physically, and that once I did that, I could do and be whatever I wanted. I could even help other people."

She stopped, staring down at her hands and picking at the nails. With her voice barely above a whisper, she added, "I'm still sorry about losing that baby. But I try to make my life worth that sacrifice."

Taking a deep breath, Cordelia lifted her head and with power in her voice said, "It has to be. I decided that it would be, right there in that hospital room. Once I decided, Bill and his wife, his friends, the nurses, the whole mess of them helped me. They moved me to a different hospital room where I met with the police. Before I left the hospital, my husband had been arrested. Bill kept me hidden until I could secure a divorce and that tosser could be sent to jail."

"I noticed you never once mentioned his name," Mira said with raised eyebrows.

Cordelia smiled in response. "You're a bright one, aren't you? I will refer to him by any number of terms, but I will never give him the honor of calling him by his given name again. He made a point of having me address him with his proper name with a certain level of obsequiousness. I'm sure you understand my response."

Given her experience moving past the terrorist in Paris, Mira did understand. She smiled. "It sounds like 'a right tosser' is exactly his name."

"I can think of a few more choice terms, but I've been trying to clean up my language—especially in front of you delicate Yanks." She chuckled.

"Is he still in jail?"

"No. He spent half his sentence in jail and then got out on licence."

"Does that mean being on probation?"

"Yes. He was monitored. Unfortunately, or fortunately, he didn't follow the conditions laid out for him—he tried to contact me. That got him sent back to jail. He's since finished his jail time, but he hasn't bothered me."

"That's good. Do you ever worry about him coming back?"

"Thankfully, no. You see, Bill never stopped being there for me. His wife died a few months after we met, and he channeled his grief into making sure I would be okay." She laughed out loud. "When that tosser tried to find me when he was out on licence, Bill's 'friends' found him instead. Going back to jail became the preferable option. He actually turned himself in."

"Wow. It pays to have good friends. I'm guessing your imaginary boyfriend has something to do with this?"

Cordelia laughed. "Yes. I don't have to use him much, but if I'm ever uncomfortable when a man approaches, I start talking about my burly boyfriend. Scares them off nice and quick. It helps me feel a little bit more in control, if that makes sense, even though I'm using an imaginary person to do it."

"I think I understand."

"Once I get to know people, I drop the pretense. But it has become natural when I'm meeting anyone to make sure to bring him up in conversation. Sorry I did with you. It's a habit I haven't decided whether I want to break or not. He was Bill's idea."

"I remember Bill being rather protective of you. It makes sense now."

"Yes, and that isn't the half of it. After leaving the hospital, I moved into this flat. Bill's friend owned it. He let me stay for free until I could afford rent. It became such an important symbol to me that he let me buy it from him when I could—at a bargain price. Bill never admitted it, but I'm pretty sure he paid the difference between my price and the actual worth of the place. Eventually, I was able to buy other places to rent out. It was a tough decision to rent out this place. But that became my final bit of healing—that I felt safe enough in the world to move on, to leave this safe cocoon. I still love this little garden, though. It's sheltered and secluded. It was my peaceful place from the first day I moved in, and it still is to this day." She pulled her knees up onto her chair, hugging them to her. Mira could feel the peace Cordelia was talking about as she took in the bucolic setting around her.

"Well," Cordelia laughed slightly, "I bet you weren't expecting quite such a long, dramatic story for this little chinwag, were you, luv?"

"Maybe not, but I knew the truth was somewhere in that vicinity. I'm glad you told me. You are the happiest, bubbliest person I've ever met. It's easy to assume that means you've had an easy life, a pretty bad assumption it turns out. I guess the reality is that you've chosen to be happy despite your difficult life."

"Probably because of it is more likely. I've seen the darkness, and I know how wonderful the light is by comparison. So, I've had to make a very conscious choice about which side to embrace. The result is that my life is literally brilliant. I admit to having moments where those past experiences haunt me, that's why Bill still feels the need to check up on me. But I've learned how to get past those moments."

"How do you?"

"By helping someone else." She said it as if it was obvious. "I don't rent out these flats to tourists to make money. I mean, it is my livelihood, but I do it to help them. I make sure they have all the maps and directions they need to have a good time and make the most of their trip. If I just took their money and ran, I couldn't live with myself." Her tone had been light until she added, "Otherwise the darkness would swallow me."

They sat silently, pondering those thoughts when Cordelia let out a squeal. "Oh, blimey! I haven't told you about Bibi and Kailani. If anyone needs help, it's those two."

CHAPTER 28

How could they have both forgotten about Kailani and Bibi so quickly? "What did you find out? How can we help?" Mira asked, anxious now that the two of them had come back to mind.

"I don't know *how* to help them yet because I don't know what's going on, but I did learn a few things. I handle real estate, obviously, so that's where I started. The owner of that building is a friend of mine. We didn't even know Bibi's last name, so I wondered if her lease might at least tell us that much."

"And ..." Mira said impatiently.

"Well, it's not her name on the lease!"

"Whose is it then?"

"The name is Thomas Davies."

"Who's that?"

"Exactly what I wanted to know. My friend got cagey when I asked about who Thomas Davies is. He clammed up, saying it's complicated and he didn't want to get into the middle of it."

"Oh," Mira said, disappointed. "I was hoping we'd learn more."

"Well, luv, I'm not done yet. Do you think I would give up so easily?"

"Oh, sorry. You're right. Go on."

"Thank you. Anyway, I wondered if Thomas was a father, ex-husband, or something like that. Thomas Davies isn't exactly a unique name, but Bibi is. I eventually found a marriage record for Bibi Cooper and Thomas Davies nine years ago."

"That's fantastic!"

"There's more. I found a birth record for Kailani Davies born to Bibi and Thomas Davies eight years ago."

"Even better." Mira was grinning from ear to ear until she saw Cordelia's knit brow. "What's wrong? That was fantastic."

"Honestly, it's not. We've learned whose name is on the lease, but not much more. We don't know why that's complicated or what Bibi's concerns really are."

"Oh, you're right. Could Thomas be an ex-husband? I never saw any sign that it was anything but the two of them in that flat. Do you ... do you think he might have been abusive or something?"

"That was an idea that crossed my mind. But I also know that just because that happened to me doesn't mean it happened to her. It's tempting to see other's lives through the filter of my own. It is my first instinct—one I have to fight."

"So, what now?"

"Well, I searched the records some more. I found no record of a divorce. But that's where my trail ends. Bibi is scared of something, but I don't know what. Oh, blimey, there was one more thing. When I first contacted my friend, he assumed I was interested in leasing or buying that flat from him since that's my business. So, he let slip that the monthly payments on the place are often overdue, hinting he might be willing to dump the place. Of course, once he realized I was asking after the people and not the flat, he clammed up right away."

"Well, where's her husband, and what's going on with the place?"

"Yes, that's what I'd like to know too."

"What do we do now? I wouldn't even know what other kinds of records you could dig up. Cordelia, would your friend tell us more? I mean, if he understood how important this is?"

"How important is it?" Before Mira could respond, Cordelia held up her hand. "With the few facts we have, how important would this appear to anyone else? We see someone who needs help, but other than our gut feeling about that, what can we honestly explain? We have nothing solid to go on."

Mira slumped in her chair. Cordelia was right. "Why does this have to be so hard? All we want to do is help," she said with a sigh.

They sat in silence pondering the dilemma before them. *Where is that peace I'd found?* Mira wondered. In her mind, she retraced her steps to peace, and that prompted her to pray. Silently pleading for help, she found herself naturally adding to her prayer all that she was grateful for.

"Cordelia!" Mira exclaimed, throwing her eyes open wide. "It's not all that complicated. We just need to get help ourselves."

Cordelia tilted her head and raised her eyebrows. "Oh, luv, you've gone a bit mental on me. Getting help so we can help? You need to sit down."

"If you haven't noticed, I am sitting down. Just listen. I don't know what to do, and you don't know what to do, but I'm heading out to dinner in a few minutes. I'm going to see Dylan and Olivia and the whole rest of their family. If we put our heads together, I'm sure we can come up with something."

"Well, it's worth a try. So, are you just going to ask them at dinner?"

"No. Tonight is supposed to be about Olivia. She's basically engaged, and she's going to quit her job and open a bakery—none of which she's told her family about yet. So, I don't want to steal the stage to talk about Kailani.

"But … I was already going to ask you if you wanted to get together for a girl's night or girl's outing. Dylan has heard all about you from me. She'd love to meet you, and I'd love for you to meet her family. Honestly, you're all like family to me now. So, why don't we talk about Kailani and Bibi then? If you want to join us, that is."

"Wow, that's a switch."

"What?"

"I'm the one who's usually on the go, the one going like a blue streak. But look at you. Did you forget you're the visitor here, and I'm the local? Yet, you're inviting me to get together with your friends." She was shaking her head in mock annoyance. "I never knew that timid thing I first met would turn into this."

Mira beamed. "I'll take that as a compliment. I have changed a bit since then, haven't I? But this is the real me, I'd just forgotten that. At least that's part of it. The other part is … well, it's who I've decided to become, I suppose."

"No complaints here, luv. What's Warren going to think?"

"Well, I'm guessing he's not going to have a problem with the new me either. He remembers when I was like this, before I collapsed inward. I'm pretty sure he's going to be my biggest champion, or already is, for that matter."

Cordelia nodded. "That's good," and she said it with a seriousness that Mira now understood much better.

"So, what about getting together with my other newfound sisters? You didn't answer yet."

"I'd love to. I've got things to take care of tomorrow morning, but after that I'm free."

"Brilliant!"

Cordelia winced. "So, that word fits, but I'm still not sure if I like it coming out of the mouth of a Yank."

. . .

Mira was still smiling about how uncomfortable she'd made Cordelia by spouting her own slang back at her as she walked out of the flat a short time later, brolly in hand. She was meeting up with Dylan's family for what promised to be an interesting evening. Olivia had decided to tell the family her plans over dinner at Bill's pub, *The Red Fox*, hoping the relaxed atmosphere would put her at ease. Mira's only concern was that Olivia might have a hard time being heard over the general din of the place.

Olivia had winked and said, "Well, that's not really a downside."

They'd decided to meet about 7:00. Mira determined to head out early so she could talk Bill into grouping some tables together for them in the quietest corner, if there was such a thing.

Lost in these thoughts, Mira almost missed her. Kailani was sitting on her steps, nestled up to one side, almost hidden by the shrubs in front of her flat.

When Mira spotted her, she didn't hesitate but made a beeline to the child. "Hi, Kailani. I've missed seeing you." She didn't whisper, but she didn't speak loudly enough to announce her presence to others either.

Kailani lifted her head to meet Mira's gaze. "I missed you too. I didn't know if I'd see you again."

"I'm sorry about that. I should have told you I was leaving and that I'd be back." Mira noticed the stuffed blue whale in her arms. "Do you like the whale I gave you?" Kailani nodded vigorously. "I don't want to get you into trouble with your mum by talking to you. So, do you want me to leave?"

Kailani didn't hesitate. "No. Please don't. My mum won't be mad. She's just scared, that's all."

"Okay. Can you tell me why she's scared?"

She shook her head. "She doesn't tell me."

Mira sat on the step beside the little girl, reaching down to gently brush Kailani's hair back with her hand. She thought of something she hadn't before. "Kailani, I want to help you and your mum, but I don't want to butt in where I don't belong. So, do you think your mum needs some help?"

Kailani immediately nodded, peering up into Mira's face with plaintive, pleading eyes that nearly broke her heart. She gathered Kailani into her arms. "Okay. It's okay." She held her while Kailani's little body shook with tears.

When her shudders stopped, Mira loosened her embrace and pulled back so she could face Kailani. "I need to ask you another question, and it's very important. It's more of an adult question than an eight-year-old's question, but I'll bet you can answer it. You're not a typical eight-year-old." Kailani brightened at the compliment. "Okay, here goes. Your mum needs help, but do you think she'll let me help her? Is it okay if I try?"

"That's two questions," Kailani replied.

"You're right. I do that sometimes, ask more than one question at a time. So, first question: Do you think your mum will let me help?"

"I'm not sure about that question, but I like the other one. I think you should try."

"Okay. I'll try. I have some friends that I can get to help me with that. You met one of them, Cordelia, but I have other friends too—a lot of women who were once eight-year-old girls just like you. Is that okay?" Once again, Kailani nodded. "All right then. I need to leave. I'm going to meet some of them right now. We're going to get together tomorrow, and I'm sure we'll come up with a plan." In her head, she thought, *Just as soon as we can figure out what's wrong in the first place.*

CHAPTER 29

Walking the rest of the way to the pub, her thoughts swung from Kailani and Bibi to Olivia. The plan was for Dylan and Mira to sit on either side of Olivia at dinner. She was understandably nervous. Hopefully, they could give her the support and encouragement she needed since all three of them were concerned she might back out.

Bill was more than happy to accommodate Mira. As he deftly directed the rearranging of tables, Mira tugged on his arm. "Bill, Cordelia told me about her life and your part in changing it drastically for the better. You are a good man."

He shrugged off the compliment. "I was just doing what my Irina would have done. Just what she would have done."

"No, Bill. You could have easily focused only on your wife dying, but you made a different choice. You took the time to notice Cordelia and do something about it. Most people are content to look the other way. You were the good Samaritan, and I'm sure you've made your Irina proud. You, Bill, are a good man."

The rough exterior melted away, as he grabbed her hand and squeezed it gently. He was at a loss for words for several minutes. Finally, he softly said, "Thank you." Then he dropped her hand, turning his attention back to his staff.

Mira watched him busy himself again. But he surprised her by turning back. He caught her eye, smiled, and nodded before resuming his duties.

Mira was still smiling to herself when she heard a familiar voice. "Mira!" Avelyn was stepping through the door. She reached Mira in a few steps. "It's so good to see you. I'm sure you're sick of people asking how you're doing since that horrible event in Paris, but I'm going to ask anyway. How *are* you doing?"

"Surprisingly well. It's not a pleasant memory, but I've found so many good things to focus on since then. It's been a transformative couple weeks since the blast. Wow! It will be two weeks tomorrow. It feels as if it happened yesterday and at the same time it seems more like a lifetime ago. I know people say that, but it's true."

"Yes. Timewise what happened is recent history, but I'm suspecting in terms of growth, you're a different person now."

"You're right. I hadn't thought of it that way before, but I think you hit on the key. I'm just so grateful now—for everything. And I have a new perspective on life. Avelyn, you know as much as anyone how much I want children, but I'm okay if it doesn't happen the way I want it to. I'm willing to let life come to me on its own terms."

"That's good, Mira. That is so good. And you know, if you're not so stressed about a baby, it might just happen on its own. The whole 'a watched pot never boils' kind of thing."

Mira hadn't noticed how the whole family had filed in around them. Avelyn had made her feel as if she was the only person that mattered, the only one there. "I think we're holding up the crowd, aren't we?"

"No matter. They can always wait for what's important."

"Thanks, Avelyn," Mira said, giving her a big hug.

Soon everyone was seated and poring over the menus. Dylan and Olivia had managed to save a seat beside them for Mira. Few words passed between the three of them, but meaningful glances were plentiful. They were well into their meal when Dylan cleared her throat. "The three of us had a wonderful time in Rome, and more came out of it than you might expect. Olivia?"

It was a planned introduction, but Olivia wasn't quite ready to step into the spotlight. She turned, panic-stricken, to Mira. "Go ahead. You got this."

Olivia took a deep breath. "Well, I have a surprise for you. I met this guy—"

"You met someone in Rome?" Zita said.

"Oh, how romantic!" Tiana said.

"No, no," Olivia said, trying to hush everyone. "I met him a while back. I just told Dylan and Mira about him when we were in Rome. So, he's a great guy. His name is Asher." Despite her nervousness, she was having a hard time hiding her smile.

"Oh, Olivia, that's wonderful!" Avelyn said. "When did you meet him?"

"Umm, about a year ago."

"A year ago? And you're barely telling us now?" Avelyn's voice wavered, threatening to lose its warmth.

"Yes, mother," Dylan chimed in. "We can be a little much, you know. Sometimes our expectations get in the way of reality. So, Olivia waited to tell us about him until there was something about him to tell."

Olivia smiled appreciatively at Dylan. "She's right. So, Asher's funny and he's smart. He listens to my ideas. We can talk about everything and anything. We take long walks, and there's nowhere else I'd rather be than with him." Her smile was getting wider and harder and harder to suppress.

"That sounds like you're in love to me," said Tiana. And Caleb, his fingers entwined with Tiana's, smiled in agreement.

"Maybe there'll be a wedding?" Avelyn said, raising her eyebrows.

Olivia beamed and nodded. The others squealed with delight, enough that Bill came over to investigate.

"Is everything all right? You're all so subdued."

"Yes," Mira said. "Olivia here is going to get married!"

"Well, that's just brilliant! Just brilliant! We'll have to toast that for sure, and I'll send out pudding for the lot of you!"

When the hubbub had died down a bit, Olivia cleared her throat. "I have a bit more to tell you actually." Everyone turned to give her their full attention, the expressions on their faces expectant but cautious. "Asher and I have a dream." She hesitated, but both Mira and Dylan nodded their encouragement. "We're going to move to Ohio, closer to Mom and Dad to carry out this dream." She stopped again.

Avelyn spoke, and her voice was soothing and comforting. "Go ahead, dear. What is it?"

"Well, we want to open a bakery. We've been doing a lot of research, and we have a very good plan. We've saved enough start-up money, and we are super excited about it."

"Would you keep working while Asher ran it?" Elijah had gone right to the heart of it.

"Well, Dad, we're both going to be working full-time in the bakery. We've decided that's the best way to make a go of it."

Elijah was silent, contemplating her announcement. The others awaited his reaction. "So, your degree meant nothing? The good job you have means nothing? Are you going to try to go back to it when the bakery takes off? Was this *his* idea?"

Avelyn answered before Olivia had a chance to. "Elijah. Is that really what you meant to say? I think congratulations are in order." She turned to Olivia. "I can tell you're excited about the prospects, and I know you well enough to know that you would have researched this thoroughly. I trust you. I just hope it's close enough that we can become your first regular customers."

The tension was broken. Elijah steamed slightly in his corner, but the rest of the family peppered Olivia with excited questions. Soon Asher's picture was circulated amid smiles and sighs. By the end of the evening, even Elijah was smiling again.

Olivia pulled Mira and Dylan aside as the group was leaving the pub. "Thank you for making me go through with it. Dad reacted pretty much the way I expected, but it wasn't as bad as I thought it would be. It's a load off having told everyone. Now the burden is Dad's, not mine."

"That's a good way to look at it," Mira said. "Oh! I almost forgot—our girl's get-together."

They quickly gathered Avelyn, Zita, and Tiana. "Olivia, Dylan, and I thought it would be fun to get together with just us and Cordelia, my landlord is I guess the best way to describe her. She's free tomorrow in the afternoon or evening. Are you guys in?"

Everyone nodded. "Tomorrow is a good idea," Avelyn said. "We're all going home in three days."

Mira's face fell. Everyone had to go home sometime, but would she see them again once they did? "Yeah, I guess so," she said without much enthusiasm.

"What's wrong?" Dylan said.

"Going home. I can't wait to go home and see Warren, but …"

"You didn't think about us going home, did you?" Avelyn said. At Mira's distraught expression, Avelyn put a hand on her shoulder and added, "Don't worry. We always keep in touch with family. Illinois and Ohio aren't that far apart."

Mira smiled weakly. Then she remembered there was more to their gathering. "I almost forgot to tell you. Cordelia and I have been talking about a little girl and her mum that live across the street. We'll tell you about them tomorrow because we need your thoughts and ideas. So, how about meeting at my flat tomorrow at 2:00? Then we can decide what to do from there." It was quickly agreed, and the group left amid hugs and kisses.

It was dark as Mira exited the pub, the sky threatening rain. She hesitated, deciding to open her Rosetta Stone brolly. As she did so, the door of the pub behind her swung open.

"Are you walking home alone?" Bill said.

"Well, I was planning on it. It's only around the corner."

He gave her a reproachful glance. "Since it's so close, it won't take me more than a minute or two to go with you then, will it?" Before she could refuse, he poked his head inside and hollered to someone that he'd be right back.

Mira hated to admit it, but she was grateful for the company on this dark night. They chatted briefly about Cordelia and soon were at the base of Mira's front steps. "Thank you, Bill. You really are a good man."

He shrugged. "You said some people would be content to ignore what goes on around them. I'm only content the other way. I learned that from my Irina." Then he straightened up and with a mischievous twinkle said, "Just don't go spreading that around, okay?"

"All right." She unlocked the door to her flat then stood in front of it, watching Bill retreat down the street. It wasn't until he disappeared that she heard the raindrops plopping gently on the top of her brolly. She hastily ducked inside.

Closing the door behind her, she paused, watching the water droplets fall to the ground from the brolly she'd just shut. One drop, two drops, … ten drops—running together forming a larger puddle. She'd come a long way since she first came to London, when the concept of her name meaning ocean was an overwhelming one.

She wiped up the puddle and put the brolly in the stand by the door before going into her bedroom and changing into pajamas. Thus attired, she nestled into the warmth of the couch with a throw blanket wrapped around her. Pulling out her phone, she searched for the site she had bookmarked weeks before.

The name Mira has two main origins. The first is from South Slavic languages, coming from Mir which means world or peace. The other is from Hindi, originally from Sanskrit, where its meaning is sea or ocean.

This is really where her journey had begun, seeing herself maybe not like the large world or ocean yet still a very significant part of it. It was comforting to see the progress she had made.

She smiled to herself as she moved to close the bookmark, ready to call Warren. But something caught her eye. She stopped, her finger in mid-air. She read the meaning of her name again, then again, to be sure. Mira also meant peace!

The revelation washed over her like a comforting wave. Peace. Peace is what she'd felt lately. With the other meanings of her name—ocean, look, and wonder, she'd learned the meaning then found how that meaning was part of her, even made it part of her. For once, she discovered this piece of herself first, and it was the most wonderful part of all—made possible by the stepping stones of her name that had brought her to this point.

She hugged herself, smiling and laughing. She was a valuable person, not insignificant, but worthwhile. And she'd learned to look around her to see others so she could help them. She'd learned to be grateful for who she was and what she had in her life without expecting things to be perfect. All those things, every step along the way, had led her to this. She was peaceful. She felt calm in the midst of the storms of life. She was content.

But what about everyone else? She wanted nothing more than to share this feeling with everyone around her. Cordelia was at peace, and it seemed Bill had found peace after the death of his wife by helping Cordelia. Olivia had found peace in her confessions tonight just as Dylan had by expressing her love and appreciation for her mother. Peace made everything better, or if not better, possible or bearable.

If only she could help Kailani and Bibi find a bit of that peace for themselves. Hopefully with everyone's help the next day, they'd be able to find a way to do just that.

. . .

Warren answered the phone after a single ring. Mira found it incredible how much there was to tell him—about Cordelia, what she'd learned about Kailani and her mum, about Olivia's announcements to her family, and finally about her peace. It was amazing what had happened in a few short hours. He listened patiently as she relayed it all to him.

"You know, hubs, Cordelia wondered if you'd be okay with the new me, but I figured it wouldn't bother you. I mean, part of the new me is honestly the old me, rediscovered."

"Yes, it is, but when you say it that way, I'm not sure you're giving yourself enough credit. Many people would have withered that first day alone in London, but you didn't. And Paris, well, I don't think I would have come out of it on top the way you have. How are your headaches, by the way?"

"Better. I still get a twinge, a nice reminder of what happened every once in a while. But that's happening a lot less often."

"That's good. And, to be honest, it's probably going to take me some time to adjust to the new you, but I'm definitely okay with it."

Mira smiled. "I figured you would be." Her thoughts turned to Dylan and the others. "I didn't tell you yet that Avelyn said they're going home in three days, on Sunday. I've gotten so used to having them around that it feels strange to think of London without them."

"You could come home then too," Warren said, hopeful.

"I've thought about it, believe me. On Sunday, it will be four weeks since I left. I miss you so much."

"But ..."

"You know me too well. I need to make sure things are right with Kailani and her mum. My original flight leaves in ten days. I hope that will be enough time."

Warren sighed. "I understand. I know I helped you set this up in the beginning, and five weeks didn't sound so bad then, but they've been some of the longest weeks of my life. But … I would honestly be disappointed if you came home before you found closure with Kailani. It's the biggest reason you needed to stay after Paris."

"Thanks for understanding, hubs. I honestly don't know if I can help, but I want to at least try."

"I know, and I'm guessing you'll find a way to help. I hope whatever it is, it's enough—for them and for you. And as long as you're staying, you could fit in some of the day trips outside of London you'd originally planned to take."

"That's a good idea. I'd kind of lost track of those plans. It would seem a waste to come all this way and not get a few more sights in, but they're not as important to me as they once were. And I've learned that sightseeing isn't as much fun to do alone. Maybe I can convince Cordelia to go with me." Mira yawned.

"That sounds like a plan. But Mira, you should go to bed. I heard that yawn. You've had a long day."

"You're right." She yawned again. "And I need to write in my journal before going to sleep. If I wait 'til tomorrow, I might never catch up."

Reluctantly, they hung up. Mira snatched her journal and began to scribble as quickly as she could, wanting to record the events and discoveries of the day before her eyelids drooped shut. She ended with:

Peace. It's a word that gets bandied about—world peace, a peace sign from the 60s, peace out, peace talks—yet it means more than we think. It has an external meaning. Outside of myself, peace often means the absence of war or strife. It's a physical state and certainly a desirable one. But while it's something I can influence, it's not something I can control.

Internal peace is another matter altogether. This peace can be hard to achieve too, but in this case, other people or events may influence it, but I control it. I can be at peace when all the world around me rails and rages. If I look for it, I can find it.

It hides in plain sight. It's in the prayers I offer. It's in the attitude I carry and the gratitude in my heart. It's in the reach I extend to help others. It's warm and light, and I hope to always keep it near now that I've found it.

Mira closed her journal and held it close to her heart, enveloped by the thoughts and emotions she'd shared on the pages within. Struggling to keep her eyes open, she gently set the journal next to her phone on the table in front of the couch.

Too tired to even move into her bed, Mira curled up on the couch, wrapping herself in the throw blanket. An alert dinged on her phone— Aissa responding to her email. Smiling, she fell asleep thinking, I'll read that first thing in the morning.

CHAPTER 30

Mira sat stunned. She reread the email, certain she must have misread it. But she hadn't. She hadn't been awake long—only long enough to stretch, wonder then remember why she was on the couch, stare at her tired yet happy face in the bathroom mirror, and settle at the kitchen table for breakfast with her phone in her hand.

She'd been eating cereal, but it had since gone soggy as she stared at the message from Aissa.

Mira,

Thanks for your email. I appreciate the kind things you said about me, but I have to be honest with you—they're not deserved. Don't misunderstand. I'm glad I could be there to help you, but in reality, I was the one who was saved. I haven't wanted to say anything, but your continued gratitude has made me uncomfortable, so I feel I must.

About three weeks ago, I hit a crossroads. My boyfriend of five years broke up with me, although if he hadn't broken up with me, I would have broken up with him—we weren't getting along. Suddenly, however, I was alone. Even if it was supposedly for the best, I was still alone. I walked through the city streets three nights in a row. No one knew me. No one noticed me. I had no purpose and no dreams for the future. I had a job as an interpreter, but the people I met changed from day to day. Such a job made no lasting connections.

If I didn't call into work, they might have to scramble a little, but they wouldn't care. If I wasn't there walking the streets, no one would notice. I just didn't matter to anyone. I love my family, but they live out in the countryside, and I don't get out there much. We have gotten used to not seeing each other and not being in each other's lives.

If I just stopped living, no one would miss me. No one would care.

I weighed various ideas about how I would take my own life. The thought of something violent bothered me—someone would have to clean up the mess. So, I settled on pills. I could swallow them and wait for death to take me. Thursday, the day before the bombing, I had gathered enough pills. I was ready to die. I was going to have one last look around the city on Friday then fall asleep for good that night.

I wasn't supposed to work that Friday, but the boss at work was flustered because of the explosion. She needed someone with impeccable English skills since they knew nothing about you other than that you had an American passport. And it was bigger than the terrorist attack, even though that was bad enough. The situation could easily turn into a political disaster if France didn't handle it correctly because an American was injured on their soil. I was the most seasoned English interpreter, so she called me, forgetting that I was taking time off.

For the same reasons she called me, I couldn't turn it down. It was about France. So, I accepted the assignment and went to the hospital. All was confusion and chaos. Police were there. Medical professionals were there. Politicians were there, and so was the media. I almost backed out and left, but then I saw you. You weren't dead like we'd considered to be a possibility, but you were alone—like I had been alone. I couldn't leave you.

So, I decided to take one more job. I stayed at the hospital during the nights, sleeping on any empty bed they would give me. I went home once to simply gather several changes of clothes and my toiletries, but I didn't dare stay there. And as I hurriedly grabbed those items, I tried not to look at my bedside with the pills lined up, ready for me, waiting for me.

It was simply one more job, I kept telling myself. When it was done, I would finish things. I spent two days wandering the halls of the hospital, checking on you periodically, but you weren't awake yet. I contacted your hotel, ran interference, and waited.

I was waiting for you and waiting until the time I could follow through with my plan. But you changed that. I started to care what happened to you. I learned you really were all alone in Paris, alone in France. I had to somehow save you, even if I couldn't or didn't want to save myself.

Did you notice how I always seemed to be close by? It wasn't just that I was staying in the hospital; it's that you were my only assignment. My office didn't call to give me another—I assume because they remembered I was on vacation. So, I decided I would do my very best for you. Then I could leave this world, going out on top.

Why did you give me those earrings? So I could stand out in a crowd? Did you know I felt invisible in a crowd? You said things about me and you saw things in me that I hadn't seen in myself in a very long time. You made me question all my conclusions. You made me imagine a future where I was somebody. You made me imagine a future!

After we dropped you off at the airport, I had the driver take me back to your bakery. I sat in a corner and sobbed. I probably drove away all their customers, but Jean and Monique didn't care about that. They talked to me and sat with me. I hope you don't mind, but Jean lets me call him Papa too.

I finally went home and threw away those pills. Then I called Jean and Monique because they made me promise I would. Then I called my family and talked to them. I didn't tell them what I had planned to do, I just talked to them. We laughed about so many things, so much that we cried.

I go back to the bakery whenever I start to slip and fear that I might be a danger to myself, but I also go there other times too, just because I want to. My bakery papa and maman have encouraged me to talk to a therapist, and I have scheduled a visit with one later today. It has only been about a week since you left, but my life is entirely different already—in all the right ways.

You don't realize how wonderful you are. Because of you—your kind words and example—I am learning. I am learning to be okay with the ups and downs of life. I'm learning to be content with whatever might come. It's not easy, but I'm trying.

You saved me, Mira. You saved me, and I should be the one to say that thank you can never be enough.

With love,

Aissa

The email still dumbfounded Mira, but with a growing sense of wonder, she recognized what Aissa was describing—she was working on finding peace. That thought made her smile.

Mira wasn't sure how to respond. You never knew, did you? The need to help Kailani and her mother burned with an even stronger intensity than before. She hadn't known that was even possible. And if she'd had any doubts before about leaving her accounting job to focus more on helping individual people, those doubts were completely washed away.

She played with her soggy cereal, trying to think of the best response to give Aissa. When nothing particular came to mind, she decided to respond with whatever came out the end of her fingertips.

Aissa,

Thanks for your email and for being so honest. I'm sure what you said was hard to share. I will say it caught me by surprise. I had no idea what that happy exterior was hiding. But I am so very, very glad and relieved that you've decided to stick around. The world would have had such a hole in it without you, even if you didn't realize that.

I guess I'm okay that Jean lets you call him Papa, but it does have a consequence. Now you're stuck with me. Since he's your papa and he's also my papa, that makes us sisters. And I never let go of family. To be honest, I already viewed you as a surrogate sister, but this just makes it official.

Thanks for telling me your story. It has opened my eyes and brought with it a whole slew of emotions. I am sad for you and happy for you. I'm nervous and excited. I'm even feeling emotions that I don't know how to describe.

Tell me how your therapy goes. And about your life—the little things and the big. I've never had sisters before I made this trip to Europe, and I'm all about making up for lost time on that front. When I say you're stuck with me, I mean it. Sorry, not sorry. ;)

To be honest with you, I came on this trip because I needed "sisters"— other women I could connect with on a personal level. I sometimes lose sight of the idea that other people might need me as much as I might need them. Although, the more I think about it, the more that's what this trip has become.

I'm going to be in London for another week and a half. I have so much still to see, but I'm more concerned about a little girl who lives across the street. Her name's Kailani. I don't know what's going on in her life, but something isn't right. I need to try and fix it before I go home. Your email has cemented that feeling within me even more than it was before.

This may seem strange to you, given what you've just told me, but your email has forever changed me. We don't always realize the impact of our actions—for good or ill. If I had acted differently toward you, things could have turned out horribly. I had thought all those nice things about you, but if I hadn't had earrings from my husband to give you, I might not have said them. That terrifies me.

I'm probably going to annoy people the rest of my life now by being in their faces and telling them what I see in them (at least the positive things). But I don't think it will be possible for me to make any other choice from here on out.

Hey, do you want to come to London? I know that was out of the blue, but I have a comfortable couch you could sleep on. Cordelia, my landlord, won't mind if I share if I give her a heads up. You'll like Cordelia. I've adopted her as my sister too ... so, technically, that means she's yours as well ... and ... there are a few other sisters, but they leave town on Sunday. So, if you hurry ...

Well, I've rambled enough for one email. I'll write more later. And email me back!

Love you, Sis.

Mira

Mira sat back, emotionally exhausted. She wanted to pick up the phone and call Warren. He'd be as awestruck as she was about this turn of events. It was too bad he was likely sound asleep back home.

She dumped out her uneaten breakfast and picked up a bagel to idly nibble on. She had several hours before she was getting together with Cordelia, Dylan, and the others. It gave her enough time to go visit or revisit some famous London landmarks, but that idea didn't appeal to her. What to do instead?

With a sudden stroke of inspiration, she grabbed her bag and her brolly and took off out the front door. As always, she glanced up the street to see if Kailani was outside, but she wasn't. So, she took off in the opposite direction.

Mira hoped she wouldn't be a bother when she knocked on the door, but that concern wasn't enough to turn her away. While waiting, she realized she should have stopped by that favorite bakery of theirs first and brought something with her, but the door opened and it was too late to change plans.

Madge's eyes opened in surprise from the open doorway. "Mira, isn't it?"

"Yes, I'm glad you remembered. I've been away from London for a couple weeks, and I head back to the states shortly, but I wanted to visit you again. I mean, if that's okay?"

Madge hesitated. "You're kind of an odd lot, you Americans."

"Is that good or bad?" Mira asked, concerned.

"You didn't know us, and yet you talked to us that day and here you are back again. However, I invited you in like a stray cat, so I guess I deserved this."

Mira scanned Madge's face to see if she was upset, but then Madge's face broke into a wide grin.

"Come on in, girl," Madge said while waving her in. "I don't have a problem with you one little bit. But I did tell one of my sons about you helping carry our bags home and sharing tea with you. He thought I was barking mad, he did. Afraid he was going to have me committed somewhere right on the spot."

"Oh, I'm sorry," Mira said, slightly horrified at what she'd caused.

"Oh, don't bother about him. He's just trying to scare me into being more 'careful,' as he would say." She suddenly turned on Mira. "You don't want to rob us blind, do you?"

Caught off guard, Mira stammered a reply. "Um, no, I ..."

Madge burst into laughter. "I didn't think so. Come on into the kitchen. I was just reading a bit of the paper." Then she added in a whisper, "Harold is awake in the next room, but he's pretending to be asleep so I don't fuss about him getting dressed." She winked. "He doesn't know I'm on to him. But I figure it does no harm, so I let him stay put as long as he wants.

"Here. Would you like a crumpet?"

Soon they were both enjoying their crumpets and sharing the mundane stories that make up most people's lives. "Do you have a picture of your Warren? I'd love to see what he looks like. Then I can picture him as you tell me your stories."

"I do!" Mira searched in her bag for the little flipbook Warren had included as a gift in what Mira was now thinking of as his bag of tricks. The book held three or four dozen photos, most of them silly pictures they would normally throw away.

Together they turned the pages, laughing. Warren and Mira appeared in joint selfies or captured by the other one, often while in a compromising position—Mira in mid sneeze with droplets spewing from her mouth, Warren setting up a tent that was in the process of falling on top of him, and so on.

"These aren't the pictures we normally keep," Mira said, somewhat apologetically.

Madge looked at her in surprise. "But these are the best pictures of all. They show who you are, your personalities, your ability to laugh at yourselves. These are the best kind of memories." She glanced toward the bedroom where they could hear Harold stirring. "Trust me, I know."

Mira followed her gaze. "Should I leave before he's all the way up? He won't remember me. I don't want to startle or upset him."

Reluctantly, Madge nodded. "That's probably best, but I've enjoyed our visit so much."

Mira picked up her flipbook then stopped. "Wait, I have an idea." She started pulling the photos out of the sleeves in the flipbook until they were all gone but one of her and Warren. "Here's a picture so you can remember me. But fill the rest of the book with pictures of your family. Maybe it will be something your husband can flip through that will be comforting and familiar—except that picture I've left of me and my husband. You might have to take that out and put it elsewhere."

Madge accepted the book. "What a lovely idea. We have some photo albums that he enjoys, but they're big and a little overwhelming at times. This should be just the right size." Madge flipped through the blank pages as if she could imagine the pictures that would soon reside there.

"Didn't you say he doesn't always remember your grandkids?" Madge nodded. "Do you have any recent pictures of them or even older pictures? Maybe it would help."

"Well, it certainly won't hurt." Madge paused to consider the matter. "You know, if I put in two pictures of each of them, a younger picture facing an older one, that might work." She nudged Mira. "If it doesn't, at least I'll get a glimpse of my grandchildren a bit more often."

As more noise started to come from the bedroom, Mira hastily stood up, stowing her photos safely in a pocket of her bag. "I better get going."

"Mira," Madge said, grabbing her arm so she couldn't leave just yet, "I didn't expect to see you again, but I'm happy I did. Thanks for the picture. I'll always remember you." Then she added with a twinkle, "Even if I start to lose my marbles, like my Harold."

She let out a huge laugh and said, "I think I'll add a picture of a young, handsome bloke so I can convince myself when I'm doddering that he was my husband. Oh, and I'll have to add a picture of a beautiful young thing to be myself when I was younger ... but, of course, not until after Harold's gone."

Madge was still laughing at the thought when Mira said her goodbyes, making her way down the front steps. She stopped at the bottom step and whirled around. "Madge, you're incredible, you know. With taking care of your husband and all."

Madge smiled sadly. "Thank you, dear. It isn't easy, but I love the old fool. What else could I do?" As Madge turned to go, Mira heard her calling out, "I know you're up, Harold. Ready or not, here I come."

Mira decided to make a detour before heading home, stopping in the bakery nearby where she'd first seen Madge and Harold. She bought bread to go with her lunch and a variety of pastries for their afternoon powwow.

Back at her flat, she was slicing cheese to go with her bread when she heard a frantic knock at the door.

Opening the door, she was surprised to see the small form in front of her. "Kailani? I didn't ... I ... I'm glad to see you. Are you okay?"

She didn't answer, but her eyes darted around nervously with her arms wrapped around herself as if she were cold.

"Do you want to come in?"

Kailani shook her head but again said nothing.

Mira bent down so she was at Kailani's eye level. "What's wrong? You can tell me."

"My mum." Her eyes moved in the direction of her flat.

"What about your mum?" Mira quietly asked while gently putting her hands on Kailani's arms, softly rubbing them in a calming motion.

"She … she was on the phone and she was worried or mad or something. She said, 'I can pay the rent if you just let me know.' When she hung up the phone, she was real gutted."

"Do you know who she was talking to?"

"No."

"Does your dad usually pay the rent?"

Kailani stared at her with a knitted brow. "What?"

"Isn't your dad Thomas Davies?"

Kailani cocked her head. "That's his name, but he's dead."

Mira put a hand to her mouth. "Oh, I'm so sorry, Kailani. I didn't know."

Kailani shrugged. "It's okay."

"This *is* complicated," Mira said to herself.

"What?"

"Never mind. Kailani. Your dad …" She didn't know how to approach his passing. So, she chose to address the problem at hand instead. "Kailani, with the phone call, has this kind of thing happened before?"

Kailani nodded her head, her little lip quivering.

Mira pulled Kailani into a tight embrace. "Oh, you sweet child. Oh, you poor, sweet thing."

She wanted to ask her more questions—about her dad, when and how he had died. Did she miss him? Did her mum miss him? What was he like? Mira's heart ached for this innocent child. But more than her desire to have answers, she wanted to protect her. "Does your mum know you came to talk to me?" Mira knew the answer, but she felt the need to ask anyway.

Kailani quickly shook her head, fear building in her eyes again.

"Okay. It's all right. I'm going to help you. I'm going to find a way to help you. But right now, you better get back."

She nodded, and before Mira could say another word, Kailani had scampered off home, disappearing through her front door in a flash.

Mira slowly retreated inside her flat, wondering about Kailani's situation. She barely had time to sit down when there was another knock at the door. For a split second, she thought maybe Kailani had come back. Hurrying to the door, she heard laughter and a mixture of voices on the other side. She glanced at the clock. The cavalry had arrived.

CHAPTER 31

The living room felt rather small once everyone was packed into it. Cordelia sat in the easy chair. Avelyn, Tiana, and Zita were on the couch while Dylan and Olivia sprawled on the floor in front of them. Mira stood, trying hard not to pace in agitation.

Mira and Cordelia took turns laying out the story, as they understood it, of Kailani and her mum, Bibi. Mira surprised even Cordelia by adding the information she had gleaned from Kailani's short visit, not even sure what it meant.

"At first, I assumed from what we'd learned that Bibi was having trouble paying the rent, but what Kailani overheard was different than that. 'If you would have told me, I could have paid the rent,' or something like that? What does that even mean?"

"Right. And what about her dad? Why is the lease still in his name?" Tiana said.

"Do you think he just recently died? That might explain it," Zita added.

Mira shook her head. "I thought about asking, but it felt more like prying than caring, so I didn't. But it doesn't seem recent based on Kailani's reaction. She was surprised that I didn't know he was dead. In fact, she was kind of matter-of-fact about it."

"Well, it's really plain and simple," Avelyn said. Everyone turned to her, wondering how it could possibly be simple. "We need Bibi to tell us what's going on. We can speculate all we want. We can make assumptions and guesses, but Bibi knows the truth. She just needs to talk to us and tell us what it is."

It was that simple and yet not even remotely so. "How?" Mira wanted to know while several sets of eyes turned to Avelyn expectantly.

Cordelia surprised the others by responding before Avelyn could. "We need to get her out of that flat and onto more neutral territory." She glanced at Mira. "Bill was able to reach me because I was in the hospital instead of my own flat. The neutral ground helped me not be so defensive."

The others didn't know what Cordelia was referring to, but Mira nodded her head. "I hadn't thought of that before. But how do we accomplish that?"

"Do you think she'd accept an invitation to a picnic? For Kailani's sake?" Dylan said.

"It's worth a try. We could do it at Regent's Park." Then Mira's eyes lit up. "I have an idea." She ran from the room, coming back a minute later with something in her hands. "I bought this stone bracelet for Kailani when we went to the natural history museum, remember? I bought her two things. I already gave her the stuffed whale, but I didn't give her this yet. I could take it over as a sort of peace offering."

"Well, there's no time like the present, child. Go over and invite them," Avelyn said. "It's Friday. We're going home on Sunday. That means if you want our help, it's got to be tomorrow."

The reality of how little time there was—to help with Kailani, to spend with Avelyn and her whole clan—shocked Mira into action. "Okay. I'll be right back."

Walking across the street and down a couple doors, Mira could feel the eyes of the other women upon her. She hastily said a prayer. "Dear Lord, help me say the right things, and help Bibi be willing to come."

She knocked on the door to their flat and Kailani answered. "Mira!" She seemed slightly calmer than when she'd been at Mira's door a short time before. She leaned in closer. "Are you here to help?"

"I hope so. Is your mum here?"

She nodded. "She's working on a painting."

"She's a painter?" Mira couldn't believe she hadn't learned this piece of information before.

"Kind of. She does watercolors that go in children's books."

"Oh! She's an illustrator."

"Yeah, that's what it's called."

"Can I talk to her for a minute?"

Kailani glanced hopefully at the item hastily wrapped in tissue paper in Mira's hands. She tried to suppress a smile then turned and ran back into the flat.

A few minutes later Bibi appeared. She wasn't smiling. Her hands were multi-colored from her work, but she put her hands on her hips anyway. She raised an eyebrow at Mira but said nothing.

"Sorry to bother you in the middle of your work. I had no idea you were an illustrator." Tentatively she added, "Do you ever let people see your work? I would love to see it if you wouldn't mind."

Bibi's face softened ever so slightly. "I guess so. Come on in."

Mira followed her into a back bedroom that had been turned into a studio, along the way noticing once again the watercolor above the couch. She'd noticed before that it was similar to Bibi and Kailani, now she realized it was them, likely painted by Bibi herself.

Bibi's current work lay on a slanted drawing table next to a window. A picture was starting to emerge. Pale blue sky sat atop a quiet meadow, kissed with just a slight breeze that bent the wild grasses and flowers. The beginning shapes of a toddler sitting in the grass were appearing. He held a frog in his pudgy fingers, while his toes dangled in a penciled-in stream meandering lazily through the scene. What wasn't painted yet was lightly drawn with pencil, giving Mira a sense of the finished painting, compelling in its loving gentleness.

"That one is for a book cover. I'm doing the inside illustrations as well."

"It's charming," Mira said with genuine awe. "The soft tones are so relaxing and peaceful. It makes me want to read the story that goes with it."

Bibi beamed like Mira had never seen before. "I don't always do watercolors. Most of my illustrations I do on the computer. It's faster and I can change things easily." She walked over to the table, lovingly fingering her work in progress. "But, when a client is willing to pay for watercolors, I prefer them. They have a warmth and a life to them that I can't replicate as well digitally."

"I am so impressed," Mira said. She heard a clock chime in the other room, and it reminded her of the women waiting back in her flat and of the task she needed to accomplish. "Would it be okay if I came back again to look at more of your pictures?"

Bibi nodded but said nothing more.

"I don't have much time right now. I came over for two reasons. I almost forgot that I had bought two things for Kailani, but I'd only given her the whale. If it's okay with you, I'd like to give her this other present?"

Kailani's eyes sparkled, and she looked to her mother for approval. When Bibi nodded, Kailani reached for the gift. When she saw the stone bracelet, her mouth opened. She loved it immediately and slipped it onto her wrist. "Thank you, Mira!" She threw her arms around Mira.

Mira glanced at Bibi to see if she would object to her daughter's show of affection, but she smiled approvingly. When Kailani let go, Mira said, "I told you I came over for two reasons. The second was I'm hoping you will join me and my friends for a picnic in Regent's Park tomorrow. It's just a bunch of women who have become my friends. One is Cordelia who came over with me before. The others are from the States, and they're going home Sunday."

Kailani looked up eagerly at her mother. When she smiled her approval, Kailani squealed.

"I take it, that's a yes?"

"Yes."

"We'll bring the food. We could walk over from here around noon. Do you have a blanket or something we could sit on?"

Bibi simply nodded, but she was smiling.

. . .

Mira still hadn't been able to wipe the smile off her face when she opened the door to her flat. The expectant faces inside startled her. She'd forgotten she wouldn't be walking back into an empty flat like usual.

"Well? What happened?" several voices said at once.

"They're coming!" The group of women cheered. "And I just learned that Bibi is an illustrator. She showed me a watercolor she's working on. It's beautiful. She does it in a small studio in a back bedroom."

That revelation opened a flood of curious questions, most of which Mira couldn't answer. But that talk led to other topics and then still others. Before long, multiple conversations were happening all over the room.

It wasn't until Elijah called that they realized it was almost time to meet the rest of the family for dinner. They had chosen an Indian restaurant not far from the flat, the same one Mira had planned on going to weeks earlier.

"You are coming with us, Cordelia, aren't you?" Avelyn said.

"I'd love to. I think it's more like, just try and stop me."

"Good. Now, let's get busy." In a rush, the women hurried to clean up and get ready for dinner.

The pastries Mira had picked up were all gone, but the resulting crumbs had found their way onto the furniture and carpet. Cordelia pulled out a vacuum, and they all fought over who would use it. In the end, they took turns—mostly so they could take turns in the bathroom.

When it was Mira's turn to freshen up, she brushed her hair then pulled out the red scrunchie to secure it. Dylan came to the open bathroom door. "Hey, slowpoke, are you ready yet?" She said it with a grin, knowing Mira had barely entered the bathroom.

"No, I have a lengthy cleaning and makeup routine. You're all just going to have to wait." She tried to say it with a straight face, but it didn't work.

"Hey, I recognize that! Didn't you use that on the airplane?"

"The scrunchie? Yes. I was trying to keep from swatting you with my hair again, don't you remember?"

"Oh, yeah," Dylan said with a laugh. "I didn't appreciate it at the time, but I'm grateful now. I'm sure your guilt from hitting me is the only reason you consented to talk with me."

Mira nodded her head, laughing. "That must be it." She smiled at Dylan then reached up to remove the scrunchie from her hair. "You know, I don't have anything that matches this, but you do. Your red hair will always match a red scrunchie." She offered the scrunchie to Dylan.

"You already gave me things," Dylan protested.

"No, I gave you things to give your parents. I haven't given you anything that's for you. Take it. I mean, it is only a scrunchie."

Dylan surveyed Mira a moment then took the scrunchie from her outstretched hand. "I'm not sure my hair is long enough to warrant a scrunchie, but that's not the point, is it?" She slipped the scrunchie onto her wrist. "You know the blood ritual men do of cutting themselves and sharing their blood so they become blood brothers? Well, a red scrunchie might just be cheesy enough to substitute for us. What do you think, sis?"

"Cheesy sounds appropriate. Works for me too, sis," Mira said.

• • •

A slight breeze danced with their hair as they walked down the street together in the direction of the restaurant. Mira made a point to pull Olivia off to the side. Despite all the conversations that had gone on in her flat, Mira hadn't been able to have a private moment to talk to Olivia. It wasn't very private walking down the street, but it was the best opportunity she'd had so far.

"Olivia, how is your dad? After your bombshell last night?"

"He's getting used to the idea. When he thinks I'm not looking, he gets a child-like grin on his face. I think he's actually excited, but he's not ready to give in yet. A little pride is getting in the way."

Dylan chimed in from behind them. "A little pride is right. He's always bragging about his kids' college educations and what we're doing. He won't want to admit to his friends that you're quitting that great job of yours. However, I wouldn't worry too much. I think in his head he's just reframing what to brag about. Pretty soon, he's going to be telling all his friends about your awesome new bakery or café or whatever it turns out to be. He's not going to leave them alone either until they've gone there for themselves. It'll be easier on everyone if you just make t-shirts for the bakery for him to wear."

"You're right," Olivia said, laughing. "I can see him wearing them everywhere! He'd probably even wear them to church if Mom would let him." Olivia glanced at her mother a few feet in front of them to see if she'd overheard. She didn't appear to, being lost in conversation with Cordelia.

Olivia leaned over to Mira. "Now I just need to tell Dad we're going to Rome for about six months before we move and open up the bakery café."

Avelyn came to a screeching halt in front of them. "What?" She whipped around to face her daughter. "You're doing what?"

"Umm. Asher and I are going to Rome on our honeymoon and then stay. The tour guide we told you about, she owns a restaurant with her husband. They're going to teach us more about the business ... for about six months."

Avelyn threw her arms up in the air. "Wonderful! We'll just have to come visit! You can find us a place to stay. Then we can hire your tour guide and see Rome for ourselves!" She turned to Cordelia and started to excitedly chatter about the possibilities.

"Well, that went better than expected," Olivia said.

"She did seem fascinated when we told her about the things we saw in Rome," Dylan said.

"You're right. I had no idea ..." Olivia put her hands up and shrugged.

"Yeah. You just got lucky," Dylan said. "But ... make sure you find a separate place for them to stay if and when they come. Asher doesn't need his in-laws living with him within the first six months of being married."

"Good idea."

. . .

At the restaurant, Dylan, Olivia, Cordelia, and Mira sat around a table together, while the others grouped themselves around neighboring tables. When they were all settled and waiting for their food, Olivia got up to approach her dad. He was seated with her mom, so Olivia hoped the support would be there for this last tidbit she had to share. "Hey, Dad. There's something else I want to tell you."

"Oh?" Elijah tensed. "What is it?"

"Nothing to worry about. This is all good stuff." She took a deep breath. "After Asher and I get married, we're heading to Rome for our honeymoon. Our tour guide there ... well, we met her husband and her son. They have a restaurant. We're going to work there for six months. They're going to teach us about running a restaurant."

"You're going to spend six months in Rome? Even though you don't speak Italian? To do what? Learn about the restaurant business?"

"Yes, Dad." Olivia saw her mother put a calming hand on Elijah's arm.

"Okay," Elijah said slowly, pondering this announcement. "Then, you mean, you're training in Italy before opening up your place?"

"Yes, Dad."

His face broke into a huge grin. "That's amazing! I don't know anyone opening a restaurant that has trained internationally! That's fantastic. Do you know what my friends are going to say? They'll say you're the best! Wow."

Dylan leaned close to Mira and Cordelia. "He doesn't know *anyone* who has opened a restaurant and wouldn't have a clue where any of them have trained. You gotta love him."

Elijah was still excitedly asking Olivia questions when their food arrived. Only then did Olivia return to her seat.

"I'm shocked, just shocked," Olivia said to her tablemates. "You know Dad would support whatever I did, but that doesn't mean he'd be happy about it. I had no idea this would make everything better. I'm pretty sure all his reservations have now disappeared. He was even asking me more about Asher. He's never met him, but he's already decided that he's 'a fine young man,' to use his words."

Everyone congratulated her and began to talk excitedly among themselves about Olivia's future plans. "You know, you can always stop off in London on the way there or the way back. I've got some nice properties for rent ..." Cordelia said.

Olivia laughed. "We'll probably take you up on that offer."

The meal was flavorful and spicy, and the time together passed all too quickly. They were sampling a variety of desserts when Mira checked her phone. She had some new emails and one new text.

"Hey, you remember the interpreter in Paris I mentioned?" Mira said. She hadn't told them about Aissa's email, that was too personal, but she had told them how helpful Aissa had been. "I just got a text from her." She scanned the message before sharing it. It was short but wonderful.

"I don't believe it! She's getting on a train right now. She'll be here in about three hours!"

"That's great," Dylan said.

"No, wait a minute. This text was sent two hours ago. She'll be here in an hour!" Mira squealed. "Cordelia, is it okay if she shares the flat? One of us can sleep on the couch."

"Certainly, luv. That couch is actually a pull-out bed. It's got sheets and everything."

Mira squealed again. "Oh, I've got to call Warren and tell him. So much has happened. He's going to love it."

Mira's eagerness being obvious, they hurriedly left the restaurant and returned to Mira's flat where everyone grabbed the bags and jackets left there. They hustled out the door so Mira could get ready for her guest and call her husband. Cordelia was the only one who stayed back. She was busy opening closets and pulling out the extra pillows, bedding, and towels Mira was likely to need.

Mira had texted Aissa several times—making sure she had the correct address, asking if she needed anything, was she hungry, and so on—anything Mira could think to ask.

■　　■　　■

By the time Cordelia left and everything was ready for Aissa's arrival, Mira only had about fifteen minutes to talk to Warren.

"Warren, you're not going to believe it. Everyone is coming together to help Kailani, and Aissa is coming from Paris tonight! I don't even know how long she's going to stay, but she's coming!"

Warren shared in her enthusiasm, eagerly asking for more details. "I love hearing your voice sound like that, Mira. It has so much life in it again."

"I admit, it feels good. Hey, what happened with that proposal you were working on for your boss, hubs?"

They slipped into their comfortable daily conversation, sharing updates on the little and big happenings in their lives. All too soon there was a knock at Mira's door with a simultaneous text from Aissa saying, "I'm here."

Despite Mira's excitement to see Aissa, she was reluctant to hang up when they'd barely gotten started. "Love you, Warren."

"Love you too, babe."

Mira smiled to herself on the way to the door, remembering how at the beginning of this trip they'd been so worried about the cost of their phone calls. They'd long since thrown caution to the wind in that regard.

"Aissa!"

"Mira!"

Aissa kissed Mira on each cheek. Mira responded by pulling her into a strong embrace. Realizing what she'd done, Mira quickly let go. "I'm sorry about the hug." She grimaced but couldn't restrain the grin. "But I can't believe you came. I'm so happy you did!"

"How could I not? Your invitation was too tempting to pass up."

Aissa brought only a small backpack filled with her stuff. "I can only stay the weekend—tonight and tomorrow night. I have to be back at work Monday morning." She sounded apologetic.

"Hey, that's great! I'll take anything I can get." Mira was grinning from ear to ear. She couldn't believe her good fortune.

Before long they were sitting cross-legged on the pulled-out bed, sharing a bowl of popcorn between them. "I'm ashamed to admit how little I know about you, Aissa. Tell me about your family. Do you have any siblings? How are your parents?"

"My maman and papa are good people. They have a small farm and some animals. It keeps them busy," she said. "I grew up helping gather eggs from the chickens and milking cows in the mornings before school. It motivated me to study extra hard. I wanted to move to the city as soon as I could and have a job that didn't involve dirt or manure.

"It amazes me how much I miss all that farm work. I'm going back for a visit in a couple weeks. I'm actually looking forward to shoveling a bit of manure. Can you believe that?"

"I understand. I didn't grow up on a farm, but my parents always had a garden. One of my chores in the summertime was to weed it, and I hated it. But now that Warren and I have a small place, one of the first things I did was plant a vegetable garden."

"Do your parents still grow vegetables?"

"My dad does. My mom died in a car accident a couple years ago, only a year after Warren and I bought our place. It's cathartic for Dad to tend to his garden. In the wintertime, he plans the garden and starts seeds inside. The house is full of houseplants. We kid him that he's living in a jungle now. Personally, I'm terrible with houseplants, but my summer garden is a different story."

"Nothing like the taste of fresh-picked vegetables, is there?"

"No, nothing quite the same," Mira agreed. "You didn't say if you had siblings. Do you?"

"Yes. I have an older sister and a younger brother. My brother lives near my parents and works the farm for them—the part of the farm that's commercially successful. I think he'll eventually take it over and expand it. He's been buying up local farms as they become available. He'll never be rich, but he'll always be content.

"My sister is another story. She's happy but she's much more high-strung. Being with her makes you tired because she can't sit still." She shook her head, but she was smiling. "She's married and lives close by Maman and Papa too. She has two adorable children, and my parents love being grandparents. They were hoping my boyfriend and I would get married and have a family." Aissa shrugged. "Sometimes I wonder if I wanted that more for them than myself. That's probably why I stuck with him as long as I did."

"Did they pressure you for children?"

"No. They would mention it from time to time, but it was really me. I was the child that moved away. I convinced myself that I needed to make up for that somehow. But as I've been talking to my parents this past week, I realize they're proud of me. They don't wish I'd stayed out in the countryside with them at all. I don't understand why we so often make life harder on ourselves than it actually is. I've wasted so much energy trying to please them somehow that I missed the fact that they're already pleased." She shook her head.

"Well, I guess at least you *did* figure it out, thankfully while you're still young. Did you meet with the therapist today?"

"Yes, I like her. She said she can tell I'm in a better place than I was a couple weeks ago from what I described, but I already knew that. I mean,

I'm not trying to commit suicide anymore. But it's more than that. I have hope."

"You've been finding peace, making peace with your life."

"Yes, I think that's it."

There was so much more to talk about. Aissa asked Mira more about herself, and Mira eagerly shared her own story. It was two in the morning before their yawns started to get the best of them, having swapped stories back and forth non-stop until then. They'd eaten through all the snacks and all the chocolate in the place in the process.

"We'll have to go out for breakfast. Oh! Plus, I almost forgot, we've got to grab enough food for everyone at our picnic."

"Oh? What picnic?"

Mira laughed. "We've talked all this time, and I never even told you there are already plans for tomorrow. I'm sorry. Were you hoping to go sightseeing?"

"Not really. I've been to London before, and I can come again. So, tell me about the picnic."

"Did I mention the girl across the street I've been worried about? Kailani?"

"You did."

"Well, I think I also mentioned my friends too, my other adopted sisters. Anyway, we're getting together tomorrow with Kailani and her mum, Bibi. We want to see if we can figure out what's going on and what we can do to help."

Despite their yawns, Mira laid out what they knew about Bibi.

"Okay. I'd like to help too. We'll see what happens tomorrow."

Mira nodded and started to head off to bed when she thought of one more thing. "Aissa, I appreciate that you can speak English. Not only did you help me in Paris, but we can connect because you took the time to learn my language. When I get back home, I want to start learning French."

Aissa smiled. "I think you would like French. And I would like that very much too."

CHAPTER 32

It was an effort to drag herself out of bed in the morning. When Mira saw the clock, she panicked. It was 10:30, and she needed to gather a whole bunch of picnic foods in an hour. Cordelia was going to bring pies or pasties, but Mira had insisted on bringing the rest, knowing that Avelyn's family was getting ready to fly home the next day.

She quickly called *The Red Fox.* They would prepare potato salad and fruit salad that she could pick up on her way back from the supermarket. Aissa sat up groggily during her phone call, so Mira frantically explained her plans before heading into the bathroom for a quick shower.

When she came out, hair still wet, she was met with a smiling Aissa. "What's up?"

"It's all done. You left Cordelia's phone number out, so I called her and got directions to the supermarket and the pub. I've got drinks, snacks, biscuits, paper plates, utensils, napkins, and the salads from the pub owner himself, Bill. You'll have to tell me about him. He seemed to take a personal interest in making sure they were just what we wanted."

"Yes, he's an old friend of Cordelia's. He helped her out of a jam a few years back and has been protective of her ever since. I've also learned that any friend of Cordelia's is immediately a friend of his."

Mira followed Aissa into the kitchen where she saw the enormity of what Aissa had bought. "Wow! This is fantastic. Let me at least pay for it."

"I think not," Aissa said.

"Well, at least let me pay half," Mira responded.

Aissa narrowed her eyes at Mira. "Now is that any way to talk to family? It's paid for. All right?"

Mira threw her hands up. "Okay. But dinner tonight is on me."

"Fine," Aissa said in a mock tone of exasperation. They looked at each other and burst into laughter.

They spent what little time they had left before noon getting ready. Aissa had barely emerged from the shower when Cordelia showed up, who was shortly followed by Avelyn and her daughters. After everyone had been introduced to Aissa, they packed the food into two coolers Cordelia had brought and headed out the door, Dylan and Olivia carrying one cooler and Aissa and Zita handling the other.

Kailani was waiting on the front steps. As soon as she saw Mira emerge from her front door, she ran back inside her own, loudly calling, "Mum, they're coming!"

By the time she came back out, dragging her mother by the hand behind her, Mira's group had gathered at the bottom of the stairs. Avelyn had warned them not to overwhelm Bibi, but there wasn't any way around the size of their group.

Mira took a step up toward Bibi. "Here, let me quickly introduce you to everyone." Bibi remembered Cordelia and then nodded politely at each new person who was introduced. Last came Aissa.

"This is my new friend from France. Her name is Aissa. She was my interpreter when I was in Paris."

Bibi raised her eyebrows, the unspoken question of why and how an interpreter had suddenly become a close friend written on her brow.

Mira met her gaze and shrugged. "She's become like a sister to me."

Bibi's expression still registered confusion, but she moved down the steps to join the group regardless of her feelings. Kailani bounded in her wake.

When their lunch was spread out on the blanket Bibi brought along, there was little room left for any people. Cordelia winked and produced a spare blanket, "I brought it along, just in case," she said.

Sprawled out on the two blankets, everyone dove into the food. Aissa and Mira were hungry, not having had time for breakfast. Tiana breathed a sigh of relief at the sight of the food. "I'm *so* hungry all the time," she said, but couldn't be persuaded to touch the potato salad. "I'm sure it's good, but I craved potato salad at the beginning of my pregnancy, and now the thought of it is just disgusting. Sorry."

"No need to apologize, luv," Cordelia said. "We're all friends here."

Zita subtly moved the potato salad as far away from Tiana as possible. Tiana mouthed a quick, "Thank you," to her.

Kailani had a little of everything but not a lot of anything. She was more interested in chasing butterflies or running over to the water to watch the ducks. Everyone kept a careful eye on her as if she had nine mothers instead of one.

When the eating slowed down, Cordelia and Mira packed the food back into the coolers. They exchanged glances, wondering who should start and how. Avelyn spoke before they had a chance to wonder further.

"Kailani is so precious. You've done such a good job as her mother."

Bibi blushed. "Thank you."

"I'm not quite a grandma yet," she said, looking over at Tiana's growling belly, "but I will be lucky if my grandchild is half as sweet as Kailani."

For some reason, Bibi stiffened at the comment and didn't respond.

"Are you okay, dear?" Avelyn asked. "Is something wrong?"

"No," she answered brusquely. "We're fine." Whatever door had been opening had just slammed closed.

Avelyn, sensing that she must have said something wrong, got up. "I'm going to check out the ducks with Kailani. I'll bet she can tell me which one is her favorite. And then we might have to get ice cream from the kiosk." They watched Avelyn join Kailani at the water's edge, stooping down to talk with her on her level. Zita, Olivia, and Aissa purposely got up to join them, leaving a much smaller group with Bibi. Tiana rolled over on the blanket to take a nap.

"Do you ever bring your paints here and paint the ducks and the scenery?" Mira asked, trying to steer the conversation to what she hoped was safer ground.

Bibi relaxed and began to talk about her work while Dylan and Cordelia asked her one question after another. Eventually, the conversation turned to her studio space in her flat. She'd had the equipment since before her marriage, but it had been boxed up for several years.

"I had a regular office job for a while, and besides, there wasn't room to set anything up in our flat. But after my husband passed, I moved

Kailani in with me and turned her room into a studio. I wanted to be home with her when she wasn't in school. After losing Tom, I hated having her out of my sight."

"How did he die?" Dylan said.

"He had juvenile diabetes that was never controlled well when he was younger. That caused all kinds of problems—with his heart, his kidneys, you name it. Even though he was controlling it better, too much damage had been done. His body just gave out." She didn't cry, but the pain was still raw.

"I'm so sorry. How long ago did he pass away?" Mira asked gently.

"It's been over a year now. You'd think I'd be over it by now, but I'm not. Kailani seems to have bounced back. It's helped having me near her. She feels more secure that way."

"Do *you* feel secure?" Cordelia asked.

Bibi turned to Cordelia for a second before responding. "It doesn't matter if I feel secure. Kailani's the only thing that matters right now."

"Excuse me if I'm being a bother, but since I manage properties, I ... inadvertently learned that the rents in your building are often overdue. With your husband passing ... well, do you need any help? I have lots of ways to help at my disposal."

Bibi didn't bristle like Mira thought she might, but she didn't respond either. She merely gazed off into the distance. Finally, she turned back to Cordelia. "No. My in-laws kindly take care of that."

"But ...," Cordelia started to say.

"I'm fine," Bibi said, more forcefully this time.

Something clicked in Mira's mind, and she spoke before thinking. "Is your father-in-law Thomas Davies? The same name as your husband?"

"Yes, why? How did you know that?" Bibi asked, suddenly wary.

Things were not going well, but Mira understood Bibi's reaction. She probably would have reacted the same way if the tables were turned. But how could she recover from her mistake? They had been digging into Bibi's private affairs, regardless of their motive. "I'm sorry. I didn't ... I just ..." She was flustered, fearing she was alienating the very woman she wanted to help. How had it all gone so wrong?

"Ice cream, anyone?" Avelyn said as she, Kailani, and the others approached, their arms laden with enough ice cream for twice their numbers. It broke the tension, but the underlying problem remained.

Mira watched Bibi out of the corner of her eye while she ate her ice cream. Kailani was talking excitedly about the ducks in between taking licks of her ice cream. Bibi was eating her ice cream, but she was tense in her movements.

When Kailani finished, she ran off to visit the ducks again. Mira said, "I'm sorry, Bibi. I only wanted to help."

Bibi turned on her. Her tone was low and seething, as she said, "I'm not sure what you think you're helping with, but leave me alone."

Mira pulled away, feeling she deserved Bibi's ire, but a tear coursed down her cheek all the same. She didn't know how Cordelia or anyone else felt because she couldn't bring herself to look at them.

The coughing began suddenly. Kailani was immediately by her mother's side. In between coughs, Bibi said, "The ice cream ... I shouldn't have."

"Kailani, is your mother allergic to milk?" Mira said, now anxious.

"No, but it can make her coughing worse if she's upset."

"Well, she's definitely upset," Mira said under her breath.

"What do you need? What can we do to help?" Cordelia said.

"Home. Just get me home."

"Take her," Zita said. "We'll gather everything up and be right behind you."

With Cordelia on one side and Mira on the other, they followed a concerned Kailani back toward her flat. The others soon caught up with them.

But with each step, Bibi's coughing intensified. Leaving the park and arriving back at a main street, Cordelia suddenly stopped and faced Bibi. "You are not going to be okay back at your home unless you have some medicine there. Do you?"

Bibi didn't answer, just continued to cough. But Kailani tugged on Cordelia's sleeve. "Her medicine is all gone. She didn't get any more because she doesn't want people to know she's sick."

"We only want to help," Mira said, pleading.

Aissa came up beside Bibi as she continued to cough. "You don't know me, and I don't know you. But I do know Mira. She literally saved my life. She is genuine. She means no harm, I assure you. If she says she wants to help, that's exactly what she wants to do."

Bibi considered Aissa then relaxed slightly just as another paroxysm of coughing began.

"We're taking you to A&E. One's close if we turn the other direction. Can you make it or should I call an ambulance?" Cordelia said.

Surprisingly, Bibi didn't fight her. She simply turned obediently and walked the other direction, clearly giving her answer.

A&E, it turns out, stood for the accident and emergency wing. Fortunately for everyone, they got there quickly. The women took turns entertaining Kailani while awaiting news on Bibi.

Finally, they were allowed in to see her. Cordelia and Mira took Kailani back to see her mum. Bibi's face was pale, her hair soaked with sweat. Every time she took a breath it was visible in the labored and almost exaggerated rise of her chest. She didn't look good.

Kailani jumped up on her mother's bed and gave her a big hug. "I love you, Mum."

"I love you too." She brushed the hair out of Kailani's eyes so she could look directly at her. "Could you do me a favor, lamb? Can you let me talk with these two alone for a minute?" Kailani glanced at the women in the room, curious, but scampered out as her mother had requested. Mira watched Kailani until she safely rejoined the others.

Nervously, she turned back to Bibi, awaiting her wrath … but it didn't come. Bibi appeared more scared than angry. "I need you to help me," Bibi whispered, staring at the doorway, her gaze wide and frantic. "They want to keep me in hospital for a couple days. You've got to get me out of here." The fierceness in her eyes was startling.

"What's wrong? We'll help you, but we can't if we don't understand what's going on?" Mira said.

Bibi eyed the open doorway again, ensuring they were alone. Then she stared at the two of them, seemingly making a decision. "Okay," she finally said. "I have asthma. I had it as a child, and with treatment, it went away. But the stress of my husband's death brought it back. I went to the doctor and got an inhaler to use when I had an attack. But, as Kailani said, that has been used up."

"Okay … I don't understand why—"

Bibi stopped her with a wave of her hand. "That's not the problem. It's Kailani. They're going to try to take her from me."

"Who? Kailani's fine," Mira said.

"No! You don't understand! Listen to me. It's my in-laws. They're horrible people. They hated me from the moment Tom proposed. And they are terrible grandparents. They didn't even meet Kailani until she was six months old even though they live ten minutes away. They couldn't be bothered. But every time they did come around, they were controlling of everything. Nothing anyone did was ever enough. My cooking tasted terrible. My home looked messy. They had my husband jumping up and catering to them like a servant. It was bloody awful.

"But when Tom died, they seemed genuinely sad. They told me they wanted to help. So, they had the flat transferred into their name. It's a nice place, and it was taking both our salaries to pay for it. There was no way I could pay for it on my own. I considered moving, but his parents said they hated to see us disrupt our lives. They offered to pay our rent for as long as we wanted and not to worry." She shook her head. "I should have seen there was something dodgy about it, but I was so gutted by my grief that I believed them."

"I'm guessing they weren't actually that nice," Cordelia said, with only slightly disguised contempt in her voice.

"No, they weren't. Pretty quickly it went to pot. They paid the rent for the first couple months without any problem, but then they would 'forget.' Only I wouldn't find out about it until there were late fees to pay. At first, they apologized and paid for it, but I knew that couldn't last. So, I started building up my savings so we could move to a cheaper place.

"But just when I think I've built enough reserves, they skip a month or two on the rent. I have to pay up out of my savings and, of course, cover the late fees. I live in constant fear of being evicted. And I don't know what to do." Bibi was on the verge of dissolving into tears and broke out in a new round of coughs.

When the coughing subsided, Mira said, "That's awful. How does the asthma tie in with this?"

"When my asthma attacks came back after Tom's death, they watched Kailani while I went to the doctor. They seemed helpful and kind at the time, but then they started making comments like, 'We're not sure if you can handle raising a child with your health condition.' They're going to try to take Kailani from me, I know it. They don't care about her. They don't love her. They probably want to have her as a servant around the house or take her just to spite me. I told you they hate me. They'd like nothing more than to make my life miserable.

"Do you know they even blame me for Tom's death? As if they cared! They say I didn't take care of his diabetes. They're the ones who didn't help him when he was young. They're the ones who did this!" Her voice had gotten steadily angrier and angrier. It brought on another round of coughs.

"But they wouldn't be able to take her away just because you have asthma," Mira said.

"They're subtle and crafty. It would start with keeping Kailani overnight while I'm in the hospital. Then they'd find excuses not to bring her back. They'd bring in experts and psychologists to say whatever they needed them to say—that I'm not a fit mother, that I can't provide for her or take care of her. They would do it. All they're looking for is an opening."

"I'm guessing they have money on their side?" Cordelia said. Bibi nodded as she coughed. "Well, then I guess we'll just have to outsmart them, won't we?"

Mira smiled for the first time; Cordelia surely knew people who could help. Then she said to Bibi, "Why don't you stay in the hospital like the doctors want. Get better. Let them help you. I'll keep Kailani with me. We won't tell anyone. Your in-laws don't even need to know."

Bibi closed her eyes, her whole face relaxing. "Thank you." She tensed up again and added, "But you can't go to the flat to get any of her things. I'm worried my in-laws have got the owner of the building and maybe some of the other tenants watching me. I don't trust them."

"Okay. I won't go back to your place. We can pick up some things from the store on our way home, and we'll take a taxi back so we can hop inside my flat before we're seen. Does that sound okay?"

Bibi nodded. "Yes, thank you."

"Will they think it's strange that you aren't there, that no one's at your flat?"

"I've been talking about taking Kailani on a short trip somewhere, so it should be fine. Kailani's friends at school kept talking about going on holiday, so we've been trying to come up with something we could afford." She seemed apologetic. "I'm not sure we would have been able to afford anything, but I kept hoping something would work out for Kailani's sake. I think I knew it was a lie from the start, though." She hung her head, but at least her coughing seemed to be letting up.

"Well, it's good your neighbors won't be too concerned. I'll make sure they don't see Kailani without you. We'll figure out some way to help you, I promise." Mira wasn't sure why she added those last two words. She didn't want to get Bibi's hopes up if she couldn't deliver. But she felt a growing sense inside her that they could help, that they would help. Somehow this was possible. They were going to fix this.

While Kailani spent a few minutes alone with her mum, Cordelia and Mira updated the others and held a whispered conference as to how to proceed. They concluded that divide and conquer would be the best approach. Avelyn would take Kailani shopping for clothes and Tiana and Zita offered to go with them. Mira and Aissa would go back to the flat to get things set up for Kailani, stopping at the supermarket on the way to pick up toiletries, food, and anything else they could think of. Cordelia had a cot Kailani could use, but it was at one of her other properties. Olivia and Dylan offered to help take the coolers they still had with them back to Cordelia's car and then help her gather the cot and linens that might be needed. Everyone would end up back at Mira's flat as soon as they accomplished their various responsibilities.

Once it was decided, Cordelia left with her group while Mira went back to check on Bibi. Kailani was sitting on her mother's bed, telling her stories. Nurses bustled in and out, getting ready to move Bibi to a hospital room, making it somewhat chaotic. But in the midst of it, Bibi looked up at Mira and smiled.

"Come in."

"Hi. We've got things all worked out. Everyone is pitching in." She turned to Kailani. "Would you like to go shopping for some new clothes with Avelyn? She's the one who was watching the ducks with you."

Kailani face lit up. She turned to see if her mother approved. "Yes, you may go," Bibi said.

"And then, Kailani, your mum said you can spend the night at my flat while she's here getting better. Is that okay with you?"

Her eyes got big. "Mum? Can I really?"

Bibi brushed aside Kailani's hair with her hand. "Yes, lamb. You'll be safe there."

Kailani's excitement was contagious. They all beamed at each other. But as they left the room, Kailani rushed back. "Mum? Will *you* be safe?"

Bibi studied Mira before she answered. "Yes, my lamb, I believe I will be."

CHAPTER 33

The flat was ready for Kailani long before she arrived. Cordelia had not only picked up a cot with bedding, but she, Olivia, and Dylan had also stopped at a toy store. Kailani's bed was now adorned with stuffed animals; a doll; a sparkly, sequin pillow; and a soft, fuzzy blanket. Nearby, a stack of books, craft kits, and a jewelry making kit threatened to topple over. They all knew they were spoiling her, but Cordelia said what everyone was thinking, "It's about time."

While they waited for the others, the women chatted and got to know each other better. Aissa hadn't had much of a chance to do that yet.

But something else was on Mira's mind. She excused herself, going to the bedroom and picking up her journal. She couldn't understand Kailani's grandparents. How could someone not love or care for a child, especially one's own grandchild?

Dear Mom,

I miss you. I miss talking to you and being with you. But mostly I miss what is yet to be. I miss the thought of you being a grandma, a grandma to my children—assuming we ever have any. I know you would have loved each one before you even laid eyes on them. You would have gathered that newborn son of mine into your arms, cradled him, sung to him, read stories to him as he grew.

You would have taken my daughter onto your lap while you brushed her hair and told her stories about when I was her age. You would have laughed with her and snuggled her close.

How can there be grandparents in the world who don't do that? I don't understand. Avelyn will be such a loving grandmother to Caleb and Tiana's baby. She couldn't be any other way! And you, if given the chance, would have been just like her.

Oh, Mom, I don't understand. It rips my heart in two.

The tears flowed freely. She didn't even wipe them away. She could hear the laughter coming from the other room, but she had no desire to join them. She prayed in earnest. "Please Lord, help us fix this. Help us give them a life."

Gradually her tears dried and she felt light. With a peace she couldn't explain, she knew they would find a way. Even in the short time she had left in England, it would be enough.

A text from Zita interrupted her thoughts. "We're in a taxi heading back to your place. ETA five minutes. Can you be ready to open the door? Then Kailani can dash right on in."

Mira jumped up and made a beeline for the front door. "They'll be here soon," she told the others by way of explanation. Everyone huddled around the front window, watching and waiting.

"There's the taxi," Aissa said. Mira flung open the front door, and soon everyone was inside, talking over each other. Kailani stood in the center of them, wearing a smile of supernal bliss.

When they settled down enough to drop into chairs and onto the floor, Cordelia took Kailani back to show her the bed they'd made up, along with everything else they'd purchased. A few minutes later, Kailani emerged carrying a jewelry kit in one hand and a craft kit in the other. Her eyes were sparkling. "Can we do these?" she asked Mira.

"You bet we can. How about we start tonight after dinner?"

"Yes!" Kailani pumped her fist.

"It looks like you guys had fun shopping. So did we," Tiana said. "I know I just want a healthy baby, and I've said I don't care if it's a girl or a boy, but they make the *cutest* clothes for little girls. I hope the stuff for little boys is half as cute."

"It isn't," Dylan said. Then she burst out laughing. "Just kidding. My friends with little boys say it's getting better all the time. And thankfully there are a lot of cute clothes that are nice and unisex."

Tiana drew a sigh of relief. "Well, Kailani, do you want to show them your clothes?"

Zita retrieved several bags from beside the front door. "Here you go. Do you want to put them on and show everyone?" Kailani eagerly nodded. Zita helped her carry them into the next room.

"You let us know when you're ready, okay?" Dylan said.

While they waited to see the first outfit, Avelyn said, "We figured if she's not going back into her flat for a day or so, she'd need everything. So, we bought underwear, socks, pants, shirts, even a pair of pajamas. But she loved the dresses. We couldn't decide on our favorite, so we bought all three, and of course, a pair of darling shoes to go with them."

"No wonder it took you so long," Mira said. Kailani now had way more clothes than she would need for a couple days, but that wasn't the point, and they all knew it.

When Kailani was ready, Dylan made a drum roll sound. "Presenting, the glorious, stupendous, fantastic, brilliant Kailani!" Everyone cheered.

Kailani entered the room shyly at first, but the welcoming smiles boosted her confidence. By the time she modeled the last outfit, she was striding into the room as if she were on a catwalk. Avelyn had even bought her a little purse that she modeled with it.

All heads swiveled toward the door at the sound of a sharp rap. Cordelia hopped up. "Ah, that would be Bill. I ordered dinner for us." Uncertain, Kailani nestled against Mira while Cordelia opened the door.

Bill stood at the door with two of his employees. They had brought enough food for an army. "Wow, there's so much. We'll have to have Elijah and the others join us," Avelyn said.

"Even Jeremy would find enough to eat with all this," Olivia said.

When they'd transferred the food to the kitchen counters, Bill sent his workers back off to the pub. Then he turned around to face the group of women. His eyes drifted to Kailani, still glued to Mira's side.

"Hello, sweet pea," he said in his softest voice. He sat down on the floor right where he was. "You stay right there with Mira. I don't want to scare you because I know you don't know me."

He grew quiet and couldn't speak for a moment. Tears welled in the corners of his eyes. Finally, he choked out, "Sweet pea, you and your mum deserve to have a happy life. You deserve a happy life. I'm sorry your dad isn't here anymore, but that doesn't mean a whole lot of other people can't love you just as much." He reached into his pocket for an envelope. "We took up a collection—me and my staff and the regular customers that came in tonight. We figured you could use this." He handed the envelope to Cordelia to pass along. It was bursting with bills.

Kailani's eyes grew big when she peeked inside. "I've never seen this much money in my life!"

Bill chuckled. "Well, it's not as much as it might seem, but I'm pretty sure there will be more coming." He wiped his eyes. "You take care now, sweet pea. Take care."

Cordelia walked Bill to the door, but Mira called out after him. "You're a good man, Bill." He turned to smile in her direction, then once again looked at Kailani and gave her a wink.

At Cordelia's urging, and with Kailani's approval, Avelyn called her husband and invited the men in the family to join them for dinner. The food was still warm by the time they arrived by taxi.

"We figured we should go ahead and eat. That way you can have what's left," Avelyn said, specifically directing her comments to Jeremy. Without hesitation, he made straight for the food laid out on the counter.

Caleb was more concerned about his wife than he was about the food. "How are you doing, honey? It's been a long day for you."

Tiana let herself be wrapped in his arms. "I am exhausted … and exhilarated. Do you see that little girl? She is the sweetest thing. We got a chance to make her life just a little bit better. I'd do it again in a heartbeat." He held her a little bit closer. "Now, go eat. I'm fine."

While the men ate—standing or sitting anywhere they could find, Mira cleared off a small space on the coffee table. Then Zita said, "I've got this," and tenderly began to help Kailani make a small bracelet from her kit.

"Look, Mira! Look what we made!" Kailani showed off her shiny new bracelet.

Zita slowly got up from where she'd been working by Kailani's side. "I know we have to go, but I don't want to." She gently touched the top of Kailani's head. "Making that bracelet with you was my favorite thing I've done on this entire trip. I will never forget you."

Kailani wrapped her arms around Zita's legs. When she let go, both of them were crying. "Here, I want you to have the bracelet. It's so pretty on you," Kailani said.

Zita wiped away her tears then slipped the colorful bracelet onto her wrist. It fit perfectly. "Thank you, Kailani. Is it okay if I write to you?"

Kailani threw her arms around Zita again in response. This time there wasn't a dry eye in the room.

A sinking feeling hit Mira's stomach. It was time to bid them goodbye. How could she let them go? Dylan, Olivia, Avelyn, and all the others had come to mean so much to her. She reminded herself, *Okay, Illinois and Ohio are close. We will see each other again.* Dylan was another matter, living in California, but she'd already assured Mira she wouldn't let the distance come between them. They'd figure something out. Mira told herself, *This isn't goodbye for good, only farewell for now. It's going to be okay.*

Hugs, farewells, tears, laughter, well-wishes, more hugs, more tears until they couldn't put it off any longer. "Mira, we will see you again," Elijah declared. "And you must introduce us to Warren. He's a very lucky man."

"I love you! I've written about all of you in my journal. Originally, it was so I could visit you again in those pages. But I know that's not enough. I will see you all again." She turned to Cordelia and Aissa. "I know I'm not saying goodbye to you yet, but I'll find a way to see you again too." And bending down to Kailani, she added, "And of course, you too, little pumpkin." She surveyed the room around her. "I ... I ..." Tears flowed in torrents down her cheeks. "I love you all."

.   .   .

Mira watched from the front window as the taxis pulled away, taking her family away. She picked up her phone and texted Warren. "So much has happened today. We're figuring out how to help Bibi and Kailani. Kailani is spending the night here while her mom's being treated for asthma in the hospital. But it's way more complicated than that. I'll have to talk to you tomorrow and explain everything. I need to go see to Kailani. I don't think I could talk now anyway. Dylan's whole family just left. They're flying home tomorrow. I can't speak. I'm just gutted. That British term is so fitting. I love you!"

Cordelia stayed and took turns with Aissa and Mira making more jewelry with Kailani. She was such a bright child, and so eager and full of life. They laughed and smiled all evening. It was almost enough to make Mira forget the hole in her heart left by Dylan and the others.

They bid Cordelia farewell, then Aissa offered to empty the dishwasher while Mira put Kailani to bed. Kailani took Mira's hand, pulling her into the bedroom behind her. "Can you help me with my prayers?"

"Sure. You start and let me know if you need help."

Kailani knelt beside her cot and folded her arms. "Dear Heavenly Father, It's me. I'm praying from my friend Mira's flat tonight, but it's still me. My mum's in hospital with her asthma. Make her better real quick, okay? I'll keep trying to take care of her, but I don't think I have to do it by myself anymore.

"Thank you for my new friends, for Mira and Avelyn and Cordelia and ... Issa and ... Tina and Zita and ... Dylan ... and Livia ... and Bill. Thank you for my new clothes and my new toys and my new blanket and my new fancy pillow. Please help my mum be happy. I'm already happy. That's it. In Jesus' name. Amen."

She hopped quickly onto the cot and in between the sheets. As Mira started to close the bedroom door, Kailani said, "I love you, Mira. Are you like my second mum?"

"No, pumpkin. I'm like your big sister."

CHAPTER 34

Aissa and Mira had once again talked well into the night. Not surprisingly, a lot of their talk centered on helping others rather than their own background, like it had the night before. Kailani and Bibi took up much of that talk, but they also talked about their "Papa" in Paris and his impact on their lives. A shared anxiety about helping Bibi out of her situation still existed, but they were hopeful for a bright future for her and her daughter.

Kailani woke Mira in the morning. She was standing beside the bed when Mira opened her eyes. Mira suspected a small poke had awoken her, but that was okay. "Good morning, Kailani. Did you sleep okay?"

"Yes, I did. Did you sleep okay?"

Mira chuckled. "I did. Are you hungry?"

Kailani nodded. "After breakfast, can we visit my mum?"

"You bet. I think that's exactly what we should do."

While Mira set out milk and cereal, her phone rang. It was Cordelia. "What are your plans for the day?"

"Well, Miss Kailani and I are eating breakfast, although it looks like she just woke up Aissa." She gave Kailani an eye roll. She responded with a shrug and a smile. "I believe after that, we're going to head straight to the hospital, likely in a taxi cab."

"Don't bother with the taxi. I'll swing by and get you. I have some things I need to work on this afternoon, but I was hoping we could see Bibi before then."

. . .

Bibi was happy to see them, especially Kailani who rushed in to give her mum a big hug. Bibi was breathing much better, and they heard no hint of a cough. "Did you have a good night, lamb?"

"I did, mum. I made you this." Kailani produced one of the necklaces she'd made the night before.

"Oh, it's brilliant! I love it!" She looked up at Mira. "How was she? Was she a bother at all?"

"No. She was an absolute angel. But her first thought this morning was you. For that matter, her last thoughts last night were about you—in her prayers."

She smiled, gazing at her daughter. "That's my Kailani."

"How are you doing? You look so much better," Aissa said.

"I am, thank you. It took a bit to get my coughing under control, but we did. And I had a very restful sleep."

"I thought asthma meant you had trouble breathing, like you would be gasping for breath," Cordelia said.

"That's what a lot of people think. Mine shows up as a cough. I don't think Tom's parents believe I have asthma because of that. They told me so much even as they hinted I wasn't well enough to care for Kailani. I imagine they were implying mental illness. But I guess, honestly, I don't care what they think."

"Bravo!" Cordelia said. "Kailani has something else to give you. My friend Bill brought it over for you and Kailani last night." Kailani pulled the envelope out of the purse Avelyn had bought her and handed it to her mother.

Bibi opened her mouth then covered it with her hand while shaking her head. "Why? This is so much money. Why?"

"Because you need it right now. That's what good people do. They help when it's needed. Bibi, do you have family of your own? Do you have somewhere else you can go? I think you have to get out of that flat."

"I do … I mean, I agree I need to get out of the flat. My family … I haven't seen any of them in years."

"Can I ask why?" Mira timidly said.

"Well, I didn't tell you that Tom and I got married because I fell pregnant. That's part of why his parents hated me, but clearly, it's not all of it. My parents weren't much better. They felt Tom was wrong for me, that he was a terrible person. They told me if I married him, they didn't want to see me ever again.

"I think they were bluffing initially, expecting I would leave him simply because of their threat. But I loved him, and they had him all wrong. When I chose him over them, they were gobsmacked, and not in a good way. They didn't know what else to do other than follow through on their threat. So, they haven't spoken to me since. I tried to call and tell them when their granddaughter was born, but they hung up on me before I had the chance." She said it matter-of-factly.

"I don't even ... I ...," Mira stammered.

"What was your husband like, Bibi?" Aissa said.

"Oh, he was gentle. Sometimes children grow up to be like their parents, but Tom was just the opposite. He didn't want to be anything like them. That's what first attracted me to him. He wasn't perfect. He didn't know how to stand up for himself, especially around his parents, but he was trying. And he was a great father, wasn't he, Kailani?" Her daughter nodded.

"I wish my parents had gotten to know him. Me being pregnant wasn't what they expected. I wasn't living at home at the time, so they'd only met Tom a couple times. They had heard of his parents. They assumed ... well, you can imagine."

"I'm so sorry," Cordelia said. "Do you think they'd let you back into their lives?"

Bibi shook her head. "That bridge was burnt down to the ground. It will take a long time to rebuild it. I'm afraid if I reached out now, they'd just say, 'We told you so,' even though Tom was a good husband. They'll blame me for marrying into his family. In a way, they would be right."

"Oh, don't think that way," Aissa said. "It's not your fault Tom's parents are horrible people. Is there anyone else you can turn to?"

"I have a sister, though she went along with my parents. She did send a baby gift, but we haven't spoken in all this time."

Mira, Aissa, and Cordelia exchanged glances. "Can we reach out to her? To see if she might want to see you or help?" Mira ventured.

Bibi studied her daughter. "I guess that would be okay. I need to do something. Her name is Paloma. I follow her on social media, so I'm pretty sure she hasn't moved, and thankfully, she doesn't live with Mum and Dad."

"Do you have a phone number for her?" Cordelia asked.

"Yes. In my phone. Somehow, I've always held out hope that one day … well, maybe this is one day."

They left Kailani with her mum while they went out into the hallway to confer and make plans. "Are you sure this is okay, Aissa? I imagine you weren't planning on coming to London to play social worker," Mira said.

Aissa frowned at her. "After all that talk last night? You think I'd want to do anything other than this?"

"Okay, you're right. I just … I was wrong, okay?"

Aissa nudged her. "Okay. Now can we get back to solving this problem?"

"Yes, let's. So, Paloma? Any ideas?" Cordelia said.

"Well, if we call, she's not likely to answer. She won't recognize any of our numbers. And if we called from Bibi's phone … Well, she might be even less likely to answer," Mira said. "However, she doesn't live too far away, and it is a Sunday. We might be able to find her at home. So, I say we try to visit in person. Maybe we can appeal to her that way."

"That's a good idea, but we'll need to split up. We have Kailani to think about. It would be a gamble to take her with us. It might turn the tide in Bibi's favor, but if not … Kailani doesn't need to see another family member rejecting her," Aissa said.

"You're right. I … hmm. You know, I just thought of something. I need to run a side errand," Mira said. "Do you think you and Kailani can hang out together, Aissa?"

"Sure! She has several crafts we haven't tried yet, and I'm guessing she'll be up for more jewelry making. Why don't we ask Kailani if it's okay with her?"

Reentering the room, it was clear Kailani was enjoying being with her mother, but Bibi had the wan look of someone completely worn out, even though it was still morning. "Kailani, why don't we let your mum rest. We can come back later today," Cordelia said.

Kailani bid a reluctant goodbye to her mum, who tried to hide her apprehension. Despite her fatigue, it was obvious the separation from her daughter tore at her heart. "I love you, Kailani. Be good, lamb."

"I will."

Walking back to Cordelia's car, Aissa held Kailani's hand, swinging it back and forth. "Now, *ma petite princesse*, my little princess, would you like to do some crafts with me while Mira and Cordelia run errands?"

"Yes! That's brilliant!"

Aissa grinned. "Now *that's* exactly what I want to do with my time in London," she said, looking directly at Mira. Mira threw her hands up in mock surrender.

.   .   .

Once they made sure Aissa and Kailani had all they might need for lunch, snacks, craft supplies, and the like, Mira and Cordelia took off for Paloma's. Bibi had been able to produce an address from the contacts on her phone. They hoped she was right that Bibi's sister hadn't moved.

When they knocked on the door, a middle-aged man in shorts and a wifebeater t-shirt answered. "Uhh?" is all he said.

"We were looking for Paloma. Is she here?"

"Ehh?"

"Paloma Taylor? Does she live here?"

"Judith, Paloma?" he grunted over his shoulder.

A woman in a housecoat came up beside the man. "You want Paloma?"

"Yes, do you know where she is?" Cordelia said.

"She moved to a different flat. We still get her mail sometimes. Hers is that one over there." She pointed across the grass to another building in the complex.

"That could have turned out a lot worse," Cordelia said to Mira as they made their way toward the indicated door.

They knocked and waited, then knocked and waited again. "Now, *that* could have turned out a lot better," Mira said. "Should we risk calling her? We don't have a lot of time to solve this."

"I wish I knew, luv."

"Hey, what are you two doing on my doorstep?"

Mira and Cordelia spun around. Except for the blond hair, they could have been looking at Bibi. The woman in front of them carrying grocery bags had the same big eyes, small nose, and full lips.

"Hi." Cordelia's careful tone sounded like she was talking to a pet she was afraid might run away.

"Hi, who are you?"

Mira waited for her to get closer. "My name's Mira."

"And you're an American," Paloma observed.

"Yes. Is that a bad thing?"

Paloma considered her before responding. "I guess that depends on why you're here." She turned to Cordelia. "And who are you? You're at least British, but I still have the same reservations."

"I'm Cordelia," she said, extending her hand before realizing Paloma's hands were both full with grocery bags. She recovered by adding, "Do you need help with your bags?"

Paloma eyed her, hesitating, then shrugged and handed her a bag. "Sure, why not?" With her free hand, she unlocked her front door. "Come on in. You can set the bag on the counter in there."

After depositing the bags, Cordelia said, "We're sorry to bother you on a Sunday, and we wouldn't if we didn't have a really good reason. We're friends of your sister, Bibi. We're assuming you're Paloma? You look so much like her."

"She always was beautiful," Paloma said with a straight face, but the sparkle in her eyes gave her away. "So, what now? Did that no-good husband of hers leave her or something?"

Mira and Cordelia exchanged glances. "Well, it turns out he was actually a very good guy, but I suppose you can say he left her. He died last year," Mira said.

"Oh! I didn't know. I ..." Paloma collapsed onto her sofa, covering her mouth. She eyed the two of them. "How did you know he was a good guy?"

"Mostly we're taking her word on that, but you should meet their little girl. She has turned out to be an incredibly sweet and caring child. That's got to count for something," Mira said.

"Kailani?"

"You know her name?" Cordelia said.

Sheepishly Paloma nodded. "I check out my sister's social media sometimes. She's a beautiful little girl. I guess I should have known Bibi's husband died. I don't read her posts. I just look at the pictures. There haven't been any for a long time. I guess I understand now." She grew thoughtful then added, "The pictures of the three of them, you know, with Tom, well, they looked happy. But looks can be deceiving."

"Tom was a good husband and father from all we can tell," Mira said, "but your family was right about one thing, about his family." She hoped this admission would make Paloma more willing to step in to help.

"What do you mean?"

"They're controlling and manipulative. Right now, they're making your sister's life miserable. She's in the hospital with asthma and could use some help."

"Asthma? She hasn't had problems with that since she was a child."

"The stress of her husband's passing and dealing with her in-laws has brought it back full force," Cordelia said.

"Right now," Mira added, "her in-laws are the only family she has, and they're not helping as family should. They're hurting instead." She didn't know if the guilt trip would help sway Paloma or if it would swing her more firmly to the other side, but she had to try.

Paloma sat quietly thinking. "How did you two become involved? How did you even get to know her? I mean one of you is an American."

"Kailani," Mira said. She let that sink in before continuing. "I've been visiting from the States, and I met Kailani my first day here. She said something to me that changed my outlook, something I desperately needed to hear at the time. I'm going home in a week, and I'm trying to do for her a little of what she did for me. I can't bear the thought of leaving her on unsolid ground."

"As for me," Cordelia said, "Mira introduced me to Kailani and Bibi. I'm the one renting her a flat while she's here. Mira can be quite persuasive and passionate. But in the end, I fell in love with Kailani as well."

When Paloma said nothing, Mira played her trump card. "Bibi is afraid her in-laws are trying to take Kailani away from her. None of us want that to happen."

Paloma visibly stiffened. "I'll think about it."

"Here's my phone number, and this is Cordelia's," Mira said while scribbling the numbers down on a piece of paper. "We can explain more if you want to help, but time is of the essence."

Paloma took the paper with the written numbers on it. She didn't say another word, simply nodded and showed them out.

"What do you think?" Cordelia said when they got back to her car.

Mira smiled. "Kailani has hooked her too. She'll call. I just hope it's sooner rather than later."

They each had an errand to run, so they did them together then headed back to the flat. Aissa and Kailani were so involved in the project they were working on—a butterfly mobile—they barely looked up when Mira and Cordelia entered.

"Hey, we're back. Did you notice?"

"Sure, but we're busy," Aissa said, with a grin on her face.

"Wait 'til we show you what we've made," Kailani said, jumping up. She showed them two new bracelets and a small paint-by-number.

"Did you two even pause for lunch? We've only been gone a couple hours," Mira said.

"Yeah, we ate while we worked. We didn't want to waste any time." Aissa was concentrating on attaching a string to a small orange butterfly.

"When Aissa finishes, can we go see my mum again?" Kailani said. "I want to show her what I've made."

"When Aissa finishes? Just who made these things anyway?" Cordelia teased.

Kailani giggled. "I helped her with some of them, and she helped me with the rest."

"That's a good answer, luv," Cordelia said.

• • •

They found Bibi sitting up in bed with a splash of color in her cheeks when they entered her room. Aissa leaned over to Mira and said, "We have to stop making a habit of visiting hospitals together. They're not actually my favorite place." She sounded serious, but her smile belied her words.

"So, I have good news," Bibi said. "I get to go home tomorrow. I'm doing so much better. And they're loading me up with medicines to take with me."

"What about the future?" Mira said.

"Well, no problem. As long as I don't get stressed, I should be able to stay out of here. So, it's all tickety-boo!" She laughed, and the others joined her.

"We're going to try to help with that," Cordelia said when they'd quieted down. "We have—" The door to Bibi's room slamming open interrupted her words.

Thinking the worst, they all spun around. With her arms flung wide open, Paloma stood in the doorway. "I've always wanted to make an entrance like that," she said.

Bibi gasped. Kailani glanced from her mother to this new visitor and back again. "You look like my mum," she said, confused.

"Kailani," Bibi said, "I want you to meet your aunt. This is my sister, Paloma, your Aunt Paloma."

"I have an aunt?"

"Yes, remember, we were talking about her this morning."

While this exchange happened, Paloma stayed in the doorway, her jittery hands and feet contradicting her bold, grand entrance. "I came, Bibi. Do you want me here?"

Overcome with emotion, Bibi's eyes filled with tears as she opened her arms wide. Her sister ran into the embrace. Laughter mixed with sobs while the two clung to each other.

Kailani raised her eyes to Mira for an explanation. She tousled Kailani's hair. "They haven't seen each other for a long time. Sometimes that happens—we forget how much we love someone."

Kailani seemed to understand, and in response, threw her arms around the two of them, attempting to make it a group hug. The sisters loosened their grip on each other so they could include Kailani and envelop her within their arms.

After a few minutes, Kailani called out, "I need some air, people."

They laughed and released each other. "I can't believe you're here," Bibi said.

"Well, I can't believe it either. Mum and Dad would be hacked off if they knew, but that's going to be their problem I decided."

"Good, but how ...?"

"Your friends came and visited me today. They told me you were in hospital ... and about Tom too. I'm sorry about your husband, little bee. I really am. I should have told your friends when they were at my place that I would help you, but ... you know how stubborn I am, or at least used to be. I'm trying to be different."

"Little bee?" Kailani said, giggling.

"Yes, lamb," Bibi said, mussing up her daughter's hair, "my sister always called me little bee."

Paloma laughed. "When your mum was born, I thought the name Bibi sounded like two little bumblebees. I couldn't understand it, but she did make weird sounds, so ... I started calling her little bee."

"How did you know where to come?" Cordelia asked.

"Well, I've known where Bibi lived for a long time. This was the closest hospital, so I hoped this was a reasonable guess."

"You could have just called us," Mira offered.

"And lose my grand entrance? I don't think so." She winked. "But, if I had been forced to admit defeat, I suppose I would have called you," she said with an exaggerated sigh.

"Yes, that would be my sister," Bibi said, shaking her head.

"Now, little bee, tell me everything." Paloma pulled up a chair close to Bibi's bed. She motioned for Kailani to come over and lifted her up to squeeze into the chair beside her. Then she wrapped an arm around her as if they'd been familiar family all along. Kailani didn't resist but rather snuggled up against her aunt instead.

Mira, Cordelia, and Aissa silently slipped from the room, giving them time and space. "It will be dinner soon," Cordelia said. "I'm going to find us all something to eat, including Bibi. Hospital food can be terrible."

"Why don't I come with you? I can help carry it back in," Aissa said. Turning to Mira, she added, "Call your husband. You didn't get a chance to talk last night."

"How did you ...?"

"I notice things too. Call him."

Mira didn't object further since that was exactly what she'd been wanting to do all day.

.　.　.

"Warren? Oh, hubs, it's so good to hear your voice. You won't believe what's happened."

It took a while to relay everything that had gone on in the last two days. When she finished, Warren said, "Wow, Mira, I'm exhausted just listening to all of that. And to think, I assumed this was just an ordinary little weekend."

"I think they're going to be fine, Warren. I really do. It looks like Bibi's sister is going to be there for her. I hadn't considered that biological sisters might need to find each other too."

"Can they stay at Paloma's place?"

"Maybe for a few days, but it's not big enough for anything longer than that. Bibi doesn't know yet, but Cordelia's trying to find a better rental for her and Kailani. She's got the connections to pull it off, I think."

"That would be great."

"I know. She and Aissa have been so helpful." A disheartening thought occurred to her. "Aissa has to go back home tonight! It seems so short, and we've been so busy. Although, we have stayed up late talking the last two nights." She sighed. "I'm getting tired of all these goodbyes."

"The reason the goodbyes are hard is the connections you've made are so good. You should be proud of yourself, Mira."

"I guess you're right." But understanding that didn't lessen the sadness of parting. She tried not to think about the partings still ahead of her. Pushing that thought aside, she changed the topic. "We should get Bibi and Kailani settled one way or another tomorrow. Then come Tuesday ... I won't even know what to do with myself. I still haven't been off to see anything outside of London. Maybe I can go out far enough to finally catch a glimpse of the ocean or the channel."

CHAPTER 35

Aissa's departure was every bit as difficult as Mira supposed it would be. Aissa became so flustered by it that she reverted to her native French, only realizing several minutes in that Mira hadn't understood a word she'd said.

"I'm really going to have to learn French now," Mira said. "I mean, look at you in a moment of crisis. You won't be a lick of good."

"I . . ."

"See, totally useless."

Aissa narrowed her eyes playfully at Mira. "I shouldn't have bothered interpreting for you in that hospital room. I should have just told you whatever I wanted to say, and the same with the doctors." She shook her head, then continued in a mock sweet voice, "Doctors, she's insisting she wants an enema. I don't know why, but you know these Americans— stupid and demanding. Oh, well. I was told to do whatever it took to make her happy. Oh, and she's insisting on a liquid, salt-free diet throughout the remainder of her stay."

The two of them burst into laughter, but Mira's laughs soon turned to racking sobs. "I don't know when I'll see you again." She clasped Aissa in a tight embrace, which Aissa did not resist, until a knock at the door indicated her taxi had arrived.

"Not goodbye, but so long. We will see each other again," Aissa said as she waved goodbye and disappeared down the stairs and into the waiting car below.

Mira watched her go, noticing the darkening sky outside. Cordelia would bring Kailani back from the hospital soon. She hoped it wasn't raining when they arrived.

Before leaving the hospital, Mira had asked Kailani if she wanted to sleep on the pull-out sofa bed tonight since Aissa wouldn't be using it. But she said she preferred the cot in the same room as Mira. So, Mira went into the bedroom to make sure the cot was ready for her.

"We're back!" Cordelia's voice sounded from the living room.

At least I don't need to say goodbye to them yet, Mira thought as she came out of the bedroom to greet them.

"It's late, so I'm going home. I'll pick you up in the morning to go get your mum, okay, Kailani?"

"Okay," Kailani said, hugging Cordelia before she left.

After the door closed, Mira smiled down at Kailani. "We should get you into bed, pumpkin."

"Do we have to? Can you tell me a story first?"

"I don't think I could come up with a story to tell."

"Then tell me about what it's like to live in the States."

"Hmm. How about I tell you about my house and my husband." Kailani nodded, her eyes bright. "But ... after you get ready for bed."

Kailani was off in a flash, her teeth brushed and her pajamas on in no time. She climbed onto her cot and said, "I'm ready."

Mira climbed onto her own bed. "Here, why don't you snuggle up beside me on the big bed."

Once Kailani was settled, Mira pulled up the photos of home on her phone. "This is my husband, Warren."

"He's kind of dishy, isn't he?" Kailani giggled.

"What? You're only eight. Where did you learn to talk like that?" Mira teased.

"My friends at school. There's this one boy ... if he wasn't ignoring me all the time, I think I'd like him."

"Well, give him time," she said, pulling Kailani closer.

They spent the next thirty minutes scrolling through photos while Mira told Kailani the stories behind them. Then Mira remembered the pictures she'd taken out of the photo flipbook and pulled them out of her bag to show Kailani. They dissolved in giggles over the silly photographs.

"Can I have one of these?" Kailani asked. She was holding a couple pictures of Mira and Warren together.

"Of course you may." Then Mira had an even better idea. She reached inside her bag and pulled out her camera. Things had been so crazy lately that she'd taken a few pictures with her phone but hadn't used the camera. She checked to make sure she'd uploaded all the pictures she'd taken.

"Would you like to have my camera? I'll bet your mum can show you how to download pictures onto the computer. That way you can send me pictures of yourself."

"Yes! Brilliant!"

"Here, let me show you what to do." Mira took a few minutes to teach Kailani the basics. "I'm sure your mum can teach you even more, but right now you need to get some sleep."

"Can I sleep right here?" Kailani said, burrowing down under the covers.

Mira laughed. "It's good I'm not going to be around forever. I would spoil you rotten. Okay. You can sleep here."

Long after Kailani had fallen asleep, hugging one of her new stuffed animals, Mira watched her—the rise and fall of her breathing, the pure innocence of her young face. Mira gently brushed the hair off her face with her hand. She was so small, so vulnerable, so perfect. She fought falling asleep herself, filled with a burning need to stay awake and protect Kailani.

.　.　.

The sun was just peeking around the shutters when Mira stirred. Kailani had turned sideways, managing to take up three-quarters of the bed, leaving Mira a little sliver at the edge. She'd also managed to monopolize the blankets. Mira, only half covered, woke because she was cold.

Slipping out of bed so as not to disturb Kailani, Mira climbed into the shower to get ready for the day. She had just gotten dressed and was combing her hair when her phone rang. It was a call she'd been hoping would come, and it made her smile.

.　　.　　.

Cordelia showed up as they were cleaning their breakfast things. She had Paloma in tow. "Hi, Aunt Paloma!" Kailani said as she rushed over for a hug.

Paloma scooped her up into her arms. "I can't believe I missed out on this," she said to Mira and Cordelia. "I owe you a thank you."

"Let's go get my mum!"

"Great idea, luv," Cordelia said.

They gathered Kailani's new clothes, toys, and bedding before heading out the door. "Stow it in the boot for now," Cordelia said. Then they piled into her car. "We're going to have to squeeze to fit your mum in, but I imagine we'll be fine with that." And then they were off.

When they arrived in Bibi's room, she was dressed and ready to go. They only needed to wait until the doctors officially released her.

"Well, that gives us time to talk over a few things first," Cordelia said. "I made an assumption, but I need to ask. Would you rather not go back to your flat?"

"Well, yes," Bibi said, "but I don't—"

Cordelia stopped her with a wave of her hand. "You forget I manage properties. I know people. So, I was talking to my friends. They have some flats farther out of the city. They're less money than you're paying now, but Kailani would have to change schools come the start of next term. I figured location didn't matter so much for you, though, since you work from home."

"That would be great!" Bibi turned to Kailani. "Are you up for a change, lamb?"

"Yes, mum," Kailani said, smiling.

"I could get you into those easily. Those friends owe me. However, after I met Paloma, I explored a different option. You know I rent places out short term, usually to tourists. I have a couple flats I could turn into long-term rentals for the two of you. Mira and I visited them yesterday with you in mind, and I think they'll work. They're still farther out, but I thought of them because they're not far from where Paloma lives."

"Yes, absolutely!" It was Paloma who had chimed in this time. "I mean … if you want that, Bibi."

"That would be amazing!" Bibi beamed.

"Okay, then you have some decisions to make. One is a three-bedroom. So, you could each have your own room and the third bedroom would make a great art studio. They're small rooms, but they should work. The other option is a two-bedroom. You could have a setup like you do now—share one bedroom and the other will be your studio."

"Two-bedroom?" Bibi asked Kailani, who nodded.

"Okay, then—"

"Wait. How about the three-bedroom?" Kailani said.

"This from the girl who insisted on sleeping in my bed last night?" Mira said.

Kailani laughed. "I think I can sleep in my own room now. Don't you, mum?"

"Yes, lamb, I do." Bibi was smiling, but her eyes were moist.

"But can I climb in bed with you if I get scared?" Kailani hesitatingly asked.

"Of course."

"One more thing about the flats—they're furnished. You're welcome to keep any of the furniture. It will be yours. Or I can have it moved out. I just thought … well, I thought you wouldn't want to spend too much time at your old flat gathering things."

"Thank you." She reached for Cordelia's hand and squeezed it. "I … I have a few items that remind me of Tom that I'd like. We need to grab clothes and personal items, and I'd need everything from my studio. But I'm fine leaving the other furnishings behind, relieved actually. Mostly they're hand-me-downs from Tom's parents they insisted we take. Half of them are broken anyway."

"I was hoping you'd say that. I've arranged for some men to meet us at your old flat. You can tell them what you want, and they'll pack it up and take it to the new place."

"How can I ever repay you for all of this?"

"Luv," Cordelia said, putting a hand on Bibi's arm, "someone once did this for me. I'm merely returning the favor. Down the road, you might be able to do this for someone else. I'm sure you'll find a way to lift someone else's burdens."

Paloma moved in next to her sister. "I'm sure we will. Thank you." She put an arm around her sister. "Little bee, you can come stay with me until your new place gets set up. You two can share my bed, and I'll take the couch."

"Oh, I forgot to mention one thing," Cordelia said. "Paloma, could you take any time off work? I mean, right now?"

"I already did. I'm here because of that. When I explained a little of what was going on to my boss, she said to take all the time I needed. That means solve it in a week's time, but I'll take the week."

"The thing is, I have friends with rental properties scattered around Britain. Bibi mentioned going on holiday, and I have tenants in the three-bedroom unit for a couple more days. If you were to take the week and spend it on holiday ... well, we could have your new place set up and your things delivered before the week's out."

"Blinding! We could go on holiday?" Kailani squealed.

"Yes, luv. When you get back to your aunt's place, I can show you the different places available. With a few phone calls, I should be able to get you set up proper." Kailani bounced around the room, but Bibi was speechless.

Mira quietly watched this great blessing unfold in front of her. What she had to offer didn't seem much in comparison, but she knew it was important. "Bibi, I need to introduce you to some friends of mine—Madge and Harold. I met them a bit ago, but they have a son who is a barrister. I talked to Madge yesterday, and she called her son. He in turn made some contacts. I got a call this morning from a good friend of his who practices in London. He's going to help protect you from your in-laws. He told me that by the time he's done, they won't dare come near you unless you've given them an engraved invitation."

Bibi's mouth dropped in surprise. "I do have one favor to ask, though," Mira said.

"Name it."

"Harold is in failing health, and he's having memory issues. His wife Madge takes care of him, and she could sure use a friend. I'd be so grateful if you would check in on her from time to time."

"I'd be honored to," Bibi said.

"Me too," added Paloma.

The door swung open, and a nurse entered. "Everything is set. You're free to go."

•   •   •

Paloma parted from them at the door of the hospital. "I'm going to hop a bus and get things set up at my place, and even clean up a bit. Do you have any preferences for dinner? I don't cook often, so now's your chance."

"Do you know how to make Mum's shepherd's pie?"

"I do, little bee. It'll be hot and ready at six."

The first stop the rest of them made was at Bibi and Kailani's old flat. Bibi threw enough things into an overnight bag to get her and Kailani through a week. As she finished, there was a knock at the door. Bibi stiffened, but Cordelia swept open the door. "This is the crew I hired, don't worry."

Four burly men entered the flat. Bibi glanced out the front window and could see their plain panel truck parked on the street. "I'm Joseph. What do you want to take with you?" the eldest of the crew asked. He held a clipboard, a pen, and blue painter's tape.

It didn't take long for Bibi to walk with him through the flat and designate what to keep and what to leave behind. When she indicated something she wanted, Joseph wrote it down and marked it with a piece of blue tape. When they finished each room, he directed his workers to pack what had been marked. They had already loaded up several items in their truck before Bibi and Joseph finished cataloging the whole flat.

"All of this will go into storage for a few days," Cordelia explained. "Once my tenants leave, I'll have these blokes empty the third bedroom in your new flat. Then we'll put your studio items in there for you. The other things they're boxing up will be put inside, and you can do with them what you want." She pointed at the watercolor of Bibi and Kailani. "If you'd like, I'll have that hung above your new sofa."

"That would be lovely," Bibi said. "Thank you. I didn't realize we could do this so fast."

"That's the idea, isn't it? We don't want your in-laws to get a chance to do anything to stop you or to keep you from collecting your own possessions. If your landlord or your neighbors are watching you, as you suspect, we want to leave soon, before your in-laws have a chance to arrive." Cordelia eyed Bibi. "Remember, I own the new flat. If you need anything, anything at all, you just ring me up."

"Hey, is anyone hungry?" a familiar voice called through the open doorway.

"Bill! You're always in the right place at the right time, aren't you?" said Mira.

"Of course I am. Of course I am. But this time it's because Cordelia rang me up."

Kailani had been kneeling on the window sill so she could watch the activity going on outside the window—the boxes and items being loaded into the truck. She turned at the sound of the new voice. "I remember you!" Kailani said, scrambling down from her perch. "Mum, this is the man with the envelope."

"And I remember you, sweet pea," Bill said, winking. "Now, how about that lunch? I can bring you something here, or you can come over to the pub."

"Let's get out of here," Bibi said. She'd been nervously pacing ever since Cordelia had mentioned her in-laws, the bag holding her medication clutched to her chest.

.   .   .

They ate a quick lunch at *The Red Fox*. Bill found a quiet corner for them, for which they were grateful. But after a whispered conference, Cordelia and Mira felt it best to get Bibi to Paloma's. It had been a stressful day, and stress was exactly what she didn't need more of.

When they got to Paloma's, Bibi collapsed gratefully into an easy chair. Cordelia and Mira were determined to only stay long enough to make sure everyone was settled and to talk briefly about travel plans.

When Brighton came up as an option, Paloma said, "Let me take them there. Bibi can sit in a chair on the beach and rest while I play with Kailani. Bibi doesn't need a busy holiday. She needs a restful one."

Mira smiled to herself as she watched Paloma and Cordelia work out the details. They were trying to think of everything. Paloma wanted to bring Bibi back on Saturday to make sure there was plenty of time to get her comfortably settled in her new place before Paloma had to return to work the following Monday. Cordelia was going to make sure the flat was thoroughly cleaned and was even going to have the locks changed as an extra precaution.

Mira watched it all come together. There hadn't been time to introduce either of the sisters to Madge, but Cordelia had met Madge when they'd stopped by the previous day to ask about her barrister son. Cordelia would make the connection for her.

Paloma may have been out of the habit, but she was already the sister Bibi needed. And just like Bill always being watchful of Cordelia, Cordelia would do the same for Bibi. The truth washed over Mira in an unexpected but not unwelcome wave. Her unfinished business was complete.

It was bittersweet. She wasn't ready for it to be over.

Kailani sidled up to Mira. "Can I take your picture?" She was holding the camera Mira had given her.

Mira wiped the tears that had formed. "Of course you may. Why don't we hold it out in front of us and take a picture of both of us together?" And while Bibi drifted off to sleep in her chair and Cordelia and Paloma planned, Mira and Kailani took picture after picture with Kailani grinning from ear to ear and Mira squeezing out a smile hopefully strong enough to stem the tide of her tears.

CHAPTER 36

Mira rolled over in the late morning to the reality of her empty bed. She sat up. The cot was gone. Kailani was gone. They were likely already on their way to Brighton. Mira would have one last chance to see them—on Saturday when they returned, one day before she left for home. It was the parting she dreaded the most.

For a change, Warren had been the one to call her last night and before their usual time. "I have a meeting scheduled soon. I'm assuming you have a lot to tell me, so I called early," he'd said.

She'd updated him on everything that had transpired, but when she got to those last moments with Kailani, she couldn't get out the words. That told him more than the words would have.

After giving her a minute, he gratefully changed the topic. "Do you have plans for tomorrow? Have you decided what you might want to do before you fly home?"

She hadn't given it much thought. "I guess that's what I'll do tomorrow, figure out what to do with my time." It was as definitive an answer as she could give him.

They had hung up shortly after that, and Mira had alternated between sitting and staring at a blank TV screen and wandering around the flat, feeling lost. She ate cereal for dinner then dished herself up a huge bowl of ice cream, but she couldn't finish it. She thought of calling Cordelia, but she knew Cordelia was going through the flats she owned to find the most suitable furniture to put in Bibi and Kailani's new place.

Finally, she had pulled out her guidebooks and a map. What *was* she going to do for the next few days?

When Mira moved around the lonely flat the next morning, the guidebooks and map still sat where she'd opened them. She was no closer to answering the questions they posed than she had been the night before.

Putting off those decisions, she climbed into the shower, letting the warm water clear her mind. She had just finished brushing her teeth when there was a knock at her door. Cordelia had mentioned coming by to gather some of the newer kitchen appliances for Bibi's flat.

"Coming," Mira called, feeling grateful she wouldn't be alone anymore, even if for just a short while.

She swung the door open wide, but Cordelia wasn't standing there. In front of Mira was the most welcome sight she'd seen in all of Europe. Warren stood on the doorstep, bags at his feet.

"Warren!" She squealed and grabbed him in a huge embrace, almost knocking him to the ground.

"Surprise!"

"Wow! I can't believe you're here," she said, dragging him inside.

"I'm guessing with that greeting it's okay that I came?"

"Yes! Why wouldn't it be?"

"Well, after Paris …"

"Oh, yeah, I'm sorry. I was pretty adamant then about you not coming, but that was for different reasons. I'm glad you didn't listen to me." She squealed again and kissed him long and hard.

"How long have you been planning this?" she asked once she'd come up for air.

"I made the plane reservation on Thursday when you got back to London, but I wasn't certain I was going to use it, so I bought a refundable ticket. I didn't want to get in the way of what you were doing."

"You would never get in the way."

"Maybe, maybe not. This trip has been about you finding yourself again. I didn't want to disrupt that. But when I talked to you yesterday … well, you'd done what you needed to do."

"When did you leave? I was just talking to you last night."

"I called you from home, not my office. I was packed and ready, but I had to make sure before I came that it was the right thing to do. As soon as I hung up, I took off for the airport. I hope you don't mind my little white lie about a meeting. I mean, I was gathering with the other passengers," he said, looking sheepish.

"I'm sure I'll find a way for you to make it up to me." Mira grinned.

"Mira, I have missed you so much. I love you, babe." He was smiling widely, his dimples pronounced.

She had missed those dimples, that handsome face, the nearness of his voice. "I love you too, Warren." Then he took her in his arms and kissed her again.

·   ·   ·

The rest of the day flew by. Mira thought she'd shared with Warren everything that had gone on, but so many details had been missed in their relatively short phone calls. She filled him in while he peppered her with questions. They also made plans about how to spend the rest of their week, squeezing in as many sights as possible in the few days available to them. They were shaping up to be the tourists Cordelia usually hosted.

But one thing was non-negotiable. On Saturday they would be in London. Kailani and her mum were due back that day. "I can't wait to introduce you to Cordelia and Kailani and Bibi."

"I'd really like to meet them after everything you've told me," Warren said.

"Hey, I wonder what happened to Cordelia. She was going to stop by today."

"Well, actually she isn't."

"What?"

"She may have told a little white lie for me."

"Explain," Mira said with raised eyebrows.

"Well, I didn't want to chase you all over England. So, I asked Cordelia to make sure you stuck around for today." He shrugged. "I can make it up to you for that too."

"Oh, I'll make sure you do," she said with a mock-serious tone of voice. "So, how long has she known about this? I can't believe she kept it a secret from me."

"I only called her from the airport yesterday, since I wasn't sure I was coming before then. And, to be honest, I didn't know if she could keep the

IN SEARCH OF SISTERS

secret any longer than that. It probably wouldn't have been fair to ask her to either."

"You're right. Boy, you're a sneaky little devil, aren't you? I had no idea you could be so devious."

Warren laughed. "You see what you've reduced me to. This is what I'm forced to do for you."

It was good to hear the sound of his laughter. She had missed that. "Not likely, hubs. Not likely." She kissed the top of his forehead. "If you think you can stay awake after your jetlag, why don't we eat at *The Red Fox*. Bill will want to meet you."

"Bill? Who's Bill? Should I be jealous?"

"I didn't tell you about Bill? The guy who owns the pub and—" She stopped when she noticed him laughing. "You know about Bill. You're shameless, you know, Warren. I'm going to get ready for dinner."

She was finishing her makeup when Warren came to stand in the open bathroom doorway. He stood there watching her, mesmerized by her every movement.

"This isn't much of a show, you know. It's only makeup."

"It's not the makeup. It's you. You make me better, Mira. Even from afar, your care and concern for others, your kindness in gentle ways. You inspire me to try harder, to reach higher. I can't imagine the person I would be without you."

She smiled in response before returning to her makeup, using her mirror compact to apply the finishing touches. A sudden thought struck her. It was all so clear. How had she missed it? She abruptly turned to her husband. "It was you, Warren. All along it was you."

He raised his eyebrows, but she gave no further explanation. Instead, she pushed past him into the bedroom, still clutching the mirror in her hand. Wordlessly, she reached down beside the bed and pulled up the bag Warren had given her. It had once been filled with presents. She sat on the bed and overturned the bag in front of her, but only one remaining item fell out—a small stuffed rabbit.

She turned to him with tears in her eyes.

274

He sat down beside her, gently cradling her. "What is it, Mira? What's wrong?"

She shook her head, unable to speak at first. "Nothing's wrong," she finally whispered. "But *I* was wrong. I was lost on that ocean, not seeing, not understanding. But you ... you saw more than you know."

Puzzled, Warren said, "What did I see, babe? I don't understand."

"Look at all this," she said, indicating an almost empty bed. "I mean, all that was once in this bag you gave me. Start with this," she said, showing him the compact in her hand. "You gave this to me. And with it, I've learned to see myself, but not only myself, I've begun seeing others again—seeing past myself.

"You know me like no other, Warren. You gave me Hello Kitty band-aids and a strawberry ring pop because I liked them when I was a kid. Elijah adored that ring pop. He even wore it." She stared at her hands and fiddled with her wedding ring. "He and Avelyn have been married for 40 years. I think that's a good goal to have, don't you? To still be thinking of what's important to each other several decades from now?"

Warren nodded. He drew her hand to his lips and kissed it.

"And remember the four-color pen? It was the same thing. You bought me one before, knowing it meant something to me. Then you'd conveniently 'lose' it and then 'find' it for me."

"What? Me? I never lost that pen before?"

"Of course you didn't." She rolled her eyes before growing serious again. "You didn't lose me either. I lost myself. But you've been helping find me again."

"I didn't really think about ..."

Mira put a hand to his lips. "It's not that you thought through what those things would mean. You didn't have to. It's just you, Warren. You bought me large hoop earrings because you'd joke about losing me in a crowd, but I know you've only ever had eyes for me. You gave me a scrunchie to keep the hair off my face because it was an excuse to tell me everything you loved about me.

"Do you have any idea how incredible you are? You have wiped my tears," she said as if he could see the pocket tissues he'd given her. "You've watched out for me, making sure each day that I had my lunch and that my water bottle was filled. You've shown me a light in the darkness, helping me to see the way forward one step at a time." The water bottle and the small flashlight seemed to appear before their eyes, spread out on the bedspread before them.

"I've been keeping track in my journal of the things in this bag and where they've ended up. But that's secondary in importance to why you picked them in the first place. You picked them for the emotions they trigger. You did it without even thinking because I am as much a part of you as you are yourself. All of this," she said, indicating the imagined items spread out on the bed, "all this, leads back to you.

"I once said that you weren't enough, Warren. It's my 'sisters'— they're the ones who aren't enough."

"That's probably just a matter of semantics."

"But it isn't. Our relationship is the foundation. I had it wrong. I thought I needed sisters. And I do. I really do. But I felt I needed those sisters to make this relationship—the one between you and me work. The reality is those relationships are working so well because this one already does.

"That bag of yours held even more. You gave me a camera and a photo book and a memory stick. Those all capture memories. They help us remember things we would otherwise have forgotten. I've always been good at remembering appointments, but I seem to have lost hold of the more important things in life." She reached for her purse and pulled out the remaining goofy pictures from the flipbook. "This is so us, Warren— not perfect, but happy. I guess I'd forgotten that, or maybe forgotten to appreciate that."

He held her in his arms and kissed her tenderly on the forehead. "I don't think you lost those things. They just got confused with everything else you were dealing with."

"Confused or lost, I don't know. Regardless, I had to rediscover them. Thanks to you, I have."

"You give me too much credit, but I love you for it, anyway."

"That's the thing. You always love me. I gave away one more gift—a key chain, a key chain of ruby red slippers. There's no place like home, Warren. There's no place like home."

He nodded and smiled. "We made plans, but do you just want to go home? I'll take you if you want."

She surprised him by shaking her head. Then she reached down to the bed and picked up the only item actually sitting there—the stuffed rabbit. "Why did you buy me this, Warren?"

"Well, probably because it was on clearance, left over from Easter," he chuckled.

She shook her head at him. "Warren, why did you buy me this?"

He was quiet for a minute. "I bought it because your favorite book when you were growing up was *Watership Down*, a book about a group of rabbits. Your mother read it with you. A rabbit would always remind you of your mom, of being loved."

"Do you know what a rabbit's home is called?"

He shook his head.

"It's called a warren. Your name means home."

His eyes met hers. "*You* are home, Warren. Whenever and wherever I am with you, I am home."

He glanced at the bedspread and all the items that could have been there when she'd emptied his bag. He looked up into her eyes. Then he took her face in his and kissed her.

She'd never been more at peace.

ACKNOWLEDGMENTS

A book, at least with me, is never the product of a singular mind. While I can blame no one else for the final words, I couldn't have achieved putting all these words on the page without the help of many others— Chloe Bramwell, my fellow Black Rose Writing authors (who are like family to me), and an assortment of other editors, proofreaders, and so on. Of course, none of this would have been possible without the support and encouragement of my daughter, Amy, and especially my husband, Allen, who believed in me before I believed in myself.

ABOUT THE AUTHOR

Mary Ellen Bramwell, an award-winning and best-selling author, has been writing short stories since she was ten. She is the mother of five and currently lives with her youngest son and her husband of over 35 years in the Mountain West. She enjoys reading, jigsaw puzzles, and playing games but is passionate about her family and alleviating the suffering of others.

NOTE FROM THE AUTHOR

Word-of-mouth is crucial for any author to succeed. If you enjoyed *In Search of Sisters*, please leave a review online—anywhere you are able. Even if it's just a sentence or two. It would make all the difference and would be very much appreciated.

Thanks!
Mary Ellen Bramwell

Thank you so much for reading one of Mary Ellen Bramwell's novels.

If you enjoyed the experience, please check out our recommendation
for your next great read!

The Apple of My Eye by Mary Ellen Bramwell

"A mature love story with an intense plot.

This book has something important to say."

-William O. Shakespeare, Professor of English,

Brigham Young University